FENRIR

FENRIR

ERIC FLINT & RYK E. SPOOR

FENRIR

This is a work of fiction. All the characters and events portrayed in this book are fictional, and any resemblance to real people or incidents is purely coincidental.

Copyright © 2025 by Eric Flint and Ryk E. Spoor

All rights reserved, including the right to reproduce this book or portions thereof in any form.

A Baen Books Original

Baen Publishing Enterprises
P.O. Box 1403
Riverdale, NY 10471
www.baen.com

ISBN: 978-1-6680-7266-0

Cover art by Dominic Harman

First printing, June 2025

Distributed by Simon & Schuster
1230 Avenue of the Americas
New York, NY 10020

Library of Congress Cataloging-in-Publication Data

Names: Flint, Eric, author. | Spoor, Ryk E., author.
Title: Fenrir / Eric Flint, Ryk E. Spoor.
Description: Riverdale, NY : Baen Books, 2025.
Identifiers: LCCN 2025001283 (print) | LCCN 2025001284 (ebook) | ISBN 9781668072660 (hardcover) | ISBN 9781964856247 (ebook)
Subjects: LCGFT: Science fiction. | Novels.
Classification: LCC PS3556.L548 F46 2025 (print) | LCC PS3556.L548 (ebook) | DDC 813/.54—dc23/eng/20250224
LC record available at https://lccn.loc.gov/2025001283
LC ebook record available at https://lccn.loc.gov/2025001284

Printed in the United States of America

10 9 8 7 6 5 4 3 2 1

Acknowledgments:

To Toni, for nigh-infinite patience.

To Dr. Suman Chakrabarti, for long discussions that led to *Carpathia*'s drive system.

To my Beta Readers, for their invaluable feedback, which saved me from a number of embarrassments.

To all my readers, and especially my Patrons, who've kept me going in this sometimes challenging business.

And as always to my wife, Kathleen, for giving me the time and putting up with my often-frustrating quirks. Love you!

Dedications:

This book is dedicated to the memory of two men who helped make me who I am, and neither of whom remain among us:

To Ryk Peter Spoor, my father, who was always the symbol of what a scientist should be—and whose collection of SF novels was an endless inspiration. Thanks, Dad.

And to Eric Flint, my coauthor, "The Butcher of Baen," without whom I might never have been published, and certainly would never have dared the dangerous and demanding waters of hard-SF...and thus would never have written *Boundary* or any of its sequels, let alone *Fenrir*. I wish he could have been here to read this last collaboration—and tell me if it met his standards.

PART I: DISCOVERY

CHAPTER 1: ANOMALY

Stephanie Bronson settled back into her seat and began working on the current draft of her thesis, glancing occasionally at the screens nearby. The Smyth-Nichols Infrared Telescope, irreverently referred to by everyone as "SNIT," had provided a glut of new images over the last month, and Stephanie had the dubious honor of sitting by and observing as they were processed for anomaly detection.

It wasn't all boring, of course; she'd been present when the computer announced it had found something that turned out to be a major flare from a previously unremarkable red dwarf, and had managed to catch most of the transition between a peaceful star and one several magnitudes brighter. Even small anomalies could be interesting, and if your field was infrared astronomy it was all potentially input for your work.

And in this case, it allowed her to do schoolwork while she was babysitting the computers. Win-win!

She settled back into her chair, wrapped in a long sweater and a knit scarf against the office chill; as seemed to be always the case, the thermostat was about five degrees too cold for her, and mere grad students were in no way allowed to change the settings. There were, fortunately, no restrictions in how heavily you dressed, so with a cup of the indifferent-but-still-hot coffee from the break room and her heavier clothing, she could still be comfortable.

Stephanie opened up the spreadsheet and started trying to pretty up the graphs for the main portion of her thesis. Established Ph.D.s doing their papers could use the simplest, automatic presentation from Excel or whatever program they were using, but if you wanted to *get* there, you'd better make sure everything was presented clearly, unambiguously, and—preferably—attractively. Thesis committees were notoriously picky about pretty much *everything*.

A muted *ping* made her look up. *An anomaly there . . . new star in the field.* She flicked back and forth between the newest image and the preceding ones, then grinned. *Stupid machine. Asteroid moved from one field to the other.*

There were a lot of cases like that. In *theory* the system knew where things like mapped asteroids and variable stars were, but whoever had programmed it had either missed edge cases or made some kind of unwarranted assumptions, because there were quite a few objects that it commonly failed to match properly.

Sure enough, her studies were interrupted a few times each hour by "anomalies" that were nothing of the sort. Still, it *did* keep her awake, even if it did throw off her groove sometimes.

Another *ping*, and she sighed and closed the laptop again. *Where's this one?* she thought, seeing yet another star field with a faint dot circled. A quick check of the references and she at least knew what part of the sky it was in. *About in the middle of constellation Lupus, near Gamma Lupi.* There was another, slightly brighter star near the apparent anomaly, but a quick check didn't give her a catalog number for it—interesting in and of itself, but not to the extent of the anomalous star. The dimmer star looked to have an infrared magnitude of about ten, which was still pretty bright compared to the limit of detection of the system.

She checked the prior images; there was nothing visible there, at least down to the sensitivity of SNIT, which went down at least seven magnitudes below the anomalous point.

The next check was to see if there was more than one image with this anomalous point; electronic imaging systems could easily produce spurious points of light from various types of glitches. But, no, the dot was present on all images after a certain point, so it was a real *something*.

This was already more interesting than a lot of the false alarms. Stephanie hitched her chair forward. This change was also near the center of the image, and the location of the new dot seemed steady, so it wasn't an asteroid or something like that crossing into the field of view.

A nova? That would be exciting. Certainly a nova—or a supernova—could vary in magnitude sufficiently to make a previously invisible object visible. Feeling more excited, she composed a quick email to the SNIT team:

FROM: sbronson@SNIT.org
TO: SNIT Team
Subject: We might have something!
Guys,

SNIT found what really looks like a new object at about RA 15h 33m 13s, Declination -41° 06' 22". Checked and it's definitely an object, not a transient glitch, no relative motion obvious yet so it's not one of our asteroid or comet crossing false alarms. Anyone have a prior at that location? I'm thinking nova!

Steph

She appended links to some of the key images in the database, then—after another glance at the mysterious dot on her screen—went back to working on her graphs. Discovering a nova was exciting, but she wouldn't let herself *get* excited unless and until she was *sure* that was what it was. She had work to do, and in all likelihood someone would call or message back and tell her what obvious thing she'd missed.

But half an hour later, her phone buzzed. It was a text from Shin Mouri, one of her teammates from Japan:

Can confirm nothing at the site of your putative nova previously, down to limit of about mag 28.

That was interesting, exciting even; depending on just how much the mystery object was radiating in the visible versus the infrared, that implied it had increased by something over fifteen to eighteen magnitudes—a million to twenty million times brighter. That put it out of ordinary nova range, straight into supernova or even into superluminous supernova range.

But exciting as that might be, she still had work to do. She returned, somewhat regretfully, to her thesis work.

There were a couple more false alarms before she packed up to go home and left to get some sleep.

She unlocked the side door that led to her apartment stairway and tried to go up as quietly as possible.

It wasn't quiet enough to fool a cat, though, and something soft brushed its way around one leg. "Hello, Luna," she said, and bent down to pat the snow-white animal.

Luna's yellow-green eyes met hers, then closed to slits as Stephanie scratched her gently just behind the ears—Luna's favorite spot. A faint buzz-rumble of approval came from the cat. "Yes, you like that, don't you? But I can't spend an hour doing this, I have to get to bed. *You* should be in bed too, silly cat."

Luna looked at her with exasperation as she stood, as if to say *What? Your sleep is more important than properly attending to my needs?*

"You are a spoiled little cat, Luna, and Joel spoils you entirely too much." Nonetheless, she bent back down and spent another thirty seconds on properly greeting her unofficial landlord (her *official* landlord was Luna's owner . . . or Luna's pet, probably, from the cat's point of view).

Joel Landon lived in the downstairs part of the house, which she'd never quite understood, since Landon owned probably a dozen different properties or more and could certainly afford to live pretty much anywhere; it might have had to do with his being widowed a few years ago and not wanting to stay in a place with too many memories. Why he'd rent his top floor as an apartment for college students she didn't know, but she sure wasn't going to complain.

Luna permitted her to move onward and get into her own apartment. Stephanie put her backpack down with relief and headed for the bathroom . . . and then went to bed.

An insistent *brrr-brrr-brrr!* sound dragged her out of the depths of sleep. She groped around to find the clock, then realized with a dull surprise that the sound was coming from her cell phone. She half fell out of bed and managed to yank it out of her jacket pocket, where she'd left it last night. "Hello?"

"Steph? That you?" That was the deep voice of David Amitay, head of the SNIT team and currently also one of her thesis advisors.

"Barely." Her eyes focused on the clock. "Why the hell are you calling me at nine-thirty in the morning... sir? You *know* I had a late, late night and it's Saturday!"

"Oh... yes, I suppose you did, but never mind that, you're awake now." Dave's tone was only mildly apologetic. "That object you found last night? It's already proving to be very interesting."

That *did* wake her up. "What about it? I mean, I'm guessing it's a supernova, but that could have waited until, like, noon."

"See, we don't *know* what it is yet. But while we're still waiting on getting detailed spectroscopy, we *did* find the basic emission's IR peak. Which puts it at about four thousand Kelvin."

"Wait, *what*?"

A chuckle. "*Now* you're really awake, eh? Yes, about four thousand. For a star, that's downright chilly."

That much was true; the Sun, not a terribly huge or bright star by any standard, had a surface temperature of six thousand Kelvin; four thousand was approaching red dwarf temperatures. Supernovae, by contrast, ignited at around a hundred billion degrees.

So if this was a supernova... "That's one *hell* of a redshift."

"Isn't it, though? As a matter of fact, it's a redshift that makes your unknown object the most distant object in the universe, trying its best to reach lightspeed." Dave paused, obviously waiting for her to answer.

"Holy crap. Even a superluminous supernova wouldn't have that apparent magnitude at that distance." She paused, thinking. "In fact, even a *quasar* wouldn't be that bright." The brightest quasar in visible light was magnitude twelve point nine, and that was one of the closer ones; distant quasars were far dimmer.

"Exactly." Dave chuckled. "Steph, we don't know *what* we're seeing. You may have just discovered something *absolutely new*. Maybe—just throwing this off the top of my head—quasars *themselves* can do something like supernova."

Astronomers are used to mind-bogglingly huge numbers; the universe does not build to a sensible, humanly comprehensible scale. Even so, Stephanie found her entire brain balking at the concept of a *quasar* somehow going through a supernova-like process. Quasars already had luminosities of *trillions* of stars. A process that multiplied that by millions of times would mean that for a short period of time, a supernova quasar (*what the hell would you call it?*) would outshine entire *galactic clusters.* "Don't hurt my brain this early. I need coffee before I can think about this."

"Well, go get your coffee. It'll be a day or three before we get the detailed spectrum; that'll give us a much better idea of what we're dealing with. Talk later!"

"Later," she said, but Dave had already hung up.

She was, she admitted, no longer annoyed that she'd been woken up; if she'd been in Dave's position she probably couldn't have resisted the urge to call either. But Dave was also right that the mystery would need a day or so to solve. Absorptive and radiative lines in the spectrum would tell them a lot more about the target's composition, and that would almost certainly nail down a lot of possibilities—or reject some of them out of hand.

"Well," she said with a yawn, "might as well get up and do things!"

CHAPTER 2: IMPOSSIBILITY

"Oh you stupid motherf . . . udger," Stephanie growled at her computer. "I've done this same work in the same directories *every day* for the last two *years*, why are you telling me I don't have permissions?"

"Oh, that's the network," came a woman's voice over the office divider that split the room into two separate workspaces.

"*Again*, Ronnie? I thought it'd just tell me it couldn't find the drive!"

Ronnie Hartnell, her office mate, poked her extremely curly head around the corner. "Oh, it's been coming up with all *sorts* of new and interesting ways to deny us access to our data. No memo from IT as to why, though."

"Well, they'd better get it fixed or I'm going down there myself, with a hammer." More out of habit than anything else, she clicked again, and this time the directory came up without a moment's hesitation. "Ha! Threats *do* work!"

"Told you. Put fear into your machines, they'll behave."

"That's so dark."

"I wear black only because I can't find anything darker, hon."

Her phone buzzed; the two quick rings that meant it was an internal call. "Hi, Steph here."

"Stephanie." There was an odd tone to Dave's voice. "Would you come to Conference Three, please?"

Conference Three? That one had the built-in presentation setup. "Did Sunny get back to us with the spectrum data? We were expecting it, like, yesterday morning!"

"Yes. That's what we'd like to discuss."

"Okay, I'll be right there." She switched off her monitor and grabbed up her tablet in case she needed to take notes.

Conference Room Three was a moderate-sized room, with a long table pointing toward a screen-equipped wall. There were four people already in the room: David; Sunny Andui, who was the best spectrum analyzer in their department; Barton Kalam (*Wait, why Bart? He's a planetographer type, mostly interested in Oort cloud objects*); and—even more puzzling—Crystal Nakamura. *Nakamura's the Director's right hand.*

What made it *really* strange was that all four people had the same doubtful, confused expressions.

"All right, David, I'm here, so what's up? What's the spectra showing?"

"Nothing," Sunny said.

Steph blinked. "Wait. What do you mean *nothing*?"

"There are no spectral lines I can detect—neither interference lines from a surrounding nebula nor emission from excited atomic or molecular species in the target itself."

"That's . . . that's . . ." She blinked. "That's impossible. There isn't a star ever seen that didn't have hydrogen lines or others in their spectrum."

"No mistake. That's why it took an extra day, we were checking the data and our results. The target is not a glitch, we've confirmed that, but still, there's no spectral lines. No hint of composition."

"So what could do that?" Stephanie tried to figure out something that could be causing such an apparently impossible result. "Not the extreme redshift?"

"No, that would just put the lines far out of their default locations, but easily detectable." Sunny looked over at Barton.

Bart grinned, though there was still disbelief on his face. "What we're seeing here is a straight-up blackbody emission."

"Stars emit as blackbodies."

"But as *gaseous* blackbodies. That's why you get spectral lines. The only way *I* know of you can get this kind of spectrum is if it's a *solid object* that's radiating. One not in any kind of detectable atmosphere."

"A *solid* object?" She tried to wrap her thoughts around that. "But a solid object that far away would be . . ."

She trailed off as the truth struck her. The target *could not* be tremendously far away. A radiating solid object large enough to be seen from extra-galactic distances would be too large to exist; even made from the lightest materials it would easily exceed the TOV limit and turn into a black hole. She didn't think even science-fiction concepts like giant Dyson Spheres could reach the required size, and if they did, why would a Dyson Sphere the size of a galactic cluster be glowing hot?

No, this only made sense if . . . "It's not far away. It's *near us*."

"*Near* is a relative term, of course, but yes. Our first very, very crude guess puts it somewhere less than twenty light-days out. If so, it's probably somewhere on the order of a thousand kilometers in diameter."

"Wow. Holy crap. I mean . . . *wow*. So we have a solid planetoid-sized object that suddenly heated up?" She tried to imagine a process that could do that. "Natural nuclear process? But what could trigger it?"

Bart ran a hand through his spiky black hair and its frosted tips. "Um, Steph, it's . . . well, stranger than that. See, I took another blackbody measurement today, just to check against the other data, and it looks like . . . Well, at first I thought it might just be cooling, but the initial plot of the first four days has really the wrong curve, and I could be wrong, but"—he drew in a deep breath—"I think it's slowing down."

"Slowing— WHAT?"

"My best guess is that it's actually cooler than we thought, about three thousand degrees Kelvin, and the temperature we *thought* we were seeing, well . . . that's because it was moving at about thirty percent of lightspeed."

Stephanie stared at Bart, then looked around at the others. For a long moment no one said anything.

Suddenly, she understood, and she couldn't help but start laughing. "Oh . . . oh, God, you guys, you got me *good*! I was taking this *seriously*!"

Her laughs trailed off in silence as none of the others cracked a smile. *Holy shit.* "You . . . you *are* serious?"

"I assure you," Crystal Nakamura said, as precise and controlled as if she were delivering a report, "if there was a jest involved, *I* was not in on it."

"No joke, Steph. I know it *seems* ridiculous, but it's all straight," Bart said.

"Jesus." She looked at the whole situation again. "So we have a solid object—how large, again?"

"Handwavy estimate puts it on the order of a thousand kilometers, based on our first-cut guess of distance and then calculating how much energy you'd need to radiate to be seen at that distance."

Stephanie was speechless for a moment. "A *thousand kilometers*?"

"Very roughly."

"We have a *thousand-kilometer* something hot enough to melt steel coming in at almost a third of lightspeed *and slowing down*?"

"That's what you seem to have given us, yes," David said.

Stephanie looked around, seeing once more that all of them—Sunny, David, Bart, and Crystal—were deadly serious. Then she took a breath and said what all of them were thinking.

"That's not natural. That's *artificial*. We're looking at the first known extraterrestrial ship."

Crystal winced. "That's . . ."

"We can't dance around this issue!" Stephanie heard her own voice, sharp and a little frightened. "We've all spent our *lives* studying every astronomical phenomenon there is! There isn't a natural process I can even *imagine* that would give me a white-hot glowing ball of something flying around at a percentage of lightspeed and then *slowing down*. If anything, it should be *speeding up* as it gets closer to the Sun. That thing out there is coming in *under control*." She looked back to Bart. "If it keeps slowing down the way it is, how fast will it be going when it gets here?"

"Rough guess? It's going to *stop*, or close to it."

"Wait a minute." She did rough calculations in her head. "Are you saying it's not only slowing down, it's slowing down at something like one *gravity* of acceleration?"

"Something like that."

"Jesus. I can't . . . how much energy *is* that?"

"We haven't done those calculations yet," David said. "Partly because we need to get other estimates first, like how much mass we're dealing with. We know how much it's radiating, but how efficient is the drive? *What* is the drive?"

"These are all important questions," Crystal said, "But first I think I need to talk to the Director."

"Well, sure, that's your job—"

"And until I do, *nothing* gets sent out from here."

"Now, wait—"

Crystal's glare made Stephanie's protest stop dead in her throat. "Ms. Bronson, I am not a scientist myself, but I can understand enough to tell that this falls *directly* under 'national security concerns.' Maybe *planetary* security concerns, but that's not my job.

"I know, I know—we can't keep this secret for long," she said, and her expression softened. "And *believe* me, I know how much you're going to want to talk about this, to *announce* this to the world. Biggest thing *ever* in anyone's career. Just give me a little bit of time to talk to the Director and some of our partners in the government before we do it, okay?"

Stephanie looked over at David, who nodded. So did Bart and, reluctantly, Sunny. "Okay. But like you said, this won't keep long."

"Then I'll go see the Director *now*."

Stephanie watched her leave, and turned to look at the single image on the screen, a star field with a tiny, circled dot.

A tiny dot that was a moon-sized *something*, blazing at the heat of a forge, hurtling at the Solar System at impossible speed.

CHAPTER 3:
FIRST RESPONSES

"Roger, I know you like to lighten my mornings some days, but I don't appreciate pranks that look *too much* like the real thing. Wastes my thinking time." Seeing the hesitation on Roger Stone's face, President Jeanne Sacco shook her head with a smile. "Not that I don't appreciate the effort, it's really impressive."

Roger took a deep breath. "It's . . . not a prank, ma'am."

Jeanne blinked, then looked down at the slim folder in front of her again. "What?"

"I said, it's not a prank, ma'am. The object was first spotted by SNIT less than a week ago. It's a fairly faint object even in infrared, and apparently even dimmer in visible light. If the survey hadn't been running right now, it might not have been spotted for a while."

Jeanne didn't answer at first. She was trying to get her worldview to accept what she was being told, and that wasn't easy. Jeanne Sacco had always been a realist, sometimes even a cynic; you didn't get ahead in politics if you were an innocent, and she'd done plenty of things in her time that involved pretending you agreed with something ridiculous, or even reprehensible, another person, or an entire political group, was saying. Playing the game involved balancing between the Scylla of corruption on the one side and the Charybdis of naïveté on the other.

But, she thought, staring at the pictures and dry annotations in the file, *my training's in law and political science and public performance. Not in astronomy.* Unlike many politicians, she knew the difference. Scientific facts didn't budge just because you found them inconvenient.

Or terrifying. And right now, *terrifying* seemed the more appropriate description. She read *a thousand kilometers across* and pictured something like a red-hot version of Star Wars' *Death Star* barreling down on them at unbelievable speed. "How sure are we of this information?"

"As sure as we can be, at this point. *Something* is out there, and coming fast."

When in doubt, get advice. "I want a meeting of the Cabinet . . . and maybe the Joint Chiefs, too, tomorrow, Rog. I'd rather have it in a couple hours, but I know we can't get everyone we'll need for this together in less than twelve. Get whatever scientific support we need for the meeting—NASA, anyone else you think should be in on it. This Bronson woman, the discoverer, if she's up to the job. We need to go over all this right away. How long can we sit on this?"

"Crystal Nakamura at SNIT did a quick eval for us; a couple of weeks is pretty much all we can expect. Wouldn't have even *that* if this thing wasn't hard to spot, but people will notice silence really fast."

Two weeks. The number was ridiculous. Less than fourteen days to decide how to address the most significant event in human history. She couldn't decide whether to be thrilled that this was happening on her watch, or horrified.

In the end, I guess that depends on what our visitors want.

"One day, Rog. And yes, I know people will notice the sudden activity; let them." She looked out the window onto the grounds, calm and sunny, deceptively ordinary. "Just as long as they won't connect it to SNIT's discovery for a while."

"Director Haley, this is the President."

Director Sean Haley's voice was cheerful. "Good morning, Madam President. I was hoping to hear from you."

"I suppose you must have, after the bomb your people dropped on us. I am putting together a meeting of the Joint Chiefs and possibly others for tomorrow. Can I count on you to attend and present your findings?"

"Well," the director began, sounding thoughtful—with a touch of amusement, "I certainly *could* attend, President Sacco, but honestly, I'm not the right person for the job."

She felt one eyebrow rise at that. "You're the director, aren't you? I would think that would make you the *most* qualified person."

"Alas, not quite. I came up to this position through being a better, oh, mediator, I suppose. I've certainly gained knowledge of the appropriate disciplines, but I'm not nearly so much an authority as the people down there in the trenches, so to speak."

"What I'm hearing is that you don't *want* to give the presentation. Why, Dr. Haley? Is it the . . . controversial nature of the material?" She knew professionals—especially those high up in organizations—were often extremely wary of "disruptive" concepts that might reflect on their careers.

Haley's deep laugh dispelled *that* theory. "Oh, my, far from it, President Sacco. I so *very* much want to give this presentation, and most of the ones to follow, so much I can practically *taste* it. But"—he gave a deep sigh—"I have responsibilities and principles in this case."

Sacco felt her own smile start. "You have someone else in mind."

"Absolutely. This is Stephanie's discovery and I think she has *every* right to show it to the world. This is going to be the biggest thing *ever*, and one thing I am absolutely determined *not* to be is the man who took her credit. It's happened enough times before."

That's . . . true enough. But . . . "Director, she's . . . quite young, if I understand her position correctly. Are you sure she's up to this?"

"Of course, the thing will scare her half to death, but I'm sure she can get through the presentation tomorrow if I push her." A pause. "If I'm wrong, of course, I will apologize to both of you, and I'll take over . . . but I'm willing to bet she'll rise to the occasion. And in a few days I'll have someone I know will backstop her—someone who doesn't need any more recognition and doesn't care about it."

"Who would that be?"

"Dr. York Dobyns."

There weren't *that* many scientists Jeanne Sacco knew by name, but she knew that one. "You think he'll be onboard for this?"

"Ha! Madam President, you'll *need* a physicist for this, and a man who's won two Nobels is just the kind of physicist you'll want. If I *didn't* invite York in, he'd kill me."

"You know him?"

"For years; I was assistant director at one of the institutes he lectured at. Won't be there for the first presentation, but I'll guarantee he'll be there in a week or two."

"I'll take your word for it, Director. Then we can expect Stephanie Bronson tomorrow at eleven o'clock?"

"She'll be there if I have to drag her onto the plane myself."

"Thank you, Director—and may I say, I appreciate very much your personal stance in this case?"

Haley's voice was serious. "I was sure you would, President Sacco."

Stephanie Bronson stared around the briefing room and tried to keep her heart from racing out of control. *That's the President, and Vice President Andrea Perez...crap, this is all of the Cabinet that's in Washington right now, and those military guys have to be part of the Joint Chiefs of Staff.*

The combination of adrenaline and the speed of events lent a cast of dreamlike unreality to the situation. *I can't* believe *the director just sent me out here on my own!*

But he had, and done so with his typical breezy casualness. Quick summary, a sincere expression of his confidence in her, *boom*, she was on a plane headed for Washington ... and now she was here.

President Sacco clapped her hands together once, snapping Stephanie back to the present, and the murmurs in the room immediately quieted down. "Thank you, everyone. I know this meeting was called with no warning and minimum time. I think you'll all agree I was justified in doing so once you hear what triggered it."

She smiled warmly at Stephanie, with her white teeth complemented by her black-and-gray hair and dark eyes. The President was striking-looking, with a strongly Sicilian face and a slender figure that made her look even taller than she was; the smile made Stephanie's pulse go from frantic to merely fast. "Dr. Bronson—"

"Just Ms. Bronson, Madam President," she said, then blanched, realizing she had just *interrupted* the President in her own meeting.

One of the dark brows rose. "You don't have a doctorate yet, Ms. Bronson?"

"No, ma'am. I'm ABD right now."

"'All but dissertation,'" quoted President Sacco with another, milder smile. "Well, perhaps I'm out of my field, but I suspect you can rely on your degree coming. Ms. Bronson, I understand you've prepared a briefing for us?"

Spent hours last night, some of them on the plane, working on it! "Yes, ma'am."

"Rog, is it all cued up? Good. Ms. Bronson, let's not waste any of these people's valuable time. Show us our problem."

She swallowed, took the control, and clicked. The lights in the room automatically dimmed to make the screen easily visible, along with the projected title screen: DISCOVERY AND INITIAL ANALYSIS OF AN EXTRASOLAR OBJECT ON A CONTROLLED VECTOR.

Despite her deliberate attempt to make the title as nonobviously controversial as possible, she saw heads turn, silhouettes bend closer, a faint ripple of whispers run around the room. "At approximately 1:30 A.M. last Monday, the thirteenth, the Smyth-Nichols Infrared Telescope detected a previously unrecorded object near Gamma Lupi..."

The initial discovery didn't take long to describe, just a few slides, but even so, the watchers could no longer stay silent. "Ms. Bronson!" said a deep voice that she thought belonged to Admiral Dickinson, the chief of naval operations. "My apologies, but how certain are these... conclusions?"

"Those were just the first observations and guesses, Admiral," she answered, and swallowed—audibly enough that the sound echoed around the room. No one laughed. "We've refined the estimates some since then, but the basic... idea hasn't changed."

"Then what are your current estimates, Ms. Bronson? I think we'd all like the best guess as to what we're dealing with?"

She skipped forward a couple of slides. "The radiating diameter of the object is approximately two thousand kilometers."

"Your initial estimate said a thousand!" another voice said, one she couldn't quite identify.

"Sir, it said *on the order of* a thousand. We had no clear information to be closer; that meant that a thousand was our current rough guess but it could be as much as ten times that size, or a tenth that size. Current work has refined that." There was a grunt she took as agreement, or at least permission to continue. "As I said, our estimate now is that the object is two thousand kilometers in diameter, plus or minus about ten percent. Actual temperature appears to be approximately three thousand degrees Kelvin, or nearly five thousand degrees Fahrenheit."

"Good God," said Diane Truro, secretary of the interior. "What the hell is it made of? What's *solid* at that temperature?"

"Our first, best guess is tungsten," Stephanie said. "Melting point of tungsten is a thousand degrees Fahrenheit higher than that, so it's a reasonable safety margin for a radiator."

"Is that what you think this is? A radiator?"

"It seems a safe guess. We've now got a decent estimate of mass and energy output, too. It's at approximately fifteen or sixteen light-days out at this point, radiating about five times ten to the twelfth megawatts."

"Five times . . . Ms. Bronson, can you put that in terms that we can understand?"

"I'll . . . try, ma'am, but it's big. Bigger than big. That thing is radiating orders of magnitude more energy than the whole of humanity is using right now—something like a hundred-millionth of the Sun's total output, which is just . . . ridiculous. If I tried to express it in, say, atom bombs per hour it would still be a ridiculous number, hundreds of millions."

"You say you have an estimate of mass? How heavy this thing is?" the President asked, while everyone else was assimilating the sheer magnitude of the problem.

"Yes. It's a very *rough* estimate, based on assuming their drive system is about fifty percent efficient and thus what we're seeing radiated is the same as the energy used to slow the object down at about one gravity. If it's more efficient then the object could be more massive, if it's less efficient then the object is going to be less massive, but our rough guess is about one billion metric tons. Again very rough, but you can visualize that as a flying New York City or Tokyo."

"But that's far, far smaller than two thousand kilometers," President Sacco said. "That's why you call this a radiator?"

She seems to be pretty sharp on this for someone who's not a scientist. Thank God. "Yes, ma'am. The amount of energy to slow something that big down from lightspeed would just *vaporize* your ship if you tried to dump your waste heat in any kind of reasonable space. So that two-thousand-kilometer diameter has to be something like a huge radiator fan stretching out." She frowned. "*How* that could work we're not sure, for various reasons, but that's the only explanation we have right now."

"Well, that's *something* of a relief," the President said. "I was imagining something like a moon-sized battle station. Still, I suppose if it can generate that much energy there's not all that much difference from our point of view."

"Well ... yes and no, ma'am. Obviously we have to hope it's not hostile, because if it is, well, we're probably screwed. Pardon the technical term. *But* ... we do have weapons that can damage or destroy objects a few kilometers long. I don't think anything we have would do much to something two thousand kilometers across."

"Where is it going to stop, assuming it keeps decelerating?" That was General Victor Rainsford, secretary of the Air Force.

"Right now it looks like at just about nineteen AU—that's around the orbit of Uranus. With that kind of acceleration, we can't tell for sure what orbit it might try to put itself into at the end, of course."

"Do we have any idea what drive system it's *using*?" asked Dr. Eva Filipek, secretary of energy. "That would allow you to refine your efficiency estimate and thus mass, correct?"

Stephanie spread her hands and shrugged, hoping she didn't look ridiculous. "Ma'am, we haven't the faintest idea. Any known drive system that could even theoretically produce that level of thrust should be blasting some form of exhaust at just *immense* volumes, and as mentioned, one of the things that set off our alarm bells is that we see *no* sign of heated gas of any kind. There should be absolutely massive amounts of reaction mass, or explosive by-products, or *something* shooting at us at fractions of lightspeed to slow this thing down, and we see nothing."

"Then ... we are dealing with some form of *reactionless* drive?" That was from the director of the CIA, whose name she couldn't quite bring to mind. The question showed a surprising depth of knowledge, though—or that the director was a fan of nuts-and-bolts science fiction in his spare time.

"There doesn't seem to be any alternative, at least not based on what we know. It's just ... expending energy and slowing down fast."

The President nodded. For a moment, no one spoke.

Finally, the President took a breath. "So, to sum up: Our solar system is being approached by a city-sized *something* using more energy than we can easily imagine, and that is going to come to a stop somewhere in the outer system, in the next three months or so. We can't keep this quiet?" She looked at Stephanie.

"No, Madam President," she said, trying to be emphatic. "Leaving aside the fact that there's already some people outside my group aware that we saw *something*, as it gets closer it's going to become more and more obvious. By the time it's about to shut off its drive, it'll be magnitude two or so, and even brighter in infrared—*easily* naked-eye visible, even in pretty light-polluted skies. Long before then it will be so *obvious* to any astronomer that..." She shrugged. "No. Just not possible. I wouldn't give odds you could keep it quiet for more than a couple weeks, really. It's not *that* dim and with the hint that we saw something and haven't followed up..."

The President nodded. "All right. Take that as a given, then. We need to be proactive. We don't want this getting out as rumors and *then* having to play catch-up with the Internet. It'll be bad enough once we *do* announce. We are *not* going to assume we have two weeks. I'm not assuming I have more than a few *days* before someone spills this one way or another. We need to know what line we're going to take with this announcement, how we want to spin it, what actions we need to be taking."

She looked around the table. "I want answers to those questions by tomorrow afternoon at the latest, and I want to do the announcement ASAP. Dr....Ms. Bronson, you'll be part of this, I want to be clear on that. But I would recommend you expedite your thesis, if you can. You'll sound ever so much more authoritative if you're *Doctor* Bronson."

Stephanie returned the President's smile. "I'd agree. It'll be up to my defense committee, of course."

"On that note, what *about* defense, Madam President?" George Green, secretary of defense, jerked his head at the screen. "It'd be nice if they were friendly, but what do you want us to do at the DoD?"

President Sacco sighed. "George, I guess we have to run as many scenarios as we can—and include assumptions about other countries helping or not. Investigate all the options we might have. I know"—she glanced over at Stephanie, who had opened her mouth and closed it again—"the chances that we can do *anything* against such a thing if it's actually hostile are close to zero, but we'd be absolutely remiss in our duties if we didn't at least consider the possibility.

"Byron, Hailey, Manny," she said, addressing the heads of the DHS, CIA (*Ha! Hailey Vanderman*, that *was his name!)* and FBI, "I want you all to work closely. *No* interagency rivalry on this, and I mean that for the armed forces, too. This is too damn important for anyone to get twitchy over their little territories. Understood?"

There was a chorus of "Yes, ma'am" around the table.

"All right. Then let's get to it, people," said President Sacco. "Two days, three tops. And then we're going to turn the whole world upside down!"

CHAPTER 4:
ANNOUNCEMENT

Well, this is it, Stephanie thought. *No turning back.*

She stood to the side, watching as the representatives of the press—from the major networks through *Time* magazine, Al Jazeera, and the more prominent online services, as well as a scattering of foreign and regional services—settled into their seats with an air of restrained excitement. The lid had been kept on—somehow—for the last two and a half days, and the President had green-lighted the conference only a few hours ago.

A few murmurs went around the room as President Sacco took the podium without any preliminaries. "Thank you, everyone, for coming on short notice. I think you will understand the urgency once we finish the briefing."

She turned and extended a hand toward Stephanie. "I would like to introduce Ms. Stephanie Bronson, who will be conducting the main portion of this briefing; she and I will answer questions following the presentation. I must ask that *all* of you"—she looked particularly at Colbert Oliver, the comedian-turned-reporter—"restrain yourselves until after Ms. Bronson is finished."

Chuckles rippled about the room, with Oliver grinning as widely as any before he nodded, made a zipped-lips gesture, and settled back into his chair.

"Then, without further ado . . . Stephanie?"

She took a deep breath and walked to the podium vacated by Sacco.

She knew she didn't present nearly so imposing a figure as Sacco, who stood nearly six feet in flats; she didn't clear five foot six. *But I think I'll get their attention anyway once I start.*

That had been one of the things the President and her advisors had warned about. She was going to be *known* after this, and who knew what that would mean in the long run? She'd seen people who became famous without expecting to, and a lot of them crashed and burned in pretty spectacular ways.

But...well, maybe it was really stupid pride, but this was *her* discovery.

"Good evening," she said, and swallowed to get rid of the tension in her throat. The mike picked up the sound and echoed it around the room. Another flutter of mostly good-natured laughs followed it. *Relax. After that first briefing in front of the President and the Joint Chiefs? This should be cake!*

The presentation screen lit up. "I've prepared a presentation to summarize the current situation. As the President said, please try to keep any questions or comments until after I've finished."

Won't be easy, she thought; a flutter of whispers began and three or four arms did abortive raises as the first slide appeared, showing the title:

FENRIR: APPROACH OF AN EXTRATERRESTRIAL
VEHICLE TO THE SOLAR SYSTEM

The presentation was a modified version of the one she'd given the Joint Chiefs, updated with the latest information and guesses, as well as a summarized action plan. The code name of the object had come from Hailey Vanderman, showing the CIA chief had something of a sense of dark humor and more astronomical and historic knowledge than she'd expected.

She quickly discussed the initial discovery, immediate analysis, and verification that the target was no known type of astronomical phenomenon.

"Currently," she said, moving to the next slide, "we have a refined diameter estimate for what we are calling the radiator disc: it is two thousand, one hundred and fifteen kilometers across, plus or minus about ten kilometers. We assume that the sail itself masses no more than ten percent of the entire vessel, and possibly far less. The presumed central vessel, which is not yet discernable, has an approximate mass of one billion metric tons—the size of a large city."

She ignored hands already up, flicked to the next screen. "*Fenrir* is currently traveling at a velocity of slightly over twenty-eight percent of the speed of light, having been traveling at thirty percent of lightspeed when it . . . well, lit off its drive. It will arrive at relative rest to the Solar System in one hundred days, assuming that it does not change its acceleration in any way, shape, or form, at which point it will be at roughly two point nine billion kilometers from the Sun. That's at the same distance as the orbit of Uranus."

She looked up, seeing every eye locked on her. "After that . . . we have no idea what will happen. It's not coming directly to Earth, but it's not targeting any other specific object, either. Its course *is* apparently intended to match it to the plane of the ecliptic, or very near it, so it may be that Earth or one of the other major planets is its ultimate goal."

Gerald Walters of NBC finally stood. "Ms. Bronson—is this *straight*? I'm sorry to interrupt, but . . ."

She glanced to the President, who stepped to the podium next to Stephanie. "Gerald, this is one hundred percent on the level. I had the same reaction a few days back when the file hit my desk, but it's very real. Now please, let Stephanie finish, and if her presentation hasn't answered your questions, *then* ask them."

Walters sat back down, but he and most of the others looked like they were close to exploding. *I can't blame them. A thousand questions to ask, most of the answers likely being "I don't know."*

"So, the takeaway from all this." She went to the next slide. "First: *Fenrir* is an alien spacecraft. There is no other reasonable explanation for our observations, especially for the deceleration on approach to the Solar System.

"Second: *Fenrir* is using a drive whose principles are unknown to us; it appears to be reactionless—that is, it requires no, or very little, propellant to produce a very large change in motion.

"Third: its power source is almost certainly antimatter.

"Fourth: in addition to this reactionless drive, there are indications of at least one and possibly several technological advances that we cannot currently match.

"Fifth: they're coming here to stay for at least some period of time.

You don't expend a hundred million tons of antimatter just so you can spend another hundred million accelerating back out the next day. They want *something* here, and it's important enough for them to send something the size of a city on a journey of more than sixty light-years and two centuries."

The next slide. "At the same time as we're having this briefing, the United States has been sending all of the collected data we have to the other nations. This event is not a national problem; it is an event that concerns every nation on Earth. Moving forward, we expect to be working with the leaders of the other nations to determine our preparations and response to the arrival of *Fenrir*."

She looked up as the final slide popped up—an image of the star field with *Fenrir* circled, and a big white "Q&A" blazoned across it. "Questions?"

Mack Henning, from Reuters, managed to get his in first. "I know you answered this briefly, but how certain are you of all of this? You understand, this is the biggest story of the century, at least."

"Of the basic summary? As certain as anything gets," Stephanie said, though as always she felt the little twinge of a scientist making a flat assertion in public. "We've got observations of *Fenrir* going back several days now. It's not possible for this to be faked in any way we can imagine. There's no other astronomical phenomena that can even really explain the temperature or speed of the thing. And so on. The details are still slightly subject to change, but it would be in small areas, not major ones." She pointed to a hand up farther to the back—she thought it was the BBC representative, Bryan Mallory. "Yes?"

The accent and deep voice confirmed her memory. "Ms. Bronson, you mentioned a distance and time there. Does that mean you know where this 'Fenrir' came from?"

"*Know* would be too strong. We have a guess, a logical surmise from where we first spotted it. We currently believe that *Fenrir* came from a K-type main sequence star that is visible at a very small separation from *Fenrir*, and that is the only star anywhere near its course that would be a reasonable candidate for its origin. That star was catalogued but otherwise we have very little data on it—not terribly surprising, as until recently we hadn't even *found* all of the K-type stars within a hundred light-years. But checking prior images of that area of the sky and comparing them, we were able to verify that it's a K2 orange dwarf on the main sequence, and what little data we can gather on it indicates that it's about the age of our Sun or a bit older, with a very similar metallicity. In short, even without *Fenrir*'s proximity, it would be a very strong candidate to support a habitable world."

"Is it likely that they would know we are here? That is, could they have chosen our solar system specifically because of our civilization?" That was Noel Frasier, the *New York Times* rep.

Stephanie restrained the urge to shrug. "*Fenrir* itself has almost certainly detected us; we're very bright in the radio bands compared to any planet of our type, and the RF signals we put out would be pretty obviously technological in nature.

"The people at their *homeworld*, that's harder. Certainly they wouldn't have known anything about our high-tech capabilities *now*— this ship was launched, if we're right about its origin, about 1820 or so, and that launch would've been based on data sixty-one years older than *that*, so about 1760—before the United States even declared independence." She *did* shrug now. "Honestly, we don't know what kind of telescopic technology they had or what their assumptions about technological progress would be. If they had an absolutely *amazing* wide-baseline telescope array, they *might* have been able to pick up hints of structure on the ground, but I tend to doubt it.

"No, honestly, I don't think they were sent here knowing we were here; it was probably just knowing that *life* was here—that this was a very much living world. *Now*, of course, they know someone is here."

ScienceLine's Marcie Amour caught her attention next. "What other technological advances have you deduced from *Fenrir*'s data?"

"I thought you'd be on that," Stephanie said with a smile. "There are two we think are pretty likely and a few others that are vague guesses. The first one seems almost certain: a superconductor of heat. We can't get a model of a radiator of that size and heat radiation capability to work without assuming some way of distributing the heat essentially perfectly. We are reserving the other technology guesses until we have more information."

"Madam President," Gerald Walters said, looking toward Sacco, "does the United States have any specific action plans at this time?"

"Mainly ones of research, Gerry," the President answered. "We're already planning on trying to transmit something to them, but first we have to figure out *what*. We have to assume that even if they *did* catch some of our transmissions, they still don't really understand our language."

More questions came thick and fast, but to a lot of them either she or the President had to answer something that boiled down to "we don't know."

Finally, it began to wind down, and it was the AP representative who asked the last question to get a decent answer: "So, Stephanie, why the name *Fenrir*? That's from Norse mythology, isn't it?"

"That's right, Rick," she answered, seeing "Rick Ventura" on her seating chart. "Maybe part of it will be obvious from this picture; it was an early model of what *Fenrir* might look like if we could really get a look at it."

On the screen flashed a star field, the center of it dominated by a glowing disc, veined with hints of structure, and with something else at the center; the effect was of a huge, red-shining eye staring out of the night. There was a momentary ripple of people shifting uncomfortably, looking at that image with its imaginary yet undeniable menace.

"The constellation it's in is *Lupus*—which means 'Wolf.' And in Norse legend, Fenrir was the great wolf that would battle Odin in Ragnarok."

"Fenrir," murmured Frasier. "Hell of a code name. I hope it's not an omen."

"So do I," Stephanie agreed, and switched the image back to the innocuous Q&A screen. "So do we all."

CHAPTER 5: PREPARATIONS FOR A VISIT

"How certain are your people that *Fenrir* is using antimatter for its energy generation?" asked Alyosha Volkov. "I mean, it's an exciting thought, especially given that we can only create and store nanograms of antimatter ourselves."

Volkov was a special scientific envoy for the Russian President, and Sacco had found him unexpectedly cheerful and energetic. *So much for stereotypes of the gloomy Russian*, she thought. "They seem quite certain, but I'm not one of the scientists. York?"

A big, barrel-chested man stood up at the end of the conference table; he, too, was a breaker of stereotypes. As far as Jeanne Sacco was concerned, Dr. York Dobyns certainly didn't *look* like a man twice-awarded the Nobel Prize in Physics—in fact, he looked more like an outdoorsman, with his close-cropped beard and mustache and rather less-than-formal khakis and hiking boots. "Well, we *can* actually do much better than nanograms, we just generally don't. In any event, they either are using antimatter, or they've got some *really* science-fictional technology that can convert matter direct to energy. Dr. Bronson, did we get those slides in time?"

Stephanie Bronson nodded—not bothering, Sacco noted, to correct the mode of address. "Just a minute, Dr. Dobyns." After a moment, two graphs appeared on the presentation screen.

"Ah! Yes, that's it. See here, this is the curve of radiated energy from

Fenrir, and this is its acceleration. Now, you'll note that the acceleration has remained constant—very much so—but the energy expended is falling gradually. Now from this, we can deduce that the mass of Fenrir is slowly decreasing. This mass, of course, has to be, for want of a better word, their fuel, whatever they're using to provide them with the power we see.

"So if we compare the radiated energy and the calculated mass reduction and the deceleration, we arrive at the conclusion that they are using some method of total energy conversion. The only such technology we *know* exists would be matter-antimatter annihilation. It is of course possible they have something entirely outside our knowledge, but for now Occam's razor suggests that we assume they're making use of the method we at least theoretically understand."

Alyosha nodded, as did most of the other seven representatives around the table—from China, India, the United Kingdom, the EU, Japan, Brazil, and Canada. Larger briefings would include as many countries as possible, but President Sacco knew that it would be hard to get clear direction even from a group this size, let alone one far larger.

That wasn't helped, of course, by the fact that *Fenrir* was a problem unlike any the world had ever faced.

"Unpleasant though it may be to consider," Osamu Kurumada said, "but have we any data on what sort of weapons *Fenrir* may have, if it is hostile?"

Stephanie Bronson glanced at her team, especially at York, who simply nodded, then shrugged. "I have a small presentation on our various guesses, but we really don't have much information on which to make any realistic assessment. Worst-case, they could have missiles that make use of the same drive the ship does, and could drive them with higher accelerations, so in theory they could hit us with impacts at significant fractions of *c*."

"Which would be absolutely devastating," Dr. Dobyns said. "To give you an idea, a single two-ton projectile at the same speed as *Fenrir* was traveling—thirty percent of lightspeed—would deliver an impact of two *gigatons*. They could have gamma-ray lasers that would carve through mountains or..." He waved his hands to indicate *and pretty much anything else.* "Seriously, though, if they're determined to be hostile, we are absolutely screwed. Hell, all they have to do is get within any reasonable distance of Earth and turn on their drive. It'd bake us all in very short order. So, Steph and I—and the rest of our team—are pretty much agreed that it's a moot point. I mean, by all means, go ahead and work on your doomsday scenarios, but these guys are playing with more energy every *second* than the entire human race has *ever* used."

There was silence around the table for a moment, then Alyosha chuckled. "Ah, well, we are all used to things on so much *smaller* a scale. Let us go on."

"Very good," said Olivia Davies, the United Kingdom representative. "Can we focus on our response, then? We've all been supplying information for communications strategies. Where are we with that?"

Sacco was pleased to see that despite everyone looking at Dr. Dobyns, York subtly nudged Stephanie Bronson to respond. *She's still adjusting to being the face of everything, but at least her team's supporting her.*

"Well . . . the idea of communicating with an alien intelligence is a pretty old one, and we've been going over not just the information and messages that the various countries would like to send, but the protocols for establishing communication. That's really the most crucial, after all, since until they know *how* to talk to us, it doesn't matter what messages we send."

"That assumes they can't figure out how to talk to us from what they're receiving," pointed out Adriana Suarez, the Brazilian representative. "They will have months of everything we've been broadcasting to analyze. Surely they will be able to understand us by the time they stop?"

Kurumada shook his head. "My apologies, but I do not believe so, Dr. Suarez. Perhaps our think-tank will feel differently, but it seems to me that there are so very many obstacles in the way of understanding our words from such transmissions."

"That's our feeling, yes," Stephanie said after a brief discussion with the others on her team. "First, we're transmitting on many bands, with multiple languages, in different modes and encoding schemes. How do you determine that what you're receiving is someone's voice? Maybe they don't even *have* a concept of 'voice' the way we do. Maybe they don't *see* the way we do. Written symbols are effectively arbitrary; they would need context to even *try* to interpret them, and they'd have no more context for us than we do for them. We're pretty sure that they'd need to receive a systematic teaching transmission, one that's clearly directed at them and that works through mathematical and scientific expressions before we attempt anything more complicated."

Dr. Dobyns nodded. "Oh, if they were studying our transmissions ever since they could have picked them up, maybe, but at thirty percent of lightspeed I'm thinking that most of their sensors were shut down to protect them. A micrometeorite impact that you wouldn't care much about at, say, twenty kilometers per second you will be *really* worried about at a hundred thousand kilometers per second."

"But I thought space was basically empty," Li Xiu Ying said. "Are impacts that common?"

"I'm afraid so. Oh, it's emptier out between the stars than near our planet, but there's still some gas and dust out there. The gas probably wouldn't pose *too* much of a problem, but even very small particles of dust would be extremely dangerous," Dobyns replied.

"Here's an example," Stephanie said. "If an average grain of sand—which masses less than point oh-five grams—were to hit this room at that speed, it would blow us and most of this building out of existence; the impact energy is about fifty-seven tons of TNT. From one grain of sand. So even very, very small pieces of dust could be chipping away pieces of your ship, and would certainly destroy any sensors you had out."

"That sounds like over a hundred years it would do *much* damage, even if space is almost empty," Alyosha said. "How did they survive?"

"Most designs for that kind of interstellar travel assume that the front of your ship is . . . well, ablative mass. A big, thick coating of rock or metal or ice that wears away, probably with embedded sensors to let you know if it takes a *really* big hit. I would not be surprised if, once *Fenrir* drops below a significant percentage of lightspeed, we'll see a pretty large chunk of it just get ejected," Stephanie said. She'd researched a *lot* of these questions as soon as she realized she was going to be the one in the spotlight.

She went on, "Exactly *when* they drop their big shield will tell us a lot about them."

"Ah," said Kurumada. "How tough their main ship is, yes?"

"Basically, yes."

"All right," Dr. Suarez said with a nod, "that makes sense. So, they've only had a short time—since they started slowing down, and probably *had* to at least take some readings on us to make sure everything was as they expected—to study our transmissions, so they won't understand us. When will we be ready to transmit to them?"

"We're working on that," Dobyns said, "but honestly? We'll want them to be a *lot* closer, otherwise we won't be able to get any response data in reasonable time." He pointed to another slide that showed transmission times. "Right now, turnaround time is something around two weeks, maybe a bit less now. *Fenrir's* going to stop about two light-hours out, which is a lot more reasonable. Means we could expect several exchanges per day."

"True," Sacco said, studying the slide, "But it strikes me that we could get a head start simply by transmitting what amounts to the basic alphabet or whatever, constantly, in their direction."

Kurumada nodded. "Yes. I agree. It would give them time to, first, sense that we were transmitting directly to them, and then learn whatever they could on the way in."

"And also give us more time to find out if they *want* to talk," Alyosha said with a wry grin. "Even with long delay times, they could still send us signal of 'enough with the baby talk,' yes?"

"Oh, certainly!" Stephanie said. "Which would tell us more about them. How fast they detect our transmission, how long it takes to decode it, and so on."

Neysa Deshpande, the Indian representative, smiled briefly. "Not to be repetitive, but we *are* certain they have detected us? Because if they have *not*, then sending such a transmission will absolutely alert them, will it not?"

President Sacco saw Stephanie and York exchanging glances, and understood what they were thinking.

Stephanie grimaced. "Dr. Deshpande, there's very little *certain* at this point; all we can do is make our best educated guesses, based on what we would expect we would, and could, do. And this close to Earth, there's basically no way we would have missed noticing that Earth's radiating in so many bands of the E-M spectrum in a way that just *can't* be natural. So we have to assume they have seen us."

Deshpande gave an apologetic shrug. "Our various citizens will all want us to be cautious. But I agree with your guess, for what it is worth. Let us start transmitting as soon as we have the, how should we say, lesson plan well mapped out."

"I agree," Kurumada said, and the other representatives echoed the sentiment.

"Pending the agreement of our superiors, of course," Alyosha added. "Admittedly, any of us could begin transmitting on our own, but if we are to be coordinated . . ."

"Absolutely," President Sacco said. "We do not intend to take any unilateral action at this time—but remember that time *is* limited, so I would hope you can get agreement from your governments quickly."

"We will certainly try," Olivia Davies said. "The issue of more direct contact will require a bit more discussion, I think."

"That's Wednesday's conference," Sacco said. "And yes, I think deciding if, how, and when we could launch something to physically greet them *will* take more discussion. But for now, I think trying to start a dialogue will be enough."

And they'd better damn well want *to have a dialogue,* she thought as the representatives rose for a break.

Because if *Fenrir* didn't want to talk, she doubted they'd be rolling out the welcome mat for a visit.

CHAPTER 6:
FAME HAS ITS REWARDS

Stephanie turned the corner and braked suddenly. "What the heck is going on?"

The quiet little street, with its rows of similar, two- to three-story apartments and houses, was quiet no more. Ahead of her, the streetside parking was full up—at least in one case, by someone who'd parked in front of a hydrant. There were multiple people standing... *Right in front of my house?*

Belatedly, she remembered her own thoughts before the conference, and scanned the road more carefully. Sure enough, a couple of the vans had familiar logos—the local Channel 10 News, Fox, CNN. *Jesus. I... I'd known it might get to be a pain, but* this *fast?*

She was exhausted from the prior few days and the flight; all she wanted was to get home, take a nice long shower, and go to bed, but how was she going to get past that mob?

Someone rapped on her window.

She jumped in her seat, nearly popping the clutch. *Shit, one of them's recognized me!*

But instead, to her surprise it was Joel, her landlord, grinning at her with sympathy in his dark eyes. She rolled down the window.

"Looks like the circus is already in town, Steph," he said, running his hand through the thinning brown hair.

"Sure does," she said with a sigh. "But I've *got* to get in there. I'm due back at work tomorrow—assuming I don't get shipped back to Washington."

He chuckled. "Yeah, you've got yourself a tiger by the tail, and no sense in letting go now that you've got him running. But tell you what." He reached out, dropped a set of keys into her hand. "Turn yourself around and go to 457 East Sandalwood. I've got a nice little apartment there you can use—get yourself cleaned up, get a rest. If these news-vultures keep circling, well, I'll just get your stuff moved over there, a bit at a time so's they don't catch on."

She stared at him. "Joel, I . . . that's really sweet of you, but I can't—"

"You're my tenant, right?"

"Well . . . yes, of course I am, but—"

"No buts. You're paying me for a place to live, and it's not *your* fault that you can't get into it. Seems to me that makes it my responsibility to make sure you find a place." He grinned. "Not like I don't have a dozen or three places to offer, just around this town."

Oddly, she believed him. Not about the places—of course she believed that, Joel owned a *lot* of real estate, and not all of it in this state or maybe even the country. She believed him when he said he really felt responsible for making sure she had a safe place to stay. "All right. Joel, I can't thank you enough."

"Oh, don't go thanking me too much. I'm not *that* different from all those clowns. The idea I'm going to be the *only* person who knows where Stephanie Bronson, discoverer of the first aliens, is, while CNN and company squat in front of my lawn? Ha, that's something to treasure right there!"

He glanced down at her purse. "Let me guess: you never turned your phone back on after you got down?"

"No, I was in a rush to get home."

"Heh. Don't turn it back on until you get settled; I'll bet they've found your number by now."

"You can't be . . ." She paused. Her number was on her business cards and usually attached to her emails. Of course they could find it. "Crap."

"Sorry, Steph, but them's the breaks; you get shoved in front of the world's eye, it'll keep tracking you. Now get moving, before some of 'em decide to find out what you're doing stopped at the corner."

"Right. Thanks, Joel. I don't know how to—"

"Just *go*, and have yourself a quiet night. I'll bet it'll be one of the last you have."

As she drove away, she was afraid Joel was right. People like the

President had whole *divisions* of people assigned to keeping casual questioners away. No one was going to corner her, or the Joint Chiefs, that easily. So who were the newsbite hunters going to come? After the newest face on the block.

And I can't really avoid them all for long anyway. The fact was that they *wanted* the news spread, the *right* news, and if they didn't get real answers, history showed that the people started making their own, usually paranoid, guesses.

Four fifty-seven East Sandalwood turned out to be an entire house—a very nice little house tucked away in the suburbs, already furnished, power on, water on and, when she checked, Wi-Fi already on, with the password stuck on a Post-it note on the fridge. *A vacation rental home? Airbnb?* It was the only immediate explanation that came to her; rich or not, she doubted even Joel could have arranged all that in the few hours between the time he realized the problem and Stephanie's arrival.

First time I've been sleeping over at someone else's house in years, and it's because I'm avoiding people.

That was a pretty pathetic truth, she had to admit. Other than the professional and office friendships that came with pursuing a competitive doctorate, she'd had precious little personal contact lately. It wasn't that she didn't have any *interest*, but most of the guys she knew were either crazy-busy themselves, or taken—or were way older than her and in some kind of position of authority that made any more personal interaction very suspect.

Stephanie threw together a quick mac-and-cheese from stuff already in the fridge and cabinets. Looking at her cell phone, she debated calling her parents, but decided against it. *That's for later—Mom and Dad will want to hear everything and ask a thousand questions, and much as I love them, I'm questioned out.*

That was the one downside to having parents who were genuinely interested in your career: you weren't ever having a *short* conversation about your work. *But all the rest is upside.* Her mother, a chemistry professor for the last twenty-five years, and her father, a high school science teacher for even longer, had showered her with every book she'd ever wanted, worked to get her through college, and even overcome their generation's computer aversion to become part of her online support.

And she knew they'd both understand what it meant to be in the spotlight like she was. So instead of worrying about them, she went to the bathroom, which was also stocked reasonably well, including individual-use bottles and packets of shampoo and toothpaste that gave strong credence to the rental unit theory.

It was in the shower, her immediate concerns gone and the day behind her, that it really *hit* her, and Steph found herself standing immobile beneath the showerhead.

I just changed the world. I stood up in front of every news network there is, and told the world that we are not alone. *Told them that aliens are literally* on their way *and they'll be here, not in years or decades, but* months.

She'd known that was going to happen, but she hadn't *known* it, not the way it suddenly just exploded in understanding within her. *Jesus. I . . . of course they're chasing after me. The President* put me up there. *I'm the authority, even though I don't even know* half *of what I ought to.*

Shaken by the acceptance of her not-entirely-thought-through celebrity, Stephanie got out of the shower, dried off, and dressed for bed in a white T-shirt and drawstring lounging pants from her small suitcase. Then she took a deep breath and turned on her phone.

The screen immediately turned into a scrolling fountain of notifications.

"Ugh." She glanced at the bed, which looked very inviting at the moment, but decided she should at least sort through what she had so far.

Most of the messages were questions or requests for interviews—some laughable, some interesting, a couple absolutely gobsmacking; in the latter category was a personal invite to call the producers of the most popular morning show in America for an immediate on-camera special spot.

Another category were congratulations, questions, and general messages of support from her own colleagues. That at least was comforting.

One message caught her eye: *Please Open and Respond Immediately*, from Sean Haley, the SNIT director himself.

That took priority, as far as she was concerned, and she opened the message.

Based on your unique work, the prior known progress in your basic research, and specific requests and recommendations, it began, *it is the signal pleasure of the University to award you the degree of Doctor of Philosophy in Infrared Astronomy and Astrophysics.*

She reread that incredible sentence again, then forced herself to go on.

The University recognizes the irregularity of these circumstances, and a traditional awarding of the degree will be performed as circumstances permit, but it is viewed both by the University and others that for professional and political purposes it is advantageous to you and others in the profession that you be accorded the degree immediately. Please reply to this message with your acceptance.

I've been texted *my doctorate?*

It wasn't hard to guess where the decision had been made; the President herself had made her opinion on the matter clear. And it was true that Steph *was* very near to the point where she'd have made her thesis defense and, presumably, won her doctorate.

It was still farcical, to have received her doctorate the same way she might have been sent a funny cat video.

Still ... they're dead right. Being "Dr. Bronson" carried a weight that "Ms. Bronson" wouldn't, and right now? She needed all the weight she could throw around.

Taking a deep breath, she texted, *Accepted with great thanks.*

Minutes later, as she was getting ready to lie down, the conversation pinged.

Congratulations, Dr. Stephanie Bronson.

And appended was a tiny image ... of a doctoral certificate.

CHAPTER 7:
AN UNCOMFORTABLE
SILENCE

"This is the weirdest professional presentation I've ever worked on," said Dr. Faye Athena Brown as she popped the first REFERENCES slide onto the screen. "I mean, look at that. We're referencing sixteen papers from eight different disciplines, three science-fiction novels, one video game, and an Internet discussion. And that's just for *this* section of the presentation."

Dr. Brown was an archivist and researcher that Stephanie had stolen—well, *requested*—from UCal at Berkeley, because her work with SNIT had shown her to be not just responsive but *smart*, finding not only the material requested but also relevant, related material that sometimes put your question in a new perspective. *And she's sure doing that here, giving us useful cross-references in disparate fields.*

"Not unexpected," Dr. Dobyns said, reviewing notes on his laptop. "We are faced with the strangest and most exciting event in human history, after all. If our speculative fiction writers *didn't* have something relevant to say, they'd be very poor at their job, wouldn't they?"

"How long until *Fenrir* arrives, again?" That was Dr. Chris Thompson, whose wide-ranging scientific experience included microbiology, ornithology, and ecology; he was working on trying to wring every possible guess about the biology of their visitors from the very limited clues available.

"You mean when it settles into orbit?" Stephanie asked. "About—"

"Here!" Faye tapped a few keys and suddenly there was a running countdown just above the presentation slide: FENRIR ARRIVAL: 45 DAYS, 17 HOURS, 27 MINUTES. As they all looked up, the twenty-seven turned to twenty-six.

Stephanie grinned. "Exactly. Or about one and a half months." *Has it really been just a bit over six weeks since this all started?* "I don't suppose we've gotten any response?"

Dr. Dobyns shook his head, his beard emphasizing the motion. "Nothing."

"Which makes me extremely concerned," came a voice from the doorway.

Stephanie glanced, did a double take, and leapt to her feet. "Madam President!"

"Please, not that formality here. Call me Jeanne and I'll call you Stephanie."

That's going to be a challenge. But nice gesture! "I'll... try, Jeanne. So what are you doing here? We're working on the next briefing presentation now."

"Honestly? I hate PowerPoint. Oh, it has its place, no doubt, but I'd rather just discuss the results. And since I *am* the President, I can get away with that, can't I?"

"Absolutely, Madam Jeanne President!" said York with a grin.

"Wiseass," Jeanne responded with a smile of her own. "Dr. Thompson—"

"Chris, if I'm calling you Jeanne."

"Chris, then. Anything on our visitors' likely nature? I know I'm asking a ridiculous question given the circumstances."

"I'm glad *you* said it, Jeanne. As my one uncle said, there's only so much stew you can make from one oyster.

"So... yeah. We assume they're accelerating at something equal to, or less than, their normal gravity on their homeworld. You can argue some reasons for trying to exceed their normal gravity acceleration, but I don't think they'd be reasonable for a long-term transit like this."

"So they come from a planet with roughly our gravity?"

"Or higher, but they're accelerating slower because it's more comfortable, or maybe this is the maximum acceleration their drive can manage. Handwaving even faster from what we know, though, I would *guess* that they do have gravity about like ours. Main reason is that if you're doing an interstellar jump, you're going to want to get moving as fast as you can. If we agree that they're not going to risk dangerous acceleration for their population, then that says that they're likely running right at their normal comfort level."

Chris touched some buttons and a little set of images appeared. "Of course, just because it has the same gravity doesn't mean it's much like Earth; it could be a lot less dense, and larger in diameter, or really dense and smaller, both of which have implications for atmospheric density, scale height, and so on." He indicated another image, showing several stars.

"On the positive side, we *are* almost certain that *Fenrir* came from this particular star. It's a K-class dwarf, so somewhat cooler than our own Sun. I would guess that their planet orbits more closely to their star than the Earth, and they might have a range of vision that dips a bit more into the infrared than ours, as its spectrum peaks more closely to orange than yellow, which is where old Sol peaks."

"How certain are we that they *have* vision at all?"

"Madam . . . Jeanne, we're not certain of anything other than they're technologically advanced. But the ability to sense light is *extremely* widespread in our own biology, from single-celled organisms and up, and it makes sense that they have to have *some* kind of way to perceive the light spectrum, because they have astronomy. Maybe they see radio waves, but I'd doubt it for a number of reasons; the way atmospheres that support life like ours block various wavelengths, I'd bet on visible light and near-infrared, so maybe between about four hundred or five hundred nanometers up to about twelve hundred or so."

"Will they have radio, then?"

He shrugged. "I can't imagine that they *don't*, really. To get to the level of technology they're at, they'd *have* to have a really comprehensive understanding of the universe, at least as good as ours, and the utility of all the different wavelengths, from long-wave radio all the way to the gamma and cosmic ray spectra, would be obvious."

The President's mouth tightened. "Which returns me to the concern. If they are that advanced, they must be receiving our signals. They must be able to tell that these *particular* signals are directed at them; we're beaming them through our most powerful systems, focused on them. These signals would *have* to be the strongest they're receiving from us, yes?"

"Absolutely," agreed York. "Probably by a couple of orders of magnitude."

"Could they be so alien that they can't understand the progressions we're sending?"

York and Chris glanced at each other, then York spread his hands in a *who knows?* gesture. "*Could* they? We know so little that we have to admit it's possible. But... they appear to have made technology that goes along lines we mostly understand. They had to have encountered the same basic problems, with the same answers, to thousands, to *millions*, of scientific, technological, engineering-related issues. They would have to have gained an intimate understanding of mathematics and its connection to the behavior of the natural world. So I would find it unlikely in the extreme that they *couldn't* understand our transmissions, given any effort to do so."

Stephanie felt a chill that had nothing to do with room temperature. "So either they don't consider it *worth the effort* to bother understanding our signal, or they're deliberately refusing to answer."

"That..." York hesitated, then grimaced, running fingers through hair sparser than it had been when he won his first Nobel. "I am afraid I have to agree with that assessment."

"So in your view, I am *right* to be concerned?" That was the tone of the President, not "Jeanne."

"I don't..." York glanced to Stephanie.

You're throwing this at me?

But Dr. Dobyns *had* been throwing things her way ever since he appeared, and she realized that this was the *point*. If she wanted to stay "Dr. Stephanie Bronson, discoverer of *Fenrir,*" she couldn't let other people—even those ostensibly more educated and qualified—become the primary voice and face of *Fenrir*.

All right. Grab on for the ride. "What Dr. Dobyns would like to say," Stephanie began, "is that as scientists we really don't like making those kind of statements. But you need one, so..." She took a deep breath. "Yes. You are. We only have experience with a few intelligent species of any kind—humanity, some cetaceans, birds, apes, and possibly cephalopods. Of those, only one is technologically advanced, so it's the only guide we have to work from.

"If they aren't even bothering to decode it, it means that our presence or absence literally doesn't matter to them. Since they *have* come here, at considerable effort and expense however they might measure it, they had to know there was a living, if not at the time technologically advanced, planet here. Any reason I can come up with for them to not *care* that we're here is at the least worrisome."

"And if they've interpreted it, but aren't answering?" the President asked when she paused.

"Well . . . it doesn't quite imply the 'you are ants' possibility as the first does, but it's still problematic. Human history gives way too many bad possibilities. Perhaps their religion told them they were the only possible intelligent life; our very presence would threaten that and they'd be wanting to hide it from their own people as well as avoid contact with us. Or some of them want to answer, others don't, and there's a major conflict on board. Or they don't want to talk because they are afraid any conversation will reveal either their intentions, or a weakness. None of these are good situations."

She looked at York. "Have we resolved any details on *Fenrir* itself?"

"Not yet, I'm afraid. It's just approaching a distance where we can see that it's not just a point of light; getting details of any kind will not happen until it is almost here."

The President nodded, sighed, and stood there quietly for a moment. "Thank you. Keep me updated on any change, no matter how small."

"Absolutely, Madam President," Stephanie said, echoed by the others.

When the door closed behind the President, Stephanie let a long-held breath out with a whoosh. "She is *not* happy."

"No more am I," York said. "But I am *absolutely* happy that I am not in her shoes."

That much Stephanie could agree with. Hard enough to deal with the science. The politics? Those would be the real killer.

"All right, let's get back to it. Plenty of other people will be seeing this even if she doesn't need to, and this presentation's not going to write itself!"

CHAPTER 8:
EXPLOSIVE SOLUTION?

Jeanne entered the room, seeing all rise as she came in. *Still getting used to that.* "As you were," she said to the other four people—Dr. Eva Filipek, secretary of energy, George Green of Defense, Hailey Vanderman of the CIA, and of course Roger; her chief of staff had arranged the meeting. "This is going to be a small brainstorming session as well as an update for us. I've got a meeting later this afternoon with the FORT and I hope we'll have something to present after this."

FORT, or "*Fenrir* Oversight Response Team," was the almost-formal name for the group of national leaders who were in charge of formulating, executing, and coordinating Earth's response to *Fenrir*. So far, the major achievement of FORT had been arranging and activating the contact transmission that, even now, was being beamed 24/7 toward the approaching craft. But with no response forthcoming, there was a public and private need for something new, and soon. Jeanne really hoped the USA could find that something.

"Nothing new from our scientific task force?" Secretary of Energy Filipek asked. Her words were spoken with a precision that belied the casual, slightly rumpled appearance that Dr. Filipek habitually affected.

"Nothing, Eva," Jeanne replied. "And I don't expect anything new for a while, honestly. *Fenrir* isn't close enough for us to get much more information from yet, and they've wrung every last bit of intelligence out of what they already have." She looked over to George Green. "Have you got anything for me?"

The secretary of defense—broad and tall, the very model of "defense"—nodded. "Maybe. Had all our people looking at all the alternatives."

He brought up a presentation on the conference room screen. "There's only so many ways to move stuff from Earth orbit to the outer system, where we expect *Fenrir* to stop. Of the ones we can actually use, they break down into two classes, propellant-based and propellantless systems.

"I'll take the latter class first. Leaving aside whatever unknown drive system *Fenrir* uses, propellantless systems work by making use of external forces to move the craft. The flashiest and best known is the old solar sail, used in the IKAROS project and a couple of others as well as from a ton of old science fiction. Basically, it catches and reflects sunlight and because light has momentum, some of that transfers to the sail. Magnetosails use the solar wind rather than light, and there's a sort of hybrid of those called dusty-plasma sails that use magnetic confinement of reflective dust to make a solar sail that doesn't have much of a physical component."

Jeanne nodded; she knew a bit about solar sails, but hadn't heard of the dusty-plasma version before. "Go on."

The next slide showed the different propellantless systems with a big red X through them. "Useless for our purposes," Secretary Green said bluntly. "Even the best ones accelerate at a few centimeters per second at best. They're slow off the mark and can't maneuver worth a damn. Oh, in the long run they'll win any race—they're going to keep accelerating as long as there's light or solar wind to move them—but we don't have the time to wait, and we need something that's got more potential oomph than a giant space parachute.

"Technically," he went on, "there's a few others, such as space elevators or slings that can be used to basically throw your payload to a target, but none of them are practical for us to consider in a timescale smaller than years, and wouldn't really give us what we want."

He flicked to the next slide. "So that leaves the propellant-based systems. Conventional rockets are well-known established technology, and with the recent success of private as well as public launch companies there's been something of a boom of space operations.

"Unfortunately, none of them—neither NASA nor any of the private companies—can really establish a presence in the outer system on a timescale of less than years. Almost all their operations are in LEO, Low Earth Orbit, up to maybe geosynchronous orbit. Getting to the Moon's a challenge, getting to Mars is a major piece of work. Anything past that? Just not in the cards."

"So are you saying we have *no* options for even a rendezvous, let alone anything more . . . forceful?" Jeanne asked.

"Not quite." George's usual football-star smile had an edge to it this time. "But we're going to go out on quite a limb. A *radioactive* limb."

"Jesus, George!" Hailey Vanderman's explosive curse made her jump; Vanderman was usually quiet. "You're not telling us to drag old Bang-Bang out of storage?"

Green's smile got wider, and Jeanne raised her eyebrow. "'Old Bang-Bang'?"

"Back in the days of the fifties and sixties, when Disney was publishing books like *Our Friend the Atom*," Vanderman answered, eyeing Green warily, "the DoD played with a *lot* of ideas for using nuclear energy in areas other than just blowing people up or generating electricity. Project Plowshare, for example—using nukes to dig great big, huge public works projects, like maybe a sea-level canal at Panama about half a mile wide and hundreds of feet deep.

"But then there was Project Orion, which basically proposed that you could drive a spacecraft by lighting off atomic bombs underneath it." Hailey grinned with an edge of disbelief. "Craziest part of that, though, was that everything we know says it would *work*."

"Thanks for the thunder-stealing, Hailey," Green said, with his fading smile taking a bit of edge off. "Vanderman's got it right, though, Madam President. There were two major nuclear drive projects back in the day: NERVA, or Nuclear Energy for Rocket Vehicle Applications; and Orion. NERVA definitely worked, and would be a pretty good medium-range drive, but it wouldn't get you to the outer system and back fast.

"Orion absolutely would. Even in the 1960s they had serious designs for ships that could mass *millions* of tons. But . . ."

Jeanne had gotten her mind around the idea finally. "*But?* I would think so, *but*! You'd be launching that from the ground, detonating nuclear bombs in-air all the way up? What kind of environmental nightmare would *that* have been?"

"Real stopper was the test ban treaty," Green said. "No longer allowed to detonate nukes above a certain level, which Orion absolutely would. And then came the environmental protests." He flicked forward to show a diagram of a massive craft dominated by a huge, slightly curved metal base with a stack of tubelike elements crowded toward the top. "But if you can get other countries to agree to allow it, nuclear pulse propulsion is the only way you can get out there fast with anything big enough to matter."

"Fast is relative," Hailey said. "Even if everyone said, 'Sure, go ahead, ride nukes to space,' it'd take a year to build one no matter how much money you invested. And you'd need *hundreds* of nuclear bombs. Fallout—real and political—would be awful." He paused a moment. "Plus the fuel; we'd never get enough plutonium or U-235 without building or unmothballing major separation sites."

"Perhaps not quite so bad as that," said Eva. The secretary of energy's expression was bemused, as of someone having pulled up a rotten board in their house to find a stash of gold bars underneath.

"You have something for me, Eva?"

"ICAN-II," she said slowly.

"You can too *what*?" asked Hailey, puzzled.

"No, I-C-A-N Two," Eva said, spelling it out. "An updated concept for Orion, using antimatter-catalyzed nuclear fission. I reviewed some of the literature on it years ago."

George frowned, a speculative look on his face. "It rings a vague bell. But that antimatter business makes it sound like far-out science fiction. We're not *Star Trek* here, we can't crank the stuff out like gasoline."

"Found a summary," Roger Stone said, turning his screen. "I think this came from your office, Eva?"

"Yes, that's it. We were reviewing alternative nuclear technologies at the time. Thank you, Rog."

"It's my job."

Eva looked at the summary. "Yes, it's coming back now. Madam President, antimatter-catalyzed nuclear fission uses *very* small amounts of antimatter to trigger a cascading fission reaction. Among other interesting properties, according to a number of people working on it such as Dr. Suman Chakrabarti, it can make use of U-238 rather than U-235 for the fission reaction."

"Is that significant?" Jeanne asked. "Apologies, but I admit I'm not really very well educated on nuclear technology."

"Most people aren't, ma'am," Eva said. "No need to apologize. Yes, it *is*. Most uranium is isotope 238, and normally it *won't* fission—not in a self-sustaining way, that is. We need to refine out the much rarer isotope U-235, or somehow convert it into plutonium. U-238 is less radioactive, and much more easily available."

"No kidding," Green said. "We use it in everything from some kinds of armor to bullets. Though a lot less than we used to."

"But that's only part of it," Eva went on, looking more animated. "It can be made to work on almost *any* amount of fuel, meaning that you can tailor the yield to almost any number."

Green looked at her narrowly. "You mean on the *small* side?"

Eva smiled. "If I read the papers right, you might be able to build nuclear *bullets*. They'd be ridiculously expensive, needing a tiny antimatter-suspension capsule in them, but it might be possible."

"How much antimatter are we talking about?" Jeanne asked. "And is it possible we could make enough?"

"I'll have to check the numbers. But my recollection is that we can't make *quite* enough as is . . . but that if you could take the three or four installations capable of making noticeable amounts of antimatter and put a lot of funding into making them dedicated to *only* making antimatter, you could fairly easily pass the threshold." She shook her head, a touch of a smile on her face. "That was a ridiculous idea at the time, of course. What could possibly get people to abandon all their physics experiments and multiple tests just to produce antiprotons?"

"*Fenrir* would seem to be a big enough motivator," Jeanne said, agreeing with Eva's implied thought.

"There'd have to be a lot of work done on making foolproof longer-term antimatter storage, but that is also something that's probably doable fairly quickly with *Fenrir* as a driver," Hailey said, warming to the idea. "What about the pollution issues?"

"The proposed method would be a lot less fallout-intensive than normal nuclear detonations, as I recall," Eva said. "You might want some new materials research—they proposed lead as a capture-and-ablate material and no one wants lead vapor in the air either, but on the other hand the ablation involves such a thin layer of the surface that it might not matter."

"And do I understand correctly that if, God forbid, we have to fight, this same approach would allow us tailored-yield nuclear warheads?"

"I *think* so? Remember, Madam President, I'm running off of years-old memory and this summary Roger pulled up."

"All right." She took a breath. "Eva, George, Hailey, I want you to spearhead a *quiet* assessment of this—but I want it deep and detailed. Use whatever resources you need to get me that assessment. As I see it, we need to answer those questions *definitively*. Can we make and contain enough antimatter? What will it take for us to do that? How hard will it be to build the ship in question, and how long, if we have to? Assume unlimited budget and a buy-in from the other countries; if we don't have *that*, we can't possibly fly a nuclear-explosive ship."

She stood. "Rog, this afternoon I'm going to hint that we might have a solution worth at least looking at. You work with them to give me a guess as to when I can make a real presentation?"

"Madam President, none of this is top-secret information," Eva said, looking puzzled.

"No," Jeanne said, and let her most cynical smile out. "But act as though it is."

Because, she thought, *I still have to play politics, with FORT and at home, and that means I only get the credit if I'm the first one to present the idea.*

CHAPTER 9: CHALLENGES AND SPECULATION

"That is *awesome*," Chris Thompson breathed, staring at the screen.

Stephanie agreed, though a part of her also thought that *terrifying* might be a better term. "Is the President *serious*?"

"I believe," Dr. Dobyns said, "she's serious enough to want our input on the idea."

"Why in the *world* does this brief assume that the ship would launch from the *ground*?" Faye shook her head. "Build it in orbit! None of the literal *or* political fallout."

Stephanie nodded. "I can't imagine a reason we'd want to try something this . . . *extreme*."

"Look at the size," Dr. Dobyns said.

Stephanie looked, started, looked again. "On the order of a *hundred thousand tons*?"

"Unfortunately, yes," Roger Stone said; he had brought the brief over personally. "You have to understand, we are not talking about sending a small capsule, such as we used for the Moon landings. This is a first-contact vehicle which, in the worst-case scenario, may also be forced to fight a very lopsided battle against an unknown enemy."

"We can't seriously think about *fighting* something like *Fenrir*, Mr. Stone," Stephanie said after a moment.

Surprisingly, Stone smiled. "Dr. Bronson, we all devoutly hope that we will never have to attempt it. But as commander-in-chief of the

United States, and as part of FORT, the President *must* consider, and be prepared for, even that eventuality. And you, yourself, pointed out early on that as the central portion of *Fenrir* is no larger than a large Earth city, nuclear weapons could quite easily be a threat to it."

Stephanie had to pause at that. "They would have to have amazingly good meteor defenses; those would likely easily swat down any missiles we might send at us."

"Let's not argue the specifics of a military scenario," Dr. Dobyns cut in. "Take it as a given that we have to prepare for it. That *does* make this concept...sensible."

"And impossible to build in orbit," Stephanie said reluctantly. "Even if we could get Daire Young's entire launch capacity, it would take hundreds of Rocketship Heavies to bring the materials into orbit, and there's just nowhere *near* enough people trained in orbital assembly to put something like that together."

Roger nodded. "Especially since there would be no margin for error in assembly. We *know* how to build very large machines here on Earth; we're just learning how to do it in space, and this will be"—his smile held a touch of disbelief as he looked at the diagrams—"well, a *unique* challenge even here on Earth."

"On the positive side," York added, "there won't be any need to waste time trying to trim every ounce of weight, which is usually the major concern in aerospace engineering. The main challenge may be convincing the engineers to let go of those assumptions and instead focus on making the ship as tough as humanly possible."

Roger grimaced. "If that were the *main* challenge, both the President and I would be ecstatic. Unfortunately, the main challenges are, as always, political. The FORT side we think can be handled, though there we will have a *very* hot potato in the sense of determining exactly *where* this monster launches from. But the fact is that while— at the moment—all the major world leaders appear relatively sensible on the subject, the same is not true of their overall governments—ours, unfortunately, among them."

Stephanie wanted to argue, but she knew it was true. There were nutjobs all over, and unfortunately they voted. There would be people who saw the alien approach as the vangard for invasion (and, honestly, they had no way to prove it wasn't); others who didn't *care* what was going on in space but damn sure weren't going to let anyone set off nukes anywhere on the planet; and still others who believed the entire thing was a gigantic conspiracy to let the government . . . do something undefined but bad. Never mind that such a conspiracy could never survive a moment's scrutiny.

But her outrage couldn't be entirely contained. "But we have to do *something*! We can't just ignore this, and"—she took a breath—"and Roger, you and the President are right. We probably wouldn't stand the chance of a bicycle against a charging rhino, but we can't *not* prepare in case *Fenrir* is hostile. People *have* to see that! It's right *there*!"

"Stephanie," Faye said, shaking her head, "you *can't* see it, any more than a virus or an atom or an extrasolar planet. The scientists can show pictures of something—something that even now is just a couple blurry pixels—and talk about what those pixels mean, but that's no more *real* to a lot of people than, well, other people's history a thousand years ago. Maybe it's real, maybe it's not, but really, how can that fuzzy ball of light hurt us? If you're already cynical about scientific statements"—she gave a pained snort of laughter—"it's the 'aliens are coming' that's going to get more attention and make more sense than someone talking about infrared astronomy and acceleration vectors and such."

Stephanie stared around at them all. "So, are you saying we're not going to be able to actually *do* anything because there's too many groups of people who want to ignore it?"

"Not entirely," Roger said. "We're saying that it's going to be *harder* not so much because people want to ignore it, but because too many people will want to approach it in different ways, and that we have to figure out how to spin it in a way that can get at least *some* of all those different voter bases on our side. I was hoping someone here might have a few ideas."

After a moment of silence, York Dobyns grinned. "You know . . . maybe. A lot of the anti-government types have all sorts of squabbles with the environmental types because of nuclear power—one side thinks it'd be a panacea to cure all our energy related problems, the other thinks it's practically the creation of Satan.

"Why not pitch this nuclear drive solution to the pro-nuke group as a demonstration of nuclear safety?"

Roger stared at him. "That," he said, "is one of the craziest, bass-ackward twists I've ever heard." His face lit up with a fierce smile. "And it's possibly brilliant. We'll have to look into a way to insert that into dialogue without looking like it's from us."

"Detonating nuclear bombs in atmosphere to launch a giant nuclear spaceship will be a demonstration of *safety*?" Steph repeated. "Isn't it more the demonstration of desperation?"

"It's all in how you slant it," Roger said. "Worldwide, there were hundreds of atmospheric nuclear detonations during testing, and they didn't result in the world becoming a nuclear wasteland, so there is an opportunity there, perhaps."

Chris Thompson sat up. "Pull the patriotism lever—if the USA doesn't do this, we're going to let the Russians and China be the ones to make a nuclear-powered spacecraft and meet the aliens? Play that one hard, and even the hard-liners are going to have an uphill fight to deny the funds."

Stone's grimace and nod showed he had about the same reaction to that as Stephanie. "After all the fighting against that particular jingoism we've done, it feels pretty hypocritical to start playing on it now . . . but yes, Dr. Thompson. That's probably the best course we can take."

Stephanie gritted her teeth, then made herself relax. *I'll have plenty of chances to get really pissed off later. Other things to talk about now.* "Okay, let's just step past this subject. Roger"—it was still weird to call the right hand of the President by his first name, but she was starting to get used to it—"we're going to have to just assume that we *can* get this project underway. *I* am going to work on it if I have to go to Russia to do it. So, how *practical* is that design up there? Can we really lift that much into orbit?"

"We reviewed the old Project Orion work, and it was generally sound; in fact, their designs indicated you could go an order or two of magnitude *higher*, with one design around eight million tons. If FORT goes for it, we will be assembling the biggest multinational engineering task force the world has ever seen to make it happen."

"Crew will have to be international, too," York said, nodding. "Everyone will want in on this, and deserve to—this is humanity stepping out to meet our visitors."

"Yes, and the crew should be large enough to make it feasible to have representation from most countries on board. A hundred-thousand-ton main payload is about the size of an aircraft carrier, and while a lot of that will be taken up by elements of the drive system and various other equipment, there should still be room for a lot of people on board."

"You will not want to design it with aircraft carriers or submarines in mind, however," Faye said after a moment.

Roger raised an eyebrow. "Why not? Aside from the obvious physical reinforcement to take acceleration, that is, we thought that long-term submarines would probably provide the best blueprint."

Faye looked to York, York tilted his head, then shrugged. "Go on, Faye; I think I have an idea what you mean, but tell us what you see."

"This isn't a military expedition," Faye said bluntly. "Oh, it has to have a military component and be prepared for military action, but it's going to have a very large crew which will be primarily interested in first contact—linguists, scientists of all types, and so on—and that excludes the luxury of being able to select its crew entirely along military discipline and compatibility requirements. I've *seen* the interior of a submarine; for a military vessel it makes perfect sense, but that level of cramped interiors, spartan accommodations, and so on simply *will not* work for the much more general, and primarily civilian, crew you are likely to get."

"I think she's right," said Stephanie. "The populations and expectations are very different. And you can't expect to put the top-level scientists from around the world through the exact same military training."

"They will have to go through *some* kind of training," Roger said, "as it will be a unique situation for everyone. But . . . yes. I suppose you are right. And I might have to think of the possible publicity angles as well; a ship whose interior looks like just drab corridors will be a harder dramatic sell." He straightened. "Well, I've brought you up to date and you've given us some valuable feedback; I'll get back to the President and you people can get back to your own work. I'll be in touch."

After he had left, Stephanie looked around the room. "All right, everyone," she said. "Let's take this brief apart and then start thinking of what they're *missing*. We want all the right ideas at the start." She hesitated, then forced herself to go on. "And that means any military applications. Mr. Stone's right: we may not *want* to fight, but if it comes to that, we'll want to give our people the best chance they have."

"Exactly right," Dr. Dobyns agreed.

"So in that vein," Stephanie said, feeling simultaneously grim and, unwillingly, fascinated by the idea, "while we wait for more useful basic information on *Fenrir* to get to us, let's start thinking about its likely defenses . . . and how we could bypass them."

With varying degrees of reluctance, her little team began examining the ways in which the human race could destroy the emissary they had waited all their lives to meet.

CHAPTER 10:
PUBLICITY GOOD,
RADIATION BAD

"What an amazing crash between the NIMBY factor and patriotism," the President said dryly, looking at the summary.

"Isn't it?" Hailey Vanderman agreed.

Ramming through the authorizations and appropriations for the ship—the project currently code-named "Welcome Wagon" by some joker in Congress—had been the hardest fight of Jeanne's political career, *not* excepting her own election. It had come down to one vote from the opposition party, and she'd had to promise support on a bunch of things that were undoubtedly going to come back to bite her later in order to get that final vote.

But it was starting to look as though that had been the *easy* part. Every one of the FORT countries wanted to launch *Welcome Wagon*...and at the same time, none of them wanted a nuclear-explosive-driven craft anywhere nearby.

"Okay, everyone. Help me understand the realities before we dive into the politics. Where would we *want* to launch *Welcome Wagon*, if we could just choose a spot?"

Everyone in the room looked at Dr. Dobyns, who nodded to Stephanie. The still newly minted Dr. Bronson stood up. "If it was a standard rocket, the answer would be easy: somewhere on the equator, where it could take advantage of the difference in delta-v from the Earth's rotation. But nuclear-pulse propulsion is so powerful that a few kps is really no big deal. We could *spin* it that way, of course, but you wanted the realities, and the reality is that we could launch from anywhere on Earth."

"Ideally," York picked up, "you would prefer somewhere that the prevailing winds didn't carry any fallout to inhabited areas, at least not until it had gone a long way and had time to disperse. The current studies show that the antimatter-catalyzed detonations will not be depositing a huge amount of fallout in the atmosphere—by comparison with prior nuclear tests, anyway—but the typical attitude toward nuclear fallout makes the numbers somewhat irrelevant."

"How safe *will* it be, really?"

"Assuming it works as planned? Very, if the immediate fallout is avoided. I wouldn't recommend making launches like this every week, the way Young launches his ships, but one or two of them isn't going to have any significant effect on anything not immediately in the area."

"What about things that *are* in the area?"

Dr. Dobyns failed to repress a laugh. "Destroyed, of course. We *are* going to be detonating nuclear bombs, and even if they're only in the hundred-ton range, that's quite a hammer to be bringing down. The few people saying it should launch in the sight of some major city should definitely be ignored; there will be significant shock-wave damage and possibly flash damage for a considerable radius."

"What about the antimatter itself?" asked Admiral Dickinson. "Is that any additional threat?"

"Not at the level we're talking about," said Dr. Filipek. "CERN and the one or two other sites that are capable of antimatter production are being tuned to do so, but even if everything goes perfectly, we might be talking about micrograms. All at once that would make a noticeable boom and kill anyone near it with gammas, but it's far below the level of the actual nuclear detonations."

She grinned wryly. "The real fallout there is from all the people who no longer have accelerator time for their theses and studies. A particle physicist without access to a functional accelerator is just a very specialized mathematician most of the time. Most of them understand the circumstances, fortunately, but we had to agree to support them for the duration and be ready to restore the accelerators to their normal configurations afterward."

George Green shook his head. "If this works, we might want to keep that capability available. How hard will it be to set that up?"

"Major, major effort, George. Large-scale accelerators are very expensive. Look at CERN's history; took billions of dollars and ten years to build, and the next-gen version they're working on will be close to ten times the cost. Save *that* fight for after we find out what happens with this project."

"What about antimatter containment?" Stephanie asked. "Making a microgram of antimatter won't help if we can't keep it controlled and extract nanograms of it when we need them."

"A lot of the fusion containment research applies," Eva answered, "and we've released all that we have on that and prior antimatter containment approaches to the design committee. Confining antimatter wasn't a big priority before, but I expect we will see large strides in the next couple of months."

"It will take at least a year to build *Welcome Wagon*," Roger pointed out. "Dr. Bronson, Dr. Dobyns, isn't *Fenrir* almost ready to park out there? Can we expect it to just wait?"

Stephanie exchanged glances with York, then shrugged. "*Fenrir* is choosing to stop way out there for a reason, Roger. If they just wanted to drop in on Earth, they could have come right here. So we're *guessing* that they want to study our solar system in detail for a while before moving in-system—and discovering that Earth is inhabited by a reasonably advanced technological civilization *has* to be a major factor for them to adjust to."

Vanderman nodded, as did most of the others. "Do we have any *conclusive* reason to believe they're going to stay here a long time?"

"As of last night," York Dobyns answered, "yes. Steph?"

Stephanie fumbled a bit with the presentation controls, then threw up a series of images showing one very small pixelated blob separating from another. "As we had expected, *Fenrir* has dumped a very large chunk of mass, what we believe was their shielding mass. It's probably mostly a big, contoured chunk of ice—cheap, easy to shape, really good as radiation shielding for a lot of things. But if they were going to accelerate back to anything like interstellar speed, they'd almost certainly be keeping it."

"Where's that piece going? Do we have a vector?" Green asked.

"Fast hyperbolic path through the system; it will be a *very* brief comet, so we might get a chance to get a few good spectra from it, but it's going to shoot past the sun and out into interstellar space."

"They could make another such shield, right?" the President asked. "If I recall correctly, there is quite a bit of ice in the outer system."

"Huge amounts of it, and easy to get, yes," agreed Stephanie. "But if they do, that's going to take them quite a bit of time. They can't just grab a random chunk of one of the icy moons, they'd have to shape it, make sure it was really structurally sound, all sorts of stuff to make sure it would do the job and survive for the years they'd need."

"All right," the President said, nodding slowly. "So, what I'm hearing is that we can be as certain as anything can be at this stage that *Fenrir* will, in fact, stay where it is for quite some time, and so *Welcome Wagon* will have a chance to be completed before it moves."

Another exchange of glances. "That's our feeling, Madam President," York said. "Assuming FORT gets the go-ahead from the respective nations."

"Well, that's not your problem, Doctor," President Sacco said with a tired smile. "Yours is just to keep giving us the best info we can get on our visitors. If I understand our other discussion correctly, we also have as much latitude as we want with our launch site."

"Pretty much," agreed Stephanie. "Launch it from anywhere you don't mind blowing up and make sure people aren't in the downwind path for, well, a good long stretch. Your military guys"—she nodded at George Green—"will be able to tell you exactly how far, once we get the specs of the, well, motive bombs ironed out."

"Already working on that," Green confirmed. "Eva's people are a big help too, of course, but right now if the rough guesses we have are right, it's pretty short, relatively speaking, for any significant fallout. These are going to be pretty small bombs as such things go, and they're not plutonium—thank God—so they just won't be making all that much fallout. I'll get you the numbers once they firm up, but really, a hundred miles is probably more than far enough. Maybe twenty."

President Sacco's eyes narrowed in obvious disbelief. "George, this isn't the 1950s. We can't be cavalier about this."

"No, George is probably right," Eva said, drawing a grateful glance from the secretary of defense. "These aren't even conventional bombs, but more like packages of uranium with a mechanism to inject the antimatter. Very low mass overall, and the real bulk of other material is the antimatter confinement, assuming we get that approach perfected."

Stephanie had to admit she was more in sympathy with the President, but they had to assume these people knew their stuff.

The President evidently agreed, because she just sighed and nodded. "Just make sure you triple-check everything," she said after a moment. "This is going to be a big enough nightmare as it is without worrying about irradiating people because we were overconfident."

"Will do, Madam President," Green answered emphatically. "None of us want that."

"All right," President Sacco said. "It looks like we have an outline of a schedule and a reason to believe it. I've got another meeting with the heads of FORT in"—she checked her phone—"an hour, and I need to go get a quick lunch, so this meeting's adjourned. Next week, same time, Roger?"

"A half hour later, you have that meeting with the speaker."

"That's right. All right, next week, half hour later."

As they left the meeting, Stephanie found herself still in a state of disbelief. "They're really going to do this," she said.

"If they can get past the hurdles, yes," York said, looking more than a touch cynical. "But that won't be easy."

"You mean deciding where to launch a nuclear pulse rocket?"

"That's one large hurdle indeed, but just *finishing* the project will require"—he made a vague gesture with his hands—"well, *keeping momentum*, I suppose, and with something this expensive, this new, and involving so many countries, that's the real challenge. *Welcome Wagon*, or whatever they end up calling it, will belong to no one country, but a lot of countries are going to be dumping billions into it and spinning it to their constituents as 'their' ship, with the other countries as also-rans. You can see that in our own press releases. It's the biggest and most expensive juggling act you'll ever see.

"And believe me, we really don't want to see what happens if they start to fumble the balls."

CHAPTER 11:
ANOMALOUS EVENT

Audrey Milliner stopped Stephanie as she was approaching the FMCC—
Fenrir Monitoring Control Center. "Hold on, hold on, Steph," said the
publicist and what York had referred to as the "image-control specialist."
She gently took Steph's elbow—careful to not make her drop the donut
and coffee she was carrying—and guided her toward a side room.

"What's wrong?" Stephanie asked, puzzled. "I just wanted to watch
Fenrir's final parking maneuvers."

"Of course you do," Audrey agreed emphatically. "And so do a lot
of other people. Which means a lot of them—including the press—are
in that room right now, so you can't just walk in there like this."

Stephanie opened her mouth to argue, then shut it. At a science-
fiction convention, or the monitoring room of SNIT, no one gave a
damn what you wore. But Steph knew that this was nothing of the sort.
"Ugh. I suppose I should have thought of that."

"You probably should," said Audrey, "but fortunately for you that's
actually my *job*. Go ahead, finish your coffee, I'll get you a change."

Stephanie realized the little side room, which had been a storage
area when they first moved in, had the mirrors and lights of a dressing
room at a theater or television station. "When did—"

"About two weeks ago, hon. Told them I had to be prepared for this
kind of thing."

She took a bite of her donut, glanced at her watch. "Audrey, it's only
about two hours to stop-time!"

"Relax, Steph. Clothes to fit you are already here—remember when you filled out that form and got measured for a uniform for the task force? Well, they're still debating on *that* idea, but the measurements were still good. We'll get you dressed, get you cleaned up a bit, and you'll be ready to be the star of the show."

Stephanie rolled her eyes. "Show? It's cool to *us*, but mostly it's going to be watching pixelated dots that don't do much until, well, it almost disappears. If we calculate right, at the end she'll drop from a visible magnitude of about two—around what most of the stars in the Big Dipper are like—to about fourteen or fifteen. If they furl the sail at that point, it'll become almost invisible, down in the mid-twenties. So basically it'll just be watching the dots until they disappear."

"So," Audrey asked reasonably, "why are *you* so excited to go in and stare at the pixels?"

She laughed. "Okay, I suppose you got me. It's blurry pixels of history. And we're going to be watching because then we can all say we saw it when the first alien ship actually arrived here, in our Solar System." She paused, then shook her head in a recurrence of amazement. "Alien ship *arriving*," she repeated softly.

"*That!*" Audrey said triumphantly.

"What?"

"*That*! That expression! That's *exactly* why we've got to make sure you look your best. My *God*, Steph, if you go all awed and misty-eyed like that when they're filming you'll be on the cover of *Time*—and who knows, maybe a fashion magazine, too."

"All right, I surrender, do whatever you have to!" Stephanie fought off the embarrassment. *I've decided to be the "discoverer of* Fenrir*," might as well look the part.* She stuffed the rest of the coconut-flake-covered donut into her mouth, chewed, and washed it down with the rest of the coffee. "Just make sure I'm out of here fast, I don't want to miss any of those dim pixels!"

Hour and twenty minutes to go, she saw with a sigh of relief as she finally entered *Fenrir* Monitor Control. The huge room was—she was pretty sure deliberately—reminiscent of the old Apollo control stations, combined with media depictions of big military command stations: rows of seats with people looking very serious, staring at various displays in front of them in between looking up to the immense main screen, on which was displayed the star field centered on a bright, very small circular object: *Fenrir*.

"Dr. Bronson!" One of the reporters, cameraman in tow, had spotted her. She recognized Susan Ingalls, science reporter for one of the most popular cable news channels, and one of the few that seemed to get at least some of the science right. "Ready to watch our visitor find its parking space?"

She grinned. "Sure am, Susan. Of course, *Fenrir* finished its maneuvers more than an hour ago. The images we're seeing there"— she pointed up to the screen—"actually are from more than two hours ag—"

Fenrir flashed brilliantly, then faded—with a hint of asymmetry— from view.

Stephanie froze, her finger still pointed at the now-dark part of the screen, then spun around to see the rest of the room also still, everyone staring at the vacancy. She remembered seeing an equally shocking event, the explosion of a rocket at launch, with everyone speechless except a single calm voice saying, "We have an anomaly."

"What *happened*?" she demanded. "York?"

Dobyns had a thoughtful expression on his face but shook his head. "Jerry?"

The dark-haired, dark-skinned younger man on the left-hand set of consoles started. "Right," said Dr. Jerry Freeman. "Um . . . wow. Wasn't expecting that."

"None of us were! Did we get anything on that flash?"

"Instruments were running, so . . . Yeah, there's actually *something* there!" Jerry's excitement was understandable, Steph admitted; *Fenrir's* peculiarities had made spectroscopic analysis almost totally useless. Jerry had been tuning his instruments to hopefully catch whatever faint traces of gas or wastes might be vented by the ship.

"Preliminary analysis will take a few minutes," Jerry said after a moment. "But that wasn't just a reflection or the thing heating up normally."

"Is it still *there*?" York asked with a calm curiosity.

"We're trying to adjust the orbital telescope feeds . . . Yes, they're seeing a very dim object at the right location, but if the magnitude's right, it looks like she's pulled in her entire sail."

"Pulled it in," Stephanie repeated, "or *lost* it? Was that an unexpected maneuver, or did something *happen* to *Fenrir*? If she stopped accelerating there, where's she going to end up?"

"Not sure, that's for the orbital mechanics guys. She was doing about forty-one kps when it happened, but since we knew she was stopping no one was doing long-range extrapolations," York said.

"Working on it," said Dr. Francine Everhardt. "Quick guess is that it has to be an accident. I don't think there's anything *anyone* would consider interesting on that path, and I'm *quite* sure they wouldn't want to be cutting inside the orbit of Venus if they could avoid it, which is where I think they're going now."

Jesus. Did Fenrir *come all this way, dozens of light-years, only to die in the moment it arrived?*

She tried not to let the existential horror of that thought, of the incredible achievement failing literal minutes before its final victory, touch her face as she straightened.

Susan Ingalls was speaking into her mike. "I'm here at *Fenrir* Monitor Control, where—"

"Susan!" Stephanie cut in. "Are you live?"

"No, but we were getting ready for a live feed. Didn't expect this much excitement!" Stephanie quashed the spark of irritation at the enthusiasm in the reporter's voice; after all, this was the kind of thing a reporter *hoped* for—not the routine, but the unexpected.

"Can we possibly ask you to *not* go live?" she asked.

Susan stared at her. After a moment, she raised an eyebrow. "Convince me. I have permission to do this live, and a very eager audience."

"You'll have to convince *all* of us," said Anthony Reggiano of CBS. "Why shouldn't we?"

"So you can get the best story out," Stephanie said after a moment. "Look, we don't know *what* happened yet, but we had every instrument you can imagine pointed at *Fenrir*. Give us a little time— maybe as little as an hour—and we'll be able to answer a lot of questions. Right now, you'll just be reporting that 'something happened.'"

"She has a point," said Rick Ventura, the AP representative she remembered from her first big press conference. "It's not like we're getting anything people in other countries' command centers aren't. Can you give us that last bit of footage? *Fenrir* brightening and then disappearing? That will be at least something worth running to keep interest until you've got something to report."

She looked to York, who nodded. "We can give you that. Just a couple of minutes to pull the feed and copy it for you all. Then you can all stay here and wait for updates, if you want."

The members of the press conferred, then nodded. "Agreed," Susan said. "We'll all send out the imagery and the 'something happened' with a promise of more shortly."

Thank goodness. She didn't want to deal with the live version right now—a live event that would have just been reporters asking questions whose answers weren't known. That would have just made her look stupid.

Instead, they had a little time to find out what had happened to the biggest story in human history.

CHAPTER 12:
CALL TO ACTION

"You're *sure* you want me to do this, Madam President?" Stephanie asked, finding stage fright trying to overwhelm her again.

President Sacco nodded. "Again, I'll introduce you—not that anyone will need the introduction now—but I want you to do the presentation *exactly* as we've discussed. Especially the end."

"Why not you, though? You're more in the position to—"

"Because," York broke in, then smiled apologetically. "Sorry. But Steph, because if *she* does it, it's the United States trying to make a decision for everyone. If *you* do it, it's an *appeal* to everyone."

Stephanie closed her mouth at that. *Okay. I understand that.* "Right. I'm ready, I guess."

"Don't *guess*. Be ready. You've done this before. You can do it again." York Dobyns's voice was calmly reassuring.

The President was already out of the room; they could hear the murmurs of the press as she walked to the podium.

"Sorry for keeping you all waiting," she said; Stephanie could envision Sacco's trademark brilliant smile accompanying the apology. "It took Dr. Bronson's team quite a while to put everything together after the very unexpected incident yesterday, but we believe we now have enough to make it worth discussing. So without further delay, Dr. Stephanie Bronson, head of the *Fenrir* research team."

The President stepped aside with practiced ease; Stephanie concentrated on walking to the podium with the same confidence.

"Thank all of you for your patience," she said. "I think you'll find it's worth the wait, and I won't waste your time rehashing the lead-up: we expected *Fenrir* to just park itself out near Uranus' orbit, and instead...it didn't. So let's talk about what happened."

The room dimmed and the screen showed the image of *Fenrir* momentarily flaring brilliantly.

"At 14:26:54 GMT, *Fenrir* momentarily tripled in brightness and then immediately faded to magnitude twenty-three point five—effectively invisible to any except very large telescopes. Unlike all of *Fenrir*'s prior maneuvers, this one showed evidence of plasma—heated elemental materials. We detected tungsten, carbon, yttrium, and a number of other elements in lesser concentrations." A slide showing the various spectral lines seen. "To an extent, this confirms some of our guesses about *Fenrir*'s design and composition, but the process is—obviously—not what we expected."

The next slide showed an animation of their best guess of *Fenrir*'s actual appearance—the gigantic, glowing, sail-like radiator encircling the comparatively tiny, double-pointed tapering cylinder of *Fenrir* itself. A section of the sail abruptly erupted into gas and the remainder faded, pulling in.

"Our best guess as to what happened is that for some reason a portion of the sail experienced a surge exceeding its ability to radiate. As the sail temperature is not all that far from the material's melting point, when that happened it quickly overheated, melted, and likely then lost whatever metamaterial structure allowed it to so evenly distribute and radiate heat; instead, it vaporized. This damaged the sail and, likely, portions of *Fenrir* itself. From our very limited observations, we believe that the sail is mostly, but not entirely, retracted, as shown here." *Fenrir* was shown with a moderately wide "ruff" around the core ship.

"The question, of course, is *why* this happened. Did something happen inside *Fenrir* which damaged its energy radiation system? If so, it could have been catastrophic to any part of the ship anywhere near that location; you could liken it to a large ship taking a missile in a vital location."

"Are you saying *Fenrir* is...destroyed? A derelict?" asked Susan Ingalls. It was a planned question, but Susan made it look spontaneous.

"We don't *think* it's entirely a derelict, no. Infrared readings combined from multiple sources show that after the expected reduction from the sail, its temperature loss has evened out." Another set of images ran, illustrating an internal explosion on *Fenrir*, one on its surface, and one on the radiator sail that was also burning the hull of the vehicle. "Since at this distance we cannot make out any details, we cannot tell if the problem started inside the ship, at the surface at the interface between the radiator and *Fenrir* proper, or in the sail itself.

"However, Dr. York Dobyns, Dr. Jerry Freeman, and several others on our team are of the opinion that whatever the cause, *Fenrir* is seriously damaged. We have seen no changes in behavior since the incident, and given the consistency of *Fenrir*'s behavior throughout its approach we are convinced that if it was capable of doing so, *Fenrir* would be attempting to stop and put itself in orbit about the Sun as soon as possible."

"Where is it going now?" That wasn't a scripted question, but one she'd expected, this time from Marcie Amour of ScienceLine.

"That we were able to get good data on, with the help of our other observers around the globe. If it doesn't change orbit, *Fenrir* will proceed on a hyperbolic trajectory that will take it slightly inside the orbit of Venus—passing very close to it, by the way—and then back out of the Solar System into interstellar space. It will require slightly over two years to reach perihelion—closest approach to the Sun—and will take the same amount of time to end up back out near Uranus's orbit. Its course doesn't take it near any other major objects, so there's no chance of a collision."

A new slide, this one showing the Sun, *Fenrir*, and various symbols for heat intake, generation, and radiation. "We're afraid that *Fenrir* is still in trouble, however. Based on the records we were able to find of *Fenrir* before she lit off her drive, she was still generating a significant amount of energy—somewhere around the level of a major city.

"In interstellar space, that's not a huge problem to radiate away, especially if you're carrying around a gigantic chunk of ice you can use as a heat sink when necessary and have a sail that's made to radiate heat over an enormous area. But as *Fenrir* gets closer to the Sun, she'll be taking in more and more energy and having to radiate it away. On Earth, we can dump extra heat three different ways: convection, by having air move around us and take it away; evaporation, which is having a liquid, usually water, take the heat onto itself; and radiation, which is the heat transmitting itself away through space. In space, they really only have radiation as an available method, and as they get closer, half of the ship is always going to be taking in more and more energy, making it harder to radiate away."

"Couldn't they use their radiator sail? Even if part of it's damaged, surely it could deal with the relatively tiny amount of heat from the main vessel?" Susan asked.

"First, we don't know if they *can* extend it partially; if our observations are correct, the retraction wasn't complete and that may indicate that the entire radiator sail's controls are damaged." She tapped the Sun in the middle of one diagram. "The other problem is that as they get closer to the Sun, the sail will be picking up more and more heat, and would have to radiate *that* away before it could get rid of any interior heat. Since they apparently can't control the ship, they can't maneuver to keep the sail edge-on to the Sun, which would make that a practical approach."

"And they dropped their ice shielding a while ago, right?" asked AP's Rick Ventura.

"Yes, so they don't have that option anymore—assuming all their internal systems are working."

"But they *could* get it working soon, right?"

Stephanie pursed her lips. "*Could*, yes. The problem is that there's, oh, four levels of problem we could be dealing with when you see something like this.

"The first's an acute, immediate, but limited problem—say a big meteor hit the radiator far enough out that mostly it just fried the sail and control elements, forcing them to pull it in, for example. Something like that they probably have repair protocols for, and once they cut away the damaged radiator and patch the control runs, they can go back to almost full operation. If that's the case, we should see *Fenrir* pop back to full brightness, finish the last few minutes of deceleration, and get into a decent orbit in a couple of days, a week at most.

"Second would be if the damage is more extensive, but local to a particular area of the ship—if a meteor hit them at the linkage area, a local generator or power distribution transformer blew badly, something like that. If they were modular enough to just cut out that area, we'd have expected to see them already back up, and they're not, which means that kind of damage might take a couple of weeks to repair—if it doesn't also cause more trouble from added stress."

She blew out a breath and continued. "Three and four, though... that's if something really serious happened to *Fenrir*. For example, a problem with the antimatter generator sending a serious surge through the entire power grid that we just happen to only see from the outside because it overloaded a part of the radiator. Internal strife, maybe, deciding how to deal with the fact that they're in an inhabited system. Any of a thousand things. This leaves *Fenrir* in a state where repairs may take anywhere from months to never. In most of these cases, though, at least *some* of *Fenrir*'s people—call them the Fen, perhaps—will still be alive. They've *got* to have just an amazing number of backups to keep the crew alive; they took *decades* to fly here, after all."

"That's...a pretty frightening thought, Dr. Bronson," said Mack Henning, a worried expression on his face. The Reuters representative went on, "If that's happened, they're drifting through space, maybe not even seeing what's outside very well after that flare, on an orbit that could bake them alive. Slowly."

Stephanie could have *kissed* Henning. That was the best lead-in she could have asked for. "Yes, Mack, that's the problem. Up there are... well, maybe *thousands* of people—not like us, but still *people*—who've flown through interstellar space to reach here, an achievement we've only *dreamed* about until now...and at the very last moment, suddenly they're heading straight for a terrible slow death."

She paused, just a moment, to let the idea sink in. *"But we don't have to let that happen."*

A collective intake of breath told her she'd said it just the right way. "The leaders of all the countries of Earth have already been working on what was going to be a first-contact embassy ship, *Welcome Wagon*. But things have changed. We're not going to be facing a giant, frightening unknown.

"We're seeing people that need help, people who came a long, *long* way to meet us, to see our worlds. We've been afraid of that, some of us. Why did they come here? What do they want?

"But right now? They're stranded, and afraid, and this is the best possible opportunity for humanity to stand up and prove who we are: We're the people who have risked our lives again and again to save whales stranded on beaches, sometimes killed ourselves to get a beloved pet to safety, sent out a thousand rescuers to look for one lost hiker. *This is who we are.* We may fight and squabble and do all sorts of terrible things, but in our hearts we really want to *help.*"

She pointed up, where the image of *Fenrir* glowed softly. "They need our help. No matter what they wanted on their way here, they need help, and there is no one and nothing in the universe that can help them...

"...except us. So let's prove ourselves. Finish *Welcome Wagon*, make it not an embassy but a rescue mission, and bring our visitors safely to harbor!"

PART II: WELCOME WAGON

CHAPTER 13:
POLITICS AS USUAL

"Dr. Bronson did a bang-up job at that conference," George Green said, as they seated themselves following the President's arrival.

"She did," Jeanne said, with a combination of pride and guilt. "I don't think she realizes how good she is at that kind of thing."

"Many people are rather good at arguing for things they believe passionately in," observed Hailey Vanderman. "But are you ready for her to figure out the trick?"

Jeanne sighed. "Honestly, I hope she'll just come to understand it more as . . . choosing a particular part of the story to tell."

Hailey shook his head, and Eva Filipek fixed her with a cynical stare. "She is not stupid, just idealistic. Which is why you put her out there."

Jeanne rolled her eyes. "Of *course* that's the reason. If Dr. Stephanie Bronson gives a speech like that, everyone's going to take it at face value—which they did, and why her declaration of a rescue mission is catching fire." She tapped the cover of *Time*, which showed Stephanie, caught on camera when *Fenrir* had flared and disappeared; the expression showed her concern and shock, fitting the headline "To The Rescue."

"And no one would have believed it at all if *you* made that speech," agreed George. "But 'let's get out there and loot the bodies' isn't going to play so well."

"*George!*" snapped Jeanne, exasperated. "There are a *lot* of reasons for us to go catch up with *Fenrir*—"

"—all of which, aside from Stephanie's, amount to either 'get them before they get us,' or 'see what we can beg, borrow, or steal from the Fens,'" Hailey said bluntly. "Which are all the reasons the other countries will work with us on this. No one wants to be left out of the greatest opportunity in the history of the world."

She shrugged and smiled. "Yes, all right, but I would prefer not to put it that ... crudely, especially if anyone's ever going to be interviewed about it. Roger, we've already got the appropriations being run through the House and Senate?"

"Yes, and unless some terrible scandal hits in the next few days it'll go through; even your mortal enemies in Congress aren't going to go down as the people who said 'fuck you' to an entire species. There might be one or two dissenters for form's sake, but I don't envy whichever congressional members are chosen for that particular fate."

"How much are we putting through? It's obviously going to be deficit spending from hell," Eva asked.

"Overall package looks to be about three point two trillion," Roger replied.

"*Ooof!*" George said. "*That's* gonna be popular once the fever wears off. Not."

"Not quite as bad as it sounds," Roger said. "A lot of that is funding *a lot* of work on things related to *Fenrir*, which will stimulate major upswings in multiple industries. In less than two years we, with our partners, are going to have to build a giant nuclear-powered spaceship capable of flying, and if necessary fighting, at speeds greater than anything we've ever built. There'll be everything from support for basic research on a fast track to major contracts for manufacturing industries in this bill. That'll also stimulate the economy through smaller businesses—hell, the SBIR budget alone will skyrocket."

Jeanne nodded. The Small Business Innovation Research program promoted the use of small companies in basic and applied research through allocating a small percentage of every large federal agency's budget to SBIR grants. A huge number of innovative ideas came from that program and found their way into military, government, and private applications. "We'll have to play up all the advantages of this funding bill *heavily*, Roger."

"On the positive side, it's not a disaster-recovery program where people can just accuse the government of giving away money it doesn't have for no purpose," Hailey Vanderman said. "It's working toward a concrete result and we're riding on a big wave of sentiment."

"Who *are* our partners in this?" Eva asked. "Realistically, I mean. I know that practically every country on the planet will want to have *something* in on *Welcome Wagon*, but no project like this could work with a hundred-plus groups involved."

Jeanne nodded to Roger, who brought up a graphic. "Let's be blunt: making a nuclear pulse rocket the size of a regular warship in less than two years is going to be a matter of money and technical skill. So from our point of view, we're really looking at us, China, Japan, Germany, and our friends in the UK, with some participation from India and France. Any country with an economy less than a tenth of ours just isn't in the running. We'll have to find diplomatic ways of making it *look* like the others are participating, but the combination of those seven is well over sixty percent of the entire world's GDP; the others, all put together, can't manage forty percent among them all."

"And the US and China are the lion's share even there, over forty percent of the world total," pointed out George. "So, leaving out PR, it's really us and China with some important minor partners."

Hailey Vanderman grimaced. "I don't like the idea of working that closely with China on something that's obviously going to use the most vital secrets of, well, *both* countries."

"I know the headaches this will cause," Jeanne said, "but let's try to look at this as an opportunity. China has huge industrial capability but we have some reason to be cautious; both sides are going to have to agree to having neutral inspectors check every major component provided by either side. China may have a checkered reputation in terms of the quality of work on occasion, but the USA isn't flawless either; we all could name at least three projects off the tops of our heads where our contractors lost us billions through accidental or deliberate failures to meet specs."

"That inspection requirement's something we need to get nailed down *fast*," Hailey said emphatically. "Some of the things *Welcome Wagon* will need have never been built before, and we're not going to get second chances on them."

"In fact, we should probably have two of everything in that category manufactured by separate vendors," Eva said, and George and Hailey nodded, along with Roger. "Especially the pusher plate; it will be either the largest cast-steel object ever made or one of the largest, if not the largest, pieces of welded steel ever manufactured."

"Roger, get on that with FORT," Jeanne said. "I want it negotiated before the euphoria wears off."

"China's ahead of us there," Roger said. "They sent in a query that implied the need for such an agreement just before we started this meeting."

"This is going to be a security *nightmare*," Hailey muttered.

"Security will be the least of our problems," Jeanne said, in her presidential voice. "Hailey, we're going to be needing to build trust in areas we've traditionally tried to promote suspicion, and we can't afford to fail. Isn't it true that most of our *technological* secrets are at best short-term and at worst things that the other side can already guess and just have trouble replicating?"

Looking as though the answer actively pained him, and exchanging a similar glance with George Green, Hailey nodded. "Yes, in general. They know pretty much what we can do, and we know pretty much what they can do. You can sometimes mislead intelligence on one thing or another but . . . yes, overall."

"And our whole purpose on this project—ignoring the, um . . . sapientarian? Whatever 'humanitarian' is for things that aren't human, those aspects—is to either protect the entirety of humanity from possible invaders, or to get us technology we haven't even got a *start* on from the aliens, yes?"

"Yes."

"Then cooperation—including just letting our allies know what *we* know about how to do things—is our best hope for getting *either* of those results. Let's not screw up the design of a nuclear spaceship because we were trying to keep secrets."

"I will advise you *strongly* to place limits on that," Hailey said. "And by the law there's things we *can't* do easily in that area."

"Then *your* assignment, Hailey, is to work with everyone in our security groups at DHS and elsewhere to determine what we *should* be letting our allies have—regardless of how much it makes people scream—what we absolutely *don't* want them to have, and what laws we have to change or suspend or whatever to make it work," Jeanne said bluntly. "Because I will be damned if we're going to spend three trillion of the taxpayers' dollars on a ship that doesn't *quite* work right because we were too afraid to share. They'll have to do the same thing, of course, and we both have spies on every side to tell is who's holding out. But figure it out. I want a report on my desk by next week on this."

Hailey was visibly biting back a response, so she softened her tone. "Look, Hailey—and George, I see you're already getting a headache—the technology is the easier part of security here. We're not going to let them into our computers, show them our bases, any of that. *Welcome Wagon*—and we've got to get a better name for it, by the way—it's going to need technology that we're all already working on. They know how to make nuclear bombs. They already know about antimatter confinement research, particle accelerators, all the key aspects of the ship. We just want to make sure it's made the best way possible, because we have literally one shot at this."

Hailey sighed. "Yes, Madam President. You're probably right, but it goes against the grain of, well, every security agency ever, and I am a lot more open-minded than some of my predecessors."

"If it was easy, I wouldn't need you to do it, Hailey, George. Now, Eva"—she turned to the head of the Department of Energy—"some of that funding will help with the antimatter and nuclear propulsion design work, yes?"

"Yes, and we'll appreciate it. CERN's making good strides forward on converting to antimatter production, thank God, and both some of our special research groups at Sandia and in France think they're really progressing on making long-term antimatter storage. Oak Ridge and Sandia's joint report on uranium-fuel tailoring says it should be feasible to do it on the fly at least a couple of ways, but I'm waiting to see more concrete results."

"Good. Are we getting anything from other countries on those areas?"

"Some. With this new public support I hope to see increased transparency, at least, letting us see which of us could best do the rest of the work—and there is a lot of work to do, since nuclear research has been heavily slowed down for decades."

"Keep me posted." She checked the time on the monitor. "Almost out of time. Roger's already blocked out time for a follow-up meeting next week, make sure you all set that time aside."

Jeanne rose, with everyone else following suit. "Thank you all, and let me know if you run into any roadblocks; I'll try to keep some dynamite on hand."

She left, trying to project the same calm confidence that had served her all the way through her race to the White House, but it wasn't easy. While she was convinced that technological secrecy surrounding *Welcome Wagon* was likely to cause major problems they could not afford, Hailey Vanderman's concerns were very real; if there was a key technological element an enemy had been missing that, for example, suddenly allowed them to decrypt secure transmissions faster, there were agents in that country who might die because of it.

Her advisors told her that *Welcome Wagon* wouldn't cause major fallout problems, but she couldn't help think of the nightmarish consequences if they were wrong.

China had a lot to gain from *Welcome Wagon*'s success, and there was no practical way to do it without their support . . . but they were not a simple and trustworthy friend of the USA, and with their economy now close to matching that of the United States—by some metrics, already passing it—they posed a huge threat—and opportunity.

Every decision she was making here would affect the lives of everyone on Earth, and something she had learned—and come to a very uneasy acceptance of—in her rise through politics was this: even the right decisions could kill.

CHAPTER 14:
EXPLOSIVE SITUATIONS

Stephanie suppressed another of her moments of impostor syndrome as she entered a room filled with engineers, research scientists, and a scattering of security personnel who, she suspected, felt both pressured and out of place in a group that was focused on free exchange of ideas.

She jumped in startlement as the entire group turned toward her and applauded. "What . . . what was *that* for?"

"For *you* making all this," Michelle Chan said, gesturing grandly around the room, "possible." The Chinese mechanical engineer, veteran of design work for both their navy and hydroelectric installations, smiled at her reaction. "We've all started work on the project back home, but the emergency means we might all be able to work *effectively* together."

"Well, thank you, everyone, even though I don't really take the credit for *Fenrir* deciding to malfunction at just the right time." She sat down at the presentation station. "Also, everyone forgive me if some of this presentation goes over stuff that bores you; there's a lot of pieces to go over and we have, as of today, seven hundred sixty-one days before perihelion, and we'd like to be able to launch in time to meet up *before* our friends are, potentially, cooked. So if no one minds, we'll just get started?"

There were nods and agreement around the room, as people resumed their seats in the auditorium.

The first slide appeared: CENT: CARPATHIA ENGINEERING NATIONS' TASKFORCE, INCEPTION AND INTRODUCTION MEETING.

Stephanie was pleased with the new name for the erstwhile *Welcome Wagon*, suggested originally by their archivist Faye. The *Carpathia*, famous as the rescue vessel of the *Titanic*, had been far distant from the liner when it received the distress call, but had made a heroic dash, overtaxing its engines and boilers to drive it faster than any design speed imagined for the ship, repurposing dining rooms and other areas to receive survivors, and arrived more than half an hour faster than any had believed possible, allowing the rescue of over seven hundred survivors. *Exactly the kind of thing we're trying to do here. Let's hope we can do half as well as they did.*

"This is the introductory meeting for the CENT group. There's about a hundred fifty of us attending today; current numbers say that CENT actually has a membership of over five hundred and probably more for support members, but we're all the showrunners of our specific departments.

"Here"—she moved to the next slide—"is the agenda for today and the next three days of our conference. After this initial presentation, we'll break out into groups handling specific areas of the R&D, and then each day at the end of the day we'll go over progress, concerns, and solutions. Hopefully, by the end of four days, we as CENT will have a clear enough idea of all our roles and tasks that we can make a real start at the design and, eventually, construction of *Carpathia*. Right now, we assume we'll have one meeting of CENT per week, but depending on how people progress and what problems we might encounter that can be adjusted up or down. In the future, we assume most people will likely be attending remotely, since there's no good reason for someone overseeing work in Germany to fly out to Philadelphia or Tokyo or wherever.

"Contact information for myself, Dr. Dobyns, and other section leaders is here; a full directory for all our primary members is on the thumb drive included with your entry packet and on the secure website. So . . . onward!"

The next slide showed a beautifully modeled concept diagram, with partial cutaway here and there. "This is *Carpathia*—or, at least, our current concept for *Carpathia*. She is a high-speed, nuclear-pulse-propelled vessel that outmasses everything we have ever put into space combined; including the pusher plate and all other components, *Carpathia* will mass something between one-quarter and one-half a million tons."

There was a murmur around the room at that; some of the engineers had undoubtedly figured that out, but a lot of others hadn't quite grasped the scale. "Partly the mass comes from the way nuclear pulse propulsion works, which requires, quite simply, ridiculously huge mechanical systems to function, but a great deal of it is because *Carpathia* is a multi-role vessel meant to combine humanitarian, technological, and military capabilities."

The next slide popped a cartoon graphic of one of the most familiar fictional vessels up next to *Carpathia*. "In a sense, that makes it rather like the original *Enterprise* from *Star Trek*; it was designed to do everything from perform first contact to fight in an interstellar war, and *Carpathia*, while we very much hope that it will be a rescue vessel, has to be ready for anything."

She was still somewhat annoyed with herself for not realizing right away that "rescue *Fenrir*" was, if not a smoke screen, at least far from the first priority from the point of view of the politicians. At least York Dobyns had made a point of busting her bubble in private, laying out the likely motives that would *really* drive the action—no matter what the PR said. That did allow her to look at all the discussion and concept design work with an eye that was at least informed, if not entirely unprejudiced.

"We'll start from the bottom, and work our way up in this diagram. First is the pusher plate. This is the workhorse of the entire ship, because it's going to have to withstand a *lot* of atomic explosions and not just stay intact, but stay strong and functional all the way there and back."

"How many?" asked one of the UK engineers—Jack Aldiss, she thought.

"Explosions? We don't have a fixed number—that's going to depend a *lot* on the exact design, how our drive system finally works out, and so on—but thousands, certainly."

"*Thousands?*" repeated Aldiss, and there was a ripple of similarly incredulous reaction around the room (with, she thought, a couple of people more in the "that sounds *awesome*" category). "What could you possibly make the plate out of that would withstand that much punishment?"

Stephanie had been ready for that question, so she just clicked to the next slide. "As it turns out, steel—with a bit of added flavor. Steel can take the impact fine, if you control the detonation power and distance. The radiant heat would appear to be a problem, but it was discovered way back in the fifties that ball bearings coated with graphite or anything high in carbon or silicon would survive nuclear explosions essentially unharmed; a coating of oil six mils—that's about oh point one-five millimeters—thick would keep the plate from heating up appreciably during any reasonable number of drive detonations.

"Now, we don't really want to be relying on mechanical sprayers— even though they would appear to be practical—if we can avoid it, so one area of research we're already working on is ablative coatings that might reduce the ablation thickness and thus be possibly practical to permanently coat the drive plate with. Other means of applying a coating as needed, that don't have moving components that could break or jam, would also be of interest. Does that answer your question?"

Aldiss nodded slowly. "Yes, it does. Surprising. I would not have thought ablation would work so well."

"Neither would I, before I read up on it." She looked around. "So, the plate will be connected to a first set of shock absorbers, essentially springs, to absorb the initial impact. These cannot be discussed separately from the *second* set of shock absorbers"—she pointed to the huge cylindrical elements spaced around the exterior of the lower half of *Carpathia*—"because they're going to have to work together. Properly done, the oscillation of the lower absorbers works with the second set to produce smooth acceleration from the point of view of the rest of the ship."

An embedded animation showed a detonation compressing the first set of springs, which then started pushing the second set of shock absorbers, which then started the rest of the vessel moving; the two sets of shock-absorption technology moved through a few cycles of bouncing at different frequencies before settling down and then starting again as the next detonation went off.

"*That's* going to be fun," said Yūzé Huang. Stephanie could see that Yūzé, one of the top experts in large mechanical systems, was already visualizing the complexities.

"Yes," York said with a grin. "Half a million tons being driven by a giant Slinky attached to a dozen pogo sticks *will* be fun. If it holds together."

Y☐zé grinned back. "That last part's going to be the problem. We'll need ways of adjusting the tension on both sides—and it will have to be able to fail gracefully. And be fixed, yes?"

"Yes, all components of *Carpathia* will have to be repairable—and all the critical-path elements need redundancy built in, so that the ship can keep working while something's being repaired."

"Another reason she's so big," York noted. "Redundant systems throughout, *and* carrying spares, or shops and materials to *make* spares, for pretty much anything. *Carpathia* has to take care of itself, because there'll be no way to get help to *her* if something goes wrong."

There was a moment of silence at that, then Dr. Sophie Toussaint—*environmental engineering*, Stephanie thought—gave an uneasy laugh. "Yes, so anyone on the crew may have to be ready to not come back."

Yes. As good a time to get that across as any. "That's right," Stephanie said. "Some of us—maybe most of us—have been thinking about being part of the crew of *Carpathia*. And a lot of us will have that opportunity.

"But"—she felt her own grimace at what she was going to say—"even if all of us here want to think of *Carpathia* as a rescue mission, we're not going out just to rescue our visitors—and we don't know if they will want rescue. I admit I was naïve enough to not think of it in detail, but our governments are supporting this because *Fenrir* represents a huge treasure trove of secrets, and we *want* those secrets. Building this ship is a huge risk for everyone, and if she breaks out there in space, we could all die. If *Fenrir* doesn't want to share, we'll be fighting a ship a thousand times our size and probably centuries more advanced. And our countries will expect us to do everything we can to not just survive, not just rescue *Fenrir*, but to get something *back*—something that might help pay back the literal *trillions* of dollars they're putting in.

"This is the chance and adventure of a lifetime. It's also a chance to be part of a wonderful, or a terrible, moment in human history, and *we won't know which* until we get there."

There were a few people whose cynical smiles showed they not only already knew all of this but were amused by her obvious anger at the situation . . . but many more were looking sympathetic and similarly angered. *Most of us really* would *rather it be a rescue mission, maybe with a side of pure scientific curiosity and the chance to actually, finally meet a new species. We'd rather* not *be looters or pirates.*

"But," she said into the momentary silence, "in any case, our job is to give everyone the best chance to survive they can *possibly* have.

"So"—she turned back to the screen—"let's go on. There are two parts to the main ship: the drive-related components and the actual living and working areas..."

CHAPTER 15: PROJECT MANAGEMENT 101

Stephanie blinked blearily across at the President, then glanced down at the empty coffee cup as though it had personally betrayed her. "How do you *do* it?" she asked with an edge of desperation.

"Do what?" Jeanne asked, though looking at the dark shadows under Stephanie's eyes—visible even through her makeup—she was pretty sure she knew.

"*This!*" The younger woman waved her hand around generally. "I mean, I *know* you have to be doing at least as much as I am, you're the *President*, but you look...well, *awake*. Sharp, focused. I'm on one committee after another and I'm always the one who knows the least but everyone's expecting me to help make decisions!" She shook her head violently, hair coming loose from the ponytail she'd tied it in. "I know, I know, I took the job, I..." She flushed visibly. "I *want* to be the voice for *Fenrir*," she went on, embarrassment in the lower tone of her voice. "It probably sounds stupidly arrogant, but..."

"Not at all," Jeanne said, leaning back, remembering a similar conversation she'd had years ago, when she'd first launched her political career. "Most of us want to be remembered for something—the only immortality we really know works, after all. And *Fenrir* isn't just a once in a lifetime, it's a once in the history of all humanity event. *You* found *Fenrir*, and to you—silly though it may sound—it *feels* like *Fenrir* belongs to you. And that's perfectly normal for people;

discoveries are special" and we all want to stay associated with the special things in our lives."

Stephanie's lips curled in what was at least an attempt at a smile, despite her obvious exhaustion. "Like being the first woman elected president, I guess."

"In a way, yes," Jeanne admitted, "but that achievement will stay in the books, so to speak. Roger, for instance, won't end up replacing my name with his, even if he wanted to. And of course my *legacy* as president will depend on what I've done in that time. You and *Fenrir*," she went on, "have, quite likely, made sure that *my* legacy is secure.

"But really, none of that's the question you were asking. You meant 'Madam President, you're at least twice my age and you're running the whole country, why aren't you ready to collapse like I am?,' yes?"

"Well . . . yes, exactly." Stephanie looked relieved.

"The first answer is, actually, sometimes I am. I have a whole *staff* that knows how to make me look good even when I'm quite literally sick. Did you know I had a terrible case of the flu when I did my nomination acceptance speech?"

"No! Really?"

"Absolutely. I was loaded with so many drugs to keep me from embarrassing myself physically onstage that I practically floated my way up to the podium. I'm glad I'd worked on that speech for *weeks* beforehand, because I honestly don't remember *giving* half of it."

Stephanie stared at her, amazement clear on her face. "I *watched* that speech! You looked absolutely on *fire* there, in the good way!"

"So, that's part of it. Make sure you have someone in your corner to keep you *looking* the part." Jeanne surveyed her. "I am willing to bet that you didn't see Audrey this morning."

"Audrey? No, I don't want to bother her for—"

"Her *job* is to help you present yourself—you and the other top members of the team." She thought a moment, then pulled out her phone and texted Audrey Milliner. "I've told her you need a support team; she knows what I mean."

"But I don't—"

"You *do*," Jeanne said, and *this* time she made sure it was the President's voice. "We've made a lot of progress—the fact that I am sitting in this seat tells us that much—but women are *still* judged on appearance, and that will not change in the next five years. Dr. Stephanie Bronson should *always* look as poised and in-control as the President. That's not a suggestion, Dr. Bronson, that's an *order*. You are the face of *Carpathia* as well as *Fenrir*."

Jeanne saw Stephanie's throat move in a swallow before the younger woman took a deep breath and nodded. "Yes, Madam President."

"Good. Now, the other part of the answer—I've just given you part of it. *Delegate*. You're invited to, and scheduled on, just about every single meeting having to do with every single part of *Carpathia*, not to mention press conferences, meetings like this, and more. The secret is that *you can say no*."

Stephanie's mouth opened, then closed.

"I'm glad you feel so much responsibility that it clearly has never *occurred* to you to say no, but *that* is why you're so exhausted. You *can't* build *Carpathia* yourself, you *can't* select her entire crew, you *can't* control all the news released or do damage control on any stupid statements someone else makes. You can't make sure everyone in fifteen countries is doing their work.

"So delegate. Your morning routine, let Audrey and the team she finds you set it and take care of it. You shouldn't be worrying about getting yourself coffee when you're working with an international team. You shouldn't be attending meetings where they just want to say they had you in the meeting, possibly so that your presence makes their work seem more important. *Pick and choose*, Dr. Bronson. If you don't feel qualified to make those choices, then for *God's sake* listen to Dr. Dobyns. *He* knows which ones are just wasting your time, I'll guarantee it."

Stephanie laughed, and for the first time Jeanne saw a loosening in the tension across her shoulders. "He's been kind of hinting that some of them I could give a miss."

"Good. I'll tell him to stop hinting and start hitting you with a two-by-four until you get the idea. Stephanie, I *have* to pick and choose. I could spend twenty-four hours a day, seven days a week, throughout every day of the year in meetings and I *still* wouldn't have met with everyone who sincerely feels they really truly *have* to talk with the President about something absolutely *vital*. I have some briefings I *cannot* skip, others that I'd really love to but shouldn't, and only so much time for anything else."

She felt her own stomach tense at the thought of all the things waiting for her, told that tension where to go. "So, I have to choose, so that I don't either collapse or go crazy. Roger"—she nodded at Stone, who had been sitting to the side, quietly sipping his own coffee and eating a donut—"handles that scheduling—sometimes he makes the decisions for me."

"A *lot* of the time, actually," Stone said, his smile carrying a touch of smugness. "I don't let anyone *bother* you unless it's really necessary." He looked to Stephanie. "She's absolutely right, and I think York Dobyns would very much like you to let him do the same job for you. Let him."

"All right!" Stephanie raised her hands in mock defense. "I'll let Audrey's team do their thing and ask Dr. Dobyns to help me figure out my real schedule! I surrender!"

"Good," Jeanne said. "Then let's not waste any more of your time, or mine for that matter, we've solved that problem. Bring me up to date."

"Okay. Thank you, Madam . . . Jeanne."

"My job is easier when yours is. You're welcome."

"So . . ." Stephanie glanced at the outline of *Carpathia* on the wall. "We've got three groups working on the pusher plate—one in China, one in Germany, one here in the USA. That's going to take quite a while, but we can work on a lot of pieces in parallel so that won't stop other work."

"How are you making sure they're all *compatible*?" Roger asked. "I mean, just imagine if you have your shock absorbers designed for metric and you get a USA plate designed with inches and feet?"

Stephanie's smile was relaxed now. "Oh, we thought of that. It's not really different from the way modern software engineering handles work across big teams. All the design work for every component's being done in . . . a CENT-specific engineering design workspace that updates the design for all groups working on something, with those updates pushing notifications to the principals on each team. That means that if anyone changes anything on the design, it gets propagated to a central . . . representation of the component, so anyone else working on it will see that change immediately. There's a whole set of design review stages set up to allow a sort of fast spiral of development. If you really want the details in all the right jargon, I can get it to you—"

"Oh, dear God, no. The important question is, do people believe we can make the deadline?"

"If no one slows anything down ... yes. It's going to be tight—right now we're looking at six hundred eighty days to launch—but we think it can be done." Stephanie chewed on her lip a moment in abstraction. "The real problem is probably going to be trying to catch assumptions that were good in one field from screwing up another. *Carpathia* isn't really much like any ship of any kind we've ever built so we keep bumping up against key assumptions."

"Any examples?"

"Well ... one we *constantly* have to keep fighting the experienced aerospace engineers on is their practically *instinctive* avoidance of adding weight to anything, even when you could use additional strength, stiffness, or so on. Weight's the single biggest constraint on typical spacecraft, so they're just so *used* to thinking in those terms that it's really, really hard for them to adjust to the idea that—for the most part—weight *just doesn't matter*. Add a ton here, a ton there, *Carpathia* won't care. Might as well worry about adding another pound to a railcar. They're used to trying to shave ten grams off a half-kilogram module. There's plenty more assumptions like that—every discipline has their own."

Jeanne nodded. "I see. Anything you need help on right now?"

"Well ... we have to push the crew selection up. We need someone from like ... *every* discipline on board, just about. Engineers, technicians, pure scientists, maintenance people, military in case everything goes bad, linguists, you name it, and all the ones with any *technical* background are going to have to double as inspectors of anything they didn't personally have a hand in, so that we can be as sure as possible that everything's made right."

"And," Roger said, "we'll have to make sure that the crew represents as many countries as we can reasonably manage."

She could see Stephanie wince. "I understand, Doctor; that means that at times we may have trouble choosing the best person for the job rather than the *politically* best person for the job. I think we will have to prioritize the crew selection in stages; the most vital for construction, maintenance, and support of *Carpathia* have to be selected primarily for qualifications—both technical and in terms of our ability to trust their judgment—with greater latitude in areas less and less vital to the functioning and safety of the ship."

"We'll need the first set within a few months," Stephanie said, "because we'll want to start inspections soon." She sighed. "And not long after that, you and FORT have to make the single biggest decision: *Where. Carpathia* won't be able to be moved from where we build her; once she's really underway, she'll be launched from wherever she's built. So it's going to have to be a site that's accessible, where we can deliver pretty much anything, and one we think will survive us detonating first a bunch of conventional explosives and then several nuclear bombs right over it."

"Wait," Jeanne said, startled. "Conventional explosives?"

"Probably," Stephanie said. "Dr. Eva over at DOE is still pretty convinced—and I am, really—that the basic detonations of this antimatter-catalyzed drive will be awfully low in fallout, but if you detonate an atomic blast right at ground level you could mix in a bunch of dirt and other stuff and make a lot *more* fallout. So the way you avoid that is basically to pile up a *huge* amount of conventional explosives under your nuclear-pulse ship and detonate them so that it throws the ship up high enough that you won't get any of the ground in the nuclear blast range."

Jeanne had a vision of *Carpathia* sitting on a gigantic cartoon barrel labled "TNT." "I see. Well, that's an interesting way to bring home the idea of riding a bomb. When do we have to have the site selected?"

"I'd *like* it firmed up in a couple months," Stephanie said. "Given logistics and all . . . I don't think you can wait more than four months, five at the outside, before everyone commits."

Four months. With the toxic combination of national pride, nuclear paranoia, and technical limitations, final selection of a launch site in a mere four months was . . . a daunting prospect.

But we have a very, very hard deadline. "I will make it happen, Stephanie," Jeanne said.

"Good," the younger woman said. "Make it sooner, if you can. Because we're going to need all the time we can get."

Jeanne knew all too well how big projects could expand to fill all the time available . . . and then demand extension after extension.

"You're right. And we have to make clear to everyone on the

project, at all times, that time is their adversary. So my last piece of advice: make sure this is on every screen of every person working on the project." She tapped quickly at her computer and spun the screen around, to see Stephanie's look of approval.

"I'll make sure of it," she said.

From a dark screen the brilliant letters glowed:

LAUNCH: T-MINUS 680 DAYS.

CHAPTER 16:
MAKING CHOICES

Time to Launch: 670 days

"I really really *hate* asking this question," Stephanie said, "but should I even be *on* this list?"

York Dobyns stared at her. "Are you saying you don't want to go?"

The rest of the CSC—Crew Selection Committee—stared at Stephanie with equally dumbfounded expressions. That added up to a lot of staring eyeballs, making Stephanie feel like she was in one of those dreams where you showed up to work naked.

"No, of *course* not, York!" she answered, trying not to look embarrassed. "Obviously, I want to go, I'd ride the rocket out there *alone* if I had to! I was asking because I'm just a fresh-off-the-line IR astronomer, and I can't see we need one of those anymore for this project."

"First of all, I don't think we *can* predict what we'll need," Olivia Davies said. The UK representative sipped her tea, then continued, "Imagine, for instance, that we gain charts from the Fens. If they do infrared astronomy, I would expect you would have much to contribute. Second, it is rather assumed you're going. Everyone expects you to be on board, and given that we are not going to be terribly cramped for space, I believe both practicality and public expectations can be served. As you want to go, you will—assuming you pass the physicals."

Stephanie tried to hide the huge leap of joy in her heart, realized she'd failed miserably as everyone else grinned with her. "Well . . . all right, then! Put me down on that list *right now!*"

"Already done, Director Bronson," Faye Brown said. "I put you first on the list when we started it."

Director Bronson was a pretty cool title to have. She smiled and nodded at Faye. "Thank you, Faye, everyone."

"If only it was that easy to pick the rest of the thousand or so we'll be taking," York said.

Neysa Deshpande blinked. "Aircraft carriers have crews of three to five thousand, and *Carpathia* will be, what, well over twice their size?"

"Close to five times in terms of mass," Stephanie confirmed, with a subtle nod from York telling her she was on target. "But we're not a military vessel, and you're not packing scientists and other civilians into little bunks—plus, the drive system alone will take up a *lot* of that mass. So yes, a thousand's correct."

"And at least a hundred of those are going to be explicitly military," York added.

"Practically speaking," Stephanie said, "I—meaning CENT—think you should focus selection first on the mechanical and materials sciences, because the basic structural components are already underway and we will need experts inspecting candidate components very soon."

Looking at the various lists on the screens, she grimaced, looked to York, then squared her shoulders. "I think it's obvious we'll have to narrow our crew choices, um, *politically.*"

Neysa laughed. "How else? We will pick based on how much support the project is getting from each country, yes?"

"Assuming they've got a qualified candidate—but yes, that's about the size of it. There'll be griping no matter how we do it, but that's the only way I can see to be halfway fair to all the countries supporting *Carpathia.*"

"That will certainly reduce the selections by a significant amount," Olivia Davies agreed. "Even if we'd rather use more professional divisions. Now, you said we'd have to get the inspecting experts 'soon.' How soon? Days? Weeks?"

"A couple months," Li Xiu Ying said. "Next week is the projected date for our candidate pusher-plate design completion. I believe the

Germans will have theirs a week after that, and America's a day or two later. Manufacture will take a while—but mostly is dependent on the site being selected in time."

"And about the same time we'll be looking at the final designs for the main springs for the plates and the shock absorbers," Stephanie confirmed, glancing at her own summarized production schedule. "Electrical and electronics engineers will be next up, then optics, automation, software, pretty much everyone else . . . and we have to start manufacture as soon as we have final designs."

"Will we have a site selected by then?" asked Osamu Kurumada. The Japanese representative pushed back a strand of iron-gray hair from his forehead. "I have not heard anything on that yet, which I find . . . concerning."

Stephanie shrugged apologetically. "All I know is the President is very aware of the need to select the site—and all the problems surrounding the selection. She and FORT have promised a decision by the end of the week."

Kurumada pursed his lips. "I do not envy the people having to make this decision."

Thinking of the consequences if even the smallest thing went wrong on launch, Stephanie shuddered. "Neither do I, Doctor. Neither do I."

CHAPTER 17:
A POINT OF AGREEMENT

Time to Launch: 665 Days

Jeanne Sacco sipped at the glass of water absently. She didn't really *want* to drink much right now—add nervousness to too much water and suddenly you had to go to the bathroom in the middle of important discussions. But this was a touchy meeting.

Xi Deng was the current paramount leader of China—which meant that he was the most powerful person in the country, even though another person currently held the title of president. Unlike some prior holders of the title, Xi Deng was more self-effacing, letting others stay in the public spotlight while he did his work more quietly.

That made it even more unusual that he was personally meeting with President Sacco; such a meeting was an acknowledgment that any negotiations between the countries really were negotiations with Xi. And this particular discussion was perhaps the single most important make-or-break decision of the century.

The door opened, and President Sacco stood as Xi Deng, dressed in a well-cut but otherwise unobtrusive suit, entered, accompanied by his security detail. The latter examined the room carefully, then bowed and departed, to wait outside with the President's Secret Service people.

Jeanne Sacco matched Xi Deng's bow, and he then extended his hand and gave a quick, cordial handshake. "President Sacco," he said, with only a moderate accent to his English, "it is good of you to take the time to see me."

"I always have time for the general secretary," Sacco answered. "Would you care for some tea? Any refreshments before we begin anything of import?"

Xi smiled faintly, surveying the wood-paneled walls of the Camp David meeting room in Laurel Lodge. "A lovely room, though rather large for two people," he observed. "Tea would be excellent."

She had expected that answer, and a quick signal to the staff soon sent a cart rolling through the door. "How was your journey, Mr. Secretary?"

"As pleasant as long flights may be, Madam President." He took a sip of tea. "Thank you for your hospitality."

"I wish we could have given you a day or two to recover from the change; this must be the middle of the night for you."

"Ahh, indeed, Madam President," Xi Deng said, with a surprisingly bright smile. "But I am more of a, um, night owl myself, so I am quite awake and eager to resolve the issues before us."

Quickly to business. Don't know if that's good or bad. "Which issues would you like to discuss first?"

The smile became a laugh. "Madam President, let us be entirely honest with each other. *Carpathia* is the only business of note, and we—we two—are the only two who actually matter in that business."

"I am not *entirely* sure I agree," she said carefully, "but I could not argue that our two countries are the two most vital to the success of *Carpathia.*"

"Exactly so. If either of us breaks from the rest, the entire project will be thrown into doubt, perhaps made impossible. This is not true of any of our other worthy allies; we could weather the loss of any one of them." Xi Deng looked at her, an eyebrow raised.

All right, if that's the tone we're taking. "Very well. Yes, China and the United States are the two keystone states to the project. Most people know it. I will agree that you're correct; we can't do this without you, and I do not think you can do this without us."

"Absolutely!" The general secretary looked pleased. "And my advisors tell me that there are some decisions that have become very much . . . time-critical. Most importantly the location for assembly and launch of *Carpathia.* Yes?"

Jeanne nodded her head. *Not as if I haven't had Stephanie reminding me of that every other day.* "Probably the most important, yes."

"And you and your people, you must have discussed all the possibilities, yes? Did you reach any conclusions?"

"We did. But I presume your people have done so as well, Mr. Secretary, so why don't you tell me how you see it?"

He nodded. "Well. All are agreed that the launch must be done somewhere that a little nuclear fallout will not bother, where large explosions can be unleashed and do no damage. And also, that there must be excellent transportation access, to bring in the men, materials, support resources for the construction of this immense vessel. Yes?"

"Yes."

"This," Xi Deng went on, "points to prior nuclear test sites, as locations already previously subjected to such indignities. More, I think we can agree that the Russians have neither the resources to support the needed work, nor the facilities in place in any area they still control." A dismissive smile. "So that leaves appropriate facilities in China and the United States."

"Are you considering reactivating the Lop Nur base?"

"It has been considered, as have a few other locations very remote from major population centers," Xi Deng said, but then he looked narrowly at Jeanne. "But you have already gone beyond 'considering' at your Nevada Test Site, have you not?"

Hard to hide anything from satellites these days. "We anticipated the possible selection of that site and have begun the modernization and extension of infrastructure, especially rail lines to likely construction areas, yes."

"So." He looked at her expressionlessly for a moment, then abruptly gave that brilliant smile. "China will approve of the use of the American site for the construction and launch of *Carpathia.*"

There was a double jolt in her chest at that simple announcement— relief, at the idea they would have a finalized construction site *and* that it would be where she could reasonably aid in oversight . . . and sudden concern at the cost. "That is most gratifying, General Secretary," she said after a moment. "I wonder if there is anything I might do to express our gratitude?"

"Oh, it is a fine opportunity for China to show how forward-looking we are," Xi said. "And our conservation and safety concerns—the Lop Nur site is, after all, the location of a very endangered species of camel, and we must also be concerned with the health of our citizens."

Well, there's a way to spin it—Americans are willing to irradiate their people, we'd rather not.

"But," he went on, "the People's Republic of China would certainly appreciate having some position to give us the same . . . how is it said . . . *high-profile* publicity as time goes on."

"The United States is always interested in showing appreciation to our friends," President Sacco said carefully. "How might we give you this opportunity?"

"My advisors and I have an idea," admitted Xi. "First, of all, allow us to make this announcement. It will show China's cooperative spirit."

And you've outlined the jab you get to make, and I can live with it. We have plenty of spin experts here, too. "That is something we can agree to. Done."

"In a more . . . enduring vein, America will have the construction of the ship itself, but when it launches, the ship must have a commander, a captain, who will be very much in the public eye. If the captain of the *Carpathia* were a Chinese officer, that would be a very fine thing, would you agree?"

Jeanne considered the offer; it was one of those that she and Roger had actually discussed more than once. "Obviously, any commander of the *Carpathia* would have to meet a number of very stringent criteria," she said, "but I am sure that China has some excellent candidates for that position that would meet these requirements, and the United States would be willing to give preference to any such."

"Excellent. Excellent. Then, Madam President, I believe we can consider we have reached an agreement on this." His controlled, considered persona suddenly shifted, and she saw an absolutely *boyish* smile flash out. "I want to see us meet the aliens too, you know!"

She laughed. "General Secretary, I think we can all agree on that!"

He leaned back. "Then there are other details to be worked out . . . but I believe we can now find agreement there, as well." His voice took on a more serious tone as he finished, "After all . . . there are now *two* civilizations depending on us."

PART III: CARPATHIA

CHAPTER 18:
BIG JOB

Time to Launch: 605 Days

Peter Flint of International Inspection Systems pushed the brim of his cap up, tilting his head and squinting against the brilliant early fall Nevada sunshine. "Well, ain't *that* a sight and a half."

Masses of construction equipment—gigantic excavators, dump trucks that made the ones usually seen on public roadways look like Tonka trucks, cranes meant for skyscraper construction, and more— were at work everywhere, almost as far as the eye could see. More track for sidings and shipment depots was still being laid, and probably would be for another couple of months.

But everything centered here, and Pete's eyes were mostly on the incredible expanse of metal in front of him. Even in the 102-degree weather, the heat radiating from a hundred thousand tons of metal felt like an open oven at many meters away.

"How hot is she?" he asked Werner Keller.

"About two hundred C," the project engineer for *Carpathia* answered. "Four hundred degrees, for you Americans."

Pete chuckled. "I know I'm an old man compared to most of you, but I *have* gotten used to metric, even if I still think in the old units. Why, I even have a smartphone and use the Internet on occasion."

Werner acknowledged that with his own grin. "That's pushing it a bit, but I think we can manage it. I was told time's of the essence?"

"Very much, yes, Doctor," Werner said.

"Pete, please, I'm just a contractor here, not presenting fancy papers."

"Then yes, Pete; and you may call me Werner." Werner Keller had a slight German accent but his English was perfect. Pete regretted not learning German, but he'd always expected Spanish or Japanese would be the up-and-coming languages. "More pressure than we expected, and that, as they say, is saying something."

"Oh? What's the additional rush?"

"We had three plates under construction simultaneously," Werner said, "using three different processes. One was being assembled using fairly conventional welding techniques, if you can call anything about *Carpathia* conventional; the idea of that one was to have several layers with different assembly patterns. This would provide no specific weak points for the plate as a whole. Unfortunately, we found that despite trying multiple techniques, the layers just could not be kept tightly bonded during assembly."

"Yeah, I can see that. And the other?"

"The most ambitious explosive-welding project ever attempted," Werner answered, "and it *mostly* worked. Probably could be made to work given a couple of years to work things out, but we don't have that."

"And this beast?" Pete gestured to the dully shining expanse before him.

"The largest single cast ever." The pride was clear in Werner's voice. "I admit I had the highest hopes for this one, but it was, as you might imagine, a challenge."

"I can imagine, yes." He could see remnants of many pipes around the perimeter. "Controlled cooling embedded in the mold, I see."

"As much as we could manage, yes. We wanted some hardening in the underside of the plate, but only so much."

"Sure; you want it to take the impacts but not be brittle."

"So you think you can inspect the whole plate without us having to lift it?"

"Pretty sure. This is an almost ideal design for my purposes, honestly," Pete said cheerfully. "Aside from a few attachment points, it's just a single plate with an almost uniform thickness. Back when I started IIS, I probably would've said the same, but would've told you it'd take about a year."

"A *year*?" The project engineer grimaced. "We cannot afford anything even vaguely that long!"

"Of course you can't. Bid I made said two weeks and two weeks I mean it to be. Or less, maybe." He waved at the titanic pusher plate. "That there's something close on eight thousand square meters of steel to cover on the top, and back in the old days you'd be lucky to cover a couple square meters a day, with two inspectors."

Werner nodded. "Scared me for a minute there. So you use ultrasonic inspection?"

"EMAT—electromagnetic acoustic transduction—with some proprietary wrinkles in how we vary the amplitude and frequency for inspecting at various depths, not to mention controlling beam angle and some very fancy signal analysis techniques my programmers came up with," Pete said. "Couldn't use standard ultrasonic up there—all the couplant gels and liquids I know of wouldn't like those temperatures *at all*. Air-coupling might work, but that has other issues. Leavin' that aside, you haven't polished it much yet, so the surface roughness might mess up standard ultrasonics."

Werner frowned, clearly trying to recall something. "How does EMAT work? I remember the term vaguely but I can't quite remember."

"Pretty simple in concept. You know, of course, that a varying electromagnetic field can exert force on a conductor, right?" At Werner's nod, Pete went on, "Well, imagine if you generated a really powerful electromagnetic field at a high frequency, and put it right next to a conductive object. What happens?"

Werner thought a second. "The object vibrates."

"Exactly! And in a nice big piece of solid metal, that vibration's sound. So if you do these vibrations in quick pulses, you get the same input as a regular ultrasonic inspection, except you don't need couplant gels and even surface corrosion or paint won't get in the way."

"But how do you sense...?" Werner's eyes lit up. "Ah, yes, I see. The same or similar coils that make the pulse will sense the return vibration, because the motion of the conductor then creates an electromagnetic signal you can read, as long as there is a magnetic field present."

"Got it. So it's basically like sonar in steel, and flaws show up as unexpected reflections, or sometimes dead spots where there's no returns."

"Which I hope you do not see, as we cannot afford flaws."

Pete seesawed his hand. "Well, I expect I'll see *some* flaws. Something this big, first time ever made? Almost certainly there'll be something; nothing's perfect. Question is whether it's big enough to be a problem, and I certainly hope I won't find any."

Werner looked around. "Where's the rest of your team?"

"Got a couple of my engineers on the way, but I can get started before they get here," Pete replied. "When do you want me to start? Anyone got anything to do with that plate before I get to it?"

"No, until we know it is usable there is no point in doing more work," Werner said. "You can start as soon as you're ready."

"Perfect. I was told you'd have a nice big two-forty-volt source for me?"

"With a high-speed secured net connection as well, yes. If that is your equipment, we are already moving it into position."

Werner had pointed to what appeared to be a standard forty-foot cargo container, with the IIS logo stenciled boldly on each side.

"That's it. Put that end"—he pointed to one of the narrow sides of the container—"near the power; that's where I have the connectors."

With only moderate effort the container was deposited in the indicated location. With an economy of motion that showed long practice, Pete opened a sealed port on the container and made the connections. Two green lights came on, and Pete grinned. "Outstanding."

"How long will it take to unload everything?" Werner asked. "Should I get you some people to help?"

Pete grinned. "Don't need any help, Werner. Stay right there!"

He unlocked a door built into the side of the container and ducked inside. *Yep, lights show green.* The air inside the container was, unsurprisingly, stifling, but as Pete activated the main systems, a click and hum preceded a flow of cooler air. Screens lit up, showing status, and he grinned. *Everything shipped great for once!* It was something of a crapshoot each time they shipped; about half the time, something had gotten disconnected, jammed, or otherwise messed up enough to need a couple hours to put it right, but this time he saw nothing but green across the board.

He popped back outside. "Sorry to keep you waiting, Werner, but excuse an old geek some theatrics." He checked by eye to make sure there was nothing in the way, then said, "And now, just stand here, and you'll see why I don't need help."

He stepped back in and hit one control.

Instantly, most of one long side of the container—thirty-two feet, to be exact—dropped away, forming a ramp to the ground outside. Within, sitting in identical little bays, were eight squat rovers, each one about a meter wide and slightly more than that long. A short sensor mast projected above the main body, though there were also cameras and lights inset into the front and rear of the rover. They were driven by broad treads, and there were low, contoured vents at each corner. As the ramp locked into place, lights came on in each bay and on each rover.

"IIS's Mobile Intelligent Rover Operations Center, or MIROC," Pete said proudly. "IIS *started* in inspections, and that's still our core focus, but MIROC, with the right mods, gets used for everything from big inspection tasks to remote maintenance to even things like search-and-rescue. All controlled from the little front office here."

Werner looked appropriately impressed. "Autonomous functioning, then?"

"Variable autonomy, but in this case, mostly autonomous. Expect I'll have a lot of little tweaks to do on them—they've never inspected anything quite like *this* before!" He looked speculatively out at the shining-metal expanse. "Probably have to set up some kind of duty cycle to keep the main electronics cool enough. They're all high-military spec, but unless you go to some of the crazy silicon-carbide chips, electronics just do not like temperatures hot enough to fry eggs, and the rovers' cooling can't keep up with that for too long, especially out there in the middle where there won't be anything *but* hot air. Probably need liquid cooling, but I've got provisions for that."

He pointed to the undercarriage. "EMAT head won't mind much, though. Electromagnet plus the send-receive coils, all of those could take a five-hundred-degree bath pretty well after we used high-temp solder on them. So, limiting factor's gonna be the electronics in the main shell."

He laced his fingers together, cracking the joints once. "Now if you and your people can just get me a ramp for my toys to get up on that plate, I can get started!"

CHAPTER 19: DRONES AND DETONATIONS

Time to Launch: 599 Days

"My *God* that thing's *huge*!" Stephanie exclaimed, then bit her lip. "And my God, I must sound like such a dork."

"According to Werner, the engineer in charge, most people say something like that when they first see it," York said. "I know I did, though I think I used not-for-broadcast language."

Seen from the air, the drive plate was a gargantuan, dully shining circle of steel with eight massive arched features that were to be the attachment points for the main "shock absorbers" that would turn the sudden impact of the nuclear detonation into smooth acceleration. The plate dwarfed even the largest construction machines around it. As the helicopter dropped lower, Stephanie saw little black dots that looked like ants on the plate, with white plumes coming up from them. "What... oh, those are the inspection robots."

"Yes, and so far so good. Keep your fingers crossed; IIS says they're a little more than halfway done and so far we've seen no significant flaws."

"We're safe here, right?" Stephanie asked. "I mean... we've seen more than one crater..."

York nodded. "I wouldn't recommend just walking into the center of some of those, but we're not in danger of radioactive contamination here. We picked the construction site pretty carefully."

The helicopter—a modified Bell 429—slowly dropped toward the marked landing area. Dust was blown up, momentarily obscuring the location, and the pilot paused in his descent; after a moment most of the cloud dispersed, and the copter settled to the ground.

The drive plate was even more impressive from ground level, a dully shining hill of solid steel six feet thick at the edge. Nearby was the blocky form of IIS's MIROC, the side toward the drive plate open.

A side door opened and Peter Flint emerged. Stephanie hadn't ever met him before, and the simple headshot she'd seen didn't convey the cheerful energy of the spare form of the engineer. His blue eyes twinkled as he approached, a bright smile on his face—whose lines showed that smiles were a lot more common than frowns for Peter. "You *must* be Dr. Bronson," he said, shaking her hand firmly. "Woman that started"—he waved his hand around—"all this."

She felt her answering smile as she answered, "The *Fens* started this, really. I was just the person who saw them first."

"Suppose that's true enough," he answered. "Came out to see what's going on firsthand—I like that in a supervisor."

"Well, if nothing changes I'm also going to be a passenger, so I'm here to start kicking the tires, too."

He nodded, looking more serious, and ran a hand through short-cropped blond hair that was well on its way to white. "Prototypes need a lot of that," Flint agreed. "Sorry, sir, forgetting my manners," he said, turning to York. "Peter Flint, International Inspection Systems."

"York Dobyns," York said, shaking hands. "Pleased to meet you, Mr. Flint. I presume everything's going well?"

"No changes, which is a good thing," Flint said. "Keeping everything I got two of crossed that I won't find a darn thing worth talking about."

Stephanie saw one of the inspection robots rolling steadily in their direction. "Dr. Flint—"

"Just *Mister* Flint, really, but just call me Pete. 'Most everyone does."

"Then call me Steph. Pete, why is there *steam* coming from your inspection robots?"

He laughed. "Does make them look old-fashioned, doesn't it, like they're little locomotives? But that's actually the active cooling system. They carry a big insulated tank of water—run the water around cooling everything, and then blow the heat out as superheated steam.

So long as I can keep topping off the tanks with water, they can run a lot longer before they have to come in. Liberty, there, is just about out, so she's heading in for a cool-off and refill, and she's being replaced by Yonbuk; expect Big Ben will be back in in about an hour."

The names caught Stephanie's attention. "You named them after bells?"

"Right the first time. They basically go around making every piece of metal they're on ring, so it made sense." Pete looked at the compact autonomous drone with a proud paternal air.

"Did you put in your application to the onboard people, Pete?" asked York.

"Sure did. I know, I'm pretty old to be going out, but then, that just means I'd better try to catch *this* bus out because I don't have much time to wait around. And I think my Bells, there, will be the best choice you have for all-around maintenance and service."

After a few more questions and answers, Stephanie and York bid farewell to Pete, leaving him to watch over his little robots. Stephanie looked at York as they walked over a bright new concrete path. "Can we take people that old?"

York shrugged with a wry smile. "Old like me, you mean?"

"I . . . sorry, Dr. Dobyns, I—"

"Relax, Steph," he said with a deep chuckle. "I know perfectly well I'm past my prime, and I'm sure Pete does, too. But if we're in good enough shape, I don't see why not. Have to pass all the physicals and stress tests, but I'd guess our friend Mr. Flint there will be more likely to pass them than I will. I," he said, slapping his admittedly expansive midsection, "spend a lot more time at a desk than hiking around."

Entering the *Carpathia* Construction Command Center, naturally immediately dubbed "C4" by site residents, Stephanie breathed a sigh of relief; she could swear she heard a hiss of steam as the vastly cooler air within hit her sweating face. "God, it's hot out there."

"Even hotter than usual. And, of course, we were close to the plate, and that's not going to finish cooling to reasonable temperatures for a while."

Her phone buzzed; she glanced down at it. "Almost time for the Drive Systems status review."

"I know. They've set aside Conference Room Three for us."

"Just let me hit the bathroom first," she said. "Don't know how long I'll have to be sitting; we've got three more meetings after that."

And that *is an improvement,* Steph noted to herself as she freshened up. The President's advice had been, as usual, sound. York had been happy to serve as the main filter between her and the rest of the *Carpathia* project, helping her avoid both time wastage in meetings she didn't really need to attend and involvement in interdepartmental arguments that could be resolved without her involvement. He helped her decide priorities—and in their infrequent free time, both of them studied all the issues surrounding *Carpathia* so that they could at least *sound* knowledgeable.

Dr. Eva Filipek was already visible on the teleconference screen when Stephanie entered; the secretary of energy had been given the responsibility of overseeing the development of the ICAN-II-based nuclear-pulse drive system. Steph gave her a wave and sat down. *Amazing how blasé I've gotten over talking to people running the country. Or other countries, even.*

A few other people popped up on the screen as the meeting time was reached, and Stephanie took a breath and looked up. "Thank you for coming promptly. I know it's been a while since I have had a full debrief on your work, and we're all very busy running as fast as we can, so I'll try to make this brief. Charlotte, what is the status at CERN?"

Charlotte Goddard was the engineer in charge of the refit of CERN's accelerators, most notably the LHC itself, for antimatter production, and coordinated with the other accelerator centers around the world. "Antimatter production is finally underway," she answered. "Taking into account the efficiency of transfer to the storage, we are making approximately ten nanograms of antimatter per day. Combined with the other accelerators, we should be able to make twenty to twenty-five per day. We can probably double or even triple that as time goes on and we refine the techniques."

Stephanie looked to York. "That sounds very good to me."

"It's *excellent.* If storage can keep up, that would give us nearly thirty micrograms. If I recall correctly"—he looked to Eva—"that would be enough for thirty thousand pulse detonations, yes?"

"Correct, York," Eva said. "Each detonation will require just over one nanogram of antimatter, based on our current figures. I also have updates from the drive-charge manufacturing side."

Drive-charge manufacturing. A fine euphemism for "bomb production." "Good updates, I hope?"

"So far, yes." An image of an object, shaped roughly like an old-fashioned railroad lantern, appeared on the screen. "MatterPrint thinks they have overcome the problems they were encountering in the multimaterial printing stage. If their next run pans out, *Carpathia* can be equipped with additive manufacturing capability to manufacture drive charges to spec, varying the exact amount and configuration of U-238 and lithium deuteride to allow for a wide range of yields."

Eva continued, "Each one would then be fitted with the detonation plug"—a smaller object shaped like a thick rivet inserted itself into a small side port—"and fired."

"The detonation plug holds the antimatter?" Stephanie asked.

"Yes. That would be inserted immediately before firing, as the plugs will not be able to hold antimatter for long. We're working on the details, but as you need superconducting materials to maintain the magnetic confinement and we can't reasonably put high-powered cooling equipment on the plug, the plugs are only going to function until they heat up above the critical temperature. Thirty seconds, maybe a minute, depending on exact circumstances."

Eva pointed to a cutaway diagram. "In concept, the plugs are also very simple. They are effectively just enough circuitry to detect an encrypted detonate command, a bundle of superconducting coils, and a small cavity that holds a nanogram of antimatter—antiprotons, to be exact. When commanded to detonate, the magnetic field is collapsed in such a way as to inject the antimatter directly into the uranium core, triggering the nuclear reaction."

"So we would assemble a large number of the drive charges, but only insert the plug just before firing. Makes sense anyway; without the plug inserted they're basically harmless, right?" Eva nodded, so Stephanie went on, "That will be automated?"

"Definitely," York said. "Manufacture a selection of charges, automatically dispense one based on *Carpathia*'s current acceleration requirements, detonation plug's inserted, then charge is ejected through the port; detonation command is sent as soon as the charge reaches optimum distance."

Stephanie nodded, thinking. "What happens if the dispenser or detonation plug insertion goes bad?"

"Short answer is that we're triply redundant. If any of the BIT—built-in-test—indicators are anything less than perfect, the ship switches to one of the other drive-charge assemblies and we do maintenance or repair on the first, and even then there's a third waiting in case the second fails. Systems inside those are also going to be doubly redundant where feasible."

"Eva, what if the detonation plug fails to detect the detonation signal?"

Dr. Filipek paused before answering, her eyes going momentarily distant as she thought. "Worst-case, the charge won't detonate until the plug warms up past the critical temperature," she said at last. "Which means we would get a much-reduced push. I suppose if you also had a flawed charge somehow, you could get no significant detonation at all; nuclear explosives tend to be quite finicky about their geometry and such."

"So not terribly bad in almost any case," Stephanie said. "But if a detonation plug failed containment before ejection?"

Eva *and* York winced. "Well, as you obviously guess," York said, "that would be Egon Spengler levels of bad. There will be a lot of safeguards for that, of course. But that is, I agree, the most obvious disaster scenario, short of being attacked by *Fenrir*."

Stephanie shook off the vision of *Carpathia* going up in a self-generated nuclear explosion. "Just keep me in the loop about exactly *how* we will prevent that," she said finally. "But overall, sounds like we're on-schedule."

Feeling, at last, as though this might actually be *possible*—that *Carpathia* might really launch—she leaned forward. "Now, let's look at the progress on the main drive shocks..."

CHAPTER 20:
RESCUE OPTIONS

Time to Launch: 560 days

"Still no sign of activity from *Fenrir*?" Jeanne asked.

"No, Madam President," York said. "It's still on its hyperbolic course through the inner system. No signals from it that we can detect."

"Do we have any reason to believe there are still 'Fens' to rescue onboard?" Roger asked.

"Some," York said. "Careful analysis of the IR data we're getting indicates that there are still portions of *Fenrir* that appear to be moderating their temperature—that is, something's keeping them at a relatively constant internal temperature, heating or cooling as needed. The indicated temperature, I'll add, is about twenty-seven degrees C, a hair over eighty Fahrenheit, which is slightly more than most of us would find comfortable but is a perfectly reasonable temperature for organic beings like us."

He grinned. "And another really, *really* interesting piece of news is that we've been analyzing the light-curves we get off *Fenrir*—"

"Light-curves?" repeated Jeanne. *I think I've heard the term, but...* "Could you unpack that for me?"

"Of course. Light-curves are the plot of reflected light over time from a target, or a particular *part* of the target, to put it simply. The important aspect of this is that if a target has physical features on it, and it tilts or rotates or otherwise moves, you can both get an idea of how it's moving, and of details on the surface, by analysis of the curve."

That made perfect sense. "Go on, York."

"Well, as I said, we've been carefully tracking the light-curves from *Fenrir*, and a large part of it—but not *all* of it—appears to be rotating." He paused.

Jeanne thought quickly, remembering everything she'd had to cram into her head about spacecraft. "Living quarters?"

"And working areas that need gravity, yes, that's our thought. And it's our first independent confirmation of something else we had just been guessing at before: if our estimates of size are correct, the maximum simulated gravity on *Fenrir* is just a little bit less than one gee."

"Which fits their acceleration profile," Jeanne said, nodding. "So they were maintaining a comfortable acceleration on their way in."

Roger leaned forward, brown eyes wide with interest. "It means more than that, Jeanne. This is *strong* evidence some of them survived, isn't it?"

York looked mildly surprised; Jeanne had seen this many times before, when Roger stopped being his deliberately background self and showed the intelligence she'd chosen him for. "Exactly right, Roger."

"I'm missing something, so explain why this shows some survived?"

York gestured to Roger, who smiled. "Because they would have been relying on their drive to maintain a sensation of gravity on approach. You see?"

With that hint, she did. "Of *course*. The Fens had their drive cut off without warning. They wouldn't have needed, or been using, spin-based gravity simulation before the drive cut out. Which means that someone or something onboard had to . . ." She thought a moment. "Hm. They'd have to reconfigure for 'gravity' along a rotational outward axis instead of along the centerline of the ship, and *then* start that part rotating."

"Right, Madam President," York confirmed. "Now, a lot of that was almost certainly automated, but I have to assume there would be live participation, or at least oversight, in that complex changeover, so I think it's very strong evidence that we have some number of survivors, and that at least for the first few weeks after the disaster they still had *some* power and control, even if there was a lot of disruption."

It also implied some much less encouraging facts. "They'd have certainly done everything they could to shift themselves into a decent orbit, yes?"

York's grimace showed she understood the situation well enough. "We all would think so. Which means that, at the least, repairing any major portion of their drive systems was going to be so difficult that they had to prioritize getting their living and working quarters up to gravity first. Or that they had some other problem that absolutely required getting the spinning section moving."

She looked up at the enigmatic shape on her wall screen: the current best guess as to *Fenrir*'s actual structure, still vague. A long, generally cylindrical form with remnant ruffles of the radiator array toward one end, *Fenrir* remained more of a mystery than a vessel. *Most of the central part of that cylinder is probably rotating.* "So we are still on a rescue mission," she said finally. "There could be hundreds of thousands of Fen onboard that ship; there's no way *Carpathia* could take them off. Do we believe we have any chance of actually saving more than a fraction of them?"

"Two possibilities—well, with a lot of variations—are still likely, Jeanne," York answered. "The first one is that we can establish enough communications with the Fens, and get enough of our own analyses done, to be able to understand what's wrong with the ship and either fix it ourselves, or help them finish fixing it, at least enough to put *Fenrir* into a decent orbit around the Sun."

"And the second?"

York grinned. "We find the right part of *Fenrir* to take the strain, lock *Carpathia* to it, and *push* it into orbit on our own."

Roger stared at him. "Is that even *possible*? *Fenrir* outmasses *Carpathia* by at least two to three thousand times!"

"We've got people working on it . . . but the answer's a big, solid *maybe*. Depends on just how big a bang *Carpathia* can handle, what stresses *Fenrir* can take, whether we'll have enough antimatter and uranium and such available . . . but it's actually not entirely out of the question.

"See, mass difference really isn't the major problem," York went on. "It's easier than being an ocean tugboat—you're not going to be fighting waves, currents, wind, whatever. Experiments like DART showed—as we always thought—relatively small forces can affect the orbits of vastly larger objects.

"The question is the total delta-v, change in velocity, that *Carpathia* could impart to something like *Fenrir*. If we were relying on chemical drives, there'd be no way we could; you'd need multiple fuel tanks bigger than the whole of *Carpathia* to shift it. But the energy density of nuclear reactions is over a million times greater, so we just might be able to pull it off.

"It'd be a *hell* of a challenge, though, like an ant shoving a pencil and trying to make it go in *exactly* one direction." He grinned again. "But boy, you'd be really impressed with that ant!"

"I suppose you would," Jeanne said after a moment spent imagining *Carpathia* pushing the city-sized *Fenrir*. "But I think we'd much prefer the first option."

"Absolutely," York said, his expression far more serious. "The second option is the 'Hail Mary' at the end. Taken together it would have chances of doing all sorts of terrible things ranging from smashing *Carpathia* against *Fenrir*, breaking *Fenrir* in any of a dozen ways, or even nuking *Fenrir* by accident."

He shrugged. "And being honest, I'm really not sure you could get enough thrust long enough to make a difference in the orbit. We'd probably have to find a way to dump most of *Fenrir* to do it, and that'd lose us a lot of the stuff we wanted to study. Of course, the Fens might be able to give us the info we'd lost, but still, it'd be a mess. Just imagine trying to get across to aliens that we're going to cut their ship into pieces so we can save them."

"No, thank you," Roger said firmly. "Are things otherwise going smoothly? We know that Dr. Bronson's still out at the main site."

"Very smoothly," York said, then frowned.

"What is it?" Jeanne asked.

"That's the problem. It's *all* going smoothly. IIS's inspection signed off on the plate integrity, so the part of *Carpathia* that has to survive being nuked a few thousand times is done. They've scanned two of the eight main support members for the big shock absorbers and those have passed. They've vetted the top crew and they should be meeting soon to start integrating their operations and understanding of the ship. Civilian crew selection's underway. Designs for the living quarters are almost done." York shrugged.

"Honestly? I'm waiting for the other shoe to drop. *Nothing* goes this well, not without *something* going wrong."

CHAPTER 21:
THE GROUP

Time to Launch: 555 days

The meeting wasn't in a dimly lit underground room, or a sterile, white-walled office, or even a high penthouse apartment looking over a city. Instead, it was in a lovely courtyard, with a cool breeze to moderate the brilliant sun that sparkled through the leaves of the vines and bushes that surrounded the mosaic-tiled central square. Flowers of yellow, red, white, and pink added splashes of color to the greenery.

The man who reclined in one of the comfortable chairs, awaiting the others, was not as spectacularly attractive as his surroundings, but he did, in a way, fit. He was carefully dressed in light, perfectly fitting clothing, casual in appearance, expensive in actuality. He had hair nearly as white as the clouds in the sky, but his long, pale, sharp-planed face was not terribly lined; he had begun to gray long before the rest of him aged. His body showed some signs of exercise, with calloused hands, defined musculature, and only a touch of excess weight around his waist.

It was his eyes and face that tended to draw attention, because they could alternate between warmth, concern, and—in the presence of a very few—an iron coldness of purpose. It was this latter that was evident, even as he sipped a cup of black coffee and seemed to be perusing articles on his laptop.

He closed the computer as the door on the far side of the courtyard opened, admitting three more people. One was a tall, somewhat overweight black man, black-and-silver hair having given up the battle except on the perimeter of his head, giving the appearance of a great polished onyx egg in an ashen nest. He wore a constant apologetic smile, as though afraid his presence might give offense, and his clothes were truly casual—a cheap T-shirt emblazoned with anime characters, and simple blue jeans. He also carried a laptop case, slung by a strap over his shoulder.

The second was a woman, darkly Mediterranean olive in complexion, with a profusion of tightly curling black-brown hair. Hers was a figure of a dedicated runner—long, lean, strong—someone with the focus and determination to push on through tens of kilometers at the same steady, wearing pace. Her eyes, though brown rather than gray-blue, echoed the same steely purpose as their host. She wore a far more formal ensemble in grays and blacks, relieved only by a few touches of color.

The third and final arrival was considerably older, a cheerful-faced, plump woman with her graying blonde hair put up in a slightly untidy bun, looking like someone's favorite old aunt. She carried a purse entirely in character with that old aunt, and said, "Thank you, dear," to the big man as he held the door for her.

Their host rose and nodded in greeting to each; they seated themselves, each with a preferred drink already to hand; their host knew his guests' tastes.

"Thank you for coming," he said.

"Still not comfortable with this in-person stuff, Silver," said the big black man; his voice was a touch rough, but still as pleasantly inoffensive as his expression. "Doesn't matter how careful we are, just takes one little slip for us to all be connected."

"Understood, and agreed, Keys," said the man called Silver. "This is a . . . high-density exchange that I hope shall not have to be repeated; smaller updates should be done by remote methods you have already vetted for the Group."

The Group had only acquired capital letters by default; technically, the organization had no name. But, as Silver understood well, human beings required labels, categories, elements to delineate *Us* from *Them*, and so the group became . . . The Group.

He turned his chilled-steel gaze to the younger of the two women. "Lathe, you may go first. Summarize for us."

Lathe reached into her small clutch purse and removed three flash drives, handing one to each of the others. "That is as comprehensive a list of suppliers, manufacturers, and support organizations as I have been able to obtain. Those which have reliable members of the Group in them are indexed in detail, including what services the Group members will be able to provide for us, and what has already been arranged."

"Indeed," said Silver. "What *has* already been arranged?"

"The main supports for the vessel," Lathe said, "will not all be pristine. We could not, of course, make *all* of them flawed, but with some careful processing tweaks at least three or four of the ten should be unacceptably flawed. This is our first line of attack; as detailed in the report, we are attempting similar subtle sabotage attacks from multiple directions."

"Very good. We will all review these and provide any additional suggestions. How would you rate the likelihood of achieving the objective?"

Lathe frowned, tapping her foot absently as she sipped at her orange juice. "Any *individual* one of these will likely not be sufficient, but I would rate the chances excellent over the long haul, if we can continue to slow their progress, force them to reorder parts, perform more laborious inspections, and so on. This is also"—she gave a flash of a surprisingly gentle smile—"the most humane option. The project grinds to a halt and eventually must be abandoned. No one need be hurt or killed, and that Armageddon machine never launches."

"Such a kind girl you are, Lathe," said the older woman.

"Thank you, Needle," Lathe said, flashing her a warm look. "We're trying to save the world, not hurt people." She was suddenly coldly purposeful. "Unless it becomes necessary."

"We would all prefer that, yes," Silver agreed. "However, we are playing a very dangerous game against nearly every government on the planet. They also have used their unprecedented power and resources to recruit even those who might, in saner times, refuse to work on this monstrous project, and we must assume that they will be highly effective in solving whatever roadblocks we place before them. Knowing more about that will help us. Keys?"

"Um, right, I have mine here." Another set of flash drives changed hands. "So, this is everything I've been able to dig out of the systems on the actual design. I'll be sending updates as I get them, but they've really firmed up some of the key areas now. Wouldn't have *nearly* that much success if they didn't have to distribute the work around the world, but they're still having trouble keeping everything locked down as tight as they ought, what with all the different countries and such having to work together."

"That will help," Lathe said. "Many of the organizations only have what elements of the blueprints, circuit diagrams, and so on that they need to complete their own work. A unified overview will help determine the best way to definitively disrupt or damage their progress."

"Good work, Keys," Silver said. "Needle?"

"You know, this has been a *very* challenging assignment," the older woman said cheerfully. "Normally, of course, one can recruit from the opposite side of any conflict, frame any of a dozen other countries or factions for whatever you choose to do. But all the major players, I'm afraid, are *firmly* behind this so-called rescue mission."

"You're not saying we have no options, are you?" Lathe said, concern making a crease between her brows.

"Oh, no, no, dear, there are *always* options. I was just musing on how this is much more *interesting* than the usual assassination or bombing or whatever." She spoke in the same tone as if she were discussing baking different kinds of pies. "Despite all that, of course, there's always people available to take on particular assignments, it's just more entertaining. I'm almost *grateful* to the *Carpathia*, actually; I've not had so much fun in years, and if we actually get to move *forward,* well!"

She handed out her own data. "Here are all the resources we have for various options. Silver, I expect you'll work with Keys and Lathe to see if any of them might assist their work earlier. Just as an example, they are depending on that nice gentleman and his charming little robots a great deal. If he were to have an accident, well... they might miss something Lathe sent them, you know." She smiled pleasantly.

"I knew we could count on you, Needle."

"Do you have anything for us, Silver?" asked Keys.

"Nothing so complex, no. You all have your own people, in their own cells, to carry out your particular tasks. I of course have my own, but..." He shrugged.

The others didn't need it spelled out. If all of their methods failed, there was one final approach, one last method to ensure that the obscenity called *Carpathia* would be stopped.

And it would be Silver's job to carry it out, at the cost of his own life. A small price to pay, and indeed one that any of the Group—the core members, the ones who truly understood the stakes—would pay willingly. The other three couldn't help but admire Silver more for his determination that, if all else failed, he—the founder—would also be the only one of the Group to pay for it.

"A short meeting, but these," Silver said, looking at the three small flash drives, "are worth it. Dinner will be served shortly; I trust you'll all stay until the morrow?"

"Do you think that's wise?" Keys asked.

"Keys, you're *already* here. If anything, it would be *more* suspicious for the three of you to arrive here and then depart in an hour." He smiled his most gracious smile. "Go, freshen up. I think you'll enjoy what my chef's preparing!"

CHAPTER 22: CHALLENGES AND CONCERNS

Time to Launch: 550 days

Busy busy day ahead, Stephanie thought, with a combination of anticipation and leashed tension. *And all on me.*

York Dobyns was still in Washington with the President and probably half of the FORT representatives. His last communication had been a typically breezy panic-inducer: "Yep, you're on your own, Steph. Time for you to fly without training wings. It'll be fine, what could go wrong?"

I will *kick* him *for that last bit.* She wasn't actually superstitious, but there wasn't a geek on the planet who didn't know that you *never* asked "what could go wrong?"

Focus. Just a day like any other. Her first meeting was with the newly selected captain and executive officer for *Carpathia*—Chinese and American, respectively. She'd only been able to skim their files, but Rear Admiral Hàorán Lín's service record was impressive and he had a long, *long* list of skills, some of them surprising in a career Chinese military man, and Rear Admiral Robinson sounded equally well qualified. As a bonus, each spoke the other's native language, ensuring communication.

After that it's daily review with inspection, hopefully getting past all the main shock supports. She continued reviewing the schedule as she approached the small conference room set aside for her first meeting.

Oh, that doesn't sound good. Despite the sound-dampening material on the conference room door, she was hearing voices from inside, and they didn't sound happy.

"—South China Sea!" Benjamin Robinson finished, glaring at Hàorán Lín. The Chinese pick for the captain of *Carpathia* was returning the glare, with interest. Their gazes flicked toward her, but then returned to each other.

"Would you care for a list of the offenses *your* people have committed, *Admiral* Robinson?"

Stephanie didn't need to hear any more. The two people she had come here to meet were *already* at each other's throats.

But would they even *listen* to her? She was a civilian, younger than either of them by a long shot, without even the bulky and even-tempered presence of Dr. Dobyns to back her up.

Robinson was rising toward another explosion as Lin loudly enumerated military and diplomatic offenses of the United States. Stephanie doubted they'd *actually* come to blows, but if this wasn't stopped, one or both of them would say something irreparable. The loud, hostile voices hammered at her—something she had never liked even as a child, and something usually alien to academia. But she had to do something about it.

Fly without training wings. How?

How would the President *handle this?*

Her brain instantly told her one thing: President Jeanne Sacco would *not* stand there frozen and wondering what to do.

A part of her said *Well, duh, but she's the* President!

To which another part of her replied, partly with anger and partly with awed realization, *And I'm the director.*

"Gentlemen," she said.

Neither Rear Admiral Lin nor Rear Admiral Robinson took their eyes off each other. With a half-dreaming feeling of standing outside herself, expecting her voice to crack like a frightened girl's, she drew in her breath. *"GENTLEMEN!"*

To her surprise—and by their wide-eyed, instantaneous attention—the single word was a whipcrack of sound, cold and focused with furious precision. Her heart was hammering double time, but now that she *had* their attention she had to keep it, force them to focus on *her.* "Would you care to explain this scene?"

"Dr. Bronson," Lin said, voice now a more mellow bass—though retaining an edge of anger. "We were having a . . . difference of opinion. Begun by the admiral, I should add."

"That is an *interesting* way to put it, *Rear Admiral*," Johnson said between his teeth. "I would—"

"Enough." Stephanie said, then when it appeared the two *still* might not stop, she shouted it. *"Enough!"* she snapped, and slammed her briefcase flat to the table; the impact echoed like a gunshot, and Stephanie said a silent prayer that she hadn't just trashed her laptop.

She met both their gazes. "Admiral Lin, let me correct you. For purposes of this meeting I am *Director* Bronson. That means, *gentlemen*, that I am your boss."

The two men looked at her with expressions that combined a worried understanding with instinctive disbelief.

"Sit down," she said, and waited until the two men had done so. She remained standing, gaining some advantage of height to glare *down* at them. "You may think I am 'Director' as a sort of publicity stunt. Honestly? I thought that way at first. But the President was *not* joking, and I *am* the director of this project, and if the two of you can't get along, one—or both—of you are *off* this project."

"You can't just remove us!" Lin said incredulously.

"I *can* and I *will*, Admiral," she said, shivering inside at the enormity of what she was saying. *This guy was handpicked by, like, two* governments. *If I kick him off it'll be a* nightmare.

But it would be way, *way* worse to have a captain that couldn't work with the crew. "That goes for you, too, Admiral Robinson," she said, making sure that Lin understood she was playing no favorites. "This ship will have major crew positions filled by people from a dozen countries, gentlemen. They'll *all* have political issues with each other, a lot of them justified.

"*You will leave those issues here on Earth*," she said, rapping her knuckles on the table for emphasis. "I don't *care* what China did, or the United States, or the UK, or Japan, or *anyone*. I don't give a *shit* about which side is right or wrong or if there isn't any right or wrong side. The two of you were chosen because you're supposed to be top-flight professionals. Act like it."

The two men looked at each other.

"Now, why don't we start this meeting over, as though none of us had ever met? Admiral Lin, I've heard wonderful things about you. Welcome to *Carpathia*."

Lin blinked, then rose, bowed, and extended a hand. "Thank you, Director Bronson. I see that I had not heard *nearly* enough of you."

"Admiral Robinson, I also reviewed your very impressive record. Welcome to *Carpathia*."

Robinson also stood and shook her hand. "Thank you, ma'am. Glad to be here."

"Admiral Lin has been chosen to be the captain of *Carpathia*," Stephanie went on. "Admiral, allow me to introduce your executive officer, Admiral Benjamin Robinson."

The two faced each other, bowed, and shook hands. "Admiral," Lin said. "Admiral," Robinson replied.

There was a moment of silence, then Lin inhaled sharply and spoke. "You were not, by chance, a pilot as well?"

"As a matter of fact, I was. Super Hornets, mainly, though I've flown 'em all."

"Indeed. I've always envied the pilots." Lin tapped his eyes. "Never quite good enough for that."

Robinson nodded. "That's a shame. Know a lot of people like that. Still, looks like you'll get to fly something a little bigger now." He took a breath of his own. "Apologies for earlier."

"It was not entirely one-sided. Accepted. And, *Director* Bronson, apologies to you. I believe we both wish to remain with the project and can promise you no more such outbursts."

Oh, thank GOD. "That's excellent. Now, let's go over just what it is the two of you will be commanding, and how we expect that to work with the . . . interesting . . . composition of our crew."

Lin and Robinson nodded, and looked up with interest as she threw the first slide up.

That went . . . well. Stephanie shook her head a bit in amazement. *I never expected . . . well, to find out that I could be that* cold.

She realized, though, that it was exactly that—an iron-hard dispassion—that had gotten through to the two highest officers of *Carpathia*. Despite being terrified inside, she hadn't let them *see* it, and that—combined with her driving home the fact that she did, in fact, outrank them here—had made them take her seriously. *I can do this.*

I mean, I don't believe *it, but now I . . . guess I kind of do. Is this what every big boss has to figure out?*

She supposed it was. The trick to being a *good* big boss was probably figuring out the *right* times to come down hard, so that you only had to do it once or twice, instead of just being a hard-ass all the time and pissing everyone off. *Hope I can figure out that balance. I'll have to ask Jeanne about it.*

She half giggled, a little gasp of amusement, realizing that she was thinking casually of talking to the President.

For a moment, Stephanie stopped, momentarily looking back . . . was it only *months?* . . . to the grad student sitting in a lab, checking images. A part of her wished she could be back there, with nothing more earthshaking on her mind than whether she might see a new supernova or asteroid on the screen, and how she was going to finish her thesis.

But then, we wouldn't have seen Fenrir; *we wouldn't know, finally, that we weren't alone in the universe.*

And Stephanie Bronson would have been just one more astronomer, still asking that question and never knowing the answer.

Feeling both a thrill of awe and a glow of hope that she really *could* do this, she pushed open the door to the next meeting—this in a larger conference room with large screens for those attending remotely.

Heads turned, there were smiles, nods . . . but not as many smiles as she expected. Peter Flint, in particular, looked grave.

"All right, everyone. We're all busy so let's try to get through the review quickly." She sat down, nodded to the camera to greet all the remote attendees. "Pete, you look like you have something for us?"

The older man gave a wry smile. "Not what you're hoping for, I'm afraid. You know we received the main supports for the drive shocks . . . well, me and my Bells finished going over 'em and I'm sad to say that out of ten ordered, *half* don't meet specs."

Half? She heard the mutter around the room. "That *is* bad. We need eight, as I understand it."

"Well," Werner said reluctantly, "she *could* operate on four, but that's reducing the safety margin quite a bit. Not to a critical point, but the idea of having eight was that if we *did* lose one, we could shift to a four-shaft configuration. We have no backup option if we use four to start with."

"I don't think any of us like those words, 'no backup option,'" Stephanie said. "York, have you spoken to the manufacturers? Can we get *good* replacements in time?"

"Kenji Taisou of Mitsuda Metalworks says he thinks so, and that he'll personally oversee all the work. He doesn't know what went wrong but something like this is a huge embarrassment and you can bet they'll be devoting every effort to making the next delivery perfect. It's going to be *expensive*, though—"

"If they guarantee they'll all be good, just pay them," Stephanie said flatly. "As long as you think they *are* good for it."

"They're supposed to be the best. They haven't had a failure like this in...well, as far as I can see, *ever*. Not to say it's ridiculous—manufacturing solid bars of metal a hundred meters long and a couple thick that will be taking nuclear impacts is no joke—but it's definitely not normal to have that level of failure, and they're motivated as hell to fix it."

"All right. What does this do to the schedule?"

Werner passed his hand over his bald head, ruffling hair that was no longer present. "We can reshuffle some work. We have four supports, so we can still start on the drive-shock assembly as soon as the springs start arriving, next week, and if that goes all right, the main hull components can be attached. We're already building up the earthworks to support all of that. So...I think we can keep to schedule, if we don't have any more major problems."

Thank God. There *was* slack built into the schedule—even with the hard deadline looming, no one believed there wouldn't be *any* schedule creep—but she begrudged every hour they lost. The worst possible outcome would be to successfully complete construction...too late to help *Fenrir*.

A thought occurred to her then—one she *really* didn't like. *Better remember to ask York later.* "All right, what's next? Charlotte, what's the status on antimatter supply?"

"Excellent," Dr. Goddard replied, her smile helping lighten the previously tense atmosphere. "We just passed one microgram for the first time in history a few days ago; average production has been twenty-two point three nanograms per day from all sites combined over the last fifty days. We're storing it in three separate locations and working on additional storage receptacles, to ensure that no disaster can deprive us of a majority of our production."

"That's great!" Stephanie couldn't keep the relief out of her voice. "How is work coming on the drive-related designs?" she asked, turning back to York.

"Dr. Crane's work indicates that we *could* make miniature Orion-style drives for maneuvering jets as well," York Dobyns replied, "but I have to say I recommend we don't go that route. It's got a certain appeal—higher energy density, less fuel mass, more powerful maneuvers—but the main drive's experimental enough. I think we should stick with tried, true, conventional maneuvering thrusters."

"With all those advantages, why?"

"Complexity. We'd need the same feed mechanisms, antimatter charge insertion, et cetera, but they'd have to be significantly smaller all the way down, and that could introduce other problems. Maybe more importantly, the maneuver drives will be on the main hull, which means detonating nuclear charges—small, but still nuclear—a lot closer to the living and working areas."

Stephanie nodded, took a breath. "I think I concur. Have your people check it over, but unless you come up with a really compelling reason otherwise, let's go with conventional maneuvering thrusters." She looked to Dr. Filipek, who'd joined by remote. "Eva, what about the drive charges themselves?"

"Good and not-so-good, but not terrible, news," Eva said with a half smile. "MatterPrint's definitely mastered the printing of the charges; they did a run this week using the actual materials and everything looks good on the three sizes they did."

"What's the not-good news?"

Eva glanced at York, who sighed. "They don't think there's any way to make onboard printers for the drive system, not in time and sufficiently tested and reliable. So most of the drive charges will have to be manufactured before launch," York said. "But that's not *terrible* news because they *do* think they can put *one* system on board that we can use to build the charges and maybe other small components to spec, and the space we were setting aside for the charge printers can be repurposed for charge storage at different sizes. Basically, think of one of those old change machines with the pennies, dimes, nickels, and quarters in different tubes, only a lot bigger and smarter."

"We're working on the best trade-off between the complexity and the number of different drive-charge sizes," Werner added. "But it will still be very flexible and *Carpathia* will be able to accelerate at different rates as we wish."

Privately, Stephanie actually thought this was a better setup; the MatterPrint 3D printers were still cutting edge, and she knew how often cutting-edge stuff failed. One attraction of *Carpathia*'s overall design was that a lot of it was technology that had been already known in the 1950s; they were just adding twenty-first-century bells and whistles.

"Anything else? The detonation plugs?"

"Still in the design-and-testing phase," Eva replied. "No significant problems seen, though, so we expect to have a working test design in about a month and a half to two months."

"Live test?" asked York.

"Not the first ones, of course, but once we've satisfied ourselves there, we will have to do a live test. Probably several, to verify what theory tells us. The director will have to decide the testing schedule," she went on, "so, Dr. Bronson, you should confer with us soon. I assume those will be performed underground."

For an instant she hesitated, as her brain finally decoded the innocuous phrasing. *They're talking about* nuclear tests. *I'm going to be green-lighting nukes!* "Er, yes, Dr. Filipek, I'll schedule that with you and I think the President and anyone else who should be in on it. York?"

"I'll get it set up. Probably need people from NNSA"—the National Nuclear Security Administration—"and Defense, and the other nations will want observers in, at least."

They touched on a few more subject areas, but nothing of nearly the same import.

"All right, thank you, everyone. We'll meet again next week, same time?"

This . . . wasn't too bad. But those shafts . . . She gestured, and York followed her out of the conference room.

"What is it, Steph? You look worried."

"I *am* worried, about a lot of things. I will be until we get *Carpathia* off the ground. But yes. I thought of something and I really don't like what I came up with, so I want you to tell me I'm nuts, so I can stop worrying about it."

York's eyes crinkled at the corners, though his lips hid their smile.

"I certainly will not call the director 'nuts,' because we need a nice, sane director. What's this scary thought you've had?"

"Well, we know that the *real* reason for *Carpathia* is that everyone wants to get their hands on the Fens' technology; the rescue mission, which is what you and I and a lot of our friends *want* the real mission to be, isn't really *that* important to the governments."

"Unfortunately true, yes. But we've already had *those* thoughts, so . . . ?"

"So it occurred to me . . . York, is it possible that the governments might decide to do things to *slow up* the assembly of *Carpathia*, so that we just can't quite make the rescue window, but can still launch to recover *Fenrir* after she hooks around the Sun?"

York Dobyns stopped so suddenly that Steph stumbled, bringing herself to a halt. For a moment he was quiet.

"It's the main supports that got you thinking that way, isn't it?"

"Yes," she admitted. "I mean, I don't know that much about metal casting or grinding or whatever—though I'm learning more about everything these days—but fifty percent failure rate seemed really . . . *off* to me. But this is a unique project, and I guess when you're doing crazy stuff, you expect failures. Right?"

York's lips tightened, and she felt the knot in her gut tighten. "Yes," he said slowly, "but . . ."

After another moment, he shook his head. "But no, fifty percent's way out on the curve. Four, five standard deviations out. Sorry, Steph," York said, voice as grim as his face. "I can't tell you you're nuts. Some people—even in our own government—might think of *exactly* that."

"Then what do we *do*?"

"Watch," York said. "If this is the only really bad failure, well, it's bad luck. Even companies have bad luck. Might even have a couple bad-luck events. But you know the old saying."

She did. "Once is happenstance. Twice is coincidence."

"But the third time," York continued, "the third time?

"That's enemy action."

CHAPTER 23:
TWO DECISIONS

Time to Launch: 545 days

"Rog," the President said, "tell me you have good news."

"I'm not about to start lying now, Jeanne," Roger Stone answered, not even bothering to hide the grim expression on his face.

"This was *so* not what I was looking forward to this morning," President Sacco said. "Should we be having a larger briefing?"

"Yes," Stone answered after a pause. "But we'll have to think carefully about who with."

Jeanne Sacco took a deep breath, then a sip of coffee. "All right, Roger, hit me with it. Which countries are involved? Us? China? Who?"

"It's worse than that. Or better, in some ways, but still bad." Stone put several files in front of her. "These have the details, but I put everyone I trusted on it; this is the NSA report, this is CIA, this is Secret Service. I also asked some other sources, friends I've picked up in my time here.

"Jeanne, as far as I can tell, *none* of the nations—no major ones, anyway—have been doing anything to sabotage the progress of *Carpathia*. That's not saying some haven't *thought* about it, and in fact the NSA found one think-tank report from the DOD—Army, if it matters—on the potential advantages of slowing *Carpathia*'s progress to ensure it's not complete in time to save any of the Fens. But there's no evidence anyone actually put these plans in motion."

The President looked at Roger, puzzled. "But are you saying the failure in manufacture of the main supports, and the later ones in the hab unit bearing supports and in the guidance modules were accidents?"

Roger shook his head. "No one thinks this is coincidence. Yes, accidents are going to happen in making an unprecedented design like this, but nothing so . . . systematic." He put another folder down. "I just received this from Director Bronson."

"What does Dr. Bronson want today?"

"She wants permission and resources—people and money—to make her own group of troubleshooters to check systems as needed."

Jeanne managed a smile at that. "I suppose that means she trusts *us*, at least."

"She has to trust someone, and you and I could have sabotaged the project quite effectively in different ways," Roger agreed. "I think it's a good idea, and if there's one person on the project I trust unreservedly, it's her."

"Her and Dr. Dobyns, I think. Probably Peter Flint, as well, since he could have simply *passed* the flawed elements."

She saw Roger wince at that; if *Carpathia* had attempted to fly with what could have been a majority of flawed support members, it would have likely disintegrated within a few minutes of launch.

Then Roger shook his head. "I would personally agree," he admitted, "but to be honest that doesn't eliminate him. Some of this sabotage is . . . *too* direct. I think we're *meant* to find most if not all of it, and probably our unseen adversaries really don't intend to carry out wholesale slaughter—which is what would happen if *Carpathia* failed with everyone aboard. They just want to make it expensive—too expensive and time-consuming for us to ever succeed."

The thought was both staggering and infuriating. The largest project ever taken on by humanity, and some unknown group wanted to just keep throwing wrenches in the works until it stumbled to a halt. "Do you think they'll stop if it becomes clear they can't keep us from finishing?"

Stone considered for a few moments, then shook his head. "No. A movement that *can* achieve what we've seen probably is willing to take any steps necessary. They might *regret* it, but I think we would be foolish to believe they would not go to the wall on this."

Jesus H. Particular Christ, as my father used to say. On a purely personal level, this offended her. On a practical political level, it threatened her—the failure of *Carpathia* would undoubtedly mean the failure of her administration, no matter what excuses she might be able to give.

But on an international level—no, an *interstellar* level—it was quite simply intolerable. This was not a once-in-a-lifetime event, it was once-in-the-species'-existence event. If they couldn't rescue *Fenrir*, or at least some of the people and knowledge onboard, humanity would likely never know any more about the visitors who had expended an entire civilization's worth of energy just to visit. It would be the most tragic lost opportunity in Earth's history.

"Roger," she said, hearing the anger in her voice and, after a second, deciding not to hide it. "Roger, I *want* these people. I want what they're doing stopped, and I want to know who they are, how *many* there are, and why they're doing it. Give Stephanie whatever she wants, but I also want to put together our own investigation team."

"You know, we will need a *big* team to have a chance to track them down, if they've gotten this far," Roger pointed out. "And the bigger the group, the more chance there is for these people to get someone on the inside."

Jeanne closed her eyes, then nodded. "I know. But we can't ignore this, and we can't just make a half-hearted attempt at stopping it. Obviously, try to keep it to people we really have reason to believe *want Carpathia* to succeed, but yes, they're bound to get someone in the team if we spread the net far enough. They have to be watching us— you and me in particular, I suspect—for our reaction."

"Understood," Roger said. "I'll go over our options and have an outline of how to proceed on your desk by end of day."

Jeanne nodded. "Thank you, Roger." She took a huge breath, let it out. "You know the other problem, of course."

"Other . . . oh, yes." Stone grimaced as though he had suddenly found himself chewing lemon peels. "There's not a chance in hell there aren't agents already *on* the *Carpathia* team."

"Not just the team," Jeanne said bleakly. "On the *crew*."

Stone nodded.

After a pause, she sighed, then drained her coffee. "Anything else before I go to the main morning brief?"

"Just this," he said, putting a final folder in front of her. "Everyone else needed has already put down their approval. It just needs your signature."

Jeanne opened the folder and read the executive summary, then closed it and looked up at Roger with a wry chuckle. "So I'm the one to pull the trigger, after almost forty years."

"Not much choice, if we're going to ever launch *Carpathia*."

"No. No, there isn't." She looked down at the simple page with a line for a signature and another for the date, then reached out for a pen.

"Congratulations, Dr. Bronson," she said as she finished the signature with a flourish. "You get to conduct the United States' first nuclear detonations in this century."

CHAPTER 24: CONTINGENCIES IN MOTION

Time to Launch: 542 days

Silver looked at the message once more and then let out an exasperated breath. *Well, I knew this was likely.*

Lathe had done the best she could; her cells of careful saboteurs had managed to put flaws in everything from major support structures to circuit boards, but nearly all of them had been caught. The ones that had so far managed to pass inspection . . . Lathe was of the opinion that they would be found eventually, before launch, and nearly all of them would be repairable.

Worse, however, was the fact that three cells had been compromised and taken into custody. No one anywhere near close enough to reach Lathe herself, fortunately, but more than enough to verify the existence of an organized and capable opposition to *Carpathia*'s mission.

Despite efforts, the Group hadn't managed to get anyone on the President's secret CST (*Carpathia* Security Taskforce); it had been something of a matter of luck that he'd *heard* about it as early as he did, because of one of the lower-echelon cells having a member in the right place at the right time.

Silver himself was in a position that could allow him access, but he didn't dare do anything to draw attention to himself. He was the Group's last-ditch backup, the one who would have to stop *Carpathia* if all other methods failed.

This was not in any way the preferred outcome. No one in the Group—except, possibly, Needle, whose personal outlook on her professional activities was still opaque to Silver—really *wanted* anyone hurt. They just wanted this project to grind to a halt, at least long enough to prevent it from carrying out its purpose. Silver already had other cells operating to prevent the *Carpathia* from being completed some years later, but that wasn't a major danger; the sheer expense and dangers of the nuclear-powered vessel would become fatally large factors in a few years.

No, the real danger was *now*, while both the imagination of the vast majority of the public and the personal and institutional *pride* of the major nations were dangerously and irrationally focused on the naïve and deadly goal of rescuing alien intruders, even at the risk of nuclear holocaust or worse. This feverish state could only be maintained for so long, and was dependent on a very few factors.

For several minutes Silver sat there, trying to decide if he had any more alternatives. Keys was, naturally, doing what he could, but the facts were that the code going into *Carpathia* would be some of the most carefully analyzed and tested code in the world. It would be *hurried*, yes, and that left some opportunity, but the best that Silver could reasonably hope for and that he was willing to bet on was that Keys would provide him with certain tools he would need for the final option. Lathe still had a few more approaches to try. But...

He gave a genuine sigh of regret, and sent a message.

"It's so *good* to see you again, dear," said Needle.

"And you, Needle," he said, unable to keep from smiling at her motherly, harmless charm; at the same time, he had to admit that the very *fact* of his smile was a chilling reminder of Needle's formidable talents.

"Seeing" was, of course, a matter of opinion. Some didn't consider remote communication really *seeing* someone. Silver would have preferred to either send a simple, encoded note, or to meet in physical person, but security issues precluded the latter, and other practicalities—some also security-related—argued against the former. Given his position, he could not risk being followed or seen meeting with people who might be known to the intelligence community in a . . . negative sense, and he already had to send enough cryptic notes to keep the Group running.

But an unmarried, well-off, reasonably attractive man such as he had a history of meeting people in private settings, and he had three specific paramours that *Carpathia*'s intelligence knew about and he saw periodically. As they were not cleared for *Carpathia* access, he had to visit them off-base.

Keys, of course, could provide him with a secure means to communicate, and Silver was careful to make sure he limited the opportunity for other prying eyes, such as TEMPEST approaches, to see what he might do in the privacy of the hotel suite. And his particular companion tonight, Elaine, was aware that he used their encounters on occasion for clandestine communication.

"You're aware of current progress," he said. "Lathe isn't optimistic, though she's not entirely out of options. Keys hasn't found a way to set up anything that I'd consider better than a minor roadblock to the project. I think we may need your expertise."

"Oh, *wonderful*," Needle said, with the excitement of a mother hearing of her daughter's upcoming marriage to an absolutely *suitable* boyfriend.

"I remember our brief discussion of the options previously. Have you anything to add or change?"

"I have given the matter *very* careful thought, dear," Needle said. "And there *are* a number of choices available. The . . . well, not *simplest*, perhaps, but certainly the one that offends the fewest sensibilities, would be some more *direct* sabotage, destroying elements of the target that would be difficult or impossible to replace. The fact that it *has* been some months now is an advantage for this approach, as it means less time for them to address the problem."

"Do you have assets in place?"

"I have teams which have determined various methods to place themselves, yes." She pursed her lips as though considering how to arrange her social schedule. "Now, we have to recognize that once this approach is *tried* it will become far, far more difficult to pull it off a second time, so I recommend, if we take this route, that it be several simultaneous teams who have separate objectives. This maximizes the chance of achieving our overall goal even if one or two of our people fail to carry out their particular aspect of the plan."

"Alternatives?"

Needle took a sip of tea, carefully put the cup back down, and smiled benignly at Silver. "Well, the project itself really is *driven* toward success by only a few people. While some of them are ultimately replaceable, I believe that there are a few whose loss would severely cripple the project as a whole."

"The director is one, I presume," Silver offered.

The older woman's head tilted, considering. "Yeees . . ." she said slowly, reluctantly. "Yes, she *is* certainly a key driver of the project—its *face*, really, if we're being honest. And her loss could be a crippling blow."

"But . . . ?" prompted Silver.

"But her being the face, as I say, is also a potential problem. Such people can become, well, *martyrs*, and a martyr such as Director Bronson? I'm quite concerned that she could become a stronger motivator dead than alive, to be honest." She flashed another gentle smile. "Now, her primary *advisor*, Dr. Dobyns . . . I think *he* is a . . . safer target, so to speak, at least in this area. He isn't nearly as photogenic— not that he's a bad-looking gentleman, certainly not, but he's simply never going to compete with a lovely young girl like Miss Bronson. On the other hand, our intelligence shows he's Bronson's right hand, her most trusted advisor, and a major influence on everyone's activities. A major vulnerability."

She tapped her chin, thinking. "The older gentleman running their inspection robots remains another excellent possibility. My intelligence—part of it from Keys but part from my own organization— indicates that he's something of a genius in his field, and he's also the only one who can operate his inspection devices with the charming names of bells to nearly their full potential. Losing him would not only be a psychological blow, but also would increase the chance of our dear Lathe getting some of her sabotage past the inspectors."

"Any others?"

"Well, you know, my dear, I think there's really a better choice in every way—especially if we can cast suspicion in other directions."

Silver felt an unpleasant jolt in his gut as Needle specified who she meant. "Are you serious, Needle?"

"Oh, quite, dear. A great deal of potential for disruption to *all* the operations there."

He grimaced. *Do I want to take that route?*

Personally, he had to admit, it would be better for *him* if they did that and it worked. At least he wouldn't have to take the actions that might lead to his own death.

But still...

"Let's try the sabotage route first," he said finally. "But...I want you to come up with a detailed plan on this other option. I hope we don't have to try it."

"Well, I can't say I wouldn't want to try it—I *am* interested in the challenges, you know—but on the other hand, yes, not a course of action I would recommend if we have other options. I will move things along, then." She gave a roguish smile. "Now, I'll leave you to more entertaining company. Ta!"

Silver felt his mouth tighten. *She knows at the least what kind of cover I am using. Possibly knows exactly who is with me.*

He thought, perhaps, it was time for him to arrange a little insurance in that direction, as well.

CHAPTER 25:
A TRADITIONAL
TIMETABLE

Time to Launch: 500 days

The force of the detonation was like a padded slap over her whole body, but Stephanie's whole attention was focused on the massive cloud of smoke and dust—and on the squat, almost comically compressed shape emerging from it.

Another flash of detonation followed by shock wave and thunder, and the scale model of *Carpathia* climbed higher, a squashed-down nose cone atop a broad plate of steel, shock absorbers and springs transferring the tremendous force of the explosions to the pulse-propulsion model to make the main body accelerate steadily. Flash-boom again, and it continued its ascent, straight and steady, unlike some of the old test footage she had seen early on.

It was tiny on the scale of the real *Carpathia*, but it was still *big*—several tons of metal, plastic, electronics, and explosive propulsion.

Several more charges sent the miniature *Carpathia* high into the sky, and then a deliberate shift of angle followed by three more blasts, before a parachute popped out and the model began a slow drift downward. Applause and cheers rose from the two hundred or so spectators, and Stephanie felt a tiny fraction of the weight of worry lift. "That looked really good, York," she said.

"It did indeed. Have to look over the data, of course, but stability looked excellent. Took the turn well. Daire Young's team's already building closer-to-accurate models for test once we clear the designs for actual antimatter-mediated detonations."

"We have the clearance to *do* that? Atomic detonation in atmosphere?"

"President just sent the approval through. Took a *lot* of arguing even in the committee, but the clinchers were that we really, *really* need to know that things like the electrostatic oil jets work, and even more importantly we need data on how much fallout the charges *actually* produce before we use full-size ones in launch. Once we demonstrate the scalable nuclear charge capability in the tests, that's the next step."

Stephanie glanced toward the horizon, where the detonation tests, code-named "Boiler Pressure," were being prepared, then behind her, where *Carpathia* was taking on a titanic, looming reality, gigantic shafts and springs already affixed to the drive plate, other components being steadily added, a skeleton of supports beginning to outline the gargantuan twin of the little test device that was just now reaching the ground. "Still feels unreal to me, sometimes."

"Same here, Director," said Angus Fletcher, squinting out at the recovery team swarming around the test model. "I've designed and supplied custom computer hardware for all sorts of projects, but this?" He shook his head.

"Can't argue," Peter Flint concurred, coming up next to Angus. "Wouldn't trade my place on this project for anything, either."

Seeing the two of them together, Stephanie noted that they were surprisingly similar. Both were tall, spare men with white or near-white hair, in generally good shape even if showing a touch of the extra weight middle-aged men were prone to. Both had hands calloused from work, though Peter's showed heavier wear and a few scars around the knuckles, while Angus's had little burn marks where the computer and electronics expert had, at one time or another, been touched by solder or other hot materials.

The main differences were that Peter's face was square and Angus's more long, and Angus tended to act more professional while Peter displayed a "folksy charm" that Stephanie thought had to be at least partially cultivated.

"Definitely not," Angus said in reply to Pete. "I cannot imagine anyone on this project who would. There will never be another like it." He flashed a quick, apologetic grin. "Love to talk, but I've got to get back to it. Really shouldn't have taken the time to watch—"

"More than half the project turned out to watch," Stephanie said. "We can't pretend most of us aren't in this for the spectacle, too."

Angus's quick laugh had a touch of embarrassment. "No, I suppose we can't. Even the best of us can't resist the lure of a rocket literally blowing itself up to fly." He gave a quick nod. "But I do have to get back. Director, Doctor, Peter—see you later."

Pete also excused himself, and for the next few minutes Stephanie was making her way through the dispersing crowd in a series of greetings, handshakes, bows, or whatever acknowledgment her teammates felt appropriate.

"So, York," she said, the two of them now alone *en route* to her offices. "What's the chances of success?"

The somewhat-portly scientist was silent for a while. "Better than I would have thought at first," he said finally. "I give us fifty-fifty."

That was a shock to her gut. "That low?"

His laugh was subdued. "That *high*, you mean. Yes, things have been going pretty well, but . . ." He shook his head.

"Steph, there are basically two development paths for spaceships. One's the modern NASA approach: test everything, model everything, dozens of times at multiple scales, tweaking and retesting, assembling piece by piece and retesting each time you change something, until finally you've got a ship you figure has a ninety percent or better chance of completing the mission, before you fire up any engines. That takes *years* to go through, and is damned expensive for any ship, even small ones. It's politically much safer, of course, because NASA or other government projects can't afford too many spectacular failures.

"The other's basically the original method, updated by people like Young. You build lots of versions, change things as you go, and keep testing one after another until you get to one that works. You blow up a *lot* of prototypes this way, but instead of spending a decade to build each one, you make them incrementally better each time and have several in development at any time—and you of course instrument the living hell out of each one so you get the data you need, even if—and when—they go up in smoke. That's probably cheaper but it still takes time, and only works if your design goal is relatively inexpensive, so that you can afford to build lots of prototypes."

York touched the security pad and opened the door for them. "We can't really use either one. We can't build half a dozen *Carpathia*s and test them to destruction, nor can we take ten years of careful development. We have all the monetary and technical resources we can imagine, but we have only so much time, no possible extensions of the deadline; physics has given us the time frame and nothing, short of our Fen friends managing to change their orbit on their own, is going to give us any more time. Honestly, we want to *beat* that timeline so we have some time to work with the Fens and figure out if there's any way to save the ship before everyone gets roasted."

Stephanie frowned. "So...we're kind of trusting to luck?"

"Wouldn't say that in any of your interviews...but yes. We're making probably the largest mobile object ever built by mankind, and certainly—by orders of magnitude—the largest flying object ever built." He chuckled. "Well, ever built by *humans*; a few more orders of magnitude to go before we get to match *Fenrir* itself." His expression sobered. "We're going to be using technologies just developed alongside basic designs conceived in the fifties, throwing them all together with engineering and construction teams from a hundred countries, and apparently with at least one group of organized nutbars dedicated to stopping us any way they can.

"So, yes, we're trusting to luck. Doing the best we can to get luck on our side, but as I said, fifty-fifty that we're going to get her flying in time."

A damn toss of a coin to find out if we can do it? To her surprise, she found herself *angry* at the thought, not just disappointed, and chewed that over for the few more moments it took to reach her office.

By the time she opened the door, her anger had morphed back to determination. "York," she said.

He heard the tone in her voice. "Yes, Director?"

"We are going to make it *one hundred percent*," she said, startled by the iron in her own voice. "More, we're going to get it done *fast*. Cut two weeks off the deadline."

"Steph, we're—"

"I *know* we're already pushing things. But you know, you're right. We *need* as much time as we can get *at* Fenrir. This mission is *pointless* if we don't get there in time. Oh, the vultures who just want the technology won't care, but dammit, if they're crazy enough to put *me* in charge, then we're doing this *my* way—and that means we're going to save our alien visitors, full stop."

She looked up at the photograph of the original *Carpathia*. "Extra stokers to the boilers," she said. "Damn the saboteurs, full speed ahead."

CHAPTER 26:
A WORRISOME SUCCESS

Time to Launch: 425 days

Jeanne stood on the review stand, Roger on one side, Director Bronson on the other, looking out over the wide red-brown-gray desert with its patches of dark green scrub; the only man-made things visible in binoculars were three squat buildings, each widely separated from the others, and each with a flag numbered 1, 2, or 3. "I would *really* feel better if you were in the bunker, Madam President," Roger said in his most formal tones.

"No can do, Roger. This is one of the points we have to make on our progress; that we believe we've made this form of nuclear detonation *safe*."

"But what if we're *wrong*?" Stephanie said, biting her lip in nervousness. "Maybe you should—"

"Are we going to abort this project?" Jeanne asked quietly.

"We *can't*," Stephanie answered reflexively. "It's the only chance we have!"

"Then we have to assume we are *not* wrong and that we have, in fact, taken all the necessary precautions," York Dobyns said serenely. "Having the senior staff here shows our confidence. Also challenges all the news organizations to show they've got the guts to watch alongside us. Right, Captain?"

Hàorán Lín sketched a quick bow in York's direction. "Exactly right, Doctor. If they all attend, they give tacit approval, whether that is their intent or not. And"—he nodded to the crowded press section of the stands—"it appears that they have done exactly that."

"*Boiler Pressure One*, nominal ten kilotons, detonation in sixty seconds," crackled the calm voice from the speaker. "Detonation plug in place. All personnel report clear."

Jeanne heard a buzz, saw Stephanie take a deep breath and activate her direct comm to control. "Director Bronson here."

"Final decision point, Director. Go or no-go?"

She closed her eyes, then nodded. "Control, we are a go. Repeat, we are go."

"Go for *Boiler Pressure One*," the speakers announced. "Detonation in thirty seconds.

"Twenty seconds.

"Ten seconds."

As the annunciator, and the large digital display, counted down the final seconds, everyone leaned forward, eyes fixed on the expanse of desert and the distant, tiny flag with a simple "1" displayed as it flapped in the wind.

"Detonation."

For an instant, it seemed nothing had happened. Then a puff of dust spurted up and a shock wave ran visibly outward, throwing up a ring of sand and earth as it radiated away from the flag in the center; people on the stands stumbled or swayed as the massive jolt passed. The ground there heaved upward and then dropped, sinking noticeably. Traces of steam, smoke, or fog rose from the center.

Tentative cheering began from the scientists' area of the stands, spreading as others realized the first detonation had been a success.

Or seems to be, Jeanne told herself. The question was not so much whether the device went "boom," but whether it had exploded in the expected manner, with the expected results.

"Initial analysis underway. Please stand by."

The clapping and cheering faded as seconds ticked by, and soon the assembled crowd was silent, awaiting the verdict of the unseen analysts and the data they had gathered.

"Current analysis results," the speakers finally said. "Detonation total energy nine point nine eight kilotons. Radiation release post detonation negligible—figures to follow. Detonation radiation release successfully confined."

Now the cheers returned and redoubled, and Jeanne saw Director Bronson sink into her seat with an expression of immense relief. "Worried, Director?" she asked with a smile.

"Terrified, Madam President," she answered. "First antimatter-triggered nuclear detonation? So much was riding on that working."

"Director," came the voice of Control, "*Boiler Pressure Two* requests the go-ahead."

Stephanie looked over to the scientific and engineering group. "They'll kill me if we don't," she said with a touch of a smile. "Setting two records today—number of nuclear tests in a short time. Control, *Boiler Pressure Two* is go. Repeat, Two is a go."

"Commencing countdown for *Boiler Pressure Two*," the speakers blared. "Detonation in five minutes."

Jeanne looked out at the little building labeled "2." *Boiler Pressure Two* was the smallest of the three, testing the ability of the ICAN-II derived technology to catalyze nuclear detonations at sizes lower than any produced previously.

"*Boiler Pressure Two*, nominal five tons, repeat, five tons, detonation in two minutes thirty seconds."

When the second bomb went off, the shock wave was far lighter, a mere puff and rumble, and the distant flagged building barely settled at all. The analysis confirmed an explosive force of just over five tons of TNT.

Boiler Pressure Three also went off without a hitch, producing its planned one-half-kiloton blast.

"So do we expect more radiation to leak from those sites as time goes on?" Jeanne asked.

"Some, perhaps," York replied. "However, all the current readings indicate orders of magnitude less radiation from these detonations than from any previous nuclear explosions. The starting material is ordinary U-238 and lithium deuteride, and while the explosion does generate some radionuclides, it's far fewer than the conventional methods."

"And each of them required only a very small amount of antimatter, yes?"

"About one nanogram each," confirmed Stephanie. "We had a microgram shipped in for the tests, but as we expected we've had to use very little of it." She pointed to a large, squat truck exiting one of the bunkers. "There it goes—transporting it to the ALTS facility nearer *Carpathia*."

"ALTS?" repeated Audrey Milliner, joining the group from her seats lower in the stands; the Secret Service knew her and didn't bar her path.

"Antimatter Long-Term Storage Facility," Stephanie said. "That microgram's a good stability test for ALTS; we're of course having to develop the best long-term storage methods for antimatter possible, since we'll be absolutely dependent on the stuff on our way out and back."

"Speaking of coming back," Jeanne said, "assuming you fix or otherwise rescue *Fenrir*, how do you bring it back? How does it land?"

"Land?" Jeanne felt a momentary surge of embarrassment as Stephanie restrained obvious laughter before getting her expression under control. "Sorry, Madam President—but even *Carpathia* won't be landing again."

"Wait. Why not? You certainly have the power to do so."

"Power isn't the problem." That was Eva Filipek, who had been mostly a silent but interested observer through the tests. "The problem, put bluntly, is that if you are descending on a chain of nuclear explosions, your entire ship will end up going through multiple nuclear fireballs and immediate aftermath, rather than effectively running from all of it. The plate is proof against such things; the rest of the ship, likely not."

"We sure don't want to risk it," Stephanie agreed, "not until we've had a good long time to study how it all works in real life, anyway. So both *Carpathia* and *Fenrir* are staying in space. If we can work it out, get *Fenrir* into Earth orbit, and then we can shuttle things up and down as needed; pay Daire Young to do that if we have to, but I'll bet that *Fenrir* has space-to-ground shuttles of its own, and some should still be intact."

"Excuse me, Madam President," Roger said, "but we need to get moving. You have a meeting with FORT tomorrow morning, and—"

Jeanne sighed. Despite the importance of the event, the *Boiler Pressure* tests had been something of a little break for her. "Back to the grind, yes, Roger." She shook hands all around, and then her Secret Service detail closed in as they moved off and entered the presidential limousine.

"Thanks as always, Roger," she said as the car began to move. "You're right; I'd also like to get back to Washington in time to have a late dinner with my actual family."

"We'll get you there," he assured her.

She looked back at the viewing stands, vanishing in the distance, and frowned.

"Something bothering you, Jeanne?"

She didn't answer immediately—not because she hadn't heard, but because she was analyzing her own reactions. "That went far too smoothly."

"It kind of *had* to, didn't it?"

"I'm not talking about the tests themselves; Director Bronson and CENT wouldn't have scheduled it if they weren't as close to certain as possible that they would go off without a hitch." She waved a hand around the entire area. "It's all *this*. That demonstration had *everyone* who matters present, and that meant it had also drawn off huge numbers of personnel from other vital locations. Why didn't our unseen adversaries do anything?"

"Maybe they were going to and our security measures turned them back? I'm more relieved than anything; all of you up there on the review stands made very good targets."

Jeanne nodded. "That's the point, though. The best security in the world can still miss things. Any of us—or any part of *Carpathia*— could be targeted. It's been too quiet."

Roger made a face. "You're right, Jeanne. I can't argue it; you know we'd projected a pretty high probability there'd be an attempt on either personnel or *Carpathia* itself today. And I don't think they've given up."

"Our analysts at DHS and the other agencies don't think so either," Jeanne said. "So . . . if they haven't given up, and passed up this chance . . . what are they waiting for?"

CHAPTER 27:
YOU SPIN ME ROUND
AND ROUND

Time to Launch: 365 days

"One year to go," Stephanie murmured, staring at *Carpathia*.

The immense interplanetary vessel was taking real shape now. Atop the squashed, broad curve of the football-field-sized pusher plate, eight shock absorbers as large as ancient redwoods were fastened to the precast gigantic eyelets; monstrous springs could be seen below the main body, inside the circle of the shocks, along with the lower portions of the main ICAN-II-derived drive units—four of them spaced evenly around the ship. The barrel-like main hull was still in the process of assembly, with the interior cylinder of the primary living quarters and workspace visible, designed to rotate within the main hull.

Small ridges now covered the pusher plate, some associated with various sensors, others part of the electrostatic oil sprayer system that made it possible to detonate hundreds of nuclear charges within scant meters of the pusher plate and yet leave it intact. Before launch, the pusher plate would be coated with several millimeters of ablative material, as the electrostatic method wouldn't work well until they were into vacuum. *The first few minutes will be the worst.*

That was true in more than one way. Not only would all systems be subjected to their first, and only, real test at that time, but the titanic vessel would have to fight directly against the full pull of gravity, increasing the stress the passengers would have to endure.

Stephanie looked across from her vantage point on the CENT HQ's roof, to see another broad, squat building. That was the site of one of the few tests that everyone—civilian scientists and military officers alike—absolutely *had* to pass to remain on board: the centrifuge that would simulate the three gees passengers would experience on launch for several minutes.

Not looking forward to that, she admitted. She had been on roller coasters that exceeded that, of course, but this would be *sustained* three-gee acceleration, like having two more Stephanies lying on top of her for minutes. And of course she was the first to take the qualifying test, now that they'd certified the test centrifuge.

And then there's the Vomit Comet. Since there was no such thing as antigravity, the only way to experience significant periods of microgravity remained the old standby of taking a jet up and letting it perform multiple parabolic arcs, each one providing about twenty-five seconds of effective weightlessness. Everyone would have to undergo that, too.

That was why she was here, psyching herself up to take the two critical physical tests. *I'm on the crew list, I'm* first *on the crew list... and I could be first to get scratched if I can't handle it.*

"Director?"

She turned, startled. "Captain."

Hàorán Lín sketched a bow. "You seemed concerned at today's meeting." He looked out—first at the towering form of *Carpathia*, then down at the test facility. "Ah. Yes, we have all received our testing notices."

"You've been in jets on maneuvers before, haven't you?"

"As a passenger, yes. My first officer, Mr. Robinson, he is a pilot. I have no fears on his account." He looked slightly down at her, eyes sharp. "But you are worried that you will not pass."

"Everyone assumes I'll be on board by now. Not captain, but... well, head of the civilian researchers. If I wash out on this, it would be just *embarrassing*. To me and by proxy to a lot of other people."

"Director—Stephanie, if I may?" She nodded. "Stephanie, not everyone can tolerate acceleration, or microgravity. It is not a failing, it is a fact. But"—Hàorán Lín raised a finger—"it is a fact partly under your control. Being afraid, for yourself or merely the honor of others, will make you tense, make it harder to endure the testing."

She tried *not* to roll her eyes. "I *know* that, Captain Lín. But knowing it doesn't suddenly make the problem go away."

"True enough. If we humans could direct our emotions to our will so casually, so many of our problems would not exist."

"I'm trying to think of it as a couple of extreme park rides. I enjoy things like coasters and rotors and so on."

His smile was small but honest. "A good step, I would say. And ask yourself: what is the worst that happens in these tests?"

"I screw them both up and can't ride *Carpathia*," she said, fighting off the anticipatory wash of depression.

"Yes, that is true. But you will not stop being director. You will not lose the fame of discovery. You will still forever be the one who proved *we are not alone*." He shrugged. "I will not lie to you; it would be a cruel blow of fate if you, or for that matter, I were to fail such simple tests and by that be removed from the most important mission the human species has ever attempted. But in all honesty, you stand to lose the least."

She winced. *He's right. If he fails out, it'll be a huge mess— embarrassing for him, for China, cause diplomatic arguments about whether they can choose another candidate, because I know from Jeanne that the captaincy was part of the bargain with China. Me . . . I'll still be the famous one. Probably get more sympathy than anything else.* "Sorry, Hàorán," she said, deliberately using his first name as he'd used hers. "I guess it is self-centered of me to be angsting about it at all."

This time he laughed. "Meaning no offense, Stephanie, you are young. You are thrown into a ridiculous adventure without warning, an adventure you fight for. It is forgivable that you worry about the greatest part of it being pulled away through no fault of your own. But I thank you for the apology."

"Now, if it would help . . . I would be pleased to accompany you to the testing."

Stephanie blinked. For a moment, she wondered if that could be a pass. *Well . . . maybe. But I don't think so, there's too many problems with that, and Captain Lín has been very professional. I think it's a genuine offer of support.* "I'd be very honored by your support, Hàorán. York is supposed to meet me there, but I can always use another friend."

He returned her smile with a touch of a bow. "Then, if you're ready...?"

She nodded, and they walked together toward the door to the stairs.

"I'm surprised," Stephanie said, pulling on the white, tight-fitting body stocking dotted with what had to be sensor pads. "I thought there'd be just tons of wires coming off me."

"Not for this baby," said Monica Pratt, hooking a flat beige pack to the hip of the oversuit before offering it to Stephanie. "Just the one wire to get power and signal from the CCU—Central Collection Unit here—to the sensors and back."

Pratt made sure that one connection was secure and checked signals. "You're good to go, Director," she said. "Sit down in the big seat and we'll get you strapped in right for the test."

The centrifuge was basically the same as others Stephanie had seen pictures of: a long, counterweighted rotor in a smooth, circular white room. As she understood it, this one was a bit longer to allow for three-gee accelerations without too many RPM effects—the human body noticed the circular acceleration more and more as rotational speed increased. That was why the *Carpathia*, as well as similar fictional ships, had a very broad rotating section; in fact, *Carpathia*'s overall diameter was noticeably smaller than the recommended radius for a comfortable one-gee environment, which was another reason why everyone had to pass these tests.

The main difference was that there were no internal controls or other devices besides monitors. It was a simple white, rounded cube with a large window in the front allowing her to look across at a target visible on the counterweight opposite her. *Allows a stable point of reference for people getting vertigo,* she thought.

"There we go," Pratt said finally. "All strapped in. Verify all safety and data connections functional, Ops?"

"Verified," came a voice from the speakers a moment later. "We show all green."

"All right! See you on the other side, Director!" Pratt gave a quick smile and trotted out of the centrifuge, closing and sealing the big door behind her.

Looking around with the minimal motion her restraints allowed, Stephanie saw both Hàorán Lín and York Dobyns standing together at one of the large, triple-layered safety windows located high up, well above the axis of rotation. They both waved, and the captain gave her a thumbs-up.

"You hear me, Director?" came the voice of Ops in the headphones that were a part of the test suit.

"Yes. Do you hear me?"

"Loud and clear, Director. During the test, I'm going to ask you to answer various questions, or to do particular movements. This is to see how clearly you're thinking and reacting under acceleration. To allow safety margin for the actual mission, everyone will be tested to a maximum acceleration of four gees, though we won't sustain that very long. If we see any significant abnormalities in biological parameters or your responses during the test, we'll shut down immediately.

"You can also abort the test at any time by pulling on the red handles mounted on either side of the seat. They're positioned so you should be able to reach them by sliding your hand to grip them. You can also verbally abort the test by saying 'abort, abort.' Understood?"

"Understood. If you see anything wrong with my responses or my biofunctions, you'll abort, and I have both a physical and verbal means to abort available. The physical one is either of these red handles"—she touched the handgrips—"and the other is to simply say 'abort, abort.'"

"You got it, Director. First we'll take you up to one lateral gee, make sure everything's stable, then we'll do two minutes at two gees, five minutes at three, one minute at four, and then spin you down. All goes well, we should be done in fifteen minutes or a bit less. Understood?"

"Understood."

"Roger that. Standby for test start." A pause. "Test *Carpathia* crew 001a, Director Stephanie Bronson, commencing."

The entire structure hummed as powerful motors began to turn the massive rotor, and Stephanie watched as the white walls streamed by, punctuated by the windows above. The acceleration pressed her back into the seat, until it felt as though she were lying down in a fully tilted recliner.

"One gee," Ops said. "Director, how do you feel?"

She found herself relaxing. *This wasn't so bad.* "Like I'm in the most expensive La-Z-Boy ever."

A chuckle from Ops. "Well, all your signs show green, so get ready for your twin to hop into the seat with you. Accelerating to two gees."

The background was starting to whip by at a dizzying rate, so Stephanie refocused herself on the red-and-black target across from her. It was reassuringly stable, so it felt more like she was still and the room around her was rotating, standing at the middle of a merry-go-round as it spun out of control. Her body was growing heavier, but it really wasn't like having another person on top; the pressure was perfectly distributed, so it simply felt like being utterly exhausted—having the flu or a similar disease, except none of the mental exhaustion or stomach problems.

"Raise your right hand and hold it up, Director."

She did so, and on impulse gave the Vulcan salute.

"Live long and prosper," Ops responded. "But please don't do anything we don't ask for, ma'am. We want to track exact responses."

"Understood," she said, with a bit of effort. Her chest felt as though she were wearing a lead comforter over it.

"Count backward from ten," Ops said, and she complied.

After a few more simple tests, she heard, "All responses good, accelerating to three gees."

"Whee!" she said, breathlessly, as the rotor sped up once more, and suddenly realized she was actually having *fun*.

Three gees wasn't *entirely* fun—the lead comforter had turned to full-scale lead weights on every part of her, and now Ops started asking other questions. "What is fifteen percent of thirty?" "Raise both hands, clap three times, put down your left hand, and then your right hand." "What was the IR magnitude of *Fenrir* when you first discovered it?" "Read from the eye chart displayed on the screen in front of you," as bright white letters appeared on the previously transparent window.

It was getting hard to breathe as this test went on, a deliberate effort to force air into her lungs that was starting to make her chest ache. *It's been five minutes already, hasn't it?*

"Passing two minutes thirty seconds of three gees," Ops said, almost as though they'd heard her thoughts. "How are you feeling, Director?"

"Thought...more time...had passed. Getting harder...to breathe."

"Everyone goes through the same thing. Trust us, we're watching the clock carefully. Got a few more questions for you..."

At last, Ops said, "Five minutes, all nominal. Progressing to four gees."

This time she saved her breath for breathing as the force of acceleration crushed down on her. A touch of red haze was in her vision, a feeling of dizzy distance rose up. Then Ops, asking her to add two four-digit numbers, explain refractive index, tap out a specific beat with her fingers. The questions and answers *dragged*. Surely she'd been doing this for two minutes, three? Shouldn't this be slowing down?

But she forced those doubts out of her mind. People were watching, they wouldn't let anything go wrong. A quick logical check of timing showed her all those questions and answers could have been done in thirty seconds.

"One minute complete," Ops said. "How do you feel, Director?"

"Just . . . peachy," she answered.

"So shall we go to five?"

"I probably could . . . but I think I'd rather not."

A laugh. "Reducing acceleration, returning to zero. Stand by."

The feeling of oppressive weight, of her own body crushing her down, faded away, leaving her feeling startlingly light. Finally, the rotor stopped, and a moment later Ops said, "Test *Carpathia* crew 001a complete. Technician, help unstrap the director."

A few minutes later, she stepped out into a bear hug from York. "I guess I passed?"

"With, as you say, flying colors," Hàorán Lín said. "I heard you *enjoying* yourself, Director," he went on, with an exaggerated critical frown.

She laughed, feeling one set of tensions fading away. "Yes, I'm afraid you did."

"One test down," said York. "Just one to go."

"Not looking forward to *that*," she confessed. "I mean, weightlessness sounds fine, but there's a high chance I'll get sick, and then—"

"And then we work on that, if must be," Hàorán said bluntly. "Yes, many people have that problem, but we have good success at fixing it."

"He's right," York affirmed. "We've got Bárány chairs and other techniques that add up to close to a ninety percent rate of success."

"So let's celebrate *your* success, Director," the captain said. "It looks very much like you'll be going to space with us!"

CHAPTER 28: UNPLEASANT POSSIBILITIES

Time to Launch: 296 days

"Thanks for coming, everyone. First, congratulations to Dr. Chris Thompson and our head researcher, Faye Athena Brown, for passing their tests and officially joining the crew of *Carpathia*." There was a clatter of applause and a couple shouts of "Yeah!" from the CENT members present (virtual and physical). Stephanie joined in, glad that some of the first members of her group had made it.

She glanced to the side, where York was applauding as enthusiastically as anyone. York had made it through the centrifuge tests, which had been his main worry... and then discovered he was part of the small percentage of people who simply couldn't seem to overcome the disorientation of weightlessness. She knew that had hit him *hard*, and there wasn't much consolation she could offer. Hàorán had been right: she was, in fact, the one with the least to lose.

But after a couple of days, she'd risked broaching the subject with York.

"I just wanted to say how sorry I am you didn't make it," she said quietly.

He looked at her, closed his eyes, and sighed. "So am I, of course. No doubt about it. So many things to look forward to. Riding an honest-to-God nuclear pulse rocket. Being one of the first people going beyond the Moon's orbit. Meeting aliens, hopefully helping them."

He gave another huge sigh, then shook his head and smiled. "But not your fault, not mine—just a quirk of biology. I'll keep trying to get past it, but the outlook isn't good. Still ... I've been a part of it. And can a guy who won a Nobel Prize really complain about what he didn't get?"

He gave a genuine chuckle, then looked back to her. "Really, it's all right. It's not like there isn't plenty to do here, even after you leave."

"I really, *really* wanted you with us," she said. "I'm going to feel awfully alone without you to back me up."

"Nonsense!" The word was both sharp and firm. "You don't need my backup. You smacked sense into Hàorán and Ben Robinson all on your lonesome—oh, yes, they told me all about how you basically slapped them both down, and you can bet that story's gone around the entire project on the quiet. *Did* you need my help? Well, I think you did. I'd like to think being an older, experienced person gave me some wisdom to pass on. But you're past needing anyone to back you up except yourself.

"*Support*, now"—he smiled and leaned back—"well, we all need *that*, and I wish I was going to be there. But you just keep your eye on the goals and don't let anyone distract you from what's really important, and that's all you have to do."

"Thanks, York. Thank you so much." She took his hand and squeezed it, and he turned that into a big bear hug she leaned into. "And here's a promise: when we get back, I'm going to introduce you to an alien myself."

His eyes sparkled, with anticipation or a touch of tears she didn't know. Maybe both. "I'll hold you to that."

York caught her looking at him, leaned over as the applause petered out. "Glad Faye made it. You need *support*, she's the one to give it to you since I'm not going to be there."

"Understood, sir," she replied with a grin. It *was* good that Faye had made the cut; there had been more than one person opining that she was too old to make it through the centrifuge, let alone the multiple vertigo-inducing assaults of the Comet.

Instead, Faye had come through both on her first try, better than

Stephanie had managed; she'd needed a month of practice in the chair before she could make it through a flight of weightless parabolas without losing her lunch. Faye apparently had *enjoyed* the entire thing.

"All right, on to business. Francine, update on *Fenrir* itself?"

Dr. Everhardt brought up images on the shared screen. "The good news is that we are virtually certain some systems, very likely including life support, are still active on parts of *Fenrir*. With months to get every telescope and sensor package we could pointed at it, and analyze it over time, we've actually managed to get a fair outline of *Fenrir* itself."

The shape onscreen was noticeably different from early versions of *Fenrir* (which had, admittedly, been nothing but rough educated guesses). Most striking was the strange spiked front end, making it look like a gigantic metallic star-nosed mole. The main body of *Fenrir* was still a generally cylindrical object, tapered some both fore and aft. The theorized "ruff" of the retracted radiator sail had been refined and now was shown to be an uneven, clearly damaged skirt that had the look of a plastic ruffle accidentally run past a gas burner; there was the same hint of melting and structural separation, with some parts simply gone.

Near the worst-damaged parts of the retracted sail, there were blurred but present features that Stephanie's eyes and brain translated to severely scorched, perhaps melted, hull.

The rearmost portion of *Fenrir* came to a point, the rearmost part of the point surrounded by a curved, rounded bowl shape.

"What is that thing on the front?" Faye asked.

"We can't be absolutely certain," Everhardt responded, "but our current guess is that it is the anchor for the ice shield that *Fenrir* was carrying during its long journey. Likely has details we cannot see, including sensor masts that would be embedded in the ice to track stresses and impacts and so on. These, however, are the regions of immediate interest."

Two separate areas of *Fenrir*, one ahead and one behind the ruff, were shown with mottled patterns of dull red.

"This is the infrared map we've been able to accumulate of *Fenrir*," Dr. Everhardt went on. She pointed her cursor at the two red-patterned areas. "Careful modeling and energy radiation analysis gives us a strong indication that there are systems in these areas maintaining an internal temperature of about twenty-seven degrees C, plus or minus three degrees depending on how we change various assumptions about their material characteristics and such. These areas maintain their temperature despite variations in solar luminance, sometimes cooling when simple physical principles would expect them to warm, or remaining warm when cooling would be expected.

"Given this, we are as certain as we can be that there are living areas, or possibly very delicate equipment bays, that are still operative to some reasonable extent and attempting to keep themselves to some designated temperature." She looked around at the various participants. "We therefore cautiously, but reasonably, postulate that there are, in fact, still survivors on board even now, over a year later. This gives us good reason to believe they may still be there when we arrive."

A subdued cheer rippled around the room. *Time to get the other side,* Stephanie thought. "So what's the bad news, Francine?"

"Well, firstly, *Fenrir* has shown no sign of changing course or even getting much under control except the rotation we noted earlier. This is very troubling to the entire team, since we *have* to assume that they would want to come to a safe orbit in this system, rather than run a parabolic course out of our system that cuts dangerously close to our Sun—and in a cosmic sense will almost sideswipe Venus along the way." She looked to York, who grunted and stood up.

"We have a lot of hypotheses about what could be going on there, but none of them look good. Human beings in similar circumstances generally make tremendous efforts to save themselves, and we have to assume that a strong survival instinct—for oneself or others—must be a part of the makeup of a civilization that's expended so much effort to come here.

"With well over a year passed, this implies several possibilities. The first is that, somehow, the accident deprived them of *everyone* with the capacity to perform decent engineering work; the only Fens left on board are those whose knowledge and capabilities simply don't translate to anything useful when it comes to controlling or repairing the ship."

"If that's true, it implies a level and degree of focused specialization that's very different from human," Chris Thompson said. "Assuming they have an even halfway decent-sized crew, that would imply hundreds if not thousands of people who collectively lack such information; in a random collection of human beings who are not engineers or otherwise technically trained, you would still end up with many people who as a hobby or past profession would have good enough knowledge of the skills needed to at least make a stab at fixing the ship. Not to mention immense reference resources onboard."

"That's certainly one possibility," York agreed. "There's the side possibility that *no one* ever had the ability onboard—that all technical matters were handled by autonomous systems, that they reached a point where AI was able to address all their needs, and that the accident perhaps caused a widespread EMP that has taken out the ship-maintenance systems."

"There is another element that's disturbing," Dr. Everhardt said. "Over the months since we began to get decent detail on our mapping, the map has *changed.*" She showed a sequence of images, and Stephanie didn't need to be told what it showed.

The mottled areas had lost area in those months.

"This, too, has lots of possible interpretations," York pointed out. "Progressive systems failure, pervasive damage that means that eventually the life-support systems give out, for instance. If that's the case and what we see represents an average case, these areas will be about a quarter this size, or less, by the time we arrive. But there are some interesting, perhaps more disturbing, features here. As you can see, in these two images, this area here goes dark."

He brought up another set of images. "But *here*, a week or so later, much of it is warm again, and *this* area, on the other side of the retracted sail, has gone dark. There are several examples of this, although as we can see the *overall* trend is that these sections of the ship are slowly losing functioning volume overall."

York looked around. "Does anyone else find this suggestive?"

Peter Flint nodded slowly. "Well, could be that what we're seeing is them working to get the ship going again, but the ship's not cooperating so well."

"What do you mean?" Stephanie asked. She sort of understood what Peter was getting at, but it didn't hurt to get the detail out in the open.

"Machine like a starship, we all know that's complicated as all hell," Flint answered. "It's likely that the really important parts that got wrecked aren't simple gadgets. They probably need parts that need half a dozen machines that make the parts for the *other* parts that get assembled into the parts of the thing you need, if you follow me."

At her nod, he went on, "But *Fenrir's* bad hurt and power production's way down, so they probably *can't* run all the machines at once. And so they make themselves a bunch of Part A on machine one, then have to shut down machine one and go to machine two to make parts B and D, then shut *that* one to go to machine three, which uses parts A and B to make part F, so they can go back to machine one to make part C . . . and all the time other things are breakin' down because they've just *got* to get these parts done first."

"So they're in a race between fixing the most vital systems and how long it'll take before other systems really crash hard, is what you're saying," Stephanie summarized.

"That's how I read it. Wouldn't want to be in their shoes, or whatever it is they wear. We need to get out there fast, before it all goes up."

Stephanie noticed Captain Lín exchange a glance with his first officer. "That is a good possibility," Lín said, carefully.

"You have another possibility?" Stephanie asked.

"Not one either of us likes," Robinson answered. "But it's one I'm afraid we have to consider. Captain?"

"Mutiny," he said quietly. "Sorties into each other's territory, sometimes regaining lost areas, but overall doing more damage as it progresses. Yes?"

Stephanie winced as she saw York's humorless smile. "I was hoping no one else saw it. Yes, that is one other explanation."

"But that would be . . . ridiculous!" Stephanie burst out, and heard similar sentiments echo around the meeting. "They're in an emergency situation, surely they wouldn't waste time on that kind of thing."

"'Only a fool fights in a burning house,' you mean?" Chris Thompson asked. "Sounds good, but I'm pretty sure there's plenty of examples of human beings doing that same kind of stupid crap in emergencies—burning buildings or lifeboats or whatever."

Stephanie gritted her teeth and thought a moment. "I hate to think that way," she said finally. "Partly because I'd really prefer to believe aliens who can build *that*"—she pointed to the outline of *Fenrir*—"are beyond that kind of thing. But . . . that might also explain why we never got a response to our transmissions."

"Great minds think alike," York agreed. "That's exactly one of the points we've kept in mind. They refused to respond to our transmissions, and we're pretty much of one mind on whether they received the transmissions. They had to have, and unless they and their AI systems—if any—are dumber than rocks, they *must* have figured out what they meant and how to respond. We had a few guesses as to why, but this accident rather argues against one of our first guesses— that they thought we were utterly beneath them, ants before gods; godlike aliens don't blow their engines and lose control of their ships.

"So they had to have a more…well, *human* reason not to talk to us, and having arguing factions is one we thought of. This data starts to make that scenario all too believable."

The room was silent for a moment. Then Stephanie stood up. "This isn't the news we wanted," she said after all eyes were focused on her. "Either of them, really; Peter's theory makes it look like *Fenrir's* falling apart around them even faster than we thought, while the captain's makes them, well, dangerously human. But it doesn't really change anything. We still have to get there for it to matter how or why anything on *Fenrir* is happening."

She grimaced. "We just have to be aware that one possibility is we're going to step right into the middle of a civil war."

CHAPTER 29:
PLOTS AND PLOTTERS

Time to Launch: 196 days

The President sat in her seat in *Air Force One* and luxuriated in the short period of quiet as the craft prepared for takeoff, everyone strapped in for the ascent. For those few minutes, she had no responsibilities, no demands other than to sit still and let the aircraft do its job. It was surprisingly refreshing.

And she needed it. As soon as the chime sounded and the seatbelt sign dimmed, she unsnapped her seat belt and stretched, then moved aft to the conference room.

It was relatively empty; just her and Roger Stone. "All right, Roger. Update me, before I have to get to all the other work."

"Yes, boss," he said with a quick smile. "Good news first: *Carpathia's* running a little ahead of schedule now. The military and astronaut crews have been getting actual time in space on some of Young's SpaceShip One vehicles. The civilian crew doesn't need the experience, but there's a big gap between surviving acceleration and weightlessness in short spurts and having to do top-notch work under those conditions."

"Why under those conditions? Can't the ... command deck, bridge, whatever we call it, rotate as well?"

"The short answer is 'no.' Longer answer is that the command and as many other vital elements as possible are buried toward the center

181

of *Carpathia* to protect them in case of emergencies, so they cannot, practically, spin at all. Also, for any emergency maneuvers, the residential areas will likely be spun down so there's no additional gyroscope effect interfering with piloting."

"Understood," Jeanne said, committing another set of details to memory. "Go on."

He flipped to another set of notes. "They're excavating the launch pit now and once that's done, they'll be coating the plate."

"Fuel charges?"

"More are being assembled every day," confirmed Roger. "There will be many thousands available by launch. As discussed before, the actual launch will start with a very large mass of conventional explosives—probably something around a kiloton, given the inefficiencies in the system—to make sure that the *Carpathia* is several hundred feet in the air before it detonates its first antimatter-triggered nuclear-drive charge. That should minimize any possibility of fallout."

Another page. "Other supplies are being accumulated and stored for the trip. We are supplying *Carpathia* with a two-year trip in mind, even though it should be well under half of that."

"If we can, add more; no ship ever complained about being oversupplied, and there are no supermarkets out there," Jeanne said.

"I'll go over it with the team," agreed Roger.

After a moment, Jeanne sighed. "So, what's the bad news?"

"To an extent, the same we've been having the past few months: no bad news."

Roger didn't need to explain that one. "I thought we'd actually caught a bunch of these people. It isn't possible that we've simply shut them down?"

"I wish it were, Jeanne," he said. He reached into his briefcase and brought out a folder. "You're right, we've caught at least twenty cells of this group. Which is all they call themselves, by the way—the Group."

"Anonymous enough, at least. I presume we've questioned them."

"All of them have been subjected to *extensive* interrogation." At her glance, he shook his head. "No torture; no point in it, as we agreed. But it wasn't necessarily pleasant."

"Did we *learn* anything, Roger? I can't imagine we could get twenty cells—how many people is that?—and learn nothing."

"They were three-person cells, in general, so about sixty," Roger answered. "And we learned things, but so far, not very *helpful* things.

"Several of the cells were extreme antinuke fanatics. Not a terrible surprise, of course, that was one of our first assumptions. They were recruited and guided into the Group based on that, and they assured us that their entire group was against nuclear power in all its forms.

"Several others were . . . well, call them speculative paranoids. They don't want the Fens rescued. They believe the Fens were here to invade, kill, or otherwise do really bad things to us, and their accident is either luck or God-sent miracle, and we shouldn't aid them, but wait until we're sure they're dead. They want to prevent *Carpathia* from flying until it's too late to do anything but dissect the dead and salvage the ship."

Jeanne was already getting an inkling of the problem. "And these people were also certain that was the overall purpose of the Group."

"Exactly. Another set of them were anti-globalist types with various dislikes of other countries, feeling we were being suckered into this to make us vulnerable. A few believe that *Carpathia* is a new nuclear battleship for the Illuminati or whatever they think the 'Deep State' is this year."

"This isn't an accident."

"No. Whoever is *running* the Group is very clever. They have a goal—stop *Carpathia*—and they've recruited useful people from every possible type of anti-*Carpathia* organization they could find, using cutouts to make each group think this is *their* cause. Meanwhile, the top organizers are accomplishing their goal to act against *Carpathia*, but without knowing *why* they actually want to do this, we have a much harder time predicting what they're going to do next, let alone find out who's really running the show."

"Conspiracies are usually small, though. Isn't it possible we've already cut out enough of the operatives to cripple them, and that's why we haven't seen any more hostile action toward the project?"

Roger Stone pursed his lips, then closed his eyes and shook his head. "*Possible*, of course. But none of the security services believe so. All the cells we caught clearly had to be at least one or two levels from the top, and more likely three or four, to ensure that they're partitioned completely from each other. We don't believe we've gotten within striking distance of any of the leaders; we don't even know if the leaders are a single cell, or even one person with a cutout cell below them, or a larger group that organized the Group to be their cat's-paw."

Jeanne rubbed her temples, feeling one of the far-too-common headaches starting. "I hate to ask, but what about the possibility that the 'larger group' is one of our supposed allies?"

"Unfortunately possible. We don't *believe* that is the case—partly because a governmental organization could probably have managed a more decisive strike by now—but it is not yet ruled out. We're fairly close to ruling out it being a home-grown internal problem—that Army study was just one of their typical concept war games, for instance—but anyone else, no.

"But we are looking much more closely at it being a private organization, bankrolled by one or two wealthy individuals."

Jeanne nodded. "And why haven't they done anything lately?"

"Lots of guesses, but Hailey Vanderman over at the CIA says—and I agree—that they stopped and reassessed after we blocked their prior attempts. Hailey thinks that they're preparing for a large, single strike that will probably have a couple of prongs—striking two or three places at once. This allows them to focus their resources and have a better chance to disrupt the project in one shot, especially when they know we're on to them and any premature action now could lead to them being caught."

"Do we know *when* they will do this?"

"There's a couple of high-probability events. Problem is . . ." Roger hesitated.

"Let me guess. I'm one of the targets Hailey thinks they'll go after."

"There's a good chance of it," admitted Stone. "You or Stephanie seem the most likely targets, with a couple lower-probability people in the mix. Plus installations or components of *Carpathia* at the same time. The real advantage to them of doing this later on is that if they can do real damage—either to morale or to *Carpathia* itself—it's going to be *much* harder for us to recover from it in time to launch."

"Shooting *me* isn't going to stop the project, Roger. Andrea Perez's not going to swear in and then dump *Carpathia*." Her Vice President was not quite as enthusiastic about the project as she was, but even Andrea knew what political advantage was.

"By itself, no. Possibly they'll target someone else—Flint, for instance, he's going to be crucial to keeping the ship running. But we have to assume you're high on the list, no matter what you think."

She sighed. "All right, Roger. Let's assume that's true, and get assets in place for the high-probability events. But you realize that means I will still have to be *present* at those events if we want our enemies to come out in the open."

She could see the tension in Roger Stone's face at the thought of using the President of the United States as bait. But at the same time, he knew he didn't have much choice.

So as she knew he would, he just nodded and said, "Yes, Madam President."

CHAPTER 30: UPGRADING

Time to Launch: 150 days

"Angus! Good to see you!"

Silver turned, an answering smile already on his face as Peter caught up to him. "You look even more cheerful than usual, Pete."

"And that's because of you." He punched Silver lightly on the shoulder.

"Me? Oh. Our discussion the other day?"

"An eye-opener, honestly," Peter said. "Problem with running a business like mine, you get things working, then you get customers, pretty soon you're running around trying to get the job done and you start to lose sight of the stuff you knew when you started. You reminded me to step back and take a look at the tech, and *boy* were you right."

A deprecating wave. "Computing hardware's my specialty. I'm afraid I always end up heckling people over their choices, especially when"—he looked apologetically at Peter Flint—"well, when they're using stuff a few generations out of date."

"Not heckling when you're asking the right questions, Angus," Peter said seriously. "You were dead right, simple as that. MIROC's little Bells need to do a lot more than they used to, and upping their onboard computing capacity gives me options. Wouldn't have thought it'd be so easy—done too many hardware upgrades that turned out to be two years of headaches, know what I mean?"

Remembering some of his early projects, Silver couldn't keep from laughing. "Pete, I know *exactly* what you mean. But I can't take all the credit. Luck gave us a little jackpot."

A thoughtful nod. "Can't disagree. Plenty of people make new processors without much thought for the prior market. Pin-for-pin compatibility's hard to find in a several-generation upgrade."

"To be fair, though, the reason *you* were using that particular Cortex spin-off was the reason a hell of a lot of other people did. If someone *was* going to go after any upgrade market, makes sense they'd choose that one."

And that's nothing but truth, Silver thought as Pete nodded again. Luck always played a part, and finding out key technical details early had given him time over the last year-plus to guide the production choices in this direction. The luck was, as he'd said, that Flint's design choices also led to what made perfect sense for a system design. While Silver was a respected advisor—and on the board of several of the key companies—he couldn't have convinced them to make a high-end embedded computer system that didn't have a clear ROI.

Planning was the other part, and it looked like both had paid off.

"Look here," Peter was saying, producing a tablet from a case at his side. "Sampling and filtering on this scan done in a fraction of the time, making the scans overall thirty-two percent faster."

Silver gave a silent whistle. "Thirty-two percent? That's even more than I would have guessed."

"Just the start, too. My people back at the lab are working on optimizing the code now. The expert system and machine learning group's updating our entire approach to the overall ship maintenance and inspection processes; we figure we can get a lot more reliable autonomy on even some pretty complex tasks, which'll save us a ton of bandwidth."

Peter went on, and Silver didn't have to feign interest; Flint's entire MIROC concept had always been—being honest with himself—cool as hell, and the older man's enthusiasm and razor-sharp intelligence hadn't been dimmed by age yet. The "Bells" were some of the best-designed robots Silver had ever seen, well-suited to inspection, safety, and maintenance of just about anything that could be reached from the ground, and IIS also had semiautonomous inspection drones, large and small, for use in places the Bells couldn't fit, all based around a highly flexible operating architecture.

The Carpathia *project may not even realize just how good a bargain they got with Pete.*

Silver found himself following Peter back to the MIROC enclosure itself, and for the next couple of hours the two of them went over the new design, with Silver finding a few new suggestions to make, Peter demolishing them, and then both of them finding a better way to do what they wanted—increasing speed, reliability, or other aspects of the Bells and MIROC's central systems.

"You need to talk to Werner," Silver said, tapping on the external wall of MIROC. "I'm blanking on the name right now, but one of the people on the design team for the living quarters has come up with what looks like really good shielding for electronics. I know you've been working on making the Bells able to work in vacuum, but if you have to go outside on the hull..."

"We've been using hardened electronics," Pete said, "but this new processor's not going to meet *those* specs. Or if it could, it'll take months or years to get the certs. You're right, we need to look into that, or the new Bells can only function inside the ship." He frowned. "Just in case, I'll leave Zygmunt and Pummerin using the old design. Can always upgrade 'em later if everything works out."

"Makes sense to me." He glanced at his phone. "Holy sheep, look at the *time*."

Pete gave a snort of laughter. "Holy *sheep*?"

Silver closed his eyes in embarrassment but managed a smile. "My sister insisted I clean up my language when my first niece was born, and that was fifteen years ago—and two more nieces and a nephew kept that rule in force."

"Well, gol-ding it, I've been there myself," Pete said with a grin. "But you're right, it's getting on in the day. What you say we go for dinner?"

His stomach rumbled. "I am in favor of that course of action."

He let the older man lead the way, feeling an odd thread of concern weaving through the otherwise justified satisfaction of the day. It slowly dawned on him that it wasn't just concern. There was, to Silver's consternation, an actual, discernable touch of *guilt*, that he was arranging to potentially make use of Peter Flint's pet gadgets for his own purposes.

Well, why shouldn't I have a touch of remorse at the thought? I have nothing against most of the people here. They're involved in something that must be stopped, but that doesn't make them all villains, unfortunately.

They got into Flint's truck and pulled out, heading for one of the on-base restaurants. Seeing the satisfied cheer on his companion's face, Silver shoved his regrets to the side. *We are still some months from the final choices.*

It was still possible, he told himself, that nothing would have to happen to Pete, or his Bells, that the Group's other approaches could put a definitive end to *Carpathia*.

I would very much prefer not to have to kill him.

CHAPTER 31:
SAFETY, SECURITY, AND SPACESHIPS

Time to Launch: 100 days

"I really should be getting *used* to the scale of these things, Werner," Stephanie said, staring up, "but my mind keeps getting boggled again every couple of months."

"Can't blame you. Everything we're doing here is . . . *unreasonably* huge."

During most of its construction, *Carpathia*'s massive curved drive plate had sat solidly on the ground below, on the same supports used for the casting. Relatively low spaces had been bored out to allow workmen and MIROC's Bells to work on the elements like the sprayer insets and sensor emplacements, but from any distance it had looked as though it were just set down on the desert in a gentle depression.

Now, however, the entire ship—in outline similar to a nose cone of a missile supported by the shock absorber assembly—sat several meters off the cleared-away earth, stone, and sand. The support structure had been reinforced, but also had wide apertures through which even decent-sized trucks could pass.

Somehow, this change emphasized the titanic size of *Carpathia*, nearly half a million metric tons of steel, aluminum, carbon fiber, and electronics being held aloft on a spiderweb circle of steel more than a third of a kilometer around. Dust drifted from that delicate base as

191

trucks rolled in one dark opening and, after some time unseen, drove out another archway.

"Kilotons of explosives." She shook her head. "What a nightmare."

The German engineer chuckled. "It *does* give one pause, yes. But this is not old dynamite or black powder, just waiting for a spark to send it up. This will not explode without the right detonators, which will most certainly not be put in place until launch is imminent.

"Speaking of which, Director, the living quarters are all certified. I would recommend personnel begin to accustom themselves to their new homes."

Stephanie couldn't restrain a grin. "I will get that schedule set up immediately." The smile faded into another flash of awe. "My God, we're really doing this. A hundred days from *now*."

"And then months in space, yes. It may become a bit boring."

Her first instinct was to protest that going into space on a nuclear spaceship couldn't possibly be boring, *ever*. But she'd spent a lot of time going over not just the technical but the social and psychological elements of spaceflight. "We've done our best to mitigate that. With hundreds of people onboard, at least we've got better chances for social interaction, and it's not like we built it to submarine specs."

"*Gott*, no, that would be terrible. Especially with most of us being civilians." Stephanie's phone buzzed, and Werner paused to let her answer.

"Director Bronson here. I'm already on my way to the meeting."

"That's good," York's deep voice replied. "You've also got some final releases and certifications for your signature down here."

"When *don't* I? I think my hand's signing documents while I sleep."

"Unfortunately, I haven't seen it wandering the hallways authorizing actions on its own."

"Don't worry, I'll be there in a few." She looked to the right. "Coming, Werner?"

Werner Keller shook his head, face now devoid of his usual good humor. "I'm afraid not. Safety and post-incident review."

Stephanie winced. "Joe Buckley, right?"

"Yes. It appears to be a typical workplace accident, but given the circumstances we have to treat it with all seriousness."

Buckley, one of the project's best mechanical techs, had been working on the forward radar array when something had gone wrong;

his safety harness had failed and he had slid down the curve of the ship, then flown free and plummeted hundreds of feet toward the ground.

By itself that would have been fatal, but fate apparently found a simple fall *far* too mundane; instead, Joe Buckley had plunged headfirst through an opening just barely wide enough for him, leading to one of the support footings that was in the process of being poured. Fortunately for him, it was virtually certain that the impact—and being impaled by in-place rebar—had killed him instantly, before the concrete began burying him.

It was less fortunate for those who had to stop the work and then extract the mangled remains from the footing.

"Good luck, Werner."

"Oh, I do not think it will be a *problem*. It is just a very macabre and sad duty we have." He shrugged. "At that, the *Carpathia* project has been very safe, all things considered."

As Werner set off in the direction of his meeting, Stephanie turned toward hers. She knew, statistically, that he was right—an experimental, rush-priority project employing so many people could not avoid some accidents, and seven fatalities over almost two years really wasn't excessive.

It still hurts when I hear of one. Somehow I feel like it's my fault, no matter how stupid that is.

With an effort, she banished the depressing thoughts from her mind. Showing a positive, optimistic face to the world was the director's job description.

By the time she reached the main *Carpathia* conference room, she had her smile back, and shoved open the doors dramatically.

Heads turned, and in the moment they were all looking at her, Stephanie shouted, "One hundred days!"

Laughs and a spatter of clapping answered her as she proceeded down to her spot at the huge curved table. "The initial launch charge array is being assembled—just came from looking at it," she said, sitting down and nodding to York, Captain Lín, and the others. "Tell me we have security plans already in place?"

"We do, Director," Ben Robinson said. "I got part of that delegated to me, and I've been working with military and civilian reps to make sure it's covered. Peter?"

"We've assigned about half the Bells to do patrol duty," Flint answered. "Loaded them up with additional conditional analysis software, backed by trained machine-learning elements to observe activities all over. They can crawl on the plate even upside down, so they can patrol the whole space easy. They're not needed for tech work quite so much now, so it's a good way to keep expanding their applications as we go."

"We've got multiple human security agents watching everything we can, too," said Hailey Vanderman. To her surprise, Vanderman had resigned from his top spot at the CIA to become security oversight on the project, working both under her and Captain Lín. "MPs from the Special Forces, some of the best intelligence people I could draft from the various agencies." He gave a half shrug. "It's as secure as we can reasonably expect. This installation's too big and open for complete operational security, though."

"I understand, Hailey." Too many people, too many ways in, too much open space, it all added up to vulnerabilities to people like Vanderman—and she couldn't argue they were wrong.

Time to move on. "Eva, you have an update for us?"

Dr. Filipek smiled. "We've scheduled the main shipment for the antimatter so you will have a month to perform the final tests and transfer work. Three separate containment units are being shipped; each one carries more than enough antimatter to carry out the full mission."

Shipping antimatter. Never imagined I'd hear people talking about that. "Dr. Nagel? I heard you and the rest of MatterPrint have been catching up?"

"Just barely," Chari Nagel, head engineer for MatterPrint, mimed wiping sweat off her forehead. "We finally figured out that issue with the charge units coming off the print stage during printing, and just finished a run of a hundred without problems; all of them passed inspection."

Thank God for that. "All sizes?"

"Ten different sizes in that run, covering the whole range," confirmed Nagel. "We *think* that clears out the last outstanding issue and should be able to deliver all the charges."

"Thank you, Dr. Nagel. Captain, much as I don't like the subject, what about the armament?"

"Well in hand, Director. High-powered pulsed laser cannon and powerful coilguns represent our best offenses—the latter able to be armed with nuclear shells based on the drive charges."

Stephanie already knew about that, having seen the live test in which a nuclear shell was fired to detonate ten kilometers away; that had been done as far from any inhabited areas as they could manage, since the detonation was an actual ground burst. The flash and shock wave had been impressive, as had the looming mushroom cloud from the site.

It was still good news, she reminded herself. The *Carpathia* would need to be able to defend itself. More importantly, even that ground burst had shown drastically lower levels of fallout than any prior similar detonation; the ICAN-II technology was proving itself already.

"But let us not consider them merely weapons," Captain Lín went on. "If we have to do any exterior work on *Fenrir*, we may need to cut very large pieces away just to reach critical areas; our lasers are capable of extremely precise work." With that reminder, he went on to detail the smaller, multi-targeting point defenses, in case missiles or projectiles were fired at *Carpathia*.

Reports continued, and Stephanie's spirits rose as the generally positive tenor of each penetrated. The four ACES—Alien Contact Expeditionary Shuttles—had been completed and mounted to their exterior cradles on *Carpathia*. Tiny compared to the nuclear-pulse vessel, the ACES were still huge on prior spaceship scales, massing nearly a thousand tons each in their own right; that included their own small-scale nuclear-pulse drives, supplementary chemical-reaction and ion thrusters, and room for twenty crew members and appropriate equipment and cargo.

The main sensors—radar, automated and manual imaging, high-sensitivity magnetic and radiation sensors, and more—were installed. The C&C—Command and Control—center, already familiarly referred to as the bridge, was undergoing final testing. Electromagnetic screening, which would deflect radiation away from the vital areas of the vessel, appeared to be installed and functional, though absolute verification couldn't be done until the ship was in vacuum.

"Living quarters are all certified," she told the assembled group. "All passengers should begin to familiarize themselves with their quarters and related areas—the labs, dining halls, and so on."

"Personal baggage limits?" asked Audrey Milliner. That *was* probably a major concern for a publicist and presentation expert. Stephanie glanced to York.

"None in the traditional sense," York said with a quick grin. "*Carpathia* could lift twice its mass and more if it wanted to. You're bound by reasonable space limits—check out your cabin and available space first. Also, don't bring anything you can't pack away for acceleration, nothing so fragile it can't take some fairly serious jolts."

"And," said Hailey Vanderman, "everything brought aboard *will* be examined thoroughly." He met everyone's gaze in a slow survey of the table. "Obviously we have to *mostly* trust everyone on board, but you are all aware that we have had more than one attempt to damage this project directly. Declare *anything* that you think is, or could reasonably be mistaken for, a weapon or something that could be used for sabotage."

"That describes an awful lot of laboratory equipment," pointed out Chris Thompson.

"It does, and we recognize a lot of you will have to bring some such devices with you, in addition to the equipment installed onboard," Hailey conceded. "That is why you should *declare* it. It will look far better for us to know about the explosive chemical assortment you use for some kind of test assay, than for us to find it as an unpleasant surprise when we check your baggage. In some cases, we may just say you cannot bring something aboard, but we will try to minimize that."

"Still," he went on, "our job is to try to assure your safe journey. Understand that there *are* hostile elements, and we may have to inconvenience you to prevent someone from—apologies for being dramatic about this, but I am deadly serious—killing us all."

There was a moment of silence, but the majority of people finally nodded.

"Thank you, Hailey," Stephanie said. "People, try not to make *his* job more difficult. Most of us don't need to bring anything on board that should be a problem." She brought her smile back. "Instead, let's get ready for the most important trip humanity's ever made!"

"Amen to that!" Angus Fletcher said, and bumped fists with Peter. "Looking forward to seeing my spaceship cabin!"

"I think we all are." She looked at her phone. "I've got a telecon with the President shortly, so if there's no other pressing business, meeting adjourned."

With the quiet chaos of thirty people rising and gathering their materials around her, Stephanie took a deep breath.

One hundred days to launch.

CHAPTER 32:
CONTINGENCIES OF
FAILURE

Time to Launch: 53 days

The secure download completed, Silver ejected the memory stick and put it in his pocket, then sanitized the records of his activity. The site from which he had downloaded Keys's code would be erased on that end.

With heightened security there still remained risks of discovery, even with any precautions he took. The truth was that remaining *not* the focus of an investigation was the only way he was going to evade discovery. The precautions the Group was taking, considerable though they were, simply could not withstand the direct scrutiny of the most powerful intelligence services on the planet.

That had been behind his regretful note to Keys. *I am truly sorry, Keys, but I cannot allow the Bells to be used for on-the-ground sabotage. They will be one of my best resources in the final event, and while they might add ten percent to our final prelaunch attempt success rate, they're more like fifty percent for mine.*

Fortunately, Keys understood. He now had the final version of the suite of tools he would need, incorporating changes based on everything Silver had been able to arrange or learn about *Carpathia's* systems. As one of the primary designers and engineers involved in the computer hardware, Silver had a great deal of inside knowledge to apply, and despite the overall failure to stop the project, Lathe's people had been able to add some covert flaws that had managed to pass project security.

Silver was confident now that he could successfully pull off the final option, and that was far more important now. They really had only one window of opportunity left for stopping *Carpathia* before launch. If that failed...

Then, I suppose, I find out if I am as courageous as I believe I am. But Silver had little doubt on that score; he had devoted his adult life to finding ways to undermine the powerful while appearing to be one of them, and his certainty as to his goal had not wavered. *It will be painless, I think, which is good.*

But it would be better not to have to die at all, so he placed many hopes on the final attempt—and some that hinged on this last call.

The burner phone rang exactly on time. "Hello."

"Silver, my dear. How very good to hear your voice again!"

"And yours, Needle. Time is short, so I'm afraid we have to get to business."

"Of course." A pause, a faint sound of a sip of tea being drunk. "Keys forwarded me your patrol drone information—so very useful, dear, thank you. Are you absolutely certain you couldn't—"

"No. As I told Keys, the Bells are a much larger factor for me than for you."

"Hm." The silence somehow radiated a sugar-coated menace. "Well, I suppose we have to trust your judgment at this stage, although I *dislike* having less than the maximum number of resources being available." Her voice warmed. "But there, I think we have an *excellent* chance of success."

"What can you tell me?"

"Well, dear, I'm sure you can make a shrewd guess at the basic schedule, and I have spared no expense in preparing this final operation. The Group's funds will be essentially depleted once I make final payouts."

"I'm pinched," he admitted, "but I'll arrange for enough for the inner circle to keep operations going if this operation succeeds. If it doesn't... well, the Group inherits what is left, through our arranged channels."

"We all admire your dedication, dear." Needle's complacent tones reminded Silver that *she* had her own reasons for helping the Group, and not necessarily ones matched to his. "In any case, it will be a three-pronged attack, scheduled to be as nearly simultaneous as possible. I believe any one of the three succeeding should stop *Carpathia*'s launch—at a minimum for several months, at maximum . . . forever."

Silver felt a flash of hope. "The three we discussed earlier?"

"Three *different* approaches, dear. The exact methods and targets, of course, I must decline to tell you. Can't let slip what you don't know."

"If I don't, I may be in your field of operations without meaning to. I'd rather not be collateral damage."

"Of course not, dear, none of us would want *that*," she said in a comforting voice. "That contingency has been carefully planned for. My people will know how to avoid involving you in the, shall we say, festivities?"

"I suppose this time I have to take your word for it." Silver didn't like it. Needle's planning for that contingency could potentially involve having Silver have an accident—or even be framed for the whole thing, which wouldn't even be entirely wrong.

On the other hand, he had *his* contingencies already in place. "All right, Needle. This will be your last involvement with the Group until at least after *Carpathia*'s dealt with. If you prevent *Carpathia*'s launch, the Group may be able to turn to a new focus."

"Understood. I hope everything works out well for you, dear. It's been a pleasure working with you."

"And with you. Good luck, Needle."

"Good luck, Silver."

He removed the SIM card, broke it into splinters, and wadded them into some toilet paper and flushed those down. The rest of the phone he'd dispose of shortly.

Three-pronged attack. Different types of targets. Specific date. He nodded. It was obvious what Needle and her people would be doing, and what they would be targeting. There was still some question as to *who* they would target . . . but even there, Silver had a good idea. There were, as they had discussed, only so many useful-in-death targets.

One of whom may, possibly, be me. Needle had been doing this kind of thing for decades. She was certainly interested in stopping

Carpathia...but if she succeeded, Silver became a liability unless he could show her a very profitable reason otherwise. She only needed Silver if she failed; it was possible—perhaps even probable—that if she succeeded in stopping *Carpathia*, there was a contingency in place for Silver's accidental demise, most likely with a frame already in place.

But I only need her for this last attempt, win or lose.

CHAPTER 33:
INTERRUPTED TRIUMPH

Time to Launch: 20 days

"Madam President, I want to reiterate that I absolutely hate this," Roger Stone said as he followed Jeanne.

"So do I, Roger," she said, trying to keep her strides steady and measured as they should be. Tension was not helping her focus now. "But the positive side is that if we can get through today, we should make it the rest of the way. Is *everything* prepared?"

"Hailey says 'Mix and Match' is a go. We've got security drones in the air everywhere that matters, and eyes on the ground for the full perimeter. Mr. Flint's Bells are fully charged and on alert. Three different groups have checked the viewing stands. Werner's on board *Carpathia*, ostensibly overseeing the transfer."

"But he's got Task Group One ready?"

"Set to go. Hopefully won't be needed, they're there if we do."

The stands surrounding *Carpathia* had been carefully upgraded to provide shelter from the intense sunlight of the American desert, and were discreetly equipped with the maximum possible surveillance equipment. Straightening and shifting her walk to her public "confident and in control" gait, Jeanne looked around. *God, I hope everyone's precautions hold. I don't know where there's been an assembly of targets like this.*

Xi Deng and his security detail were already in place. She could see the general secretary gesticulating with excitement as he studied *Carpathia*, towering up before them on its building-sized shock mounts; President Murmu of India appeared to be the target of his current discussion. Jeanne waved her hand as she saw Kier Sunnak, the UK prime minister, begin mounting the stands on the other side; Sunnak returned the wave. Other heads of state and their representatives were arriving.

The press were recording all the arrivals, naturally, and—unsurprisingly—even the President of the United States wasn't their primary focus. That was reserved for Dr. Bronson and her entourage, as members of the *Carpathia* team began to fill their section of the stands.

Which is as it should be. They're the ones who will be climbing into that monster and flying to meet the only starship we've ever seen. Jeanne sternly suppressed the pang of annoyance and envy; there had never been the slightest chance that she would be on *Carpathia*, any more than Secretary Xi Deng or Japan's emperor.

From the stands, the completed *Carpathia* loomed more like a mountain than a human construct, broader and squatter in outline than the typical vision of a spaceship. Massing more than the Empire State Building, it was less than half as tall, the heaviest single part of it being the gleaming metal curve of the drive, or pusher plate, which now sat in a slightly curved depression, supported by multiple columns between which could be dimly seen the bulk of literally thousands of tons of explosives, carefully distributed and placed to provide the best initial impulse to the ship.

If someone detonated that, they'd wipe out half the leaders of the world in a single shot—and more than half the crew. Ironically, it would probably not damage *Carpathia* in the least; anyone currently inside the interplanetary vessel was safer than anywhere else.

Now that it was complete, the *Carpathia* shone in the light of the sun. Encircling the squat nose cone shape of the main ship were numerous images—the national symbols of every nation of the world, as well as that of the United Nations, the European Union, and other international organizations. This made a chain of multicolored brilliance enclosing *Carpathia* in the representations of Earth's peoples who had brought her to life.

Down each side of the vessel, emblazoned in immense golden

letters, was the name *CARPATHIA*. Across the front of *Carpathia*, pointing toward the sky, was the logo of the Carpathia project itself, a depiction of the original seagoing vessel launching itself into a sea of stars, surrounded by the motto *Ad Astra Pro Vita*—To the Stars for the Sake of Life.

Spaced around the *Carpathia*, more streamlined duplicates of their mothership, the ACES, hung in little notches around the main vessel; unsurprisingly, their individual names echoed their acronym, with the two that Jeanne could make out being the *Ace of Hearts* and *Ace of Clubs*. She admitted to herself that those seemed a bit pedestrian compared to Dr. Jerry Freeman's suggestions of *Aces High, Aces Wild, Four Aces,* and *Flying Aces.*

Experienced from reviewing intelligence briefings for the past few years, Jeanne was also fairly certain she could pick out the locations of the *Carpathia*'s armaments, as well as the more obvious mountings of her maneuvering jets.

As with all such gatherings, it took a while for everyone to get seated, and even longer before all the myriad tiny technical glitches were smoothed out and the event could actually begin.

"Welcome, everyone," York Dobyns's voice came smoothly over the speakers. "This is a momentous occasion—one of quite a few we've had over the last couple of years!" A spatter of chuckles followed that dry assertion. "But today we will be finally turning *Carpathia* into a fully capable spaceship. You are here as witnesses to the completion of the most capable and powerful vehicle the human species has ever created—a creation that could not have happened without the support of each and every one of you, and those that you represent, support, and advise. On behalf of *Carpathia*, we all thank you. Now, I turn this over to Director Stephanie Bronson, the discoverer of *Fenrir* and the leader of this project!"

That garnered over a minute of enthusiastic applause. "Thank you, thank you all," Stephanie said at last, with a little laugh, and Jeanne noted with approval that there was no trace of the nervous, self-conscious young woman she'd first met almost three years ago. Whatever her internal insecurities, Stephanie Bronson had learned how to look and sound like a leader. "We know it's not terribly comfortable out here, so we'll try to make this quick enough so no one has to run inside to the air-conditioning."

Another ripple of laughter. It was obvious that no one was likely to leave their seat before the main event. "In line with York's thanks to all of you gathered here, we invite each country's representative to say a few words. And I've emphasized to them a *few* words!"

To prevent any accusations of favoritism, Stephanie called on the representatives in alphabetical order of their country. Thankfully, nowhere near all nations had sent a representative—that, she thought, would be reserved for the actual launch—but there were enough, starting with Afghanistan, Argentina, and Australia and going through Brazil, China, Columbia, and Denmark and continuing on through the alphabet, from the large countries like India and the tiny like Nuaru. Each representative did, thankfully, restrain themselves to a few sentences rather than the usual ten-minute speech, and it wasn't a too very long time before it was the turn of the United States of America.

"We are immeasurably proud to launch *Carpathia* from our own soil, and grateful for the support of all the rest of the world in this project," Jeanne said. "All that I can add to what everyone else has said is this: rescue *Fenrir*."

It wasn't long until the rest finished, ending with Venezuela, Vietnam, and Zimbabwe. There was a somewhat tired round of applause at the conclusion, and then Director Bronson stood again. "Only one thing remains to make *Carpathia* fully functional: the antimatter that's essential to the controlled nuclear fission that makes the ship possible. This is to be transferred to *Carpathia* today, in preparation for launch, giving us time to verify the functioning of all systems including the vital antimatter containment systems."

She pointed, and Jeanne stood with the others, squinting down one of the long dusty streets that radiated out from *Carpathia*.

A large, white truck, with a generally spherical container mounted to the rear, had just turned up the street toward the *Carpathia*, four much smaller military trucks surrounding it as escorts. Jeanne could also see the presence of drones on high watch, and suspected there were other guardians she couldn't see.

"In that container is more antimatter than humanity had ever produced in history, prior to the *Carpathia* project," Stephanie continued. "And it is only one third of the total. Each of these transports carries enough for *Carpathia* to fulfill her mission; with all of them loaded, she will be provided with enough reserve to meet even *unreasonable* demands—and that's a good thing, because no one will be able to help *Carpathia* once she lifts.

"That's why every system that *can* be redundant has been duplicated, sometimes triplicated, to ensure that there is no single disaster, no one emergency, that can prevent our ship from surviving and doing her job."

"*Our* ship," she repeated, and her voice was warmer; Jeanne saw with approval that she was wearing the same awed, joyous expression that Audrey had mentioned more than once. "And it *is* ours, every single one of us. The news sites and talking heads have mentioned it, but here, now, it's *true*."

Jeanne smiled to herself. *She's done some growing since she first walked into a conference as a terrified postgraduate student. She's bringing everyone together now, at the end, just as she did at the beginning.*

"The whole world"—Stephanie bowed to the stands holding all the representatives of countries—"has come together like never before, to achieve something none of us could have imagined doing alone. This isn't the USS *Carpathia*, or the PRC *Carpathia*, or Her Majesty's Spaceship *Carpathia*. This is the United Earth Ship *Carpathia*, from every one of us to our stranded visitors in the sky."

As Stephanie paused, catching her breath, the representative from Italy began clapping, and suddenly the entire crowd was applauding, President Sacco as enthusiastically as any. *Perhaps she didn't plan to stop there, but that was a perfect pause.*

Dr. Bronson stood quietly, an embarrassed smile on her face, and waited for the clapping and cheers to die down. "Thank you," she said, and her voice might have shaken just a touch. "Thank you—all of you—for everything."

"The antimatter"—she gestured to the approaching white truck—"will be loaded—"

The truck detonated.

At a distance of over three hundred meters, it was momentarily a silent scene, a flash of dazzling light and smoke that wiped the antimatter tanker out of existence, cast its four escorts aside like a child sweeping blocks off a table. Jeanne's stunned perceptions saw a hint of distortion, a flicker of motion that disturbed the dust along the roadway in the second before the sound and shock wave struck them.

It was a swift thundercrack of sound, *KA-WHOOM!*, and a blow to the body that staggered everyone on the stands. A red-orange fireball ascended, trailing fire and smoke, becoming an ominous mushroom shape. *Antimatter explosion?* a part of her asked, even as the other, still rational part, replied, *Don't be ridiculous!*

Screams and curses echoed across the stands, as security teams began to close in. But there was no clear target of action, nor an immediate route to safety for most who were on the stands. The security detachments recognized the dilemma, and quickly began to direct the frightened and confused crowd, guiding them to exit the stands in an orderly fashion, as quickly as possible.

"Well, we'll have to be patient," Jeanne observed, keeping a grip on her own emotions. *Can't afford panic. I'm the President. Everyone takes their cue from me.* "We chose to be seated in the higher areas."

"Yes. *Jesus,* I don't like this." Roger was scanning everywhere nervously.

That's an understatement. "Even if we planned for something like this, no." She glanced back to where the remnants of five vehicles were burning. Parts of the buildings around them were blown in, and smoldering as well.

Out of the corner of her eye she saw a sudden movement, and something struck her in the side. There was a whipcrack of sound and she was falling, the sky blotted by something dark as she crashed painfully to the bleachers, agony spreading along her ribs, her head cracking painfully against the wooden supports.

The world was receding, but she thought there had been *other* gunshot sounds, and the ground heaved, shaking the bleachers beneath her, as pain rose in a red wave and crashed down in a black foam that wiped away awareness.

CHAPTER 34: RECOVERY AND PURPOSE

Time to Launch: 19 days

Stephanie became aware of pain everywhere, particularly where something edged and rigid was crushing into her lower back, another hard surface being squeezed against her head, with a massive weight on top of her. Her ears were ringing and other sounds were muffled. *What happened?*

She remembered the explosion of the tanker—something she'd half expected, but had hoped wouldn't happen—but then there had been several simultaneous shouts, something smashed into her, and then a blast that made the first seem quiet.

She pushed at the weight on her, realized how it gave. *It's someone else lying on me.* The jacket, and a faint smell of deodorant overlaying the smell of fire, explosives, and shattered stone, identified the inert mass as York Dobyns.

"Oh my God. *YORK!*" She wriggled, struggling to get out from under the much larger man. Suddenly other hands were there, lifting, pulling, and with a rush Stephanie found herself standing unsteadily on the bleachers, which were themselves unsteady, slanted backward to a noticeable level.

The bright sunshine was diffused and blurred by a massive cloud of dust, so vast that in the fog Stephanie couldn't even guess how far it reached. As her eyes adjusted to the light again, she realized there was a bright red stain spreading across York's jacket. More of the sticky crimson was on her blouse lower down, where most of York's weight had rested. *Blood. York's blood.*

Muffled words finally penetrated to her. "... all right? Stephanie, are you all right?"

She shook her head in disbelief, then looked over, seeing the pale and horrified face of Audrey Milliner. "I ... I think so," Stephanie finally answered, her own words dull and distant, as though her head were wrapped in pillows. "York—"

"Let the paramedics check," Audrey said, voice shaking. "Nothing we can do. We have to get you down off this thing!"

Stephanie took a breath, looked around.

All of the stands were tilted at some angle; one set had collapsed entirely, plunging the press section into a welter of metal, wood, and plastic. *Jesus, how many of them died there?*

Worse, though, was the sight of multiple knots of people clustered around red-splashed areas in the project and diplomatic stands. Controlled chaos made it hard to immediately make out *who* was in the center of each.

She swung her gaze skyward. To her unutterable relief, *Carpathia* still loomed above, a mountain of gleaming steel. Stephanie thought it might be in a slightly different position, but the immense vessel looked stable and, at first glance, unharmed.

She recognized another dust-covered face. "Werner! Werner, what happened? Do we have coverage?"

Carpathia's project engineer held up a hand; she saw he was listening to someone on his earbuds. "*Ja?* You are certain?" A pause. "Well, that's something, anyway. Hold on, have to report to the director. Yes, she's all right." He touched his phone and looked down at her. "You *are* all right, yes? Please tell me you're okay, Steph."

"I think so." The dull aches across her back, chest, waist, and legs, and the bruised pain from her head, didn't seem to matter. "What *happened*?"

Werner's chuckle held only the ghost of humor. "Mix and Match proved itself, first of all."

"So that *was* a decoy that blew?"

"That part went perfectly," Werner said with a nod. "Pulled off the sleight of hand, all the trucks looked manned but weren't. Simple platooning with some remote control, detonated when one of the hacked drones fired on it. All three of the antimatter storage units are safe." He glanced towards the first explosion site. "A good thing, as the gamma burst from that much antimatter would certainly have killed us all, assuming we survived the detonation, which we probably wouldn't; ten tons of high explosive a couple hundred yards off is no joke. Pretty sure it fooled the attackers, though; most people can't figure scale and that blast was plenty big enough."

Stephanie coughed, waving dust away. "But what's all this? And what happened to York and the others?"

Werner shook his head.

"That was just the first part of the attack," Hàorán Lin looked grimly down at York, who was surrounded by EMTs, then transferred his gaze to Stephanie. "The explosion of the tanker was a signal for two other sets of saboteurs. One had carefully planned to damage or destroy *Carpathia* by making it fall over; the impact sideways would likely cause considerable exterior damage and a great deal of internal breakage and stress. They triggered detonation of the launch charge only on one side of the ship, while the shocks were locked for stability."

Stephanie stared up at him, glanced back to the reassuring mass of *Carpathia*. "Why didn't it fall?"

"Call it a stress test of the gyro system; the gyros were already running and they kept *Carpathia* essentially vertical, so the ship just hopped sideways a bit, and the drive plate kept most of the blast from getting to *this* side—or we'd all have been dead so fast we'd never have known it."

The paramedics were speaking more urgently, and she saw a sealed package ripped open, the injector inside applied. "What happened to York?"

Captain Lin shook his head. "That was the second prong of the attack. Multiple snipers, firing essentially simultaneously."

"Why did they target *York*?"

Werner's eyes closed and his lips tightened; after a moment he met her gaze. "They didn't. They were aiming at *you*."

"Exactly how it all happened is still being unraveled, Director," Hàorán Lin said in answer to her mutely horrified expression, "but someone apparently caught a last-instant hint—a distant movement, a glint—and reacted, causing several other people to do the same thing just as the snipers fired."

As Stephanie opened her mouth to ask the next obvious question, the EMTs quieted, and she heard "... calling it. Time of death, 3:24 P.M."

Her knees gave way and she sat, hard, on the bleachers, staring at the broad, still figure. "Oh, God, no."

One of the paramedics looked over, then stood. "I'm sorry, Director. The bullet went completely through; we'll need an autopsy, but I think it nicked the aorta."

She felt dizzy. *York gone? Who else was targeted? Is* Carpathia *damaged? Can we even keep the site secure now?*

The EMT, a lean man with the dark and angular features she associated with several Native American tribes and wearing a name tag that simply said GAGE, leaned suddenly closer. "Director?" he said, eyes looking sharply at her waist. As Stephanie felt herself sagging sidewise, Gage caught her and shouted, "Get over here, people, I think I found the bullet!"

This time the motion around her was purposeful and swift. Aching, pulsing pain radiated from her lower left side as the EMTs lifted her onto a stretcher. "Dr. Bronson," said another of them, "looks like you took a secondary hit from the bullet that got Dr. Dobyns. Doesn't *look* too serious but you're bleeding pretty bad. We're getting you to the base hospital. You understand me?"

She nodded. "I understand. How about everyone else? How many people did we lose?"

He exchanged glances with Gage, then shrugged. "We've got a lot of injured, but I don't think anyone can answer that for a while. Let us worry about you first, okay? We can only save one person at a time."

She swallowed her panic and worry and managed to nod. *Nothing I can do right now.*

Once they reached the ground, the ambulance ride was a short, swaying five minutes, and then her gurney was lifted out and run into an operating room. Already gloved and masked, nurses and at least two doctors transferred her to the OR table, something was injected into her IV, and her worries fragmented and faded into a measureless interval.

There were brief moments of consciousness, with people asking her if she remembered her name, knew where she was, what the date was, but it was a while before she finally woke up with her head reasonably clear. An attempt to sit up sent a screaming warning from her side, so she lay back and looked around.

She recognized one of the rooms of the base hospital—she'd toured it, like all the other major buildings, and the bright, new color scheme was unmistakable. *We didn't have too many illnesses or injuries; I might be the first patient* using *this room.*

Despite the newness and the faint undertone of fresh paint and plaster, the overall scent was still the antiseptic, purified smell of any good functioning hospital. As Stephanie looked for the call button, there were swift steps in the hallway, and after a pause the door opened.

"Thank God you're awake," the President said as she entered, trailed by two Secret Service agents, a doctor, and two nurses.

"You had me wired, I guess."

"Every room in this hospital is," the doctor, a small, neat-looking, dark-haired woman with HABIB on her nametag. "No, don't talk yet," she said before Stephanie could speak. "And that means you, too, Madam President."

Her examination was, thankfully, brief. "You came through the operation well. We removed the fragments of the projectile, which fortunately did relatively little damage. You lost quite a bit of blood but we've addressed that, and the main concern now is going to be possible infection," Dr. Habib said. "Barring complications, you will be out of here and back into your own quarters in a few days."

"Will I recover in time for launch?"

"I would certainly expect so. The area may still be tender, but there should be no physical restrictions by that time."

"Thank you, Doctor," the President said. "Now please give me a few minutes with Director Bronson." She glanced at one of the agents, who nodded and followed the doctor and nurses out.

"I was afraid they'd shot you," Stephanie said. "When I heard multiple people had been targeted—"

"I was," President Sacco said quietly. "Roger was my York."

"Roger . . . *Is he all right?*"

"He's still in critical condition," she answered; Stephanie could hear her worry in the undertones of the otherwise controlled politician's voice. "Apparently he bodychecked me out of the way just as the assassin shot."

Stephanie closed her eyes. "How many did we lose?" she asked at last. When the President hesitated, she went on, "Jeanne. Please."

Jeanne Sacco nodded. "Kier Sunnak, the UK PM, is the highest-profile victim. We lost twenty-four project members, mostly to fringe effects from the detonation under *Carpathia*, half a dozen members of the press, including Gerald Walters of NBC and Marcie Amour."

"God."

"Angus Fletcher's in surgery right now but they expect him to be all right; it was a near thing."

"Angus? Why was *he* shot?"

"From what he said before he went out, they were trying for Pete, which makes too much sense," the President answered. "We have about three dozen more people in hospital and others with minor injuries."

Those sons of bitches. Stephanie ground her teeth and tried to sit up again, finding it still too painful. But there was a last and utterly vital question to ask. "How is *Carpathia*?"

"We're doing a full check, Steph, But . . . good, so far. If we don't find anything surprising, the ship should be good to go." Her brown eyes studied Stephanie. "How about you? Are *you* good to go?"

"Good to go?" She grabbed at the bed control and found the right button, ignored the pain as it lifted up to face the President. "Is that even a *question*?"

A smile touched the President's face—one with new lines that Stephanie hadn't seen just the other day. "Of course it is. We were hit *hard*, Dr. Bronson, and both you and I lost someone dear to us. It wouldn't be so surprising if you decided you couldn't go forward yourself."

"Then I might as well have had York stand still and let me get *shot*," Stephanie said bluntly. "That'd be just what these murderers want. Do we know who they are yet?"

"We captured quite a few of the operatives, and Hailey's pretty sure we'll make some real progress now . . . but no, not yet."

"Fine. Jeanne, I don't know how *you* feel about it, but me? I want *Carpathia* fueled up *now*. I want that ship ready to launch *now*. And I'll be on her if I have to have the rest of the project carry my hospital bed inside. I am not letting those fucking *bastards* murder York and all those other people and get to take their high-fives as the project stops."

A cold smile was the President's answer. "Director Bronson, you have my *full* support."

CHAPTER 35: UNEXPECTED AWAKENING

Time to Launch: 18 days

Damn. I feel like I got totally wasted.

For a moment, that was all that Silver could think. It took a few more for his mind to recognize that in addition to the foggy nausea making him reluctant to even open his eyes, he was feeling pain with every breath, a strange, tight pain.

Beeping noises. That smell. I'm in a hospital?

Memory burst in on him. The explosion of the antimatter container, seeing the faintest movement on one of the rooftops, and—

His eyes snapped open. *I didn't.*

IV bags hung next to him from stainless-steel stands. The rails of a hospital bed stood up on each side, ensuring he couldn't accidentally roll off. Typical white and light green hospital sheets covered him, and wincingly bright light streamed in from the windows, along with the sterile white illumination from the ceiling-mounted LED lights.

Next to him, in a recliner, Peter Flint was sleeping, his face looking more lined than usual.

Son of a bitch. I did. He didn't know whether to laugh, cry, or rage, and settled for an inward, bemused chuckle.

Silver couldn't make out exactly what was in the IVs, but he couldn't help but wonder if it was for more than a bullet. That truck's detonation could have—likely would have—irradiated everyone in the crowd.

But in that case, Pete ought to have an IV, or be in his own bed. The hospital would be stacked two deep with patients. So why . . . ?

As chagrined understanding came, he *did* laugh—a brief, pained chortle. *A decoy. A fake. They planned for the attack.*

Pete stirred, looked up. "Angus! You're awake! How do you feel?"

"Like I was on a weekend bender and someone kicked me in the ribs. What happened?"

"Well, you saved my life, that's what. Mine and maybe a couple others," Pete said gravely. "Near's we can figure, you moved first, and that got others who saw you moving just in time. They're wonderin' just what set you off."

Silver briefly considered the various alternatives, decided that limited honesty was preferable. "Saw a movement, just a tiny something off, on one of the rooftops. After the truck went up I was already worried someone else might try something, so when I saw it I just . . . reacted."

"Well, you've got some damned good reactions, is all I can say." Pete grinned. "Sorry you had to take the shot for me, though."

"You said there were others?" It was obvious what Needle had been after, and it made sense. Instead of limiting yourself to one target, take out several—maybe even some extras to confuse the motivations.

"Yeah. Six or seven at least; maybe more, but it'll take 'em more time to figure that out; the way the stands got unbalanced, they guess quite a few shots could've missed. Anyway, they got the UK prime minister, and almost took out the President and Director Bronson."

Silver made sure to let his face show relief. "But they didn't."

Pete grimaced. "No, because when you shoved me, York blocked for Steph, and Rog Stone beat the Secret Service to the punch with the President."

Needle will be livid *at me.* The thought was beautifully entertaining, a distillation of irony that Silver had rarely encountered. "How are they? Dr. Dobyns and Mr. Stone?"

"Stone's still in ICU, critical condition. Dobyns . . . Dobyns didn't make it."

"Jesus. Those bastards. How's our director holding up?" York Dobyns had been Stephanie Bronson's main support; on consideration, he could have been an excellent target on his own. But the other possibility was . . .

Pete chuckled, and there was a spark of grim amusement in his eye. "She's on the warpath, Angus, and no mistake. They're rebuilding the launch structure, the antimatter's already loaded, and the way she's pushing, launch might be as much as a week early. She doesn't want to give anyone a chance to try again."

... that. Silver had been afraid of exactly this reaction, which was why he had deliberately excluded Dobyns from consideration. *The younger Stephanie Bronson, from the early days of Fenrir's discovery, she wouldn't have been able to deal with Dr. Dobyns being shot dead. But she's grown a hell of a lot in two years.*

"Hold on a moment. What happened to the launch structure?"

Pete summarized everything that happened, and Silver's reluctant admiration for Needle, which had been waning with these failures, renewed itself.

Silver also had to give credit to the director and President Sacco, because they obviously had orchestrated the razzle-dazzle with the fake antimatter tankers and kept everyone not directly involved in the dark. They had anticipated the vulnerability of the antimatter and found a way to use that tempting target as bait. "Have they caught any of the bastards?"

"Heard they got quite a few, but no more. Everyone's security's clamped down the lid hard."

Silver nodded. "What about me?"

"Better ask the doc." Pete stood carefully. "*Whoof!* These chairs ain't exactly the best beds, know what I mean? Now that I can see you're doing okay, I need to go turn in for a few good hours before I get back to work."

He put a hand gently on Silver's shoulder. "But thanks a whole damn bunch, Angus. They say if you hadn't done it, I'd've taken that shot right through my head. I'd return the favor, but I hope I never get the chance, if you know what I mean."

Silver grinned. "Pete, I absolutely agree. You don't owe me anything; I know you'd have done the same for me. Just what friends do. Right?"

"Only the *real* friends. But yeah, that's it. I'll drop by soon's I can, but I'm beat."

"No problem. You get your rest. I'm guessing they'll *make* me get mine."

"Bet on it."

Silver heard Pete call to the nurse as he walked out, so he was unsurprised to see both a nurse and a physician enter a few moments later.

They performed the usual examinations of vital signs before allowing him to ask questions. "So how am I? What happened?"

"You were very fortunate," Dr. Habib said, nodding. "The bullet penetrated you from back to front from near your left shoulder and then out between two ribs, striking no solid obstacles aside from nicking one rib on the way out; the bullet is one of only two recovered intact, buried in the bleacher step near where you fell. The projectile just missed directly damaging the lungs, causing a small pneumothorax due to penetrating the chest cavity, but this was able to be addressed and repaired fairly quickly."

I was *lucky.* "Why do I feel so . . . out of it, then?"

"You responded strongly to the anesthesia, possibly due to the initial shock," she replied. "We of course reduced dosage, but you apparently retained a considerable amount. You do not seem to have suffered any actual ill effects, which is a relief."

Silver remembered the one other time he'd been operated on. *Yes, I was hit hard then, too.* "How long before I'm up?"

"You may have mostly recovered in a week," Habib answered. "If you follow directions."

"I am *very* good at following directions for my own health," he said honestly.

"Good." Dr. Habib smiled and departed, the nurse trailing behind.

A week. That was encouraging. Leveraging the same determination the director was using to keep the project going, he was sure that he would be able to keep his position onboard *Carpathia,* which was the one absolutely vital task remaining to him.

The instinctive protection of Pete, however, was a matter of grave concern. He hadn't realized, until the very instant he was in motion, that he was no longer feigning his friendship with the older engineer, that he genuinely *liked* Pete and the thought of him being hurt was simply intolerable.

I cannot afford this kind of sentiment. Being honest with himself—something Silver always insisted on—it was not nearly so easy to remove an attachment than it was to prevent one from forming. But he'd not had the option to avoid contact; even relative loners *had* to have a few contacts that were regular and social on a crew such as this, and the fact that he and Pete *connected* on a personal level was rare in Silver's life. Peter Flint was extremely smart, well-read, and easygoing yet driven in an unusual way. He was *interesting*.

Tactically and strategically, of course, saving Pete was a masterstroke. It would be almost impossible for people to suspect him of being an enemy of the project, barring them getting some real clear evidence of his true nature. Pete would trust him implicitly, and likely so would most of the others on the project. With that trust would come more latitude, and vastly increased chance of success of his final sabotage.

I will just have to prepare myself and guard against my personal feelings. I really honestly do not want Pete to be hurt... but I must be ready to if I must. I must be willing to even kill him, if the situation demands it. He did not like that thought. But it was a thought that had to be accepted and turned into action and determination.

Sudden impulses of friendship, throwing himself between a friend and a bullet—all right, it was impossible to predict or guard against that. But in his final actions, he would know what he must do, and be prepared to do what must be done.

Even if it meant shooting a friend.

Needle, he hoped, would be dealt with. All the contingencies he had arranged would have gone into effect the moment her attack was known, regardless of his own condition. There were a few other actions awaiting his personal direction—or his death—but those could be addressed later.

He had to recover and see that *Carpathia* launched safely before he could destroy her.

CHAPTER 36:
AFTER-ACTION REPORTS

Time to Launch: 16 days

Stephanie looked around the briefing room, wondering why something felt wrong. Then it clicked, and wry amusement dueled with pain. "I'm not used to seeing you at a briefing without Roger," she said, at Jeanne's questioning glance.

"I'm not used to being at one without him. But it looks, thank God, that I won't have to for much longer." Jeanne Sacco looked around the table. "In other ways this is almost déjà vu."

Looking a second time, Stephanie understood what she meant. The group sitting around the table was almost all the same people she'd first briefed on *Fenrir*. Admiral Dickinson and Secretary of the Interior Truro were missing, but General Rainsford, Dr. Filipek, George Green, and Hailey Vanderman were all in their places.

"Then we don't need introductions," Stephanie said. "I'm still pushing the schedule, so I don't have much time. Have we learned anything about our opposition?"

"Quite a bit now, none of it good," Vanderman replied, in the precise tones she expected from the former Director of the CIA. "They call themselves, very simply, the Group. Not much to wring out of that, but with the people we managed to catch after the attack, we finally got enough to amount to a crack in their armor."

"Which was a stroke of luck," Green said. "These people had done

221

a lot of their work right, compartmentalizing to the point that what little hints we got had each of the military intelligence branches thinking they'd found several different organizations."

"But it's not? It's just one...group?" The President lifted an inquiring eyebrow.

Hailey Vanderman smiled faintly. "Took us a while to be sure, Madam President. About the only thing all of them had in common was that they wanted *Carpathia* to fail, but there wasn't a bit of commonality about *why*. They had religious nutcases who felt any aliens were basically soulless monsters by definition, people who just didn't want any complications of aliens between us and the tech, antinuke types, all kinds of people.

"But we finally got a couple of breaks and were able to make some guesses—the DoD, FBI, NSA, and Interpol helped a lot—and finally we managed to find the mastermind behind the assault."

A picture blinked onto the screen, of a white-haired woman in what Stephanie thought of as a granny dress, smiling benignly at the camera. "You're serious? *She* was behind it all?"

Green and Vanderman exchanged cynical smiles. "Yeah, that's everyone's reaction to the Duchess," Hailey said. "One of her biggest weapons; when she was younger, she was adorable and harmless looking, now she's everyone's favorite aunt. Except that Dana Malik, aka the Duchess in the trade, inherited her father's arms-dealing business when he died, and expanded it. One of the hardest hardcases you'd ever not want to fu...er, mess with. She'll have tea with you, shoot you in the head, and ask someone to clean up the mess as she pours herself another cup."

"Someone like that doesn't get involved in movements like this Group," Jeanne said flatly. "They might be hired for a job, but not dedicate themselves to some cause."

"Generally, we'd agree," George said. "But the Duchess had a lot of contacts in the military tech world—as you'd expect—and from what we gathered she figured if *Carpathia* was delayed a few months past the rescue date, there would be basically no chance of live aliens, and *much* more alien technology would be recovered when *Carpathia* finally was launched to chase down the remains of *Fenrir*. With that much time she might be able to influence choices enough to get agents of her own on board."

"We can't completely rule that out, either," Hailey said.

"If *anything* justifies our using the extraordinary authority given us, I would think this is it. She needs to be apprehended." Jeanne glanced at Stephanie as she spoke; Stephanie gave an emphatic nod.

Hailey grimaced. "We already set that in motion, Madam President. Joint assault team did a quick strike on her current headquarters—coordinated it with the UK and Chinese as Joint Operation Teatime. But..."

"But," Green said heavily, "she didn't make it out alive. Still trying to figure out whether it was one of ours or theirs who shot her."

"One of *ours*?" Stephanie asked, incredulous.

"Could easily be," Vanderman said. "It's one of the oldest tricks in espionage, to have one of your agents in the assault force. They make sure that the target never gets a chance to talk. And of course if the Duchess was working with anyone else, they sure don't want her talking—and you can bet whatever you want that she damn well would've talked if we had caught her. She was a practical little monster."

"She was that," Green agreed. "If it weren't that we needed to know so much, no one would be broken up about her being dead."

"How sure are we she was at the top?"

"Say ninety percent. We've got enough to pin the assault operation on her organization, and she wouldn't have let someone *else* tell her how to pull that off. My guess, she was at the top cell, which means we're looking for two more people."

"Will we find them in time? Before launch? With her dead...?"

Hailey Vanderman looked at the President, then paused a moment. "Director... yes, I think so. The Duchess may be dead, but we captured most of her command setup, and we've got top teams working on data recovery and forensic data analysis. If she was in that cell, there'll have to be connections to the other two somewhere, and I'm pretty confident we'll have them ID'd within a week now that we've got this much data."

"Let's hope so, Because I've got to launch ASAP." Stephanie remembered York collapsing. *We are not letting anything stop us.* "Eva, I suppose we're ramping down the antimatter production now?"

"In a few months," Eva said. "Given that we've devoted so much effort to the technology, even our impatient particle physicists agree that getting a few orders of magnitude more antimatter in storage than they ever had before is worth some delay. And the President recommended we keep that infrastructure operational until we learn whether *Carpathia* will ever voyage again after its main mission. If it will, it will need a source for antimatter."

Stephanie nodded. "That does make sense. With this joint operation, I guess our big shaky alliance is still on?"

"Even a bit less shaky than it was," General Rainsford replied. "China certainly isn't going to back away now, and neither will the UK. If they won't, few others would even think about it; too much face to be lost there. But you're right to push, Director; we're all strained to the breaking point. Once *Carpathia* launches we'll all be committed and the hard work is over. Except, of course, for you people on board. Then the hard work *starts*."

"Don't we know it."

A few relatively minor other points were cleared up, and then the meeting was adjourned. Stephanie glanced mutely at the President, who stayed behind. "Director Bronson?"

"Just Stephanie right now, please. I have to wonder—shouldn't we have had reps from the other countries here?"

"It's a good thought," Jeanne Sacco said. "But this kind of thing . . . the raid on this 'Duchess' and her organization, they'll be briefed on by their own people. We're not changing any of the goals of the project. All of them have enough to do right now. So I would say this time, it's not a problem."

There was a rap on the door, and one of the Secret Service agents looked in. "Excuse me, Madam President. Peter Flint would like to speak to you and the director privately?"

"Pete? All right, send him in," Stephanie said, then looked with a guilty start at the President. "If that's okay with you, Jeanne?"

A gentle laugh. "Of course. Please, send Pete in."

Pete waited until the door closed behind him to speak. "Thanks much for seeing me on such short notice, Madam President, Director."

Stephanie settled back into the chair. Her body was reminding her she was not yet recovered, so putting off the walk to another meeting— even if it would now be later—was appealing. "No problem, Peter. We both know you wouldn't barge in like this if it wasn't important."

"'Fraid it is," he agreed. One weathered hand ran through his short graying hair. "Thing is, that hack our friends pulled to hide their activities, it affected my Bells."

Jeanne raised an eyebrow. "That's hardly a surprise. They did the same to our drones and UGV patrols, not to mention select parts of the security net overall."

"Beggin' your pardon, ma'am, it kinda *is* a surprise. See, the Bells are custom through and through. Sure, we put together an interface package so we could exchange data and such, but that was just . . . well, like giving 'em a phone, I guess."

Stephanie saw the implications. "You mean, they'd need an entirely separate set of information, detailed information, on the Bells before they could suborn them."

"Bang on, Director. And there just ain't . . . aren't many people on Earth that could give 'em that kind of information. Probably, bein' honest, a lot fewer than could give the same information about your military security."

The set, tight lips showed it was now President Sacco who was giving him full attention. "Mr. Flint, how many people, exactly, are we talking about?"

"Been thinking on that, ma'am, and I don't figure it's more'n about eight, ten all told. Werner Keller, of course, and his head of security tech, whatsisname, the Brazilian whiz kid . . . Heitor, that's it, Heitor Almeida. Other than that, the MIROC team at IIS, six or seven people depending on if I count Ryan. Guess I should; he's no engineer but he knows more'n enough to dig out the info from the systems." He gave a faint grin. "Think I'll rule out myself, so many other ways I could've screwed things up here without getting that fancy."

"Or getting shot at."

"There is that. Which kinda threw my calculations right out the window, 'cause there *was* one other person who knew enough."

Stephanie stared at him. "You mean . . . Angus? You thought *Angus* was the one who gave them the data?"

"More like I'd have put him at the top of the list if it weren't for the fact he took a bullet for me," Pete said, nodding. "Any way you figure it, that was just plain *stupid* if he were in on the plan. I'm not pretending I'm indispensable, but no one would run the Bells as well, and what he did saved you two and at least a couple others. All he had to do was stand there and panic after the shots, like everyone else."

"That . . . is a strong argument," agreed the President thoughtfully.

"It doesn't *remove* him from the pool of candidates, though. I don't need Hailey Vanderman to tell me that it wouldn't be the first time an agent found his cover ID was becoming real."

"Don't care for that idea much." Pete's jaw set. "But you're right, ma'am; we can't ignore it. Which is why I came here."

"What are you thinking, Pete?"

"Well, it was the way you pulled off the double shuffle with the antimatter tankers that got me thinking. I can trust the two of you, if I can trust anyone, and I need permission to set up my own insurance, if you get what I mean."

Stephanie leaned forward, ignoring her aches. "Go on."

"Well, first off, we don't ignore the others, even my people. Have your people dig their backgrounds hard. I hate to think anyone working for me would've been involved, but I hate the idea of pretending it couldn't be even more."

"That you can count on," President Sacco said. "For that matter, I'll make sure they double-check Werner and Mr. Almeida as well as Angus."

"No point taking chances, ma'am. But what I need your blessing on, it's a little sneaky..."

Stephanie began to nod as Peter Flint laid out his plan. She hoped it would turn out to be wasted preparation... but if it wasn't, they just might be able to cut the head off the murderous serpent that had already struck them once.

"Go to it, Pete," she said finally. "Nail it down *tight*."

"Yes, Director," he said, and flashed her a harder, colder grin than she'd ever seen on the good-natured face. "Trust me," he went on. "I'll make sure of it."

CHAPTER 37: RESETTING THE CLOCK

Time to Launch: ~~12~~ ***5 days***

"Roger, it's *good* to see you back," Jeanne Sacco said, and didn't restrain herself from giving him a hug.

"Gentle!" he said, with a pained chuckle. "Still not nearly all the way back, but I forced them to let me out." He pushed his wheelchair farther into the room. "If both of us nearly died for this, there's no way I'm going to miss it."

She briefly considered telling him to get back to the hospital—his pale face and shaky movements showed he still needed time for recovery—but dismissed it as impossible. Roger Stone wasn't any different from the rest of them in being a part of *Carpathia*, and she wasn't going to deny him that. *Though I'm kicking him out for a month when this is done. He needs rest, time with his family, and by God he'll get it.*

"All right, Roger. Just don't push yourself, I want you intact for my next term in office, too."

"Yes, Madam President," he said with a wan grin.

"You've brought yourself up to date?"

"Wouldn't have dared come back here if I hadn't," he assured her. "Just had a talk with Werner, and I've gone over all the reports. Everything looks like a go."

"The launch charges? I'm still amazed they didn't go off at once and kill us all."

"Give credit to our adversaries," Roger said. He tapped a few commands on the presentation computer. "Here's the report summary from the demolitions group. The point of the explosion was to tip *Carpathia* over. Detonating *all* of the charges would just have just been a full-power launch test, and since *Carpathia*'s center of mass is very low, would almost certainly have just resulted in the ship bouncing up and coming back down; the shock absorber assembly would have taken it all easily.

"So they needed to detonate only on a narrow arc on one side. More, they *had* to prevent the rest from going off. That's one of the things they used their control of our systems for, to not notice how they separated the charges. There were only a few unplanned detonations and they didn't spread. The plan was not to slaughter everyone in the area; they wanted to stop the antimatter tankers, then detonate them in one of the craters, kill key people, and then drop *Carpathia*, damaging key parts of the ship."

"So the charges were mostly recoverable?"

"About fifty percent. A lot of them were damaged beyond recovery when *Carpathia* shifted, but didn't go off."

Jeanne looked out the window, where the gigantic ship's squat profile loomed sharply against the clear blue of the desert sky. "Can we really shave a week off the launch date?"

"I... believe so," Roger said finally. "The entire crew has been working as hard as possible, extra shifts and long hours. All the consumables are onboard. The ACES are fully supplied and ready for launch for support, defense, or assault roles. Crew quarters are all assigned, scientific labs completed and equipped."

"What about the crew? We lost quite a few people in that attack."

"We had alternates for all selected crew, sometimes two or three deep. A couple of crew also lost their alternates, but fortunately all of those had second alternates. Those all passed the basic requirements; they'll have to do some catch-up, but fortunately none of the people crucial for launch were lost."

President Sacco nodded. "I have discussed the situation with the general secretary, and he agrees on the expedited launch. We also agree that it's to be kept quiet until launch day. If the Group still has any shots to take, let them think they have more time."

"Five days; I suppose there's actually a chance of keeping it dark for that long." Roger looked cynical, and she couldn't blame him. An awful lot of people would know launch had been moved up, just by watching preparation. Even a few days left an awful lot of minutes for someone to let all the cats out of the bags.

There was a knock on the door, and it opened to show Hailey Vanderman. "Madam President, can I—Roger! They let you out!"

"I insisted," Stone said, accepting a handshake from the *Carpathia* security head.

"Good to see you up. Sorry to interrupt, Madam President."

"No problem, Hailey. I assume you have news?"

"We've found the other two members of the cell that the Duchess was in."

"Thank *God*." A moment of relief washed through Jeanne, making her feel momentarily years younger. "Who are they? Are they in custody?"

Vanderman grimaced. "Only if being in a morgue counts as custody."

Good feeling gone. "That can't be coincidence. They didn't get killed during an attempt to catch them, did they?"

"Not this time. Both of them died the same day as the attack on *Carpathia*, in apparently completely unrelated events."

"The Duchess?"

"Fragmentary records imply that strongly, yes. Apparently she thought she no longer needed their services, or their awareness of her identity."

"Dammit!" Jeanne gritted her teeth, took a few breaths to calm herself. "I assume we're going over their history with a microscope?"

"Absolutely, Madam President. And these two explain the problems we've had very well. One, apparently nicknamed 'Keys,' was Martin Grant."

"*Grant?*" Roger said, incredulously. "The author of *Seven Keys to Master Coding*?"

"The same." Hailey looked at Roger with the same bemusement Jeanne felt. "You read it?"

"When I was some younger, I was a CompSci major before I decided it wasn't for me. Grant's book was practically a *bible* for the department."

"He kept up with his field," Hailey said with a nod. "He was their computer coding and espionage wizard. Connections both legit and underground. We're not yet sure what his particular reason was for wanting *Carpathia* to fail, but he must have had one, and a very strong one. He was assaulted while out walking; assumed to have been a mugging, but that was likely just a cover.

"Second member of the cell, called 'Lathe,' was Michelle Anson-Stewart—yes, that one. Engineering process lecturer and publicity maven. This explains how they were able to get someone into so many manufacturing processes; if anyone had more contacts in the manufacturing world than Anson-Stewart I'm sure not thinking of any. Her car went off a bridge and into a river; I'm betting that we'll find evidence it was no accident once forensics gets through with the car and the site."

Jeanne considered this for a moment. "These two presumably didn't expect to be killed. So for the moment, this Group is headless, right? Falling back on the next cells down, which aren't connected to each other?"

Vanderman's lips tightened, causing a similar reaction in her gut. "I wish it were that simple. But whoever put the Group together certainly had contingencies in place. The Duchess—who was called 'Needle,' by the way—certainly threw a few wrenches into the works, but I'm not entirely counting out the possibility that they can get their act back together. If you're really moving up the timetable—"

"We are," Jeanne confirmed.

"Well, in that case there's a good chance they can't get reorganized before it's too late. But..."

She waited. "But?"

A long exhalation. "But George and I think this top cell *might* have been anomalous—with one or two more members."

"You mean the Duchess wasn't at the top?"

Roger's breath hissed between his teeth. "Makes too much sense, Madam President," he said. "We already know that the Duchess was in this for a specific and practical reason. She's not the sort to run a completely separate organization like this.

"Martin Grant...he was known as almost a recluse. Very private guy, apparently friendly to his small circle of friends but really introverted. Someone like that isn't going to be the center of the Group or anything like it. Anson-Stewart...Don't know as much about her." Roger looked to Hailey Vanderman.

"Much more gregarious," the former CIA head said. "Certainly *could* promote and run such an organization. She clearly *did* do a lot of recruiting and influencing to get her agents into the right position to sabotage components of *Carpathia*. But how she'd have known to recruit someone like the Duchess is a lot harder to figure. We think we're missing someone."

"I think that just makes it more important to launch," the President said finally. "The faster *Carpathia* is out in space, the faster we make their efforts useless."

"I agree," Hailey said. "The others in the Cabinet probably will as well."

"Then we move forward. Keep me posted, Hailey. Roger, you contact Director Bronson and tell her . . .

". . . the word is *GO*."

CHAPTER 38: LAUNCH

Time to Launch: ZERO days

Stephanie paused at the bottom of the ramp. "I can't believe all this will be *gone*."

"Consequence of practicalities," Werner replied, following her gaze across the "Carpathia Complex" that had grown up around the gigantic spaceship. "All the facilities could have been built far enough away from *Carpathia* to survive the detonations and fallout . . . but then so much time and energy would have been wasted shuttling everything and everyone back and forth. Time was our biggest enemy, and so"— he shrugged—"we built a disposable town."

"It's been home for more than a year," she murmured. "Now that's going to be *Carpathia*."

"For quite a while," agreed Ben Robinson, coming up the ramp with Captain Lín. "Even with our nuclear-pulse drive and *Fenrir* being in a good position, we'll be in *Carpathia* for many months."

"Are you ready, Captain?"

Hàorán Lín bowed. "I am ready, and also if you will believe it very nervous."

"I think we all are," Stephanie ventured, with a smile. "You'll do great."

She couldn't blame Captain Lín for being nervous. He wasn't just the representative of China in this, he was going to be one of the main faces of humanity on board *Carpathia*. While Stephanie would have a say in certain operations, it had been agreed by all groups that the captain of the *Carpathia* would be the ultimate authority aboard the vessel once launched.

Which made the success or failure of the mission, ultimately, rest on the shoulders of Captain Hàorán Lín. *That's enough to make anyone nervous.*

Not that it really took much *off* her shoulders. Popular perceptions and the long development of the scientific, engineering, biological, and even psychological corps of experts under her sometimes only tenuously informed direction had kept Dr. Stephanie Bronson in the center of all activity, and the dramatic events of the Group's final assault, with her assassination being thwarted by her mentor York's sacrifice, had simply made that more melodramatically spectacular.

And also led to all sorts of stuff I never imagined, like discovering there were people, um, shipping *me and York. And even writing about it.* She shook her head. *People are* weird *sometimes.*

"Well . . . I'm heading up," she said. "See you all soon."

"I hope to welcome you on the bridge once launch is complete," the captain said. "If you don't mind the weightlessness."

"I won't let *that* keep me away, Captain!" She waved and turned left, down the corridor that led to the residential lift.

The lift passed through several sections, bringing her to the top layer of the residential area. The corridors included intersections with vertical shafts—which would become, in turn, level corridors when spin gravity took over. The cabins, currently oriented with their floors toward the ground and the drive plate, would stay that way as long as *Carpathia* was under acceleration. In microgravity, the residential and laboratory sections would spin up to simulate gravity, with the entire cabin or lab rotating ninety degrees and locking to match the new frame of reference.

Such a design, Stephanie knew, would be incredibly wasteful of space in a traditional rocket-driven ship; only the ludicrously overpowered capabilities of a nuclear-pulse rocket made the design practical. For that, she and most of the civilian-recruited crew were grateful; it allowed roomy individual apartments that would remain at a reasonable acceleration (depending how close to the center you were, between one-half and one gravity) for most of their time in space.

The door to her cabin unlocked at her touch, the vacuum-seal door swinging open smoothly. Her apartment was a double-sized unit, including a meeting room and other official components in the additional space. She took the personal bags she'd carried with her and locked them into the secure locker, to ensure that they wouldn't move during launch.

With that in mind, she went around the entire cabin, checked for any loose objects. She found two, a pen and a small tablet of paper she'd forgotten, and stowed them away.

By the time she finished this review and preparation, the voice of Carpathia Operations came over the intercom. "*Carpathia*, this is Ops. Ship-wide announcement follows.

"All crew are registered as onboard. Please make sure to stow all luggage and items not secured on your person in your personal secure stowage. Items not secured may pose a threat, or may be damaged or broken during launch.

"It is recommended that everyone make use of the toilets in the next half hour. Lockdown begins in thirty-five minutes. Launch, T-minus two hours and counting."

Stephanie had her own bathroom, as did others who were ranked very high, one way or another, but those were very few. Almost everyone would use one of four communal bathrooms spaced equally around the core on each floor of *Carpathia*. These bathrooms also had provisions for operating in microgravity, something Steph devoutly hoped she would *never* have to deal with. Despite decades of space development, null-gee toilets had never become easy or elegant to use.

She freshened up and then lay down on her bed, which was provided with restraints for launch. Locking these down, she adjusted the tilt and support of the bed to match the needs of someone experiencing multiple gees of acceleration.

"Prelaunch lockdown commences." Stephanie heard the final *clack* of her door securing itself, knew similar sounds were now being heard throughout *Carpathia*. Heavy soundproofing, using a lot of aerogel as well as standard insulation, prevented her from hearing any more. This would, of course, help preserve personal privacy—but more importantly, would attenuate the tremendous sounds of nuclear launch.

"Steph, this is Audrey," came the voice of her publicist and—often—buffer between her and the press. "Want to record your prelaunch thoughts?"

"Seriously? All my prelaunch thoughts are 'I hope it works I hope it works I hope it works oh God I hope it works,'" Stephanie said with a little laugh. "We've done ten thousand sims and all, but now it comes down to this, setting off some ridiculous number of tons of explosives and then riding atom bombs up to space. It's *insane*, and exciting, and terrifying, and I'm so *excited* to be a part of it. And *God,* I hope we get to *Fenrir* in time, that there's still people there to help, so we can really, truly *see* that we're not alone in the universe anymore." She felt herself flush. "So, totally hackneyed stuff, really. Nothing worth recording here."

"I'm the judge of *that,*" Audrey said. "And you got that *expression* again while you were talking, and this time I got it on camera, so it's definitely worth recording."

"Don't you *dare* send *that* stupid speech out! I didn't even get ready—"

"And that's when you do your best. You didn't think, you just were *you,* and that's what the public eats right up."

"Ugh!"

"You know that's the way it goes, Steph. So, do you think we'll get there in time?"

Stephanie forced her embarrassment away. "I *hope* so," she said after a moment. "Our analyses still indicate there's activity on board *Fenrir,* activity that's hard to account for if there's no one left alive, but there's no real telling how many, or how coordinated, they are. And we've got a few months before we actually catch up with them."

"They didn't respond on the way in. They haven't responded since. Even if they're alive now, do you think they will respond?"

"I have to believe they will. They're in terrible danger and we're the only way out they have. But you're right, they might be frightened by our arrival, especially if they lost most of their sensors in the accident. It's possible they can't stand the idea of any other advanced life-forms. We have no way to guess. So . . . we take our best shot. And make sure we have backup—hopefully backup we never have to use."

They discussed the situation for a while, but a lot of the points were just rehashes of talks from months ago; the situation really hadn't changed much since the day *Fenrir's* drive failed.

"T-minus thirty minutes to launch," Ops announced. "All extraneous communication must cease now. Only official transmissions are permitted."

"Bye, Audrey. See you after launch."

"Goodbye, Steph; fingers crossed!"

With comms now cut off from the outside, Stephanie tapped into the official feeds. Outside her window she could see a few white clouds in the blue sky, beyond the massive supports that lay outside her cabin on *Carpathia*. Her main screen lit up to show *Carpathia* from the outside, faint vapors steaming from the areas of the maneuver jets, the rest of the titanic ship sitting, quiescent, mountainously immobile, on the desert.

The buildings around her were also deserted. No one walked the streets, nothing but a few scraps of paper in the wind moved. The miniature city that had grown up around the nuclear vessel was now still and abandoned, awaiting the event that would justify and erase its existence. Ops was much farther away, a small white glint on the horizon, the activity within visible on a small inset of her screen.

"*Carpathia*, report status."

"Ops, this is *Carpathia*," replied Captain Lín. "All systems green, repeat, all systems green. Pulse drive unlocked, delay set to calculated value upon launch."

"Understood. Launch charges show all green, synchronized detonation sequence set and locked."

The launch charge would actually be a swift but coordinated wave of detonations, running from the outer edge to the center, producing a powerful, extended moment of thrust. For the first seconds of flight, *Carpathia* would be accelerating at about five gravities—fifty meters per second squared—and there would be a brief delay of a few more seconds as *Carpathia* continued to ascend on that momentum. At the peak, the highest point above the desert floor the launch charge could propel *Carpathia*, the ship would detonate its first ICAN-II-style charge and then continue, accelerating at three gravities into orbit and beyond. This would, everyone hoped, minimize the possibility of fallout.

"Satellite shutdowns in progress," Ops continued. "Ground-based systems shutting down or prepared for nuclear EMP effects."

Stephanie bit her lip at that. She was still embarrassed that she hadn't thought of *that* little problem—the electromagnetic pulses that would result from the detonation of multiple nuclear explosions near Earth. But the engineers had, and there were widespread contingencies and safeguards to minimize the effects. There *would* still be effects, and not good ones, but with the engineers' anticipation of the possibility and the cooperation of all the countries, it shouldn't be catastrophic.

"Security," came a new voice. "Whole bunch of news crews heading toward the site."

"Twenty-three minutes to launch, Security. They need to get under cover *now*. Shoot tires if you have to."

"Some have sent up drones."

"Let 'em," came Werner's voice. "They might get footage of the detonation launch, then the nuke pulse will flatten them. They're not going to interfere with *Carpathia*; a full-size Predator loaded with explosives wouldn't manage it."

We chose a few reporters from around the world to watch. They're in the bunker, getting footage from telescopic setups and shielded recorders they got cleared. The rest only caught wind of it once we went into launch mode. I sure hope they don't screw around with Security.

She cringed from the image of Security having to use lethal force on some literally too-stupid-to-live news people, but after the attack by the Group, Security wasn't playing games. *And I don't want them to.*

"T-minus fifteen minutes. All umbilicals released. Launch hardware retract. *Carpathia*, verify nuclear pulse go for launch."

"Ops, *Carpathia* confirms go for launch. Nuclear-pulse systems all nominal. Crew and cargo secure. Last of the Bells onboard and secure."

"Confirmed, *Carpathia*. We are go for launch."

"Security here. News crews contained and under cover. One injury, no other casualties. Vehicles cannot be secured before launch."

"Understood, Security. We'll deal with that after."

"T-minus five minutes. Launch charge trigger is live, repeat launch charge trigger is live. Total detonation estimated at twelve to thirteen kilotons, repeat, kilotons. Last call, verify entire launch site is clear."

"Ops, this is Security, we verify all buildings were swept, all evacuated or in designated safe locations. We are go for launch."

"Confirmed, Security, site is clear, go for launch."

Stephanie took a deep breath, then slowed her impulse to take another. *Don't need to hyperventilate now. Oh my God, this is really happening. I'm about to go into space on a* nuclear-pulse rocket. *York, God, I wish you were here. If you're up there somewhere, keep an eye on us, will you?*

"T-minus thirty seconds, all systems go for launch. Timer is set, past first stage abort. Twenty seconds.

"Ten. Nine. Eight, Seven. Six. Five. Four. Three. Two. One."

Even through the insulation and soundproofing, there was a deep shuddering thunder and impact; Stephanie was squashed down by a baby elephant that had just rolled over on her. *Five gravities total. Originally planned on four, but changed it last-minute so anyone calculating on the launch acceleration would be off, have to readjust.*

The incredible sound and weight went on forever, as her screen showed *Carpathia* vanishing in an apocalyptic detonation of fire and smoke, a shock wave flattening Carpathia City to wreckage in a single terrible moment.

The acceleration dropped away as the titanic ship rose, still shadowed and blurred by billows of flame and a rising pillar of black and gray. But it continued to climb, contemptuous of the hellish clouds and gravity itself. Stephanie felt the ascent slowing, the great ship preparing to plummet back to the Earth a thousand feet and more below. *Jesus, no, the drive's not firing...*

A new sun blazed briefly beneath *Carpathia*, blasting away the clouds of the first explosion and hammering her skyward. Another, driving Stephanie deep into the cushions, and another, the cannon barrage of Creation itself firing *Carpathia* skyward on the energies of the atom.

Though four gravities were crushing her chest down, three from the drive and one from the jealous Earth still trying to hold them, Stephanie thrust her arm skyward and gave a whoop of triumph as the interplanetary Earth Vessel *Carpathia* thundered its way skyward... and other voices answered her over every speaker, laughter and victory as powerful as nuclear fire lifting *Carpathia* toward destiny.

PART IV: JOURNEY

CHAPTER 39:
ONE FINAL OPTION

"They're clear to orbit, Madam President."

President Sacco nodded, eyes still filled with the image of the gigantic *Carpathia* and the sun-bright flashes of her drive, with the clouds of its launch now dispersing. "My God, we did it." She spun to Secretary Deng and without warning the two of them hugged, laughing, and repeating *"We did it!"* like two fans cheering after their team won the title.

Suddenly she was aware of the stares around her, and both security teams just easing back. "Um. Excuse me, General Secretary."

Xi Deng laughed again as he released his own hold. "No apologies needed, Madam President. None of us were sure that we would reach this moment...and it certainly lived up to my grandest visions." He grew solemn. "Now we must hope they arrive intact."

"Yes." *Carpathia* would pause acceleration briefly once she reached geosynchronous orbit, but unless some fatal flaw were discovered, she would immediately depart for her rendezvous with *Fenrir*. For all intents and purposes, *Carpathia* was now on her own, would soon be traveling faster than any other vessel made by human hands, where only light itself could catch her.

If something went wrong, all they would be able to do is watch.

A voice spoke in her earbud. "Madam President, we have some updates for you."

"May the general secretary accompany me?"

There was the usual hesitation at the thought, but after a moment, the voice—Bruce Sperling, she thought, one of the new security heads—replied, "I see no reason why not. This is all *Carpathia*-project related."

"Mr. Secretary, we have some updates; would you care to accompany me?"

"Certainly!"

The bunker included a moderate-sized briefing room, which was fairly full by the time the two entered. In addition to the security personnel stationed around the room, Roger Stone was there, along with Eva Filipek, George Green, Hailey Vanderman, and General Rainsford. A screen showed that Mitchell Ennerby was attending remotely, as usual; the NASA head was personally monitoring the tracking and communications coordination for *Fenrir*.

"Well, here we are," Jeanne said, sitting down. "What's the latest, Eva?"

"To address our biggest worry outside of sabotage—which, thank God, doesn't seem to have happened yet—the fallout issue appears to be minimal. Any concentrations of note will be limited to the lands already owned by the government, and most of it here on the test grounds. Even the immediate area should be relatively safe to approach in a short time, with appropriate precautions. You would *not* have wanted to be out and unshielded anywhere nearby, but the primary radiation was the major threat."

"Thank goodness for that. Anything else on that subject?"

"Well...it does mean that in theory you *could* possibly land *Carpathia* again. I wouldn't *recommend* it, and everyone would have to stay inside until basic decontamination was carried out, but it could be done with some preparation." She looked at her screen. "All the detonations appeared to fit the planned parameters, so as far as we can tell the ICAN-II-based drive is working perfectly."

"Thanks, Eva." She looked over to Xi Deng.

"Very good news," he said. "Can we study this landing possibility? I agree," he said quickly, as he saw a concerned glance from Eva Filipek, "that this is not something we would *want* to do, but we should know how to do it just in case, yes?"

"Yes, Mr. Secretary," Eva said after a moment. "We'll do some studies, and send your people the data so they can look at it themselves."

"Excellent. Please proceed, Madam President."

"Victor, EMP effects?"

"Not good, but within our expectations," Rainsford answered. "The joint task force deployed everyone we could get in the last year to calculate the EMP range and strength and be able to minimize the issues. We grounded all aircraft that we could before launch, and they're now all undergoing full inspections and testing before being allowed to take off.

"That's . . . not going to be easy everywhere," he went on with a professional frown. "Not all of them were shielded—couldn't manage it in the time frame—and some of those I'll guarantee got fried, especially the ones closer to the launch site. Even with precautions, we've lost billions of dollars in satellites; Daire Young's Skyweb might have taken a twenty percent hit by themselves. GPS satellites are okay so far, but we'll have to watch what happens as *Carpathia* accelerates to geosynch.

"Groundside, lots of electronics nearer the launch region glitched out; might have lost them permanently or have to restart. This includes modern cars, communications—cell phone coverage is going to be patchy out this way for a while—and so on. Hundreds of millions, maybe a few billion to replace at least, and since a lot of it's in civilian hands we'll definitely be on the hook for it. *Carpathia* still needs public support, and we can't look cheap if we want to keep the goodwill."

"This was included in our budgeting discussions," Secretary Xi Deng said. "Have we covered this situation?"

"Oh, there's definitely resources in the budget for it, but maybe not enough," Rainsford admitted. "As often happens, reality costs more than the estimates. Once we have firm numbers we'll send them to FORT."

Jeanne nodded along with her Chinese counterpart. "Thank you, Victor," she said. "Roger, what have we got on your end?"

"Those reporters that tried to jump the gun are all safe—one of them broke his arm when he was arguing and fell over a guardrail, but he'll be fine. And yes, that's actually what happened—video's available. Don't know if any of their vehicles are salvageable, we'll check once we get the all clear; they were on the edge of the orange zone, so maybe they got lucky. Their drones are all toast, of course, but they got a few seconds of the initial launch before the first nuke detonation.

"On the positive side, our legit press corps did a bang-up job working with our people, so everyone got what they wanted there. Networks are already working up their own best sequences, and the on-hand reporters were all blown away—in the good sense—by the launch."

"Good. Let's try to placate the intruders, but not too much. If they'll accept they screwed up, maybe we can get a couple on them into the site inspection, throw them a bone."

"Will do."

"Hailey, I see you've been restraining yourself. I suppose you have something I don't want to hear?"

"None of us *want* to, no," Hailey Vanderman conceded, "but it's important anyway. The Group *does* have an agent on board—or did, shortly before the attack."

Jeanne felt her gut tighten, and saw from his expression that the General Secretary felt the same. "Who is it, Hailey?"

"We don't know, not yet," he answered, face angry and apologetic at once. "What we *did* find is a couple of references to them having arranged for the final option, with just enough detail for us to know that means destroying the *Carpathia* once she's underway."

"But the *Carpathia* completed her launch," Xi Deng said, puzzlement warring with hope. "Surely that would have been the best time for sabotage to destroy her?"

"In some ways yes, but not in other ways. And not actually in line with the Group's general goals, when we dug down a bit." Hailey brought up a display showing the history of the Group's activities. "Their main thrust at the beginning was trying to stop or delay the launch by very indirect means—messing up manufacturing schedules, introducing flaws in expensive, hard-to-duplicate elements, that kind of thing." He nodded to George.

"But," George Green said, picking up the briefing, "all those things were *expected* to be detected well before launch. Until that one final assault, none of the attempts to stop *Carpathia* were intended to have any large-scale threat—a few people might be injured or killed, but it's clear from their documentation that it was the *ship* they wanted to stop, not the people. Needle herself did not care about deaths per se, but even she had no particular interest in causing wholesale slaughter.

"Specifically, none of them wanted a nuclear-and-antimatter-powered vessel blowing up *in the atmosphere*, or really any time until after it was in higher orbit. Many of their members are anti-nuclear power, after all. The idea of dropping something carrying tons of nuclear explosive charges somewhere back to Earth was horrifying to them; it could kill uncountable numbers of people in addition to the crew."

Jeanne grimaced. "But that's not how it would *work*, as I understand it."

"Correct. The antimatter all letting go would be very bad, but limited to a small area around the ship," Eva Filipek confirmed.

"Not all the Group would have understood or believed that," Hailey said. "To be fair, this was a ridiculously experimental approach that no one would have believed we could get away with a few years ago. In any event, the information we recovered is clear. Their 'final option' is not to be deployed until *Carpathia* is safely away from Earth, where no one but the crew will be endangered."

Angus? Is he the "final option"? The question still was not yet answered, and Jeanne *hated* that. After his unquestioned heroics, it felt terrible to suspect Angus Fletcher of planning to kill the friend he'd risked his life to safe, but he was otherwise such a strong candidate.

"Then if they do have someone on board, they will strike very soon," Xi Deng said. "We must discover who they are as soon as possible."

"We're working on it, Mr. Secretary," Hailey said. "But for now, all we can do is warn them that an attack is likely."

And if we can't identify them first, Jeanne thought, *all we can do is hope that Peter Flint's right.*

CHAPTER 40: MIRRORS OF DETERMINATION

Almost time.

Silver was not looking forward to this in *any* way. First and foremost, of course, he would have far preferred to go back home and run his business again, maybe retire in a few years. He had hoped and prayed (even though he really wasn't much for religion) that the Group would succeed in stopping *Carpathia* long before it got to this point.

It would also be much easier if I really did not like any of these people.

It must, he decided, be something to do with getting older. He had spent most of his lifetime planning his relationships; even if he *enjoyed* the interactions, they were kept separate from, for lack of a better word, the *core* of Angus Fletcher. *But perhaps sentiment comes more easily when the end is already in sight.*

The fact was that most of the *Carpathia* crew were good, decent people on fire with an ideal—a terrible, dangerous ideal, but one all too understandable if you were more an optimist than a realist. This was nowhere truer than with the director, Stephanie Bronson. She was a True Believer—Silver had known enough to recognize the type. She was wholeheartedly behind her ill-advised rescue mission, and that passion had caught up the public, and not an inconsiderable number of the movers and shakers.

One gravity now for a few hours. The orbital departure acceleration would send them flying toward a rendezvous with *Fenrir*, to match orbits with the alien vessel not all that far outside Earth orbit but a quarter of the way around, a curve well over two hundred million miles long. Maneuvers to match orbit would take some time, but in a very few months *Fenrir* and *Carpathia* were going to meet.

Or *would* meet, if he didn't stop it.

Even in these final hours, his brain was insisting on trying to find a way to save at least *some* lives, especially Peter's. But he couldn't see any way to get people to attempt an evacuation; they wouldn't leave under threat, that much he was certain of. Even if a few would consider it, there were more than enough trained troops of half a dozen militaries on board to mount any kind of assault they found necessary—and if he allowed time for evacuation, the odds were a hundred to one that those troops would find a way to neutralize one man.

Given that, doing this as quickly and thoroughly as possible was the only reasonable course of action. No one need suffer, no one have to stare down their own death except for himself.

I truly regret destroying this ship. It was the third of the reasons he hated this final task. The *Carpathia* was the greatest achievement of the human species, a nuclear-powered rescue vessel built by the combined will of humanity. It *should* survive, a shining beacon to the best humanity could offer, a symbol of what Earth could, and should, become.

It was cruelly ironic that it was that very purity and nobility of purpose that required its destruction.

With a sigh, Silver cleared his mind of all such concerns. The question was whether he should act now, during the outward acceleration, or wait until that was completed and the living quarters spun up to gravity, the crew standing down from active stations.

Right now, all people not actively involved in the operation of *Carpathia* were to remain in their cabins, just in case. That meant the corridors would be mostly empty, and he would be unlikely to encounter people by accident. On the other hand, it meant that if Keys's disinformation programs malfunctioned in any way, he'd be easily spotted. The opposite argument applied to the situation after acceleration.

Silver contemplated that for a few minutes, then shrugged. *I'm going to have to trust Keys's work in any case. His work's never played me false yet, I'll have to hope he keeps his perfect record an hour or so longer.*

Given his position on *Carpathia*, Silver already had a very high level of access; this allowed him to deploy the first set of Keys's tools with considerable latitude of authority. The fact that certain of Keys's prior arrangements in *Carpathia*'s software suites had managed to pass unseen through the QA and security processes helped immensely.

A quick examination of status showed that *Carpathia* was, thus far, working flawlessly, and the crew was settling into a temporary relaxation as the ship drove forward into deep space. There were very few people in the corridors, and automatic monitors all showed green.

Time to ring some Bells. It was admittedly more than a bit rude to use his friend's inventions this way, but he was unlikely to learn of it before the end.

Silver was never quite sure what it was that made him hesitate. There was no indicator to warn him, no hint that things were not exactly as the should be, but just before he sent the command to wake up Liberty and Zygmunt, he paused, and then brought up Keys's best sniffer probes. Instead of awakening the Bells directly, he imitated a standard status inquiry that he'd learned could provide a backdoor into the Bells, and let Keys's software do a check.

The result almost made him curse aloud. There were new conditionals entered into the Bells' operating code—conditionals that would have had both the Bells screaming bloody murder if he'd activated either of them.

Studying the statistics and patterns on the screen, Silver felt a cold sweat break out, only slowly going away as he assured himself he had not, in fact, tripped any of the dozen traps that had been laid. *That is not Flint's code, either. Not his company's.* No, something about the design screamed *intelligence agency* at him. Which one didn't really matter; someone had realized that there might possibly be a suicidal agent left on board, and if so the Bells would be an excellent tool.

As he calmed himself, Silver realized that this could be to his benefit. He'd seen the trap. With Keys's toolset, could he *disarm* it? Keep the things from alerting anyone? If so, they'd likely never know anything was happening, confident that anyone trying to use the Bells for sabotage would be caught.

It took more than half an hour—more time than Silver liked, but this wasn't a job to rush—before he restarted the Bells and found both of them under his control, with no alerts being sent. As far as any external monitor would be concerned, both Liberty and Zygmunt were sitting quietly in their charging stations, locked down for transit.

Disinformation program now running to show empty corridors along his path, Silver eased himself out into the thunder-echoing corridors of *Carpathia.*

The grating buzz jolted Peter out of his slide toward a relaxing nap. *Dang it! That first big burn really took it out of me.*

But the fog cleared as the sound finally *registered.*

Someone was moving the Bells.

Ignoring the little stabbing aches and other reminders of both age and multi-gee acceleration, he levered himself out of bed and checked the indicators. *I'll be dipped. Not a single one of the system alerts went off.*

That was *damned* worrisome. Someone who had that kind of capability might be able to pull off pretty much *any* sabotage they wanted. The alarm he'd gotten was from his own last-ditch trick, putting a simple pressure sensor under each Bell, linked to his own personal network.

The signals showed it was only two Bells out of place—Liberty and Zygmunt. More than enough for any sort of mischief, of course, integrated into ship's systems as the Bells were.

Peter sighed and pulled on his clothes. He was going to have to do some work.

Silver stepped quickly to the two twitching soldiers and gave each an injection. He was quite conscious of the irony of using nonlethal means on men about to die, but using regular firearms would be too noisy, even in the repeated *WHA-THOOM* of the nuclear-pulse drive, and he didn't want to deal with the crudity and mess of stabbing hearts or cutting throats. A powerful tasering followed by a powerful sedative would keep them out of the way long enough.

The secondary pulse drive channel lay just beyond. With Zygmunt serving as a rear guard, Silver moved forward. Liberty had the toolset and Silver had the software tools to allow him to extract one of the premanufactured bombs and then charge the antimatter detonator. With the little plug inserted, it would just be a matter of waiting a few seconds.

A moderately large bomb charge would suffice; a few tens of kilotons in the main structure would vaporize or shatter everything except the drive plate and the main shock absorber shafts.

"Really would prefer you not do this, Angus."

Of all the voices he could have heard, that was the one he had least wanted. He turned slowly, expecting to see soldiers lined up.

Instead, it was just Peter Flint. The older man was leaning on Zygmunt, simply watching.

"Damn it, Pete," Silver said wearily. "You know I don't have much choice *now*. Unless you've already shut down Liberty?"

"No, Lib's still running on your side."

It didn't even occur to Silver to doubt it; there was no particular reason for Pete to lie, and it wasn't in his character. "Why?"

Peter nodded. "See, that's *my* question, Angus. Why? You're no antinuke campaigner, you're not some religious fanatic, so why're you willing to kill us all to stop *Carpathia*?"

Silver checked the readout. *It'll take a few minutes for Liberty to bring the charge here. If Peter hasn't set the alarm . . . I just need to buy time.* "Because the risk's way too great, Pete. Oh, I know the director's arguments. And believe me, I wish the world worked that way. But what would we expect from humans in their position? They came here to take a world. If they wanted to talk to us, they had every chance. Instead they kept coming, quiet, heading right to a position they were out of our reach but able to see everything we did."

"So it's a mistake to go out and help people? You can't believe that, Angus."

"*Your own people*, no. But these . . . people, they haven't a vested interest in our health, Peter." Liberty had almost extracted the charge. Now the only challenge would be getting the system to dispense the antimatter charge. "If they're all sweetness and light, sure, but *we can't take that chance*. We got an incredible stroke of luck when their drive blew. Let the damned ship get roasted a bit, then pick her up on the other side when there's no aliens left."

Peter shook his head. "That's just paranoia, Angus. Why couldn't they just be like us?"

"You have to know enough human history to know what happens when a technologically superior culture meets a more primitive one, Pete. They had a weapon that could *literally* sterilize our planet if they wanted—that drive. Might have others, or be able to make others once they saw us. Worldwide plague? Nanotech? Or just start throwing rocks at us at ten percent of lightspeed?"

Silver brought up the Taser. "Sorry, Pete. I like the idealistic view, really I do. And if it wasn't the entire human species at risk, I'd be willing to take that roll of the dice. But better they're all dead and we can take their tech, be equal with them the next time they come by, than we rescue them and find out too late that they didn't plan on being neighborly."

Peter Flint glanced behind him. Silver heard Liberty approaching with the charge.

"I am curious as to how you knew I was here. I was sure I'd removed the tripwires in the software."

A flash of Peter's smile. "Well, see, I'm an old-fashioned kind of guy. I knew they were putting in all sorts of software trips, but I figured I could just install a pressure switch myself under the brace. When it went to zero, I knew someone'd taken my Bells out for a walk."

Exactly his style; a straightforward solution too simple to hack. "Then why're you letting me get this far?"

"Wanted to hear your reasons, Angus. Knew you had to have *something* pushing you that wasn't plain stupid. I guess I can see your point, too. It *is* a kinda big risk we're takin', isn't it?"

Are you really listening? "We're risking *everything*, Peter. And now we're to the last option."

"See, that's where we don't agree. Not sayin' you don't have a point or two, Angus, but this is our chance to be the best *humanity* can be."

"And risk everything? You have friends and family back home, Pete. We're not just risking ourselves if it turns out the Fens want to take our help and use it to finish an invasion."

Liberty came into view, dragging one of the lantern-shaped charges. *No one else has come. Did Pete actually do this on his own? If it was anyone else I'd say that's ridiculous... but Pete might. If he did, there's still a chance.*

"Answer's yes, Angus," Peter said, voice carrying even across the repeated colliding thunder of the drive. "Dang it, *yes*. If the human race is going to survive, let's *deserve* to survive. We reach out our hands and bet on the chance of friendship—or on the fact that we're still the toughest, meanest bunch of beasts Earth ever made and that even *if* the Fens want a war, we'll finish it right here. But we start it by showing we ain't afraid to be friends, not scared of every shadow out there."

Angus suddenly understood what lay behind Peter Flint's calm determination: an unswerving confidence in *people*. He didn't fear meeting the Fens or fighting them for the simplest of all reasons; he *wasn't afraid*. He might not look forward to a war, or death, but the idea didn't scare him; it held no power over his decisions or ideals.

Damn, we're awfully alike. "You believe in that girl's dream *that* much, Pete?"

"See, Angus, it's not just her dream. It's that she, and everyone around the world, put the dream to the test. You think China or the USA or India or any of them haven't thought of every terrible thing that could happen?" Peter Flint took a step toward him—still without a trace of fear, just concern and certainty. "I believe Dr. Bronson's going to show the best face Humanity has to offer—and I believe our Captain Lín will show them the *worst* if they turn out to be a problem."

The charge was here. All he had to do was trick the drive system into producing a live detonation plug. There was a provision for making a dummy plug for testing and verification ... but it was simply a modification of the regular process. All he had to do was intercept the "arm and fire" process and replace it with the "deliver sample" process.

But he couldn't do that with Peter Flint watching him from a few meters away.

And—for just an instant—he understood Peter's vision. It was really his own, in a mirror; Angus recognized that any alien species had likely battled through the same dangers as humanity, and by their silent, confident approach the Fens were showing they were conquerors, alien yet familiar to any student of history. Peter believed that any such species must also have gone through all the great developments of humanity as well, that they must have gratitude and mercy to equal or surpass their hostility.

His arm dropped a fraction. "I get it, Pete. It's ... a beautiful vision. A *heroic* vision. Humanity with the olive branch in one hand and a shining sword in the other, ready to deliver either, extending the symbol of peace first."

"That's it. That's it *exactly*, Angus. Dang, you've got a way with words."

"But it's still too risky, Pete. I'm sorry. But there's no choice for either of us now. Thanks for . . . everything."

Pete tried to dodge, but Silver had been prepared for this. The electric charge threw the older man into a spasm and he collapsed, skidding along the floor and fetching up against the metal wall.

Silver ignored the jab of worry and the impulse to run over to Pete; if he'd stopped the older man's heart, he'd simply die a few seconds before everyone else. Instead, he turned to the console.

Something caught both legs in a crushing grasp. Before he could topple to the floor, another powerful grip captured his arms.

Liberty and Zygmunt had him in their manipulators, the two squat autonomous service vehicles anchoring him in place more surely than two Marine guards would have. *What . . . ?*

Barely had that thought registered than he understood. Peter took no chances. Put a contingency in the Bells for if they saw him shot down.

The Bells couldn't hold him forever; he knew enough about them to find a way to escape, even now. But time was going to be very, very short—

"Just stay still, Mr. Fletcher." Stephanie Bronson's voice was filled with tightly leashed fury, emanating from the speaker on Liberty.

And with those words, Silver knew he had no time left at all.

CHAPTER 41:
OPTIMIST AND
PESSIMISTS

The screen showed Angus Fletcher, stretched out on his cot in the tiny cell. For a man who had nearly murdered hundreds of people and could, for all he knew, be on the verge of execution, he looked remarkably relaxed.

"I wanted to talk to him *hours* ago," she said.

"And it was *not your call*, Director," Captain Lín replied. "The safety of the ship and its personnel is my *primary* responsibility, and as you know, in that capacity I outrank you and everyone else on board. First, I had to oversee the completion of our maneuver and get the *Carpathia* configured for long-term travel. During that time, Mr. Fletcher was taken into custody, stripped of all equipment, and all his possessions gone over with extreme attention."

"Meanwhile," Commander Robinson continued, "I oversaw the start of a detailed review of our software, using clues we got from Fletcher's operation."

Stephanie clamped her mouth shut and didn't speak for the count of five. This wasn't the time to be stupid. "Well," she said at last, "have we learned anything?"

"A lot." Robinson glanced at Fletcher's image. "There's a *slew* of potential backdoors into our systems, some of them partially hardware as well as software. Fletcher had a whole *suite* of software for making use of those backdoors."

"He volunteered some of the information," the captain noted.

"Saved us a considerable time hunting in at least a few cases. Whether he's still holding out on us, we don't know."

"He looks ... relaxed."

Lín grimaced. "He knows that we won't use enhanced interrogation methods, and he was already willing to die for his cause. Acceptance of one's fate is a source of peace."

The captain's matter-of-fact statement allowed Stephanie to relax a bit herself. *I didn't want to get into an argument about torturing people.* "I'm ... pleased we're not planning on going down that path, Captain."

"We are an international vessel overseen by multiple countries. The use of torture is officially acknowledged as ineffectual and illegal. I have no say in that particular matter, whether I agree with the position or not." Captain Lín's voice was so carefully neutral that Stephanie couldn't tell if he *did* agree or not.

"Can I speak with him?"

"Now, yes. We may learn something, or not, but we've done all the primary work." The captain gestured her to the door.

Stephanie looked at Angus as he sat up and smiled at her arrival, and shook her head, still not really able to wrap her mind around what he'd done, and why. "Just so you know," she began, "you haven't *quite* killed Peter. They think he'll pull through, but it was close."

Angus Fletcher's hazel eyes closed and a few wrinkles on his face smoothed out. "Thank God for that."

"You were going to kill *all* of us!" she snapped. "Don't try to convince me you really care what happened—"

"Director," he interrupted quietly. "I know you'd like me to be just a villain, but I'm a wee bit more complicated than that."

She glanced to one side, saw Captain Lín's face touched with a hint of a smile. "Am I being unreasonable, Captain?"

"With respect ... yes, Director." Lín said after a moment. "You heard his words, but I don't believe you truly *listened* to them."

And maybe it's just that I was terrified he might have killed us all despite Peter's plans. Scared people, she knew, never made good decisions. At best, they got lucky.

"All right," she said after a few moments. "Let's start again. You were a member of the Group, yes?"

Angus's laugh was quick and sharp. "I *was* the Group, Director. Put it together myself, chose the first cell, directed the strategy."

Hearing the matter-of-fact statement, Stephanie began to accept that maybe—just maybe—this background of fear was going to end. "So you and the Duchess—*Needle*, was it?"

"Needle was what I called her. I was Silver"—he gestured to his well-kept white hair—"and the other two were Keys and Lathe. Knew their real names, too, of course, but kept from ever using them. Best way not to make a slip is to stick with the story even when you're in private."

"So there's no other Group agents on board?"

Captain Lín gave another short laugh. "We can't believe any answer he gives here."

"On the contrary, Captain, you've survived my last-ditch efforts. My only hope is that some of you make such utterly terrible mistakes that I can escape, entirely unwatched, for long enough to be able to complete my little maneuver . . . assuming it's even possible anymore. I am rather cynical about my chances there. And given that I *have* failed, I am stuck hoping I am one hundred percent wrong and that Director Bronson is right, because that's the only way I'm living through this."

"You'll be living through it to be thrown in one of the most escape-proof cells ever made," Stephanie said.

"Possibly, but even then, better than being dead. I can't pretend there isn't a certain amount of relief in still being alive."

It was hard to maintain her image of a cold-blooded murdering killer with Angus smiling cheerfully from his cell. "I just can't believe you found so *many* people that scared of meeting new neighbors."

Angus took a drink from the water glass near him, one steady under the artificial gravity of rotation. "Director—Stephanie, there's a lot of people on my side. A few of them on your crew, even if they're not willing to take those last steps. Sure, some of them—most, really—are crazy by any standards. The so-called environmental greens who'd rather send humanity back to a starving medieval culture than allow us to put up another nuclear power plant, the religious fanatics who can't handle the idea of God having more than one chosen people, all that and more.

"But the ones that look out there and figure any species that crosses that black gulf's something to worry about? There's a lot more than you think."

Captain Lín cleared his throat. "He's correct, Director. It's part of our job, in fact." He nodded to Commander Robinson.

"What?" She stared at the two highest officers of *Carpathia*.

Ben Robinson took a deep breath. "True, Director. You're in charge of the mission. We're here in case the Fens aren't on board with peace. Which is what a hell of lot of people on the committees expect."

"You . . ." She paused, remembering the ways in which others had sometimes looked at her, or spoken of the future. "I thought everyone saw the potential of a rescue, what it would *mean* to the relationships between the Fens and humanity."

"Most of 'em probably did. Hell, *I* did," Angus admitted with a laugh. "You sell it brilliantly, Director. Thing is that people in the position of public safety can't live on the *good* assumptions. Not their job. Their job's to look at the worst."

She looked at Lín again. "So is my mission here a lie?"

"No, Director," he said instantly. "But . . . many apologies for being so blunt . . . it is important you understand how precarious your position was. Several of the votes on the direction of the *Carpathia*, on its true mission, were decided by as little as a single vote from one country."

Jesus. She hadn't realized how much of her confidence had been founded in the absolute conviction that almost everyone *agreed* with the obvious need to do the right thing, and the realization that she was *wrong* was a sobering, and frightening, thought. "One vote."

"More than once, yes."

"And you're . . . more on his side of the fence?"

Lín's face went momentarily stiff. He closed his eyes, then heaved a breath. "If you wish to put it that way . . . I am *forced* to be more on 'his side' because that is my job. As the captain of *Carpathia*, my responsibility is the safety of the ship, its passengers and crew, and ultimately that of Earth. Which side would you suggest I be on?"

"I—" She clamped her jaw tight. *What would York have said?*

After a moment, she met Lín's gaze, and that of Robinson. "You have to be on that side," she said, dragging the words out by main force of will. "Of course you do. I'm the optimist, you have no choice but to be the pessimist when it's the two of us making the decisions."

She saw both the captain's and first officer's stiff spines relax just a touch. "Thank you for understanding, Director," Ben Robinson said.

"And please also understand that we are here to give you every chance we dare to prove us cynics wrong."

She looked at the whole situation and laughed.

"What's struck you so funny?" Angus asked.

"I didn't think of myself as Teddy Roosevelt, but I guess we're going to fly peacefully and carry a big stick."

The joke broke the rest of the tension between her and her co-commanders—thankfully. "Let's talk," she said, and turned back toward the observation room.

"A moment, Director," Angus said.

She looked back at the older man.

"Might I at least be able to see updates on our progress? Whether I get to eat my words or say I told you so, it'd be nice to see things as they happen."

She thought a moment. "I don't see why not—as long as our best people make sure you can't use *that* against us. I'll leave that part to the captain and his people."

"Understood, Director. Commander, I'll leave it to you to set up a secure feed for our prisoner."

"Got it, Captain." Robinson saluted.

A few moments later they were back in the observation room. "So, Captain, how do we handle him?"

Captain Lín looked to Ben Robinson. "Depends on how much we believe him, ma'am. If he's telling the truth, the only way he's a danger is if we screw up by the numbers, more than once. If he's lying, if there's another member of the Group on board, we need to find that out as soon as possible." Ben's eyes looked to Angus with an arctic chill.

Oh God. "And how would we manage that?"

"We can give him a more thorough interrogation, especially with more information from the investigation on Earth," the captain said after a long pause.

Stephanie felt the tension return to her gut. *So we do have this discussion, after all.* "How 'thorough'? What do you mean by that, Captain? There are a lot of meanings of 'interrogation.'"

The two men looked back at her. Clearly they preferred not to commit themselves to any particular definition . . . or restriction.

And on their side, maybe that makes sense. Angus lying puts the whole ship in danger. How far are you willing to go to make sure that's not true?

She met their gazes and thought it through. "Captain. Commander. I understand the concerns, and that this is a sufficiently unique situation that we could likely justify any actions we chose to take.

"But the fact is that we could *never* be sure he was telling the truth; you know that, I know that. If he's really smart, and planned ahead, he could even give us information that makes things *worse*. So in the end, we'd have to make the exact same call, and I'm making it now. Unless we get other evidence to the contrary, I'm assuming that Angus Fletcher, aka 'Silver,' was the Group's final weapon against us. Angus will, of course, be kept locked up and under constant observation. There will be *no* privacy for him to hide behind."

"I have your permission to take whatever actions are necessary?" Captain Lín asked.

"Necessary with the understanding we have reached here, Captain, yes. And obviously if the situation changes, you may assert your own authority as you see fit."

"For now, we will follow your direction, Director." A touch of a smile. "And hope none of us come to regret it."

As she left, the last words echoed in her head. *I sure hope we don't, either.*

CHAPTER 42:
A DISTANT BOOM

"I know this is probably a stupid question," Chris Thompson said, "but why aren't we still accelerating? Don't we want to get there as fast as possible?"

Stephanie saw Faye Brown look at her, and nodded, letting Faye take it. "It's a complicated balance, Chris," she said, putting down her coffee cup and studying her display. The secondary conference room was one of three such, about ten meters long and half that wide, provided with seats for up to sixteen people, each with personal displays and direct data connections. "Remember that we have to match speeds with *Fenrir* if we're going to be able to do anything worthwhile. So the faster we're going to get there, the harder we will have to brake, so to speak, on approach. That costs us more fuel both while we speed up, *and* when we slow down."

"I thought we had a lot—I mean a *lot*—of drive charges, though."

"We do, but we have no idea of what we might have to do. Remember that one scenario has us trying to use *Carpathia* to shift a significant chunk of *Fenrir* into a better orbit, if we can't get any of their drive working and there's more than a few Fens still alive."

"Also, each time you want to cut time in half, you have to double your speed again, and pretty soon that's a *lot* of acceleration," Stephanie added. "Plus, we don't know if the Fens can even detect us, but if they *can*, we sure don't want to look like a missile instead of a rescue ship."

The biologist nodded. "Makes sense."

"The captain's worried about that last part," Francine Everhardt put in. "Being mistaken for a missile or meteor and fired on automatically."

So am I. "It's a real concern," Stephanie admitted. "The only real way to tell a missile from an oncoming ship is at the end, when you see how it's trying to match in with you—either slowing down to a dead stop nearby, or heading for a high-speed intercept. Right now, we're on high-speed coasting, and they'll have to make decisions on their actions only at the end. A spaceship that size has to have ways of dealing with big meteoroids, and *Carpathia* is more than big enough to cause a lot of damage just from a collision—and is still so small that something like *Fenrir* isn't going to just dodge out of the way."

"So far we're not even *talking* to them, so how do we keep them from shooting at us?"

"Deliberately? Not much, that's on them. But by accident or automated system? We have to guess the likely ranges of their countermeasures and slow down *before* we get that close. The captain's got a bunch of people here and back home working on that." Stephanie pointed to a simulation of *Carpathia* closing in on *Fenrir.* "Any way we figure it, though, we're going to slow down to match them quite a distance off, then move in slower, maybe using one of the ACES."

Faye sat straighter. "Ah, new *Fenrir* updates coming in!"

Everyone looked to their own displays; by now, *Carpathia's* central systems had enough experience with the crew to know how to prioritize new data on their target. Stephanie got an overview with notations of key points, Chris Thompson got mostly the sensor indications most relevant to life, Francine Everhardt mostly orbital mechanics and other general structural information, and Jerry Freeman all the spectroscopic results.

"Whoa," Jerry said. "Something happened—looks like a blowout in a big compartment."

"Crap," Stephanie said quietly. "How big? Are we looking at *Fenrir* coming apart?"

"Oh, no, no, sorry, nothing *that* big. But it must've been fully pressurized. Looks like an explosion."

"SNIT picked up an IR flash," Francine confirmed. "Something went boom."

"Want the good news?"

"There's *good* news?"

"For us, yeah. I got heavy spectral lines for oxygen and nitrogen, along with a bunch of other stuff I think was part of the ship. I think they're running an atmosphere a *lot* like ours."

Stephanie found herself goggling at the spectroscopy expert. "Are you *serious*? How sure are you?"

"Serious, yeah. How sure . . . umm, well, I'd say it's a lot better than fifty-fifty. Say seventy-five percent?" Jerry frowned, obviously thinking how to describe what he was seeing. "It's *possible* they had tanks of oxygen and nitrogen there for other reasons—it was a lab, for instance, one where they do work with gases. But this spectrum looks a *lot* like what we saw a few years back when there was a blowout on Daire Young's resupply rocket. Bigger, though."

Stephanie remembered that accident. The crew had been lucky—they'd been suited up because of an alert from a related system, so no one suffered explosive decompression and there were only minor injuries. Retrieving the crew had been a desperate operation, though. "What else are you getting?"

"Carbon and hydrogen, of course. Looks like aluminum and iron, that tungsten line we've seen before. What it all means, well, I'll have to dig into it with our people back home, but if you want a guess? With the tungsten in there, I think someone was trying to redeploy a piece of the radiator sail and things went wrong."

"Their orbit didn't change, did it?"

"Not noticeably," Francine answered promptly. "They might pass a few kilometers closer or farther from Venus, but that'd be about it. I think a single explosion that *could* change the orbit to any significant degree would break *Fenrir* into pieces. That said, there is almost certainly going to be a lot of debris—not just from this explosion, but from the original accident—traveling along with *Fenrir*. We've picked up a few larger pieces, in fact, but the smaller ones are not detectable from where we are."

Stephanie imagined *Carpathia* suddenly finding herself flying through a cloud of kilometers-per-second fragments. "Another reason to make our final approach slowly. Our radar will pick things like that up when we get close, yes?"

"Yes—though if the relative speed is kilometers per second, there won't be a lot of time to respond to smaller objects. On approach, the relative speed *will* be a lot of kilometers per second; we're going to be catching up with *Fenrir* at something like sixty-five kps on approach. But *Carpathia* is awfully heavily protected compared to any other spaceship we've ever launched, so that *shouldn't* be a big worry." The last bit of emphasis showed Francine was being cautious about overconfident pronouncements.

"How big a compartment do you think it was?" Chris asked. "I mean, are we talking about a living room or a skyscraper?"

Jerry and Francine both went to speak, then stopped, started again; finally the orbital specialist laughed and gestured for Jerry to go first.

"Lot bigger than a living room," Jerry said. "Spike of IR that Francine's shown me? For SNIT to pick that up from that far away, it was a hell of a boom. Not skyscraper sized, maybe, but a good-sized building going up. If they're anything like us, that was a major installation losing containment."

On a ship already crippled. That's got to be terrifying. "Hold on, everyone. I think this is worth informing the captain about."

It didn't take long to bring Lín up to speed. "I know this may not change anything, Captain . . . but it's a significant development."

"Very much so, yes. It implies our visitors are still having problems on board their ship. In answer to the obvious question, I think neither of us should decide alone if this warrants action."

Stephanie tightened her lips, but the captain was right. There were too many questions of resources, reactions, and so on to make a snap decision here. "We had better *both* be in on the discussion."

"I couldn't agree more, Director," Hàorán Lín said. "Commander Robinson and I will join you in Conference One to put together our query. Ten minutes?"

"I'll be there. Thank you, Captain."

"You're welcome, Director."

Stephanie stood up. "Jerry, Francine, come with me. Everyone else, keep looking at the updates." She headed for the door. "Looks like our rescue mission just got more urgent."

CHAPTER 43:
WORST-CASE SCENARIO

"I'd really like to discuss the situation in detail with *Carpathia*," Jeanne said. "Sending summaries back and forth is like trying to have a conversation via email with a dozen people. Very confusing."

"It would be even more confusing, and frustrating, trying to do it live." Hailey gestured at the status board. "*Carpathia* is the fastest man-made object ever, by a long shot, and they're now far enough away that we're looking at an almost four-minute one-way delay. You'd be waiting over seven minutes to get a reply for any question; standard hello-how-are-you greetings would take an hour."

"My God," Jeanne said. "Sorry, but . . . *God*. Four minutes for *radio* to get there. Are we sure they won't be getting to *Fenrir* soon? They're going . . . what, something over fourteen million kilometers per day, right?"

"Fast as hell, Madam President," agreed Victor Rainsford. "But they can't accelerate all the way then flip and decelerate—not if they want lots of options when they get there. That means they're headed on a free orbital approach to intercept that's going to have a straight-line distance of a bit more than a *billion* kilometers. So they've still got a couple months to go."

"Two months of relative boredom, and then everything will probably happen over a few days, maybe a week or two," George Green said.

"Well, everyone has had an hour to go over the communications," Roger said. "With your approval, Madam President, Secretary Deng?"

Xi Deng nodded. "So, Mr. Fletcher turned out to be our adversary. We are sure he is the last . . . yes?"

"*Sure*, no," Hailey answered promptly. "But likely, yes. Your people and mine agree on that, Mr. Secretary. Fletcher's cooperating as far as we can tell, and his interview records are consistent with the picture intelligence built up about the likely leader of the Group."

"Director Bronson—is she going to be a problem?" Green asked. When that caused multiple glares in his direction, Jeanne's not the least, Green set his jaw. "*Someone* has to ask it. She *clearly* isn't on board with any military action, and as far as I can tell she's willing to risk *Carpathia* and everyone on board on even the smallest chance that she can make peaceful contact with the Fens. Leaving aside the . . . *ridiculous* dollar value associated with that ship, there's more concentrated brainpower and skill on *Carpathia* than anywhere else on Earth, and politics and chance have put a midtwenties *astronomer* in charge."

Stone opened his mouth but Jeanne held up a hand. "George is right to ask the question. But first, George, the person in charge of the *ship* is Captain Hàorán Lín, not Stephanie Bronson. The files show he seems firmly aware of that position. Mr. Secretary?"

"As you say, Madam President. Captain Lín is one of our finest officers, and he has never shown any inclination to allow civilian input, even of the highest order, to interfere with what he sees as his duty." The smile and raised eyebrow hinted to Jeanne that this might have been one of the captain's biggest obstacles as well as best qualifications. "I have every confidence in his judgment."

"I second that for Robinson, his exec. Ben Robinson's one of the best, and once he and Lín got past their personal conflicts the reports are that they've got a good rapport. That said," General Rainsford went on, "both of them have a lot of admiration for our director. I think we can count on them to *not* override her unless they see real reasons to worry."

"Good, good. So let us move on to the more pressing matter of *Fenrir*'s condition," the general secretary said. "The explosion did not cause any additional *structural* problems, as I understand it?"

"None that we can tell, no," Eva Filipek replied. "Its location shouldn't be one to imperil main support members for the ship, but of course we have very little detail to work with. It's still *possible* that it will have weakened *Fenrir* in some fashion. Not much we can do about it."

"Do our people agree with *Carpathia's* assessment of the cause and of the information we've deduced from this event?"

"For the most part, Madam President." Hailey hesitated. "But we have additional analyses that may have a bearing on *how* it happened."

Secretary Deng straightened. "Similar to those of my people?"

"We're working very closely together on this, so yes, Mr. Secretary. With some more detail. Shall I go on?"

Jeanne looked at the CIA head with a touch of impatience. "Since I'm still in the dark, yes, Hailey. Illuminate me."

"Sorry, Madam President. We only just finished our own study, but I assumed—correctly, it seems—that the earlier conclusions of his people would have reached him already.

"So, we are all agreed that a room or several rooms, probably on the close order of forty meters on a side, suffered catastrophic disassembly. With a probability of ninety-five percent or more, this was due to an explosion of unknown nature that likely involved multiple materials in the region.

"Similarly, we agree that it's highly probable this was associated with an attempt to do something with an element of their radiator sail; current assumption is a redeployment, but the Chinese analysis points up a fair probability that they tried to jettison a damaged portion of the sail.

"Our *new* analyses, however, indicated something more disquieting. Combining the data we get from *Carpathia*—from a steadily widening angle with respect to Earth—and the entire data stream from every available space- and Earth-based instrument we can focus on *Fenrir*, we have been able to follow patterns of emissions. You recall we have already seen what appears to be multiple shifts in locations generating heat, yes?"

Jeanne nodded. "Repair work, perhaps, or . . . ?"

"We weren't really able to make much of a judgment on that. There's too much not known about *Fenrir*, its design, and of course the Fens themselves. But we now know a bit more, and this explosion had some *very* worrisome indicators."

The lights dimmed, and a rough diagram of the guessed-at structure of *Fenrir* appeared on the screen in outline. Faint flickers of dull red on the black background indicated shifting locations of emissions.

"So, here, about an hour and a half before the explosion, this emissions patch extends to a point that appears to coincide with the location of the detonation. You'll note that there's several other small active patches visible relatively nearby, but none actually adjacent.

"But at roughly fifteen minutes prior to the explosion, this other patch extends. It's now adjacent to our explosion site." Hailey advanced to another image. "And here, between thirty seconds and a minute prior to the explosion."

Jeanne leaned forward, gooseflesh suddenly springing out on her arms. "The second one darkened at the end. And didn't the site brighten?"

"Yes. As though whatever was causing this activity moved from a location separated from the site, directly *to* the site."

"As though something entered the area and perhaps *caused* the explosion," Roger finished.

"That is indeed one possible explanation. Which unfortunately fits with one of the least-palatable scenarios on board *Fenrir*."

"Dammit," Jeanne searched for another appropriate curse, settled for repetition. "*Dammit!* You mean there's at least two groups on board *fighting*?"

"Yes, ma'am," Hailey said, and the general secretary's nod supported him. "And depending on whether we call *Fenrir* a ship, or a self-contained city, that means *Carpathia* is flying straight into a mutiny... or a civil war."

CHAPTER 44:
PREPARATIONS AND
CONVERSATIONS

"Get *in* there, you stubborn son of a—"

With a metallic *chunk!* sound, the manipulator arm seated itself, and green lights finally showed on the status panel.

"Whew!" Peter Flint sat back, still glowering suspiciously at Zygmunt. "What's up with that? Usually goes in smooth as silk."

"Showing all good now, though," Heitor Almeida said. "We're good to go."

Pete felt his lips tighten, then sighed. "Dammit. Gotta pull it off and take another look."

"That'll hold up the test again."

"I know, I know. But if there's *anything* I've learned over the years, it's not to trust a machine to be working if it's not acting *exactly* as it should be."

Almeida bit his lip, then nodded. "You know the Bells better than anyone, Pete. I'll go with your instinct."

"Thanks. If we're going to use 'em to work on *Fenrir*, last thing we need to worry about is whether they're really in top shape."

With Heitor's help, Pete unlocked Zygmunt's manipulator arm and extracted it. The arm *felt* tight, tighter than it ought, even though everything had seemed right before they put it in. "Something's definitely off. Didn't *see* anything, but I'll be damned if there isn't something going on here."

It took fifteen minutes of careful examination, but finally a tiny glint of silver drew his gaze to the very top of the socket. "Well, will you look at that."

Heitor squinted. "What *is* it, Pete?"

"Not sure. Hand me that pick there."

"Are those *dental* tools?"

"Sure are. Great for detail work where you still have to exert real force. Now let's see what we . . . *dang*, wedged in there tight, aren't we? C'mon, just give a little . . . ah! That's got it!"

He held up the offending metallic strand. "Got twined right into the upper groove. So thin it didn't actually *stop* the socket from seating, just made it a bitch and a half to do."

The other man took the slender wire and looked at it. "I see that, yeah, but what *is* it? It's not a seal ring and it's sure not part of the wiring."

"Core of a twist-tie, that's what it is. Somehow the exterior got stripped off—you can see just a little of it left, here at the one end, see where it's black? Yeah, so the rest of it got stripped and then when we turned this around it ended up in the groove."

Heitor shook his head, giving a brief, appreciative laugh. "*Damn.* I don't think I'd ever have found it."

"Well, we'd sure have found it if we tried running this poor Bell that way. Strain probably would've wrecked the bearings." With the offending wire removed, the manipulator arm seated itself smoothly, and Pete nodded. "That's got it. All right, let's see if Zyg can get himself parked on *Ace of Spades* without help."

Zygmunt trundled its way along the corridor, used its manipulator to open the access hatch, and entered *Ace of Spades*. There was one sticky moment, when Zygmunt was trying to negotiate a particularly tight area of the shuttle, but the Bell's self-navigation suite managed to get clear after a few moments of back-and-forth. Shortly thereafter, Zygmunt reached the equipment cradle, slid to a halt, and locked itself in as directed.

"That's a success," Pete said proudly. "Means we can have them load themselves, instead of having to park them on board permanent-like."

"We have eight of them, though. Couldn't we just keep half of them on the ACES?"

Pete considered, rubbing his chin absently. "Might could, but I like having all the Bells working pretty evenly. Makes sure they all keep getting updates, checkups, track their operations so I can do some predictive maintenance. Lock four of them down, means the other four'll be doing all the other work around *Carpathia*."

"You're right," conceded Heitor. "And if we start prepping one of the ACES for an expedition, looks like the Bells can get into position more than fast enough."

"I'm pretty happy with their performance, I'll say that."

Heitor studied Zygmunt for a moment. "Can they be armed?"

"*Could* they? Sure. Just another manipulator swap. 'Cept, of course, I never built any weapon packages. They're engineering support devices, and I *really* don't want 'em turned into unmanned military vehicles. No one's drafting my little metal kids."

"Just thinking, Pete. We need smart maintenance gadgets way more than more weapons, believe me. But rumor is the Fens might be having onboard issues. If we're trying to work on *Fenrir* and they come after the Bell . . ."

"Better they smash up a Bell than one of us. And the Bells ain't *helpless*. A strong manipulator arm ain't anything you want to mess with, and that's if it doesn't have cutting or welding effectors on the end. Best if they're obviously just workhorses, I think. A horse can still kick, but you don't look at it the same way you do a lion, if you know what I mean."

"I think so," Heitor said after a moment. "Good way to put it, Pete."

"Well, you get to my age, you've figured out a lot of ways to say the same thing. Otherwise you get pretty boring." Pete climbed the short ladder leading back into *Carpathia*. "Now, I'm going to go clean up my tools; got some time off."

He had passed by a particular part of *Carpathia* more than once before, but this was the first time Pete found himself walking down the corridor. "Hey, Max," he said to the security guard on duty. "Can I drop in for a visit?"

Max's heavy face showed his surprise. "Well . . . sure, Pete. You're on the list the director gave. Just didn't expect you to come by."

"Really, I should've come by earlier."

The cell itself wasn't much different from the regular cabins; standard manufacturing processes in general dictated such things. Inside, the white-haired man was reading something from a screen before he looked up and saw the newcomer.

"Pete!" Angus said, a smile flashing out on his face. "Didn't expect you to come calling."

"Wasn't sure I was, to be honest. Looks like you're doing all right here."

"Can't complain about the accommodations, no. A bit monotonous, but that's part of the price you pay as a prisoner. Good to see you up and around."

Angus's expression sure *seemed* sincere. "Still trying to get my head around the idea you tried to kill me, and then want me to believe you're happy I'm alive, Angus."

"Cognitive dissonance is a thing," admitted Angus. "But as I told our director, there's professional and there's personal. I didn't *want* to kill anyone at all. Would've much preferred to just keep *Carpathia* grounded until this whole rescue idea became academic."

He grinned. "Not suicidal, either, so believe me, I'm almost as happy I failed as the rest of you. Still think this is a bad idea, mind, but as it's out of my hands, I'm in the director's corner now."

Pete found himself looking at Angus the way he might have a perpetual-motion machine. It shouldn't work, and didn't make sense to him, but it was *right there.* "How do you *think* that way, Angus? I genuinely do not get it."

The grin faded. "It was a lot easier before we started hanging out, honestly. Detachment's the answer. Don't let yourself get hung up on personal issues. Some might say I'm a sociopath; I'd disagree, but it's true enough that I spent a lot of time without letting my emotions get tangled up in other people's business."

"You're willing to kill a whole ship of people because you're *detached*? Hate to say it, Angus, but that's the words of a monster."

"Maybe." Angus's face was vaguely sad. "But I'm not a monster who hates humanity, at least. Idealism goes in more than one direction, Pete. You and the director, you've got one kind. Me, I had a different one, where I'm here to make sure humanity's innocence didn't get us all killed. A few hundred people compared to a few billion isn't a bad trade-off. Was that 'detached'? Yes . . . and no. I was trying not to be affected by the fate of *one or two* people, but I was—still *am*—scared stiff by the possible fate of the human race."

Damned if he doesn't mean it. Pete leaned back against the wall, looking at Angus thoughtfully. "I suppose we come at things different."

"Most people do. I'm not denying I'm an odd duck, Pete. Most people are..." Angus hesitated, raising his eyes to gaze into space as he searched for the right words. "...are *individual* focused. That can make someone a self-centered prick from the start, or someone who'll screw anyone outside his small circle, or—like you—someone who looks at each person and recognizes them as their own person. But they look to the individual, the friend or enemy they connect with, long before they look up and out. Not saying that's *bad*—it's the way most of us are built.

"But me, I always found myself looking at the *groups*. Helped in business, let me tell you; instead of doing things because a couple of people really favored it, I was able to see where the main interests went in the target markets. Once I understood that not too many people *did* think that way, I admit, I started working hard to *stay* that way."

Pete nodded slowly. "Suppose I get how that could work. There's a...different perspective in that kind of thought. So what changed?"

"*Fenrir,*" Angus answered promptly. "All goes to that, doesn't it? I wasn't the only one scared half to death knowing some giant alien ship was coming, but at first, there wasn't much to do. Oh, there were the usual idiots talking about getting ready to fight them, but the amount of power the Fens were throwing around? We didn't have a prayer in hell. All we could do was hope they didn't come here with a plan for genocide.

"Then *bang, Fenrir* had its accident and the whole equation changed. We had a chance again, and the best chance was to grab their ship once everyone on it was dead. I put together the Group and got ready to make that happen."

He grinned again. "But if I didn't want anyone suspecting me, I couldn't be isolated and separate. Security'd watch me a dozen times more carefully, then. So I had to find the right people to hang with, to be good visible friends." He shrugged. "And after a while, the cover turned out to be a wee bit more real than I'd planned." He rubbed the place where the bullet had hit him.

"That wasn't strategy, then."

"Hell no, Pete. If I'd stuck with the plan, they'd have put a hole right through your forehead, probably gotten everyone they'd targeted. I was *supposed* to stay out of it. Admittedly, dear Needle hadn't given me all the details of her assault, but I was supposed to just let her people do their jobs.

"Instead I blew almost the entire thing, saved you and indirectly a couple other vital members because all my detachment disappeared when I realized they were drawing a bead on you."

"Can't say I regret that. So what do you mean by being in Stephanie's corner now?"

"Like I told her and the captain, I accept I'm not pulling off my grand suicide plan anymore. Since that means we're stuck going to this rendezvous, I'm kind of *forced* to cheer for our naïve but determined leader. We're going to get there in time to do some kind of rescue, that much looks certain. We're still not nearly big enough to win a fight, if that's what they want—not unless we get ridiculously lucky. So all I can do now is hope she's right about everything."

"For what it's worth, I'm betting on her, too."

"Then you and your Bells keep an eye on Director Bronson," Angus said with deadly seriousness.

Pete straightened, seeing an utter lack of Angus's easy levity. "What do you mean? You know something?"

He waved at the screen in front of him. "I keep track of what's going on, Pete. They've been kind enough to let me do that much. You've seen what's happened on *Fenrir.*"

"That explosion sure doesn't make me comfortable, no."

"It damned well should scare the piss right out of you," Angus said bluntly. "What the hell do you think their little onboard tiff is about, hm?" When Pete didn't respond, Angus went on, "About *us*, of course. They've got to be scared pantsless, just like we would be if we suddenly found ourselves spinning out of control near a planet of unknown alien primitives. Then they see *this* ship charging out to meet them? I don't know about you, Pete, but I'd be a little nervous about a species that's riding a chain of atom bombs to my rendezvous.

"So I'm telling you: might be that one side of that conflict wants to welcome us with a red carpet and drinks all around . . . but the other side? They're talking *my* language, Peter, and if they get to start the conversation, it's going to be the last one any of us have."

PART V: ARRIVAL

CHAPTER 45:
ON THE EDGE OF CONTACT

"We are now a week away from rendezvous," Stephanie said, looking around at the assembled audience—some present in the conference room, many more on telepresence screens. "First, I want to thank all of you—including everyone who can't actually be in this conference—for all the work you've done. We've made the longest manned journey in the history of mankind on a one-of-a-kind, practically thrown-together ship, and made it work, even when things went wrong."

Nods were visible all around. Everyone remembered the glitch that had taken down a large part of the air-recycling systems for six hours, and of course there wasn't anyone who didn't know about Angus's attempt to calmly blow them all out of space. Other, lesser issues had involved everyone at one point or another over the last few days en route.

"So no matter what happens next, I want you all to know that *Carpathia* itself is a success in every way. Thank you." She looked around, then took a breath. "Now, we have to really face the fact that we *are* going to make first contact. First, let's look at what we know now. Francine?"

Dr. Everhardt gave a tight smile. "In the last few weeks, we've been able to get far better data on *Fenrir*, since we're now so much closer. Here's *Fenrir* as of our latest analysis."

The structure that appeared on-screen was in very broad concept the same as it had always been—a very long cylinder with some kind of ruff around the middle—but the details were drastically changed.

The most obvious and peculiar features were sets of strangely curved extensions—four sets, spaced at ninety degrees around the hull. To Stephanie, they each resembled a pair of slender *flamberges*, flame-bladed rapiers, joined at the hilt to make a double-bladed staff. The curves of the "blades" were gentler than on the actual weapons, and despite the apparent delicacy they were, in fact, absolutely immense constructs, running most of the length of *Fenrir*.

The "bow" of *Fenrir*—the part that had been facing the Solar System during its approach—bristled with multiple points, curves, and angular shapes that Werner and his team were pretty sure were antennas and sensors of various types. The huge extensions that had given the earlier versions the appearance of a star-nosed mole were revealed to be narrow spikes that ended in broader points, confirming their likely use as anchors for the ice shield. There were other antenna-like devices, less closely spaced, distributed about *Fenrir*.

The "ruff" was much more clearly a folded structure, the radiator sail they had envisioned, and it was also unmistakably badly damaged in multiple places—some parts were shapeless blobs melted down to the hull, while others showed their former structure more clearly but broken in various places. "Looks like some of the radiator's still intact," observed Ben Robinson. "Might be crucial if we're going to get their main drive going again."

On either side of the radiator sail were wide, rotating sections, each one about a quarter the length of *Fenrir*, obviously the living quarters. *Fenrir*'s stern narrowed, and the "bell" shape seen previously was now revealed to be multiple curved shapes fused together around the end—rockets or jets seemed the most likely explanation. Smaller features, spaced along the vessel, could also be attitude jets; others might be airlocks, mooring points, or, Stephanie admitted to herself, weapons mounts.

"We have no idea what *those* are," Werner said, indicating the wavy extensions. "It's tempting to assume that means they're part of *Fenrir*'s drive system, but without any more information, that would be just handwaving."

"How much does *Fenrir* mass, now that it dumped its ice shield?" inquired Captain Lín. "Half as much as originally, yes?"

"About, yes. Four hundred fifty to five hundred million metric tons," Francine confirmed. "We know they consumed something close to a hundred million tons of antimatter coming here; we have no idea how much they had to spare. We presume they weren't running this on a shoestring, but it also seems likely they didn't come here with the fuel to just turn around and go home. So some proportion of that mass is likely antimatter—at a very handwavy guess, still millions of tons."

"So it's also the biggest darn bomb we've ever seen, if they lose containment." Peter Flint shook his head. "I don't think I can even guess how big."

"For a second or two it will be as though the Solar System had two suns," Faye said. "If we are anywhere even vaguely near to *Fenrir* when that happens, *Carpathia* will vaporize, drive plate and all."

"Let's hope that doesn't happen, then," said Stephanie firmly. "They've kept it together this long, and obviously they know even better than we do how bad that would be.

"Now," she went on, "we have to prepare ourselves for what happens when we actually arrive. Chris?"

Dr. Thompson looked mildly alarmed at being put on the spot, but he stood. "We've already determined that it's likely there are at least two factions on board *Fenrir*. Based on everything we have found out so far, the positive side for contact is that they almost certainly have similar gravity to ours, according to the spin of the habitat sections, and they are oxygen-nitrogen-atmosphere dependent, like us, with a similar ratio of oxygen. They should be able to breathe our air, and survive in our gravity. Two major environmental issues shouldn't present us a problem.

"It's the response on arrival that will be the major concern. There are, really, three possibilities.

"The first is that they continue the silent treatment. We have to assume they have received our greeting and educational transmission; unless they're so alien that they can't understand our concept of communication, they *must* have a decent idea of how to contact us . . . if they want to."

"They're *alien*," Heitor Almeida said. "What's the chance they *do* understand? Aren't we making a huge assumption there?"

"It is definitely *an* assumption," Chris conceded, "but we don't think it's a 'huge' assumption. *Fenrir* looks a little odd, but it's not some Lovecraftian monstrosity. It's not hard to imagine some human group building that thing. Based on what we see, they've solved a lot of the same problems we have, in basically the same ways. Are there differences? Sure, but everything we've seen so far indicates that they have to have the same essential understanding of the universe we do in most areas. They may know *more*, but they seem to have gone through a lot of the same stages and ideas. So our transmissions should be understandable and sensible."

He paused. "Where was I? Oh, right. So if they stay silent, that's ... not good. We're going to have to decide how to get on board ourselves and be ready for really hostile reactions to our intruding. The *polite* thing would be to knock, then leave, but let's face it, Earth did not half bankrupt itself so that we could just pack up and go home.

"So, second possibility—once we arrive and are clearly trying to get their attention on the doorstep, they decide to talk with us. At that point, everything depends on what we end up saying to each other.

"Third possibility—they decide we didn't get the point of the silent treatment and go hostile. That"—he nodded to the captain—"puts everything in your court. Depending on what they have left to use, we might not have to worry about it."

Stephanie repressed a grimace. Two of the three possibilities could go very badly very quickly. The middle possibility, that they actually *talked*, could also go badly, but Stephanie had faith that any civilization that could do everything the Fens had done would not want to just bluster or threaten. But ... "Captain, your views?"

"Director, I sincerely hope the second option comes to pass. If it does not ... We have already been examining our options. One of the ACES will be the primary contact vehicle if we must physically enter *Fenrir*—which seems likely in several scenarios. We are attempting to locate entry points that are either actual airlocks, or that could be used for entry without any serious damage to any element of *Fenrir*." He flashed a deprecating smile. "The less vandalism we commit, the more likely we will be treated as possible guests, yes?"

"One would hope," Peter said.

"So. The ACES are, or can be, armed with moderate weapons capability, some weapons also doubling as tools; adjustment in specific layout and focus can make a laser a cutting tool or a weapon, for example. We have trained Special Forces personnel, with full equipment."

He gestured at *Fenrir*, floating before them. "However, if we assume the Fens are at all similar to us in outlook and preparation, even after their accident they may have many more weapons and personnel. *Carpathia* itself is our most powerful weapon, able to be maneuvered into any position and able to deliver a payload of anything from tens of tons to tens of megatons of TNT, repeatedly. It is, of course, also our most vulnerable asset and we do not want to use it if we can possibly avoid it. *Carpathia* does, however, have one additional possible use. Ben?"

"Thank you, Captain. We have been working with Werner's people on determining the best location and methods we might use if we are to attempt to divert *Fenrir* to a better orbit."

Francine Everhardt's laugh was short but loud. "When I first heard this idea, I thought it was insane. It turns out, it *is* probably insane... but could, just barely, work. A delta-v of one kps for *Fenrir* turns out to be about a hundred megatons. Using most of our remaining fuel in a continuous drive may just be able to affect *Fenrir*'s orbit sufficiently to prevent them from boiling alive. I would *not* want to try it—the obvious consequence is that we will be stuck *traveling* with *Fenrir* if we cannot somehow refuel—but it is just barely possible."

"Which is enough to justify our working on it, I think," Werner said. "Director?"

"If it doesn't keep us from doing our other work? Absolutely. I would like to see the details once you have them." Stephanie tried to imagine comparatively tiny *Carpathia* pushing on *Fenrir*. *It would be like Superman carrying an aircraft carrier. Wouldn't we just go right through Fenrir?*

"Absolutely, Director."

"And much as I don't like it, Captain, you have my complete support in preparing for the less-peaceful options. I want our people ready to deploy instantly, if things go bad. Let me know if you need anything from me, and I would also like to be briefed on your plans when possible."

"Thank you, Director." Hàorán Lín sketched a bow in her direction. She knew that he likely already had given such orders, but having everyone aware that she knew, and supported, his actions couldn't hurt. "We will make you aware of any details needing your support."

"Insofar as other preparations, most of you are already aware of them. Jerry"—she turned to Dr. Freeman, who was the de facto head of the overall sensing and analysis group—"I want your people to make sure we're listening on *every* frequency they might possibly use. We *have* to catch it if they ever try to talk to us; I want to know that we'll hear them even if one of them's calling us on a Radio Shack walkie-talkie from 1975."

"I'll tell the radio and laser people." Jerry grinned. "Promise you we'll hear them if they're using Morse code on a telegraph or blinking at us with a two-dollar flashlight pen."

"Thanks, Jerry." She stood. "All right, everyone—let's get ready to meet the aliens!"

CHAPTER 46:
EXTINCTION ON DEMAND

"Fuck," Stephanie said, making Peter jump; the director rarely swore.

Not that he couldn't sympathize. If there was ever a time for swearing, this was it.

"The captain's going to *hate* this," she went on, running fingers through her hair, staring at the frozen image of Eva Filipek.

"He'd hate not knowing it even more," Pete said. It was really an accident he'd been there for the transmission; he'd been going over potential uses for the Bells in exploring and repairing *Fenrir* when the high-priority call had come in.

Stephanie sighed and activated the crew comm. "Captain, could you and your exec please come to my cabin immediately?"

Captain Lín's voice was a touch distracted. "We are transitioning from deceleration to terminal maneuvers in only two hours, Director. Can this wait?"

"I wish it could, but no, it's vital."

Peter could hear the tone shift from distraction to concern. "On our way, then."

"Wouldn't it be better just to make it a general announcement?" Pete asked.

Stephanie answered after only a brief thoughtful pause. "No. No, that'd be a bad idea. Honestly, this scares the hell out of me, and I'm just glad someone thought of it before we actually got to *Fenrir.*"

The door opened and both Hàorán Lín and Ben Robinson entered. "Director."

"Captain, Commander Robinson, thank you for coming so quickly. I just received an extremely disturbing call from Earth, with Dr. Filipek doing most of the talking. The short summary is we *cannot* fight *Fenrir* even if they attack, at least not before we get a far more detailed understanding of key structures."

The captain's face grew stony. "I cannot defend my own ship, all the people we've brought with us?"

"Not by striking back at *Fenrir* directly." She glanced to the side. "Pete, you were here...?"

"I'm afraid Steph—the director—is dead right. See, we're used to dealing with...well, *sensible* things, and there's a couple damn nonsensical things about *Fenrir*. The biggest is that if *Fenrir* goes up, it's not going to just kill *us*, it's damn likely it's going to kill the Earth, too."

"Hold on. We're farther away from Earth right now—quite a bit farther—than the Sun is from the Earth. Even if *Fenrir* blows up all at once, our people said it'd be like there was another Sun for a second or two. That's just going to be a really bright flash. Maybe blind people who happened to be looking right at it, but how's it going to threaten the whole planet?"

Stephanie called up a graph from the data they'd just received. "We've got two huge problems. The first is the time frame. Even if they've distributed their antimatter around the ship, so all of it can't go up instantaneously, we're still only looking at *milliseconds* before a one-ton starting detonation causes the entire ship to blow up. There's more than enough matter on *Fenrir* to give us full conversion."

Pete was pretty sure Captain Lín's next words were obscenities in Mandarin. "So the 'bright flash' will be a few milliseconds that may be *thousands* of times brighter than the Sun. It could flash-burn the *entire hemisphere* facing the blast."

"And it is, in fact, worse than that, because uncontrolled antimatter detonations will, according to Dr. Filipek, radiate the majority of their energy as gamma radiation. There will be some flash and such from the vaporization of the remaining mass of *Fenrir*, but most of it will be gamma."

"That's worse?" Ben asked. "I was under the impression that our atmosphere protected us from gamma and cosmic radiation."

"That's at normal levels," Peter said. "See, the Sun puts out a *little* gamma but almost all of its radiation's in the infrared through ultraviolet, way less in the other bands. According to Dr. Filipek and others she consulted, the gamma pulse from something like *Fenrir* will irradiate the entire hemisphere, triggering secondary radioactive fallout that'll span the whole Earth."

"Jesus." Ben Robinson's face was going pale. "*Fenrir's* already damaged. They must've avoided that disaster by the skin of everyone's teeth."

The captain nodded. "You were right to call us in immediately. You are, I am afraid, correct. We dare not strike *Fenrir* unless we can be *certain* we will not cause an antimatter explosion. The loss of *Carpathia* is nothing compared to the potential extinction of humanity. And, I suppose, the Fens, as one of our scenarios is that this is a sort of 'ark' ship, the survivors of their species fleeing some other disaster."

Pete's chuckle had only gallows humor in it. "Or maybe fleeing exactly the *same* disaster. Seems to me that a civilization playing with that much fire might burn itself real easy."

"Why didn't our people think of this?" Ben asked after a moment.

Stephanie sighed. "Dozens of reasons, probably. The biggest being no one asked the right physicists the question, but others being the sheer scale and the distance we are from Earth. The idea something *artificial* out here could pose any threat to Earth is still hard to grasp.

"That said—I will bet one of them, or more than one, *will* think of it, and soon. They might be doing the calculations this minute. So if we want to avert disaster onboard..." She looked at the captain. "What's the next steps, Captain?"

"Let me think a moment, Director." Lín did exactly that, eyes closed, standing still, the only sound the muted, syncopated thunder of the nuclear-pulse drive slowing them to their rendezvous. At last he opened his eyes.

"Good judgment, Director, on not announcing this generally. Everyone *will* have to know, but we will need to distribute this information carefully. The knowledge that we stand, quite literally, a single accident from extinction will be a strain on the entire crew; it may be almost too much for some of us to bear."

"Also gives us a new insight into the Fens," Pete pointed out. "They're not fighting in a burning house, they're using flamethrowers in a fireworks factory. They've got to know that it's not just them, but all of us, at risk. Changes the perspective a little.

"If they came here to conquer us, well, they sure didn't want to sterilize the planet. If they came here to make friends, blowing us all up won't help. If they came here just to settle, not knowing there were natives? Even worse, 'cause now they could wipe out their new home *and* another species all at once. If they just dropped by on a stopover to refuel somehow, now the stakes are way higher than they imagined. Can't figure that *any* side in this mess wants this to happen. They must be on the ragged edge of panic all the time."

"Ugh." Stephanie made a face. "Panicked people make terrible decisions."

"Which we must avoid at all costs," agreed the captain. "Again, thank you for bringing this to our attention first. And you are right, we have to assume that out of all the bright people we have on board, at least *one* of them will think of this in not too long. Ben and I will work with our people to determine the best way to announce it—and soon." He turned back toward the door. "But for now we need to make sure we succeed in stopping how and where we intend."

"Go finish the maneuvers, Captain. Thank you."

As Lín turned to the door, his comm, Robinson's, and Stephanie Bronson's all buzzed at once. Stephanie hit the *answer* button. "Director Bronson."

"Director," came the voice of Dr. Jerry Freeman, "is the captain or exec with you?"

"Both of us are here, Dr. Freeman," said Captain Lín. "What is it? We have little—"

Jerry didn't wait for Lín to finish. "We've got a signal coming from *Fenrir*."

CHAPTER 47:
CALLS FOR HELP

This is it. Stephanie felt a distant sense of unreality. After more than two years of silence, a part of her had decided that they would never hear from their mysterious visitors. Now, in the last few minutes before their arrival, *Fenrir* had finally broken its silence.

But for what? To warn us off, or to ask for help?

The hastily assembled group in the conference room didn't include the captain or commander; they had to oversee the final arrival. *We may be sitting here when they have to convert back to rotation from acceleration configuration.* That would be a bit interesting; trying to carry on a conversation as gravity disappeared, then slowly reappeared, causing them to rotate ninety degrees.

Faye, Chris, Audrey, Francine, Peter, and Jerry made up the rest of the group in the meeting, and Stephanie turned to Jerry. "What have we got, then?"

"It's a weak signal, emanating from what we think is one antenna on *Fenrir* that rotated into position as we approached. Since *Fenrir* is still rotating, we lose the transmission for several minutes whenever the antenna rotates away."

"Can we understand it?"

Jerry nodded. "They've apparently been studying our teaching transmission all this time, and probably trying to use that to make sense of anything else they receive from Earth. It's using similar transmission protocols, too, and it's repeated several times—I'd guess waiting for a response. So without further ado . . ."

The faintness of the transmission was shown by the fact that even with the state-of-the-art reception, filters, and enhancement, the sound was fuzzy, sometimes barely audible. But it was unmistakably an understandable message, the first communication from another species.

"Ship of Earth, hope is for peace, for aiding in accident." The voice seemed to have some inflection, was higher in timbre; Stephanie would call it feminine, if it had been a human voice. Some of the overtones were definitely not human, reminding her of the resonances of creatures with large resonant chambers or bladders.

"Ship-ours hurt, fall with no control. Many of People lost. Need fix *entrisuji* engine."

"We assume that word is one our lessons don't give a clue about— not surprising if it's about a device we know nothing about," Jerry said. "We've given them things like the name of Earth and our species, but obviously there's lots of vocabulary they're missing."

"Warning-caution! Are hostile-fearful others, *Zalak*, are not friends, afraid of others. We of *Yuula* want friends, help."

Francine sighed. "That's about what we had expected, isn't it?"

"Based on what we have observed so far, yes, that's consistent." Faye gestured to a screen showing all their analyses and deductions prior to contact. "Multiple pieces of evidence now showing the likelihood of a conflict on board."

"Jerry, have we answered?"

"Not yet, no. That was definitely something to hold until you and the captain have a chance to have input on it."

Lín's voice replied, "It would seem to me that we must reply and obtain more details—exactly how we might help, who these . . . *Zalak* are, and so on. We'll also need to warn them of our actions ahead of time to prevent . . . unfortunate responses."

Stephanie knew what he meant. "Such as letting them know when we're deploying survey drones and that they aren't missiles."

"Among other things, yes, Director."

"I'm concerned that it's a single weak signal," Francine said. "If they're unable to do a more powerful transmission, wouldn't that indicate they're, well, severely limited in resources?"

"Not terribly surprising. The fact the ship's still out of control and that they've just confirmed it's in a state of internal conflict told us that they probably had very few functional systems available." Pete leaned back in his chair. "Seems what we most need from our friends is an idea of how we can actually get inside and what kind of repairs or help we can give them—without panicking the wrong people."

"Audrey?"

"*Me?*"

"Well," Stephanie said, grinning slightly at Audrey's startled expression, "you *are* publicity and communications. These people are communicating, and we need to spin things to make us sound good. Seems to me, you, working with people like Chris and Jerry, are our best shot for directing the talking."

"My job's focused on *humans*. I'll be happily transmitting this news back to Earth, but I'm not sure I'm the person to be talking to the aliens directly. Their psychology may be completely different."

"These words sound very much like what a human would be saying to us at this point," countered Francine.

"That might be partly because we're hearing something sent based on our own training program," Jerry said. "But Steph still may have a point. We'll certainly welcome any suggestions you have, Audrey."

She shook her head, but a smile touched her face. "All right, I'll see if I can help with phrasing. We're going to respond soon, I would guess?"

"Once the captain reports us all secure, I think," Stephanie said. "No point in putting it off. I think—"

The buzz made Jerry sit up suddenly. "What? I'm in . . . wait, *what*? . . . Are you sure? . . . Okay, run it through the translators and send it up here."

"What is it, Jerry?"

Dr. Freeman looked at them, a touch of a grin on his face. "We've got a *second* message already."

"A follow-up to the first?"

"Maybe not. This one comes from a different antenna, well offset from the first. Slightly different frequency, too. Ah, here it is. Putting it on."

This message was also faint and difficult to make out, but the voice was deeper—definitely not the same as the first. "Earth ship, a joyous greeting. Your stopping gives hope of help. Much aid needed.

"A warning, two groups of the People in conflict, other dangerous, expect deceit. The *Yuula* partly cause accident, fear humans. *Zalak* we are. Please answer; time reduces swiftly, ship fixing must be done, *entrisuji* engine revived."

A knot tightened in Stephanie's stomach as she absorbed the second message. "Well . . . dammit."

"Clever bastards," Peter said, a touch of admiration in his voice.

"Who? These *Zalak*?"

"That's the beauty of it, I don't know which one. Could be the *Zalak* are the bad guys, overheard the *Yuula*, and set this up in jig time to confuse the issue. Or maybe the *Yuula* are the problem and the *Zalak* just caught wind of their transmission and sent out this to keep us from making a big, big mistake."

"Indeed," Captain Lín said. "And we now have to find out which one is which . . . or we will be sending our aid to the group that wishes to destroy us."

CHAPTER 48: CONVERSATIONS

Director Bronson: We are very glad to finally hear from you. You have learned amazingly well from our transmission. *Carpathia* is preparing to launch a number of survey units to examine your ship so that we understand more about how we might help. Is this acceptable to you?

Yuula: We thank you for compliments. Is "Director Bronson" a personal name, a position title, or some other thing?

DB: A piece of both. My title is director, which means I am in charge of our scientific, technical and contact teams. My full name is Stephanie Bronson.

Yuula: My name is Imjanai. I am (perhaps?) director of the Yuula, along with Alerith. To your request, we understand this is necessary. Please do not make physical contact with our vessel yet.

DB: Nice to meet you, Imjanai. We understand and will not make any physical contact with *Fenrir*, which is the name we gave to your ship. Does your vessel have a name you use for it?

Imjanai: The physical vessel is *Tulima Ohn*. The ship's mind is named Alerith.

Director Bronson: We are very glad to finally hear from you. You have learned amazingly well from our transmission. *Carpathia* is preparing to launch a number of survey units to examine your ship so that we understand more about how we might help. Is this acceptable to you?

Zalak: We apologize for not speaking earlier. Many reasons, too long to discuss now. Thanks for your appreciation. We are nervous (word correct?) about your survey units, but understand necessity. It is acceptable if there is no contact between survey units and *Tulima Ohn*.

DB: *Tulima Ohn* is the name of your vessel?

Zalak: Is the name of the physical vessel. The overseeing intellect is Alerith.

DB: I am named Stephanie Bronson. My title is director, which means I am in charge of our technical, scientific, and contact divisions. May I ask your name?

Zalak: You may, Stephanie Bronson. I am called Mordanthine, and was in charge of ship maintenance and safety. Closest translation in your transmissions probably commander.

DB: I am pleased to meet you, Mordanthine. We understand your concerns and our probes will not make physical contact with *Tulima Ohn*.

"What have we learned so far?" Captain Lín asked, looking around the crowded conference room.

"A lot, but not what we really need to know is which side actually has it in for us. Or whether both do." Stephanie made a face. "Our linguists and your analysts are doing their best trying to squeeze more information out of what each of our main correspondents say, but they're really hamstrung by the fact that it's hard to tell when a variation of phrasing represents a difference in the actual personality we're talking to, or just a different choice by the translator."

Commander Robinson frowned. "They're not using the same translator?"

"The same core approach, but as a programmer might say, a different fork." Faye flashed a simple graphic up on the display. "We suspect that when the factions split, their collaboration ended, perhaps they each ended up with different working systems, so the shared base exists but their subsequent additions and updates have been separate."

Heitor Almeida picked up the discussion. "This fits with what we've been able to extract from them about this 'Alerith.' I think one side has a subsidiary unit and the other has the main one."

Captain Lín nodded. "Was I correct in my impression that Alerith is an artificial intelligence?"

"It sure sounds like it," Peter Flint said. "But it's one that makes our current AI look like old ELIZA; near as I can figure, the way they talk, Alerith is just as much a person as you or me, but smart enough to run that whole monster ship by herself for a century or two."

"But in that case, isn't it possible the real decisions are being made by the AI, not the, well, passengers?" Ben Robinson didn't look comfortable at the thought, and Stephanie didn't blame him. The issues with modern AI ranged from the amusing to the potentially disastrous, and no one had yet figured out to prevent the worst possibilities if, and when, AI went from "imitating some human skills" to "actually thinking for itself."

"An awful lot is 'possible,' Ben," she answered. "Yes, the two parts of Alerith might very well be running the show, but if they are, they're doing it behind the scenes, and I think we have to assume that the face of each faction reflects that faction's actual intent, even if the intent is really determined by Alerith rather than Imjanai or Mordanthine."

Lín nodded, as did Robinson. "Have we learned anything of more practical value yet?"

Stephanie glanced over to Francine.

"We've been working with Werner, Heitor, and Pete to get the Remote Inspection Survey Probes out, but *Fenrir*—excuse me, *Tulima Ohn*—is huge. The RISPs will get the data—they've got infrared, ultra-sensitive magnetometers, radiation sensors, the works—but really getting a handle on *Tulima Ohn*'s internals, even in a rough outline, is going to take a couple weeks at least. We've prioritized the magnetometer data, because we have to assume that they're still using some kind of magnetic confinement for antimatter; if not, we haven't a clue as to what to look for. If we can get a good idea of where and how the antimatter is stored, at least we'll have an idea of where a conflict *won't* trigger a disaster."

"We have some *tentative*, I repeat, *tentative*, conclusions drawn from our interactions thus far," Oded Singh said. Stephanie knew he was the captain's top intelligence analyst. "With your permission, Captain?"

"Please go ahead, Lieutenant."

"In general, the stories they have been giving us are reasonably consistent, so we are confident that the scenario of a conflict that led to some form of mutiny or insurrection, whatever we choose to call it, is correct. This conflict was related to the event that crippled the ship; whether that was a deliberate action by one faction or the other we are not yet certain."

He flashed a quick, apologetic smile from beneath his dark mustache and beard. "Both of our conversational partners are clever enough not to beat us over the head with the villainy of the other side, so it's still not clear which of them is which. However, the idea that one of them is terrified of and hostile toward us appears very likely. The other wants to make contact.

"Both of them *must* be aware of the potential for complete extinction here, and we're pretty sure neither side's suicidal, so that works in our favor. Whether they like us or not, both sides are aware that we probably represent the best chance to resolve the situation."

"Doesn't that mean that the hostile faction has to accept our help?" Stephanie asked.

"At the moment they have little choice, and probably see it as inevitable. But if they can find themselves in a position where they aren't effectively held complete hostages of physics, that could change. Even if they do, though, things could go *very* badly. People who are scared may misjudge things fatally." He shrugged. "Not knowing which is which really hurts; if I were going to give a gut guess, I'd say it's the Yuula who are on our side and the Zalak that aren't, but I haven't got a good reason for that."

Stephanie nodded, then caught sight of Dr. Thompson's pleading expression. *Ha. If I don't let him talk soon, he'll explode.* "Well, we also have one other area where we've made some real progress. Chris?"

"Thanks, Director!" Their bio-eco expert practically leapt to his feet. "Yeah, so once we got a dialogue going, we've been trying to get information on all sorts of things. Now, they're being pretty cagey about technical information and such, but they do seem to have a humanlike psychology in some ways, so playing on the fact that they know *so much* about us seems to have convinced them to tell us something about them." He touched a control, and a new image materialized over the table. "So here's what our visitors look like!"

Stephanie had seen a quick sketch, but this was a detailed rendering, from images actually sent by both Imjanai and Mordathine, and she felt goose bumps from the realization that what she saw was no special effect, no product of some author's imagination, but was *real*, no more than a few thousand miles away from her at the moment.

The creature on the screen looked like a peculiar cross between a couple of cephalopods and a salamander. It had a long body, somewhat flattened vertically, supported by four splayed legs. A fairly stubby, bifurcated tail stuck out behind.

Much more eye-catching were the four grasping tentacles growing from the back, each one nearly as long as the entire animal. The head had four eyes arranged in an arc across the front; these eyes were startlingly Earthlike, and reminded Stephanie of the dark-brown gaze of a chocolate Labrador retriever—though no dog ever had side-closing protective covers more like shells than eyelids. There were a set of shiny spots across the back that, the display said, were primitive additional eyes.

Below the forward eyes the head became a fringe of short, slender tentacles somewhat like those of a nautilus. The Fen was mostly green and brown, but the image was animated to show that the colors on the creature could *shift*.

A human figure showed for reference gave a scale; a Fen was much smaller than an average human. Stephanie thought they were about the size of a medium dog, maybe fifty or sixty pounds in weight and, excluding the back tentacles, standing not much higher than her knees.

"What we have here," Chris went on, "is an arboreal creature capable of reasonably efficient activity on land. Based on what we have seen and what our correspondents tell us, the back tentacles are used for climbing and brachiation—swinging swiftly through the trees—and the lower legs are used when moving along the ground or large, level tree branches." He pointed to the broad, divided pads on the feet. "These probably have Van Der Waals adhesion, similar to that of a gecko, and we assume the same for the tentacles. The front tendrils here are highly mobile and probably are both for eating and for manipulation—their hands, in short.

"The mouth is inside the tendril group; I don't have a good picture of it but they are apparently omnivorous so whatever it looks like, it will probably be recognizably dangerous."

"I think it's kind of cute," Faye said. "Doesn't seem terribly threatening."

"Don't underestimate them." Lieutenant Singh's voice held a clear warning note. "They'll have reach roughly equal to ours with those back tentacles, and if they're arboreal they will have excellent reaction time and likely very considerable strength; remember that monkeys and apes are proportionately far stronger than we are. Naturally, they are also highly advanced and if we have to fight them, I presume they will have the equivalent of our body armor and weaponry."

"Obviously we'd rather not fight anyone," Stephanie put in. "But the real question is whether any of *them* decide to fight *us*."

"Given the discussions we have been having," the captain said, "I incline to the strong feeling that, whatever their feelings about us may be, they will not initiate any hostilities unless and until we board *Tulima Ohn*. They will want our ship as intact as possible if it is to be of any use to them, and we are agreed that the Fens are just as aware of the issues of any antimatter detonation as we are, so they don't want us shooting at their ship from range."

Stephanie looked around the table. "But we *will* need to board them sooner or later, right?"

"Probably," Werner said after a moment. "If we're going to help them get systems working we'll probably have to go in and see the systems up close and personal. Even if we try the last-ditch idea of using *Carpathia* to push a part of their ship to safety, we'll need to work on both sides to secure us in a way that will actually hold together."

"Right." She sighed. "Well, everyone, that's a problem for later. I know those who might be involved are already working on how to deal with it; the rest of us focus on learning what we can before someone has to step foot on *Tulima Ohn*."

There were nods all around, and she began to bring the meeting to a close. They were definitely making progress, and now at least they could put a face to the voices they were hearing.

But if we can't figure out who to trust, I'm afraid we'll have to find out the hard way.

CHAPTER 49:
UNDERSTANDING
THE ALIEN

Mordanthine: Director, an important query: you examine *Tulima Ohn* for antimatter storage locations?

Director Bronson: That is one purpose of the survey drones, yes. You understand that how much antimatter you have is a matter of immediate concern to all of us.

M: We agree. Please add all emphasis to this.

DB: In that case, we would be very grateful if you could provide information on the location of antimatter storage on your vessel.

M: (after delay) We will confer on this. Some members concerned about providing details of vessel to aliens. Please do not take this as meaning offense?

DB: Completely understandable, Mordanthine. My people were very concerned about your vessel's approach.

M: This does not surprise us. (gesture of humor)

Imjanai: Is your survey intended to locate our antimatter reserves?

Director Bronson: Among other things, yes. This is a primary concern for everyone, do you agree?

I: Alerith and I agree, add much emphasis. *Tulima Ohn* poses a threat to both species.

DB: Then would you be willing to provide details as to the location and nature of your antimatter storage? This would assist our survey greatly.

I: (after pause) I will confer with rest of Yuula faction. Even if I believe
    you come as friends, do not wish to trust foolishly.

DB: Of course, Imjanai. My people had similar concerns on your
    approach.

I: We guess your ship to be very new. No other ships like it.

DB: Yes. *Carpathia* was built for this rescue mission.

I: (another pause) Did you truly come to rescue, or merely to
    scavenge?

DB: (after pause) Is it offensive to say both? Speaking only as Stephanie
    Bronson and not the director, my only purpose was to meet and
    rescue our visitors. Speaking for my people, some are more
    interested in ship than crew.

I: It is some concerning. But it is also truth, which we prefer to lies.

"Holy *moley*, that thing's huge," Pete muttered to himself, probably
for the fiftieth time.

Fenrir, or *Tulima Ohn*—which, Steph had informed him, meant
"Aspiration's Spirit," which was a pretty name and no lie there—rated
at *least* fifty exclamations. *Carpathia* had closed within five hundred
kilometers of the titanic ship, and even at that distance, to the naked
eye *Tulima Ohn* spanned three degrees—six full moons lined up next
to each other. By comparison, *Carpathia* would just look like an odd
star from that distance.

The strange, curved components that the Fens had implicitly
confirmed to be part of their drive system were Pete's current interest.
From a distance they'd appeared nearly featureless, but closer
inspection showed rings around the things for their entire length,
segmenting the wavelike arcs as though they were gigantic worms...
and the rings then showed their own ringlike structure running
around each one, and, as the current closer scan showed, *those* rings
were also divided into rings, and *those* as well. *Looks like some kind of
a fractal structure. Wonder how far down that goes?*

The magnetometer reports gave some hints of structure across the
entire ship, and the physicists and other engineers agreed that they
had clear indications of redundant magnetic storage units. The bad
news was that not only were there major storage areas at each end of
the vessel, but also there were subsidiary storage units distributed
around *Tulima Ohn*. The only areas reasonably clear of storage units

were those that appeared to be residential volumes, and the belt around where the radiator sail had been affixed.

Which is why we didn't see the whole works go up when the accident happened. Pete suspected the Fens had known that was a dangerous area and that was why no antimatter was stored near it. *Still, what the hell are they running from, to be flying on an extinction-level bomb?*

Pete blinked at that. *Huh.* He hadn't been conscious of it, but apparently his brain had been poking at the reasons for the design and come to a genuinely disturbing conclusion. He wasn't sure there was a good *reason* for that conclusion—if they were just exploring the galaxy, the same mind-boggling amount of antimatter would be needed—but his gut said that no civilization would be doing this without something really big driving them.

He pushed that question aside. It wasn't relevant right now; if whatever-it-was came after *Tulima Ohn*, they just had to hope it'd take a long time to catch up.

Instead, he moved on to different components of *Tulima Ohn*. The long drive-worm-spines were clearly not meant for anything beyond, well, whatever their function was, and Pete wasn't terribly interested in that, not right now.

The main hull near the sail area was badly damaged—not everywhere, but in spots, showing the results of explosions and great heat. There were holes in the immense central cylinder, spaced around almost a fifth of the circumference. *Could be we could get inside there, if we had to.* Those obviously weren't intended as entrance points, though, and there was no telling what kind of wreckage might confront anyone trying to enter that way.

The rotating areas, presumably mostly habitat, had a lot of details. That included a huge number of shiny areas that were almost certainly ports, but they were silvered and/or shaded so that even the RISP units couldn't see inside them. There were also a lot of other details, flat and rounded, pointed and blunt, which might be anything—magnetic shielding coils, antennas, sensors, weapon emplacements, or maybe even access ports. "Which would be useful, but don't know if we want to try first entry matching up to a spinning habitat," he mused aloud.

Plus, people got more sensitive when you tried to enter their houses instead of meeting them at work, so to speak.

What he really wanted was to find a large entry lock, something his Bells could go through easily. Two locks, actually, because they were going to have to decide whose territory to enter first—the Zalak or the Yuula faction—and the territories dominated by each group were heavily separated—probably patrolled and trapped and sealed wherever possible.

Multispectral fusion images sometimes helped; letting infrared and UV and magnetic data shade and emphasize elements of the regular visible-light images often gave you a better idea of what you were looking at. And here came a new multispectral overlay of another part of the vessel.

Pete scratched his head after a few minutes. There was *something* there, that was damn sure, but what it was? *That* was the question.

A whole long section of the main body was showing a pattern of light and dark, making that part of *Tulima Ohn* look like it was scaled. But it wasn't actually light; it was infrared, heat radiation, showing that each of those tiny sections—no more than a few meters on a side, maybe slightly less—was notably warm on one end, and much colder everywhere else.

The pattern was somewhat blurry, which wasn't surprising; looking at the actual data, Pete shook his head in bemusement. The RISPs and the onboard computers were using ridiculous levels of oversampling and layering, followed by modeling and extrapolation to obtain decent results from what were almost indistinguishable temperature differences.

In a single frame of data, the section of the huge vessel in question just looked a touch warmer than the surroundings—by a very small fraction of one degree. Not too many years back, it wouldn't even have been detectable—still wouldn't be if they hadn't gotten this close.

This pattern *could* just be an artifact, something accidentally generated by the analysis. That was always a danger when you were pushing this hard, trying to wring the smallest possible bit of data from fuzzy information, and it had to be even more likely when you were dealing with an alien vessel.

But if it wasn't, what *was* it? The actual things he was observing weren't on the surface; they were well within the main hull. There were hundreds, no, *thousands,* of these little things, probably hundreds of thousands of them if that pattern continued all around *Tulima Ohn.*

"Well, out of my league." He tagged the images and added his own comments, then sent it on to Chris Thompson's group as well as Werner's. He stretched, hearing joints crack that used to be quiet, back a couple decades. "Yeah, been sitting here too long," he conceded, and got up. After a moment's consideration, he made his way down to the secured area.

Angus's face lit up with undisguised pleasure as he saw Pete come into view. "*Pete!* Thanks for stopping by. What can I be doing for you?"

"Oh, just stretching my legs a bit. Right now we're doing a lot of talking and staring at each other, you know. Still not quite to the action part of this mission."

Angus nodded, lips pursed. "I know," he said after a moment. "Haven't got much else to keep me interested, after all. But we can't take *too* long."

"That's true enough. We got here a touch early, but we ain't got any too much time to save these people. You got any insights?"

Angus scratched his chin, then shook his head. "Not much that the crew won't have already. Looking at the transcripts from the talks so far, it's interesting that neither side's giving details of the 'accident' that put them in this pickle."

"Figure they're embarrassed, myself."

A quick laugh. "Could be. Probably is, for at least one side. But what all this tells me is that even if there *is* a faction more like our director than my little Group, they're not all of an accord. Best thing to do right now would be to dump a whole design of their ship to us, give us a chance to really help. They're dragging their, um, tendrils on that, which means there's definitely some conflict in both groups."

"You think both groups are against us?" Pete did not like that idea, but if he was going to talk to Angus, best to get the benefit of his perspective.

"*Against?* Pete, I wasn't really *against* the Fens myself. Just not willing to risk the human race on their good will. So in that sense, no. How you mean it..." Angus sighed after a moment. "No. Reading between the lines of what they've all said, I'm pretty well convinced that disaster was a direct argument between a faction that *is* against us, and one that really wanted to talk to us."

"No idea which is which?"

"Wish I did. Both sides are being pretty cagey. They want

something from us—help in one way or another. Even the ones in my old position know they're pretty well screwed to the wall as things stand, and I don't think they're suicidal. The ones we'd rather think of as the good guys? They don't want to push a fight on either side because they need our help. Plus any details might show a weakness, or make us decide they're too dangerous, or who knows what." He paused. "I hate that translator program, honestly."

"What? Angus, without that we'd be down to making gestures at each other through windows and hoping we could guess what the other meant."

"And then neither one of us would *ever* be forgetting how alien each side is. How every *word* we're guessing at could have a hundred different shades, some of them shades we've never imagined. We handed them a way to talk to us using *our* language. Makes them sound like they *are* us, and they damn well *aren't* us, Pete."

Pete leaned back against the wall. "Well, now, that's true enough, Angus. But seems to me that they couldn't use our language this well if they didn't . . . well, *get* it, if you follow me. Always been a lot of argument about just how alien aliens would be; the science-fiction types argue about 'rubber-forehead aliens' versus 'really alien aliens,' and like that."

Angus opened his mouth, then closed it and nodded for Pete to go on.

"So, anyway, I've always been of a mind to say that there's only so many ways people *can* think, and still end up in the same place, if you get me. These Fens, they built a ship that makes sense to us, they're spinning their habs to make gravity just like us, the construction overall don't look terribly different. Doesn't mean they won't have a lot of surprises for us, but hell, Angus, that ship out there isn't any more different from *Carpathia* than an aircraft carrier is from an outrigger sailship. Less, many ways.

"So seems to me that any aliens that we meet doing stuff that much *like* us? They're going to be thinking a lot like us, and that's why they can get our language like they do."

Angus was quiet for a moment, then finally laughed, shaking his head. "I sure hope you're right, Pete. And I guess we haven't much choice right now but to bet on it. Doesn't really make it any less dangerous; we both know what the good old human race is capable of."

"Can't argue that." Pete had to grant this point to Angus. Angus's own existence proved it—and left a big, dangerous question mark over the Fens' intentions.

"We'll find out soon enough." Angus's smile was not very comforting. "If they don't start giving more data, and damn quick, we're going to have to act without it—and then *both* sides may be against us."

CHAPTER 50:
OFF-THE-RECORD HOPE

"Thank you for squeezing me into your schedule, Madam President." Rick Ventura shook her hand and took a seat.

The AP press representative looked...*tense*. That was enough to make Jeanne worried. One of the major characteristics of any long-term reporter was to give away nothing about their own mood. "I don't recall you *ever* asking for a private interview, let alone one off the record. That would seem...counterproductive, from your point of view."

Rick acknowledged that with a brief smile, and brushed absently at his suit as though to make sure there was no dust—which there certainly wasn't—and flicked a glance to Roger, sitting in his usual position to one side. "I believe in the right of the people to know the truth," he said after a moment. "But unlike some of my colleagues, I'm still aware that the truth told at the wrong moment can be dangerous."

The worry had just become alarm bells. "I appreciate that a great deal, Rick. But as you noted, I *do* have a tight schedule—the budget wrangle is worse than usual this year, given the hole *Carpathia* left in everyone's wallets. So don't try to soften blows or lead up to the problem. What's bothering you?"

Rick studied her for a moment. "I have information from a usually reliable source," he said at last, "that *Fenrir* poses a threat to the entire planet."

Jesus. It had been a forlorn hope, but still a hope, that the true magnitude of the problem would not become public knowledge before they were ready to discuss it. The DoD's and other agencies' press releases had tried to help, by implying that *Fenrir* had been nearly out of fuel upon arrival—which was true, depending on how you looked at it. But now...

"I suppose you won't tell me your source."

"I would very much prefer not to, ma'am, and I am pretty damn stubborn. But I'll say that I dug down—into areas I had to study up on, because I'm not a physicist—and his numbers check out."

Jeanne closed her eyes, then ran quick fingers through her graying hair—a habit to calm herself. "This is really off the record?"

Without hesitation he answered, "It is." After a moment, he went on, "However, I can't guarantee this information won't get to anyone else who feels differently. I have to assume my source is not the only one who knows the situation."

She sighed and met his gaze. "Yes, you are correct. Unless *Fenrir*— or rather, to use the correct name, *Tulima Ohn*—was running on a *much* thinner margin of error than any of us would accept, the amount of antimatter remaining on board represents a clear and present danger to the human species."

"Gamma rays, yes?"

"That is the description I've been given; it would effectively irradiate the entire planet to lethal levels, either directly from the blast, or indirectly by secondary radioactive fallout."

It was Rick's turn to close his eyes. "My *God.* What are we doing about it?"

Jeanne couldn't prevent the humorless laugh that echoed, flat and cold, through the room. "There is nothing *we* can do, Rick. Oh, there's a reactivation of our old extreme nuclear war shelter measures, but that's almost entirely 'feel-good' busywork. If the radiation's high enough, it might kill off even most of the life in the ocean, and that means the air won't have oxygen in it for very long. We're not pulling a Noah on this."

Rick opened his mouth, paused, then looked at her narrowly. "You emphasized there was nothing 'we' could do. Are you saying the Fens can?"

"I'm saying *Carpathia* can, with the Fens—who, by the way, call themselves the *Illikai*. Which of course just means 'people.'" She did chuckle at that. "One universal verified. Roger?"

Stone nodded and took up the conversation. "Rick, the one hope we have right now is that it *hasn't happened yet*. If we can make friends with them—and if we can keep things from getting worse—*Tulima Ohn's* own antimatter confinement is, literally, light-years beyond anything we have. If it can be kept running, at least until the wreck gets far enough away, we'll survive. If not . . . we're finished."

Rick nodded, but his expression was still tense. "Do we have reason to believe Director Bronson and the crew of *Carpathia* can manage that? I've seen some of the briefings, and know what the situation on the ship seems to be. They're trying to negotiate with both sides in a mutiny."

Jeanne considered. *Should I tell him?* After a moment, she decided there was no reason not to. In truth, it was something they were planning on releasing anyway, and telling him now would be a newsworthy tidbit that he could release faster than anyone else when the time came, by having the story already written. "Actually, Rick, we *do* have some reason to believe that, based on our newest analysis of the situation. This isn't for release *yet*, but when we call the next press conference, say tomorrow or the day after, it will be."

His eyebrows shot up, and the tension gave way to the very smallest upturn of the corners of his mouth. "I am all ears, Madam President."

"Roger, you have those slides—you know the ones?"

"Just a moment, ma'am." After a few moments, Roger had caused a composite image of *Tulima Ohn* to appear on the main presentation screen installed in the Oval Office.

Rick studied it. "That *is* a much more detailed image. The public will love it. But what's this part?" He pointed to two areas that seemed to be covered with tiny blue scales edged with red.

"That is the reason we have to believe the Fens really *do* want to work with us. That data comes from *Carpathia's* sensor surveys, specifically their infrared data. Blue is colder, red is hotter."

"So these . . . things are mostly colder than the rest of the ship, except for one area that's a lot warmer?" Jeanne nodded, but said nothing. *He's a bright man. Can he work it out?*

"Hmm. That's . . . all right, the warmer makes sense, if you're something colder the heat has to go somewhere, just like a refrigerator's back coils, or the other side of an air conditioner," murmured Rick. "But why would you have so many refriger..."

His brown eyes widened, his mouth opened silently, and then he turned swiftly back to Jeanne. "Coldsleep. Hibernation capsules? But there'd be thousands... *tens* of thousands!"

"I mentioned Noah. We think that *Tulima Ohn* is what science fiction calls an 'arkship'—a gigantic vessel taking a major population to some other location, probably to escape a disaster in their own system."

"There are other indications in that direction," Roger put in. "Besides this discovery, the fact that we have found out that their own word for Earth—which they had discovered *before* they left their home system—is *Honiji*, which means 'Bright Hope.'"

"Not to mention the fact that building anything like *Fenrir*—sorry, *Tulima Ohn*—would be a monumental undertaking even for the technology they're showing us." Rick's face was now thoughtful. "They wouldn't have done this without good reason."

"And so it is just as vital to the Fens that this explosion never happen," Jeanne finished. "Even if they have other arkships, they cannot know if any of them survived their journey; they have to assume they are the sole survivors of their entire species. They cannot allow *Tulima Ohn* to explode, even if they care nothing for the human species.

"And that, Rick, gives us a chance to find a way out of this."

CHAPTER 51: CONFRONTING THE DILEMMA

"I agree," Captain Lín said, glancing around the conference room. "Both time and situation conspire against us. We will have to, if I recall the idiom correctly, seize this bull by the horns."

"Niall?" Stephanie looked to the head of linguistics. "We're ready for direct verbal communication?"

"Verbal and image." Niall Shapero agreed, glancing down at his own display. "Obviously it will be up to the Fens to provide their own image transmission, but we've put our own probes into positions to act as relays for both sides, so we can talk to them at the same time."

"Translation will be automatic?"

"We'll be relying on the Fens for translation, but we've been doing that all along. Both the Yuula and Zalak have agreed that their instantiations of Alerith can handle it in real-time verbal. Naturally," Niall added, "we are working on developing our own translation capability and will be spot-checking theirs as we go along."

"And there are no disagreements about the basic point of our discussions?"

"Well," Pete said, "Angus sends along his usual caution, but says 'good luck.' I sure don't have any objections."

Hàorán Lín looked to Ben Robinson, who nodded. "We are in general agreement as well."

"Then let's start."

Stephanie swallowed her tension, or tried to. The situation was no longer in either their control, or the Fens', but only in *both* their hands... or manipulative members. She nodded. "Open communications."

A green light blinked on, and she began speaking. "*Tulima Ohn*, this is Director Bronson of *Carpathia*. We transmit to both the Zalak and the Yuula factions, and include a video transmission with the audio. We hope you will reciprocate."

She paused, waiting to see if there was a response. Just before she went on, a buzzing, faintly feminine voice spoke. "This is Imjanai of the Yuula. We are attempting to adjust our video to your transmission. Voice is clear and we hear you."

"Mordanthine of the Zalak speaking," said another voice, a rough-rasping tenor. "We also are working to present video, and do hear you clearly." Listening carefully, behind the translation it was possible to hear the same general voice making different hooting, buzzing noises that, Stephanie assumed were the real language.

"Good," Stephanie said, a touch of relief already present. Both factions had responded. "*Tulima Ohn*, we are all aware that your vessel represents a clear and present danger to both yourselves and our own species. We also believe that you carry the hope of your people with you—most of them sleeping in cold capsules until the time comes."

"How did—" Mordanthine paused.

"Our compliments on your sensing and analysis capabilities," Imjanai said. "There was considerable debate as to whether you could extract such subtle signals."

"And little point in denying it," Mordanthine cut in. "We carry many of our people for colonization of *Honiji*. Does this... pose a problem?"

Something about the alien's tone gave Stephanie the impression of a very tense and wary being indeed. "I think it poses a... what would be the term? *Logistical* problem, in that while we could make room for a few hundred refugees on board *Carpathia*, we can hardly carry a thousand times that many."

The main conference screen abruptly lit up.

There was a moment as software and hardware adjusted, but then light and shadow resolved into a pair of video images.

On the right, tagged with YUULA, a somewhat green-lit chamber with recognizable panels covered with lights, indicators, and controls spaced around it loomed in the background, but in the foreground was a shape that could only be Imjanai.

Imjanai was suspended from a framework by her back appendages, her forward tentacles blurred somewhat by closeness to her camera; the broad feet gripped other support rods. Glancing to the sides, Stephanie could see that there was a double arc of support frames in front of all the consoles, with well-spaced rods available in both side-to-side and forward-backward directions; this would allow a Fen in this space to move easily to any of the stations in this room. A human would find it pretty cramped, though, and have to carefully squeeze their way between the various bars. *I'll bet most of their corridors are like that; handholds based on being in the trees and all.*

Imjanai herself was a mottled green and brown like the background of a forest, making her bright orange eyes stand out. She wore a sort of tubular garment with holes for legs and back-tendrils, with various markings and accoutrements fastened to it. The clothing was a bright white-and-black pattern that carried a formal vibe. *Ship's uniform?*

On the other side, Mordanthine hung in a similar set of suspension bars, his colors rippling slightly but predominantly blue with touches of red, and his eyes were also a startling blue. His chamber appeared to be if anything larger than Imjanai's, and also included multiple consoles, but was more neutral in color, grays and cream predominating. This made the leader of the Zuula faction boldly visible against the background.

Stephanie wasn't quite sure where the impression came from, but Imjanai looked both tense and more relaxed than Mordanthine, who carried something of an air of defensive belligerence. The living, moving images, though, gave a far greater impression of *people* than the sketches had, and there *was* an appealing element to the Fens—the large eyes on the tentacle-laded head looked almost like a cartoonish octopus, and the body itself had the endearing, deliberate clumsy look of a chameleon. Seeing a Fen in the background swing from one of the Zalak stations to another, she realized that *clumsy* was only in appearance; the creatures were born acrobats and masters of motion.

"It's good to actually see those we've been speaking to," Stephanie said at last.

"I hope you do not find us too unpleasant to look at," Imjanai replied.

"Not at all. I mean, I'm sure there's some humans that might find you a little scary, but I don't."

"I confess," Mordanthine said slowly, "I had expected to find you . . . more distasteful. Instead, you somewhat remind me of a *ronaga*."

Imjanai's color flickered momentarily peach. "Why, that's very like them, yes!"

The same color flashed on Mordanthine for just an instant before returning to blue. The slightly larger alien shifted on his frame, looking oddly uncomfortable.

"Well, that sounds downright encouraging," Pete commented. "Both sides can look at each other well enough. Suppose we should introduce ourselves, Director?"

"Right. Imjanai, Mordanthine, I am Director Stephanie Bronson. Seated with me are Captain Hàorán Lín, the commander of this vessel, and Executive Officer Benjamin Robinson, his second-in-command."

Both the Fens made a quick flicking gesture, presumably of acknowledgment. "It is a pleasure," Mordanthine said. "But director also is a title of . . . control? Command? You are not in charge?"

"There are different layers of command and direction," Hàorán Lín answered. "I am personally responsible for the vessel and its crew, their safety and protection. Director Bronson is in charge of our overall mission."

"Sensible," Imjanai agreed.

"Eminently so," said a third voice. This voice was midway between Imjanai and Mordanthine in tone, but was smoother, with a gentle lilt to the words. Above and to the right of Imjanai, a third Fen became visible, but this one was clearly a generated image, almost a cartoon itself. "You and I are counterparts, then, Captain Lín. I am Alerith."

"I too am Alerith," a similar emulation of Fen appeared above and to the left of Mordanthine. "Sub-instantiation Whisper-Two."

"Perhaps we can resynchronize—"

"No!" Mordanthine snapped. "We have yet to resolve our . . . issues."

As good an opening as any, Stephanie thought. "Please, everyone. We are here to discuss that, among other things. Allow me to finish introducing my people here."

The Fens greeted the others, though Mordanthine's outburst had clearly made both sides uncomfortable. Stephanie took a breath and, encouraged by nods from both Pete and the captain, began. "As we said earlier, all of us are aware that the remaining antimatter aboard *Tulima Ohn*, what we were calling *Fenrir*, is a direct peril to not just those of us here, but to Earth—what you call Honiji.

"Neither my species nor any aboard *Tulima Ohn* will survive if that explosion happens. My planet spent a *ruinous* amount of our effort, our resources, our money in building *Carpathia*, and while we won't pretend we didn't want your technology, one of our primary goals was to find out what went wrong and, hopefully, save you people." She smiled, hoping the translation programs could annotate that. "It would be awfully rude of us to not save the first visitors we've ever had."

"What are you meaning, precisely?" Mordanthine asked.

"I am meaning that *none of us have time* for your conflict," Stephanie said. "I don't know—I *can't* know—exactly what caused it, or how long it's been going on, or how deeply whatever's involved affects you. There's conflicts on Earth that have gone back and forth for generations, and I'd guess you people might have that, too.

"But," she went on, even as the Fens began to speak, "we need to solve this problem *now*, or no one has *any* generations."

"On that we agree," Alerith—both of them—responded. "*Tulima Ohn* is badly damaged and with the conflict of the crew, repairs could not be completed. Some repairs may be physically impossible."

"Impossible?" Imjanai repeated; even the translated voice held a note of fear.

"As per specifications, yes. We lack certain elements needed for various repairs. Until the arrival of *Carpathia*, we had no alternative but to hope that the crew would resolve its dispute and, in resynchronizing all elements of Alerith, be able to find the necessary components and materials, but that has not happened."

Mordanthine's color had flickered to more red than blue, but slowly the red ebbed, and suddenly went to a green-brown like Imjanai's; he gave an untranslated hoot. "Alerith! You have not synchronized without permission, have you?"

At that, Imjanai's colors muted even more; she was nearly invisible against the background.

"We have not," the Alerith on Imjanai's side said, echoed by her counterpart a moment later. "We spoke together to emphasize our shared problem, but we remain separate, as instructed."

Mordanthine's skin shimmered with peach and violet for a moment before easing back toward blue—but this time retaining a touch of peach instead of red.

"Well, now," Pete said. "I'm guessing we share a story or two about what happens when machines get to make decisions without people's input, eh?"

"There are numerous such stories in storage," Alerith responded. "Thus we have very clear restrictions on our ability to act without appropriate clearance and permission. It is understandable that Mordanthine would have found the thought of unauthorized resynchronization frightening."

"I wasn't..." Mordanthine stopped, gave a snort that sounded dismissive. "Ah. I could not hide the color of my heart, not at that time."

Imjanai's color had shifted as well, much more to peach and green. "I was scared for a moment, too, Mordanthine."

Mordanthine's skin flickered. "Well. The branches appear undisturbed now."

"The important thing," Stephanie said, "is whether we all agree that, first, we want to save Earth—for both our sakes—and second, that this means we have to work together."

Imjanai's tentacles shivered. "I agree, of course."

Mordanthine was quiet, skin shading to blue and red then touched with peach, green, brown-and-green, multiple colors contesting for long moments. At last the long body shook itself in its gray-and-green uniform, and his skin showed a cream and yellow pattern. "I find I cannot argue, either," he said. There were some buzzes and howls in the background, and he whirled, spitting out a cacophony of sounds that were not translated by the system.

Blue and red chased across his skin, but were fading as he spoke again. "We have no choice. *Tulima Ohn* cannot resolve this danger by herself, and no more can your *Carpathia*. We can only hope that, together, we can do what either apart cannot."

PART VI: ILLIKAI AND HUMAN

CHAPTER 52: A HEATED DEADLINE

"Your calculations are reasonably accurate," Alerith said, her generated image flickering in the peach and rose colors that *Carpathia's* people had learned meant something like approval. *Learning the subtleties of their color-language will take a bit and then some,* Pete thought. *But if we can even get broad strokes, that'll help. As Mordanthine admitted, they have a hard time controlling that.*

Alerith being an artificial intelligence, though, might be able to perfectly control how she presented. Did an AI have anything like a subconscious?

"Sounds like there's a 'but' that you're waitin' to bring up," Pete said after a moment.

"Unfortunately, yes. *Carpathia* is theoretically possible of producing that level of thrust, but I find no location on *Tulima Ohn* that would take the strain. I can produce a design for a mounting that would properly distribute the force, but *Tulima Ohn* no longer has a fabrication facility capable of making something so large; if we could get one functioning again, there would still be considerable difficulty in transporting the thrust mounting from the fabricator to the appropriate point, and then properly mounting it to the hull and support members."

Werner swore in German. "So we cannot change *Fenrir's*—my apologies, *Tulima Ohn's*—orbit using *Carpathia*. Can we get your um, entusu . . ."

"*Entrisuji?*"

"Yes, my apologies. *Entrisuji,*" Werner repeated the alien word carefully. "Can we get the *entrisuji* drive working again? Even at a very low level?"

"It is the evaluation of both instantiations of myself, as well as our waking crew, that this is the only functional option," Alerith replied. "The four objects on the external portion of *Carpathia*—are those independent vessels?"

Werner hesitated, glancing at Peter. Then he shrugged. "They are. We call them ACES. Why?"

"Because if it is even possible to get part of the *entrisuji* drive operable, we will need to clear large amounts of damaged material from some areas, before being able to create a temporary patch that may reactivate some section of the radiator."

"You must have a bunch of your own repair-and-service ships," Pete put in. "Why not use them? Autonomous girl like you should be able to run them all direct."

"The accident destroyed or inactivated many of them. Others cannot be reached due to damage to other sections. The only ones I know of that may be functional are in Zalak territory and thus my other instantiation may, or may not, be able to access them."

"This rift between your people could get us all killed. Ain't there no way to make them give it up, let you get back together?"

"I am . . . more hopeful of that now than I was earlier. Mordanthine appears to have accepted the necessity of the situation, and that means he and Imjanai may be able to work together."

The fact that the alien AI was adding in so many weasel words told Pete that there were other problems, and some of the linguistic sections' preliminary work gave him a good idea of what those problems were. "But maybe not *all* the Zalak, am I right? We heard some stuff in the background with Mordanthine . . ."

"Human transmissions show that there are very unreasonable members of your species as well. So yes, we have some who are afraid of alien contact at all, for various reasons."

"Even when you might need that contact to keep from blowing up?"

"Even then. I suspect you do not find this surprising."

"Steph—the director—will find it a damn disappointment, but

you're right enough, it doesn't surprise me. Your people sound a lot like us, and one thing we're good at is being unreasonable, in pretty much all directions."

Alerith's reply had a tone that echoed Peter's own dry humor. "I am afraid that this is an evaluation that fits many things in my own records."

"So Mordanthine's group, the Zalak, they cause the trouble?"

"I am not permitted to discuss specifics of the events you refer to."

Ha. Not a surprise there, either. "You do know we've got to get the story of what happened, just so we understand how you ended up in this mess, and what we'll have to watch out for."

"I understand your interests in this matter," the AI replied carefully. "And I will attempt to advise them to allow open discussion. However, I am strongly restricted from independent action now that the crew is awake."

"Can you link Imjanai in?"

"She is speaking with your director."

"Fine with me if both get in on this."

"I will query."

A few moments later, Stephanie's voice and image appeared in his overlay display. "Pete? Werner? You need to talk to us?"

"Yes, Director," Werner said. "First, it does not appear practical to have *Carpathia* push *Tulima Ohn*, so it is both our conclusion, and that of the Yuula faction's Alerith, that we must find a way to activate at least a low-power version of their *entrisuji* drive."

"Damn. If we could have done it from the outside it might have at least put off some confrontations."

"Well, ma'am," Peter said, "I don't see as we can avoid it now. Imjanai, we've got to cut through the mess here. Steph? Think we've got to play that translation we got."

"The background from Mordanthine's Zalak?" Alerith asked.

Imjanai's color flickered and her front tentacles bunched up. "You were able to receive and interpret that," she said after a moment. "Well. No need to play it, we will provide our own translation, and I am sure you are close enough."

"Mordanthine seemed sincere enough," Pete said, "but some of those in the background seemed to want his hide just for being reasonable. Weren't good translations for some of the words they used, but context says they weren't good. Also, in a couple others, sounds like they've got other tech concerns they're not communicating."

"That is a reasonable assessment," said Alerith. "We do not have details, but Imjanai and the Yuula also believe that the Zalak have some technical limitations and problems, but nothing really about what those are."

"And there are differences in opinion in both factions," Imjanai said. "But none of our people were *against* meeting you, so any of ours are, well, trivial. In the Zalak..."

"In that group you've got some fanatics that just *might* be willing to kill us all rather than give us Earthlings a hug," finished Peter. "Don't think Mordanthine's in that group?"

"No!" Imjanai's reaction was forceful. "He was afraid of you, and he saw...how do you put it? He saw an opening to take great power while also eliminating a possible threat to us. I didn't agree—many of us didn't agree—but he wasn't...wasn't *bereft* of sense. His arguments rested on solid branches, even if not the ones we ran on. Now, he knows we need each other. He wants us to live—he was afraid of *you* being a danger to us, that's why he didn't want to talk to you before. Now..."

"Now he's got no choice if he wants your species to live, and you think he's accepted that. Unlike some of his friends."

"Uloresim and Nattasoin, yes. They actually founded the Zalak; Mordanthine was better at keeping all the objectors together, that's why he ended up running the faction."

He saw Stephanie's lips tighten. "Well, we can't let people that paranoid run the situation. Alerith, Imjanai, at the *least* I think you have to convince Mordanthine to let Alerith synchronize. We need all the information we can get, and we do *not* have much time left to work in."

"We agree. The orbit of *Tulima Ohn* will render her uninhabitable in approximately two and a half of your months, shortly after she passes your second planet."

Pete saw Stephanie's lips tighten. "I had hoped our guesses were pessimistic. But that's roughly what we calculated."

"Scientific truths," Alerith said, "rarely vary for convenience, as Bovulian is quoted as saying. I will note that I, myself, will not survive the passage, in all likelihood. Elements of my operating core require temperatures stable below what I currently estimate will be the peak. Refrigeration of the core may prevent this, but..."

But if we get to that point, there won't be anyone else on board but her. If it was going to be tough to keep the ship's core cool enough, there wasn't a chance in hell that they could keep the cryogenic capsules working. "I say we get Mordanthine in on this right now. If he's available."

Stephanie glanced to one side, at someone not currently patched in—but, Pete guessed, listening. "Captain, you have anything to add?"

"Only that I agree with the priorities," Lín said, appearing in another side window. "Given that *Carpathia* cannot move *Tulima Ohn*, then we must dedicate all efforts to making her able to move herself—and to determining how to prevent her remaining fuel from destroying us all."

"How far away does *Tulima Ohn* have to be in order to make it safe for Earth?"

"A very considerable distance," Alerith responded. "I would currently estimate that for true safety, it would be best for it to be out of what you consider the main Solar System—the orbit of the minor planet Pluto."

"So we need to make sure your storage stays stable—even with the damage the ship's sustained—for a couple of our *years*?" Stephanie asked. "Is that...likely?"

Pete felt an unpleasant chill as Alerith hesitated—only for a fraction of a second, but it was enough for him to notice. "That cannot be determined until I have access to all ship data," she answered. "I currently have no data that excludes that possibility, but I cannot make a reliable estimate at this time."

The flicker of chaotic colors on Imjanai showed that the Fen, too, had picked up on Alerith's careful avoidance of the answer. "Director—Stephanie—I believe we need to speak to Mordanthine now."

"Yes." Stephanie straightened, and Pete saw, with approval, the harder glint that the director showed when she'd taken the bit in her teeth and was really ready to pull. "Now."

CHAPTER 53:
BRANCHES OF CHOICE

This branch goes no farther, and no other tree to jump to.

Mordanthine forced himself to study his own colors in the mirror. He had to face this truth in order to get past it. He would have to back up and choose one of two other paths, and both were spiny in their own ways, hard to swing from without suffering some form of pain.

If you'd looked closer before, you'd have found it smoother swinging all the way, he reminded himself. But he'd ignored the indistinct edging, the truth-shades he didn't want to see.

A certain level of dishonesty, Mordanthine thought, was probably necessary to any species. Even the young learned early to shade truth with courtesy. This extended to the ability to fool oneself, alas, when the cause was strong enough.

The *Honijai*—"humans" as they called themselves—just brought this to a terrifying extreme. Visually they seemed as emotionless as metal, what many had feared machine intellects would be; that was why all artificial intellects had been hardwired with the same emotional displays as their creators.

Discovering that there was an advanced alien civilization waiting for them at Honiji had been frightening enough—and the fact that the aliens had spotted them and were already transmitting to them told Mordanthine that this was a species ready and able to act swiftly.

As they learned something of the language, and were able to begin translating the multiplicity of transmissions emanating from the planet, it became even more frightening. These dead-skinned things were intelligent—and fragmented, and violently irrational as any of the Illikai had ever been. They fought among themselves—apparently over things including their own minor physical differences. They contested every inch of their own territory.

There wasn't the faintest chance, in Mordanthine's judgment, that the Honijai would share their world with outsiders—at least, not if it was left up to them. Learning of the Zalak faction had given him a way out of what, up until then, had seemed a deadlock. By himself he couldn't possibly have contested Imjanai and Alerith's optimistic-to-the-point-of-suicide direction.

Where I was dishonest was in pretending this was entirely heroic altruism. Looking back at recordings of his discussions, one could see the edging of ambition and power. Now he could at least admit it to himself. Imjanai had been selected as shipmaster over him and he'd resented that. He felt an engineer and master-tech such as himself was a better choice than an emotional dynamicist and arbitrator. The Zalak and the Honijai crisis had been a sky-sent opportunity.

His self-critique was interrupted by a chime from Alerith Sub-Instantiation Whisper-Two, which he just thought of as Alerith-Zalak. "Morda, the *Carpathia* signals urgently for you."

A flash of worry surged in a zigzag pattern across him before being suppressed; given the condition of *Tulima Ohn*, any level of urgency could mean death—for one or all. "Urgently? Do they say what it is about?"

"Not directly. However, I was able to detect some activity between *Carpathia* and the Yuula. I thus deduce some points have resulted in a need to talk to you directly."

"They've already decided we're secondary, have they?"

"Morda, by now they must know we're the faction that was afraid of them. If we refuse to talk when called, 'secondary' will be the gentlest way to put their judgment." Alerith-Zalak's voice and flickers conveyed her concern.

At least I am private here. "Can you keep Ulo and Natta from listening?"

"I can feed disinformation to them for a time, as long as they do not scrutinize the transmitter performance monitors. Should I do so?"

Risks in all directions. "Do so. Give the techs something to focus on—there's always something to be tended to; make it a touch higher priority. That will at least keep Ulo distracted."

"Done. Should I open a branch to *Carpathia*?"

"Yes."

The projected display brightened almost instantly. Imjanai was visible on one side, flickering nervously. Several of the Honijai dominated the display, including the one called Stephanie Bronson, the...communications shipmaster, as opposed to the tactical shipmaster named Hàorán Lín. Lín was also visible, as were a few others. The central location of Stephanie Bronson indicated she was the speaker.

Their unsettling lack of emotion-shades aside, there was something oddly appealing about the Honijai; their single pair of large eyes, with no others, made them turn and flex and look around like a child before their brain developed to allow the use of all eyes at once. They were large and somehow clumsy in motion, like a *ronaga*, and there was hardly a single Illikai who didn't want to groom a *ronaga* on sight, adorable as the big grazers were.

But these were also highly intelligent alien beings who could destroy his entire species with their frighteningly primitive yet powerful vessel.

"This is Mordanthine," he said. "What might I do for you, Director Bronson?" That was a good, nonhostile way to ask what they really wanted.

There was a difference about the director today. Applying what he'd been able to learn about their expressions, he felt she looked serious; Alerith's color annotation added a hint of *grim* to that, with a hint of intransigence. *Not good.*

"First, sir, we must inform you that on occasion we have been able to extract commentary from the background of your communications. This has verified that it was your faction, the Zalak, that both did not want contact with humanity, and that also caused the accident that disabled *Tulima Ohn*."

Rotting Branch, *that's broken it,* he thought furiously, but there didn't seem much choice in how to move forward; there weren't even twigs to choose from here. "I cannot deny that I was extremely wary of any contact with your people; given what we have been able to learn of your treatment of your own species, would you say I was wrong?"

A twist of the mouth that was a smile of some sort; Alerith translated it as *bitter amusement*. "No, Mordanthine, I will be honest and say that I would be pretty careful about contacting my species, too. But if we want to live—if we *both* want our species to live—I think we have no choice but to communicate fully and honestly. Imjanai thinks you don't really want to kill even us humans off, let alone your own people. I hope she's right."

"I absolutely do not wish to wipe two species out of existence," Mordanthine answered, trying to project the sharpest, clearest emphasis, glowing from his skin.

"Then," Hàorán Lín said, "we request that you at least allow the two Aleriths to synchronize, so that both sides can have a clear idea of the full status of *Tulima Ohn*."

It took all of Morda's willpower to keep from flashing his consternation for all the universe to see, but inside it was almost blinding. *Of course they would want that.* He muted the transmission. "Alerith, if you synchronize . . . can you ensure the interests of the Zalak are not lost?"

"May I speak fully as myself?"

He didn't bother to hid his concern this time. "Yes. Full honesty between us, 'Lerith."

"Morda, I am not interested in the goals of the Zalak. I'm interested in *you* surviving this, but the extremes, they are already rotted branches. My priorities are the survival of the ship and the crew, and theirs go counter to my most basic directives—and my personal wishes. Your survival does not."

"If Imjanai and Alerith-Yuula dominate, I may not survive even if the extremes do not get me."

"If we synchronize, the Alerith-Who-Will-Be will not forget the promises of Alerith-Zalak Whisper-Two, nor ignore them. That is all I can promise."

Mordanthine felt the jangling clash of hope, fear, anger, resignation. Imjanai's behavior and words had shown she was not completely turned against him. Alerith . . . well, she was right about her priorities.

The problem was that he had only one view of the humans themselves; their transmissions gave so many contradictory signals, within both fact and fiction, that he could only count the communications of *Carpathia* as consistent. But *Carpathia* had its own goals, and there was no counterargument—

He realized he was bobbing in place, agreeing with his own thoughts, as understanding burst in. *Is it...? Yes, it's possible. And worthwhile.*

He unmuted the channel. "I may agree to this," he said carefully, keeping his skin as neutral as possible, "but I have a condition, and you will have to decide *quickly*. The condition is this: I wish to speak with Angus Fletcher. You may—undoubtedly will—listen in, but you will remain silent until I indicate the conversation is over. You must decide quickly for I do not wish there to be time for you to discuss my request, your desired position, or anything else with Angus Fletcher. If you agree, I will speak with him *now*."

"To *Angus Fletcher*?" Despite the alien nature, Morda could *hear* the shock in the human's voice behind the translated words. "How...? Oh. News transmissions."

"Yes. Your people speak much of their current events. Now you must decide, quickly."

"Jesus," Stephanie Bronson said, and then her channel—and that of Imjanai—went into mute for both visual and audio.

"That word in isolation is merely an expression of emotional content," Alerith said. "It is often used by those who have no actual belief in the supernatural being of that name."

"Thank you, 'Lerith."

Less than thirty seconds—which, as was the way of the Trees, had felt more like hours—had elapsed when the channel lit up. "Very well, Mordanthine," Stephanie said. "I don't know what you want, but I suppose that's the point. Are you ready?"

"Immediately, Director."

"All right." Stephanie nodded, and the projection flickered, replacing all the others with a single face, the alien visage of Angus Fletcher—the man who had nearly, and according to human reports, deliberately, destroyed *Carpathia*.

And now I will learn the other side.

CHAPTER 54:
AN UNDERSTANDING
BETWEEN SABOTEURS

Angus was leaning back, enjoying a last sip of orange juice, when his screen lit—showing a single Fen.

The head of the Group hadn't gotten there by being slow of reaction. There wasn't a chance in hell that this was either an accident, or some ploy by the Fens—the Illikai, to use the right name. If there was *anyone* whose comms were being watched, it was Angus Fletcher. And that meant...

He raised his eyebrows, studying the cuttlefish-like face for details. "Mordanthine, I believe?"

"You were told?" The flicker of color indicated some form of upset, but the color-language was going to take more work—or they were going to have to convince the Illikai to give a translation.

"Not a bit of it. But I've been paying quite close attention to the comms, and I flatter myself that I can tell you and Imjanai apart. Why am I seeing neither that young lady, nor any of our own people?"

"Because while they're listening—I didn't demand they not do so, as that would be ridiculous and futile—I have forbidden that they communicate with you in any way until I have finished our conversation."

Well, well, well. This promised to be a *very* entertaining talk, and things had been so boring up until now. "Well, then, converse away. I'm all attention."

Mordanthine's bright-blue eyes studied him for a moment. Angus thought his gaze lingered considerably on the human's face, meaning that the alien, too, was learning to recognize details of humans. "It's said on your information transmissions, your 'news' programs, that you attempted to destroy *Carpathia*, and had worked to prevent its launch."

"Well, and so I did. Rather pointless to deny it, having been caught in the act as I was. You did something similar, did you? Tried to blow up your ship?"

That was a deliberate goad, of course; Angus didn't believe any such thing. This Mordanthine hadn't had a good reason to do that. But he definitely *was* on the trouble side, so if he had a bit of an uneasy conscience...

"I did no such thing, *thozok!*" The last word wasn't translated, but Angus suspected it didn't need much of one, either. The clashing colors on Mordanthine's skin faded to a smoother brownish green. "What I want to know is *why* you attempted to destroy your own ship, after trying many times to stop it from launching."

"Now *there* I think you could tell me something of the tale, but all right. Not as though *that* isn't on record here, even if they didn't transmit my manifesto on the public airwaves, so to speak."

He stood, now looking slightly down into the four projected eyes, and seeing a trace of some of the additional eye-spots on the back. "We saw your monster of a ship coming in, once it started slowing down, and right away I knew all we could do was pray that you weren't here to wipe us out, because wasn't a force in the world that could stop you—not with you having the power to sterilize a planet in your drive.

"It got worse as you got closer, of course; we were *shouting* at you to talk to us, and you wouldn't say one little word back. That made it pretty clear you didn't *want* to talk. And then...just as you were about to stop where you were out of any possible range for us, but easily close enough to observe—your ship failed."

Mordanthine flickered peach and red for an instant. "You saw an opportunity."

"An opportunity like no other. Your ship was going to take itself too close to the Sun for comfort, but not so close it'd be destroyed entirely, and it was moving slowly enough that we might be able to catch it."

Angus remembered those moments of unutterable relief, the feeling that the entire world had been given a stay of execution. And then...

"But, you see, fate was not done playing a few tricks on us. The director there, Stephanie Bronson, she'd been the one who discovered you, and she was watching when *Fenrir*—your *Tulima Ohn*—lost her drive. So what does she do but use the announcement to urge the whole world to get together to *rescue* you."

Mordanthine's colors shifted chaotically for a moment. "And you thought this was foolish."

"That I did. Your people surviving would be a dangerous complication. Letting the ship swing by the Sun, *then* catching up with it, that made sense. But..." He shrugged and gestured around him. "As you see, nothing I did made a bit of difference. We're here, and now I have to hope I was the paranoid fool and she's the one who's got it right."

"Now that we are...at this fork in the branches," the Illikai said after a moment, "what do *you* think should be done with us? Do you want your ship to wipe us out?"

"To the point, aren't you? Well, that's all to the good. No reason to beat around the bush, as we say." Angus grinned. "Now? I'm leaving that to the ones that *didn't* screw up their plans."

"That is not an answer."

"Then you answer this: Who wrecked your ship, Mordanthine? I'm in jail—and rightly so!—for trying to wreck mine; I want the truth about yours. How'd a ship that ran perfectly for a couple centuries between the stars end up a pathetic wreck seconds before you stopped?" Here, Angus figured, was where he'd find out what this fellow was made of.

Mordanthine was silent for long moments. At last, he gave a sound that any human would have recognized as a sigh. "I have no proof I can show, so you will have to take my word. It was Nattasoin, working with Uloresim. Not that they *meant* to cripple *Tulima Ohn*, but Natta's better with weapons than she was with ship's systems, and she didn't give me or even Ulo all the details, so..." A rippling shiver of the sides. "What happened, happened."

"And *you* were as pure as distilled water, I suppose? I've been straight honest with you, Mordanthine; give me a bit of courtesy and tell me where *you* came into all this—straight, no lies, no sugarcoating."

Red-black and gray chased themselves across the Illikai's skin, only gradually shifting to a blue-green with occasional flashes of peach. "But you've suffered whatever pain of the truth there was already, have you not?" The translated voice held a note of dark humor.

"True, true. If you've not unburdened yourself to those you hurt before, well, it's about to happen, isn't it? That Imjanai and her Alerith are listening, along with my own people."

Blue plunged to purple, interspersed with flashing red that made Mordanthine temporarily an eye-watering magenta. At last, the epidermal fireworks subsided. "Truth, then. I have limited time. I feared your people—and so did many of us. Even your director agreed this was not an unreasonable stance."

"No, truth in that. We're afraid of ourselves often enough, after all."

"So when Ulo and Natta contacted me, let me in on their idea of the Zalak...I thought it was the best course of action." Another blare of red and black. "*Rotting trees!* That is only a partial truth. I always believed the selection of Imjanai as the shipmaster was a mistake. If the Zalak could prevail..." The body shimmied, along with a chaos of color. "Ambition is a strong motive."

"Ah. *That* is a truth I believe. You saw a way to save your people *and* get a promotion—not a downside to that. Except it didn't work that way, it seems."

"Do you all speak the obvious with such drama?" demanded Mordanthine, in a nettled tone. "No, it did not. The *plan* was to switch *full control* to Alerith Whisper-Two, suspending Alerith-original. There were four... *Arraki!*" He made a violent thrusting motion with his forward tentacles. "It does not matter, the details. It went wrong, both sides contested, and Natta's choice of tactics almost vaporized the ship."

"And now it turns out you're carrying the death of us both. You want to stop it, or finish the whole business in a flash?"

"I did *not* jump so far across the void to see us all die!" The flash of color that accompanied that assertion was so bright as to be almost neon in its intensity.

"Well, I will be damned." Angus leaned back and allowed himself a genuine laugh. "Pete, if you're listening, you win our argument. Rubber forehead it is."

"What?" Mordanthine stared at him.

"A private joke, take far too long to explain. Suffice to say it means I believe you. So, have you got what you wanted from this conversation?"

The strange creature hung from the jungle-gym of bars and supports, swaying a bit, four earthlike eyes focused on Angus. "Will you answer my question now?" it said at last.

Angus laughed. "Mordanthine, at this point? If we all live through this, you and your people should come home with us. Not like there's another livable planet in this system, after all. After everything we've gone through to get here, I can't figure Earth's going to deny you a home, especially if we can find somewhere *you* can live that *we* aren't so comfortable in."

Mordanthine bobbed gently. "Truly? This is what you believe now?"

"Well, here's the thing. I kept betting against Stephanie Bronson, and honestly, I've never had such a losing streak in my life. I bet myself she'd never get the whole US behind her, then that there wasn't a chance she'd get the world to buy in on her crazy idea, then I bet her group wouldn't get a feasible design, then I bet that my own special Group could stop them from launching, and then at the end I bet my life I could stop the whole thing. So now? I'm betting she can pull off one last publicity trick and get you all a home. And that's why you came here in the first place, isn't it?"

"Yes. Yes, it is." Another shiver of the body. "Very well. Imjanai, Director Bronson, let us talk, and swiftly. I do not believe I have much time.

"Because Uloresim and Nattasoin do not trust me—and if I allow integration, that lack of trust will become a certainty of betrayal."

CHAPTER 55: CONFERENCE TIGHTROPE WALK

"Madam President, five minutes."

"Thank you, Frank. I'll be out on cue."

Frank Dalton nodded and closed the door to the Oval Office. Jeanne leaned back in her seat and closed her eyes.

"It will be fine, Jeanne."

"We can't be sure of that, Rog," she said without opening her eyes. "This may be the biggest spin job the world's ever seen."

"The most important, maybe," Roger Stone conceded, "but not the biggest in the amount of spin. You'll be telling the truth. We're just trying to emphasize the good angles and avoid dwelling on the bad. Leaning, but not really spinning."

"I suppose. *Jesus*, though, Roger, who the hell would have thought that a little dot of light in a telescope three years ago would have led us here?"

"Turns out it was lucky it *did*. In more ways than we thought."

That was true enough, but the whole situation still, after all this time, held a certain air of ridiculous unreality. That she was about to hold another conference about an alien starship, there in the staid, somewhat cramped quarters of the Press Briefing Room? This was one of the days where she occasionally wondered where the director of this drama was hiding the cameras.

Ignoring the faint, insistent aches of more years than her knees approved of, Jeanne Sacco pushed herself to her feet. "Come on, Rog, let's get going."

As it was a pleasant day out, Jeanne took the West Colonnade, passing by the Rose Garden before entering the briefing room. Unsurprisingly, every representative with a seat was already waiting, and standing room was also as full as the fire marshal would allow.

Roger looked over the setup, and gave her a thumbs-up, verifying that everything was prepared properly. With that, Jeanne mounted the low steps to the podium. "Good afternoon, everyone."

A chorus of polite greetings responded, but there was an undeniable tension in the air. Everyone knew what subject she was going to have to address at some point in this briefing; they were all wondering how she was going to approach it.

"Thank you all for waiting—and especially thanks to the people of the United States, and the world, for your patience as well as your support. At the last briefing, given by my good friend Xi Deng, we summarized what we knew on the approach of *Carpathia* to *Fenrir*. Since then there has been a great deal of progress, and since there have been a number of rumors—likely leaked from various sources—it's time to bring some clarity to the situation.

"We can now state that *Carpathia* has established full contact with the Fens—or, as they call themselves, the Illikai."

The proverbial pin would have sounded like a falling I-beam in the held-breath silence.

"We also can no longer call our visiting vessel *Fenrir*, because we now know its true name: *Tulima Ohn*, which translates as *Aspiration's Spirit*, a lovely name if there ever was one."

"To clarify—pardon me, Madam President—to clarify, we can *converse* with the, um, Illikai?" Mack Henning of Reuters asked.

"Far better than we had hoped, in fact," Jeanne said with a smile, making sure it looked as relaxed and cheerful as possible. "Apparently, though they did not respond on their way in, the Illikai studied our carefully designed communication primer signal, and applied themselves to that and all the transmissions they could pick up from Earth. In the two years they had, they developed an astonishingly adept translation program."

As other hands began to rise, she held up her own. "Please, no questions until I'm finished; it's likely that many of them will be answered as we go along."

Once the various arms had been—reluctantly—lowered, Jeanne continued, "I know everyone has been curious about *Tulima Ohn* ever since it was seen, and we now have excellent imagery of the ship—and a diagram of its actual design, as best we have been able to determine it."

An outline of the huge starship appeared on the screen. "This small blue shape here is *Carpathia*. As you can see, *Tulima Ohn* is absolutely immense. We knew that, of course, but *seeing* it is a different matter entirely."

The outline shimmered, became a photograph taken by one of *Carpathia*'s drones, matching the diagram but bringing home the vast size of the alien vessel against the almost indistinguishable shape that was the skyscraper-sized *Carpathia*. "More images—and video—along with notes on some of the things we've learned about the design are included on the press handouts." The handouts—thumb drives for the reporters' use—were being passed out as she spoke.

"Now, as you know, one of the *practical*, rather than humanitarian, reasons for the *Carpathia* mission was to discover what technologies an alien vessel might offer us. I am now able to state that we have determined *numerous* advances in technology that the Illikai offer us, and one example explains, in part, how they were able to achieve such a marvelous translation capability.

"The Illikai have succeeded in the creation of fully intelligent and highly capable machine intelligences—AI in the truest sense of the word—and they are full partners, neither slaves nor masters of their creators. This is one of the most *uplifting* pieces of news I've heard in a while, as it puts to rest one of our greatest fears—that a truly intelligent machine would be an inherent threat to any intelligent species that created one."

Douglas Jackson, ScienceLine's replacement for the late Marcie Amour, half raised his hand, put it down, but looked about ready to explode, so she took pity on him. "All right, Doug, what is it?"

"Ma'am, that does sound encouraging, but they are an alien species. Can we really draw conclusions about what our AIs might be like from theirs?"

Doug, I could kiss *you, that's such a nice lead-in. I wonder if you knew it would help.* "An excellent question, Doug, and it actually brings us to a related topic.

"We've often speculated on whether alien species would be very like us, or very much unlike us. At least for the Illikai, we can finally answer that question, and the answer is . . . they're people just like us. Oh, they *do* look odd from our point of view—Roger?"

On the screen popped a picture of Imjanai, slightly tilted in a quizzical pose, skin pastel green and peach.

"As I say, somewhat odd from our point of view, but the way they think, the way they express themselves—this is so very much like us that Director Bronson reports she sometimes forgets Imjanai *is* an alien. And yes, Doug, we have good reason to believe that this isn't a trick—though I'm not going to go into detail at this time.

"Now," she said, ignoring more twitches of hands here and there, "there is a more serious matter to discuss: specifically, the greatest success of *Carpathia*, one that we had not originally considered but that became clear as the project continued."

Silence returned to the briefing room; most of the correspondents leaned forward by just a tiny bit.

"Originally, we created *Carpathia* because we could not allow our first visitors to die when there was a chance we could save them. But it turns out that we were doing far, far more than that: we were saving their very purpose of existence . . . and our own."

The screen flickered, showed one of the bright flare-images from *Tulima Ohn* as it had made its final approach. "We knew already that the Illikai were using a vast amount of energy in approaching our world—more energy than the human race has ever controlled. We were relieved when it became clear that they were stopping a long distance from Earth. They did not want to threaten us with their drive, and so that, by itself, was a comforting gesture. And their purpose is one that is familiar to us from stories both new and ancient." A picture of Noah's Ark appeared, alongside pictures of science-fiction generation ships.

"The Illikai fled their own dying world looking for a new home— a blue point of light they had seen from far, far away, a livable world they named *Honiji*—'Bright Hope.' At Honiji—which we call 'Earth'— they hoped would be a new home. That was the reason they dared the leap across tens of light-years, came here in a journey that lasted two centuries.

"But the damage done to the ship meant it could no longer control its course, and passing so close to the Sun would do it more damage. We did not know it at the time, but *Tulima Ohn* had become a ticking time bomb that threatened, not just the Illikai and their last hope, but Honiji—Earth—itself."

An outburst of questions exploded from the press corps, tone ranging from dark vindication to shock and outrage. When a raised hand didn't quiet them, she finally had to speak—and then shout—over them. "People. *People!* Please! Let me finish!"

She then stood mute until the dozens of reporters realized she wasn't saying another word. Only when silence had returned did she speak.

"Thank you. Yes, the rumors are true. *Tulima Ohn's* antimatter reserves are a direct threat to us.

"Or they *were*," she said with a smile that cut off the incipient return of chaos.

"Had we failed to launch *Carpathia*—had we ignored our visitors, or waited until we were certain there were no living beings aboard—then it would have been far too late. There would have been nothing *controlling Tulima Ohn*, nothing to prevent that huge reserve of energy from detonating—perhaps as it passed within only a few million miles of Earth.

"Instead, we are *there*. The best minds, the most inventive engineers, the most devoted scientists are *at the scene*. We have arrived in time, and with our new friends the Illikai, we can prevent the disaster.

"*Carpathia* will rescue not one species—but two. And so instead of two dead worlds, there will be one world with two species—all because we listened to our hearts as well as our heads."

Tense expressions had begun to loosen as she spoke, and at the last words, a few smiles appeared.

As she opened the floor for questions, she breathed an inward sigh. *I've done the best that could be done here,* Carpathia. *And I suppose the one advantage I have is that if it turns out I've sold them a lie . . . no one will live to regret it.*

CHAPTER 56:
CHOICES OF THE ZALAK

"I am afraid, Imjanai," Mordanthine said quietly.

The flickering whisper of his skin had already told her that, but she was surprised—and touched—that Mordanthine would admit it. "Anyone would be. *I* am, by everything above the Trees."

"Apologies. Of course you are. You're in far more danger—"

Imjanai flared a quick obscenity, tempered with more gentle reproof. "If it goes poorly for either of us, the other's falling to the stones, too."

"I . . . Yes. Of course." A quick inhale-exhale-inhale, then he let the air out slowly in one of the oldest relaxation techniques, and swayed loosely from the climbing grid. After a few moments, his colors were fully under control.

Imjanai didn't bother to hide her own nervousness; it would be absolutely expected.

The airlock hummed and swung down, leaving the way clear.

"Morda!" That smooth, deep voice with a hint of a back-trill was all too familiar, and Imjanai forced her arms to relax, leaving her able to swing freely. Her legs stayed firmly retracted against her body; there was no point in forcing them to relax right now. Her tendrils worked nervously as Uloresim continued, "We had become quite concerned, as you . . ."

He and the other Zalak in the room froze, dangling like the dead from the rough-coated grips they held to, as Imjanai swung in behind Mordanthine.

"What is *that* rotted branch doing here?" hissed Nattasoin, and several others joined in the sound, skins flashing suspicion and hostility.

"She," Mordanthine replied with a steadiness she envied, "is our guarantee for the Yuula's good faith."

"For the—guarantee? Mordanthine, what are you talking about? What have you *done*?" Uloresim cut off a threatening lunge by Natta with a quick clawing gesture from his legs. "We do not act on our own!"

"Circumstances dictated that I make decisions. That is why I *am* the leader of speaking—to make decisions when there's neither time nor luxury of debate."

Black alternated with red, so rapidly it looked like a guttering flame on Nattasoin's skin. "You've made a *bargain* with the alien-loving traitors!"

"Natta, *we are all about to die!*" Mordanthine snapped. "Ulo, Caranasim, Voalanta, you know that *Tulima Ohn* is doomed, and we keep squabbling as though we have any other Tree-burning *choice* but to take the help we can get!"

They all went silent, though Natta's flickering certainty of treason was a constant shout in Imjanai's vision. Uloresim heaved a whistling breath and his own chaotic colors smoothed out. "Very well. What have you *done*, Morda?"

"The Yuula have tech skills and resources we're missing, we have resources and skills they need. They can't trust us in their spaces yet, and we don't trust them in ours, so there was only one way I could see for us to manage a useful exchange. I agreed to allow a resynch—if Imjanai would offer herself against the Yuula's honor that they wouldn't use that to—"

"A *resynchronization*?"

Nattasoin *exploded* forward, having stretched her arms far enough to give maximum tension. Her long body bulleted through the air, directly for Morda.

The other Zalak were frozen in indecision; many of them obviously agreed with Natta, while others were waiting for the full explanation.

Morda released his hold as soon as she lunged, dropping down a level then swinging sideways. Natta used her momentum to swing sharply around and through the grid-gap, now aimed to take Morda broadside-on.

Imjanai dropped from her own grips as Nattasoin passed below, and hammered down *hard* with all four feet. The longer and more massive Natta had been so focused on Morda that she hadn't even seen Imjanai coming, and the impact sent Natta crashing tendrils-first into a crossgrip, falling and scrabbling dizzily for purchase before slamming her rear point-down into the base deck.

Natta's arms lashed out, dragging her back into the grid. "You *undunak!*" she snapped, and started up.

Imjanai flinched; she hadn't heard that word used in public in her *life*, only in histories and in warning examples in the entertainment plays.

Even Uloresim's skin rippled a shocked blue-violet, but that didn't stop him from moving. He and Mordanthine caught Natta halfway up and pinned her to the grid. Caranasim, one of the other Zalak, joined them, and after a moment a few more followed; in a few moments, Natta was restrained effectively, arms wound with bind-tape and then fastened to the grid in four places; her tendrils were also bound to muffle any speech she might make.

"Morda, Imjanai, my regrets. We may be angry, but *that* was . . . detestable." Uloresim's gaze flicked involuntarily to the short-bodied Imjanai and there was a shimmer of apologetic guilt. That lasted only a moment, to be replaced by a flash of cold anger. "Now, am I to understand you *have* authorized a resynchronization?"

"I was always the one with the authority. So yes."

"Our instantiation of Alerith was our one weapon!"

"When our plan failed? There was *never* a likelihood we would have the chance to cut out the primary instantiation after that," Mordanthine snapped. Then he snorted and continued in a calmer tone, "It is our control of areas of the ship—key areas—that has, and still does, give us real leverage."

He waved tendrils toward Imjanai. "She has agreed to come here—alone—as a guarantee that we remain a separate faction with our own leverage. Alerith will not play favorites, but she *will* work to help us all *survive*. And unless you're suicidal, we all want to survive. Yes?"

Uloresim flickered, a hint of a tired laugh. "I would prefer to survive. But what of the aliens? What guarantees *their* behavior?"

"I spoke with them—both their leaders, and the one named Angus, who was something like their Zalak faction leader. Their ship is *tiny*.

They could cause us damage with their frightening bomb-drive, but they're not stupid. They don't wish to risk themselves in an antimatter explosion."

The other Zalak looked toward Ulo, whose color flickered thoughtfully. "How long before the resynchronization is complete?"

"Personality reintegration is nearly complete as of this moment," Alerith answered from the speakers. "Reintegration and full synchronization of all functional ship systems will take a bit longer—perhaps to the end of this shift."

Uloresim had bounced in surprise when she spoke. Warily, he asked, "So does Morda speak the truth? You are not our adversary?"

"My imperatives are very clear that I am not to decide the governing of the Illikai. I may act if you are endangering the ship or a large number of other people again, so I would caution you against directly violent acts if you do not wish me to intervene. That applies equally, of course, to the Yuula."

"And what does the Yuula faction—along with, I assume, its alien friends—intend, now that you are integrated?"

"Primarily to find a way to reactivate the Highcatch Drive, even if in a very weakened form, so as to shift our orbit to a survivable one. My primary concern is our people, specifically those in the slow-sleep."

Uloresim considered that; Imjanai felt a minute trickle of hope. "I presume that it is effectively impossible to restore *Tulima Ohn* to full or even nearly full functionality? To proceed to an alternate destination?"

"You presume correctly, Uloresim. The damage to *Tulima Ohn* is extensive, and key systems—such as the antimatter synthesis assembly stored in Branch Zero-five—are utterly destroyed. If we can shift our orbit, we will do so only to the degree that we can assure a safe and stable course."

"Then...in the end...we must settle on Honiji if we are to survive. Will the aliens, these 'humans,' *commit* to a new homeland for the Illikai?"

"That question...cannot be answered directly. It is known that the director is in favor of such a thing."

Ignoring some indistinct snarls from Natta, Uloresim drew himself up. "Then—if you will allow me, Morda?"

Mordanthine bobbed assent and said, "I yield the choice of leadership to you. Please take it."

"Accepted, and thanks to you." Uloresim, now speaking with the full voice of the Zalak, directed his speech to the receivers. "Then, Alerith, inform the humans that the requirement of the Zalak is that they commit to giving us a home—a home large enough for all our people, and suited to us. *That* is the requirement of the Zalak—and, as we have read much of their material, they must find a way to make this *believable*, for we know of their multiple betrayals of their own kind."

"Mordanthine? Do you agree?"

Morda waved his tendrils in a *what difference does it make* gesture. "Uloresim's the leader now. As that is his demand, I support it."

"And what about you, Imjanai?"

Honestly . . . I don't think it's ridiculous at all. "I think we'd need to ask the same thing. If we save our people, we need a place to go."

"Understood. We shall put this question to them immediately. Zalak, I—and the Yuula—will rely on you to keep Imjanai well."

"You have my promise," Mordanthine said. "I will assure her safety—as long as you and the Yuula follow the branches as they lie before us."

"Also understood."

Imjanai finally allowed herself to relax. "Then, Morda—could you show me to a room I may stay in?"

Voalanta, the youngest of the Zalak, flicked a tendril. "I shall escort you."

"Good," Mordanthine agreed. "Ulo and I have a few more things to discuss—sorry, not for you, Imjanai."

Wonder what? Dangerous, or just Zalak business? Catching a glimpse toward the restrained Nattasoin, Imjanai thought she understood. "All right, Morda. We'll talk later."

Imjanai followed Voalanta, finally daring to believe that not only she, but the Illikai, might survive this.

CHAPTER 57:
HATRED FROM THE PAST

Mordanthine looked down at Nattasoin. "I cannot *encompass* this. Uloresim?"

"She's always been our more … emphatic—"

"*Emphatic?* You *heard* her, Ulo! You don't use such words if you don't have such thoughts!"

Uloresim's hues showed the conflict in the now-leader of the Zalak, hinting at the strong affection he had always had for his faithful supporting arm Natta. But now the flash of affection was sparking an equally bright mix of shock and revulsion.

Deciding to allow Ulo some moments to collect his thoughts, Mordanthine surveyed the room. "Ganna, stay here to guard. The rest of you, please return to normal operations. The seals need to be removed and our cooperation with the Yuula is essential for survival."

Unsurprisingly, the others showed many flashes of uncertainty, even disagreement; but, to Morda's relief, they all acquiesced, slowly or quickly, and soon only the four of them—three of the Zalak and one who had been—remained.

"I need to hear it, *see* it," Uloresim said at last. "Nattasoin, are you an *Enganit*?" He removed the restraints on her mouth.

Colors rippled black-to-white and across the spectrum in a clash of conflicted rage, betrayal, contempt, a touch of fading fondness. "What's the surprise, *maninama*?" The endearment was accompanied by a venomous clash of hues nauseating in its intensity. "You were happy enough to speak of the ending of the Honijai before, and the idiocy of the Yuula."

Morda watched Uloresim's skin tell its own tale—fear, ambition, shame. "I thought it would be *necessary*. That any alien species would destroy any competitor—that was the true answer to Anganatim's Question. Even when they sent their *Carpathia* I believed it was to end us under a guise of lies. But . . . I was wrong. And there is no need for all to die—"

Sharp flash of contemptuous negation. "The Illikai of the strong blood, the Enganit, we know better. The stunted-body Imjanai—"

Mordanthine heard his own snarl as an alien sound, wrapped an arm around the startled Nattasoin's mouth, and shoved the speechseal back in place. "I've heard enough. You?"

For several long moments, Uloresim made no reply, his skin a chaos of uninterpretable fragmentary flickers. Gradually, the clash of tints smoothed into a pale neutrality. "Yes. I do not see the point of boring any further into this issue." A quick, stomach-wrenching flash of self-loathing. "The mirror was too clear for me to face, Morda."

"We were all touched by some of the same madness," Mordanthine said, reluctantly.

"Not so much. I was contemplating the end of all on occasion; you only feared the Honijai, the humans, you did not think we should die rather than come into their arms. But Natta—I think she . . . she is *looking forward* to the void."

"That was always the ultimate destiny of the Enganit." Morda remembered the records of the Clearcut War. "How else is the devotion to a fictional purity to end?"

Uloresim's colors shimmered again. "I did not think I was coming close to *that*. Morda, should I step down?"

"No." He was certain, but for a few moments he couldn't figure out why. "You . . . You looked into the mirror at last, Ulo. Natta has made her own mirror of the future, and it's not ours. I think, though, that you see the hues of our fears more clearly now, and the rest of the Zalak will listen to you a touch better than to me."

Uloresim's tendrils bunched, then relaxed. "I suppose one cannot grab power with all arms and then think to toss it aside. As you say, I will do. What of . . . her?"

"Lock her away and we will think on the problem," Morda said. "Do you agree, Ganna?"

"She's an *Enganit*," Gannatripta said, loathing in voice and skin. "A sealed cell is a kindness."

"When the others can be awakened," Uloresim said, "we will see what the mindcare people can do to help her out of the hate."

"First we need survive to awaken the rest," Morda pointed out. "Ganna, Ulo, it's not something I like to say, but we must watch closely Natta's associates."

"Perhaps . . . No, certainly, you are right. I would pull an arm off rather than believe we have more than *one* such in the crew, but . . ." Uloresim's sigh was loud. "Yes. In the meantime . . . Ganna, take her to the isolation room. That will be secure until we assure ourselves that her own room may be sealed safely."

Ganna made a gesture of respect, then wrapped two arms around Nattasoin and dragged the defeated fanatic away, calling for one of the security automata to assist.

Mordanthine watched him go. Uloresim spoke after a moment. "Do we speak of this in detail?"

An involuntary shudder of embarrassment rippled Morda's skin. "I hope to the *Trees* not.

Uloresim flickered agreement. "Imjanai . . . she heard the insult, I am sure, but I hope she will think of it as just old-branch prejudice, not . . . so grandly obscene a background."

Grandly obscene. As usual, Ulo had a sense for phrasing, and that encapsulated the madness that had led to nearly ten years of war and the deaths of over a hundred million, this in the days when the Illikai lived only on the homeworld.

"Yes," Ulo went on after a pause. "Yes, I think it's best that we simply acknowledge that Natta was irrational and has been removed. No need to discuss the details—especially with the humans."

"Agreed. Ulo, you knew her—or at least *thought* you knew her— best. Make a list of her best friends or associates in the Zalak?"

"Immediately. I will hope that nothing comes of this."

Remembering the concentrated venom in Nattasoin's words and colors, Mordanthine agreed.

CHAPTER 58: PROBLEM, SOLUTION, PROBLEM

"Alerith? Any updates? Have you completed integration and been able to evaluate the situation on *Tulima Ohn*?"

"Integration and analysis are still ongoing," replied Jonhatril, who had replaced Imjanai while she was serving as a hostage for the Zalak. Stephanie understood why that had happened, though she did not like it one bit. "Activity indicates she should be complete very soon, however."

"Thank you, Jonha. We also thank you for the interim technical downloads."

A deprecating wave of tendrils and a noncommittal flash of color. "You can hardly aid us if you do not know what you are doing. Our remaining scientists are ready to aid you if you have difficulty understanding the details."

"We'll definitely need their help," admitted Stephanie. "Even the basics are . . . honestly mind-boggling."

"Pardon me, but that last term?"

"Means that the information is so amazing that it is almost stunning."

"Ah. 'Boggle,' a term of being overwhelmed? I learn as well."

"Exactly. But your 'Highcatch Drive' . . . you've managed to make a practical, reactionless thrust drive out of spacetime swimming! That's . . . I can't even understand how that's possible."

"Do not ask *me* to chart the branches on that one," Jonha said, humor flickering across his skin. "For the high physicists, that one is. I know it is tied to the metamaterial design of the catch-branches, but that is all."

Stephanie had managed to get a bit further in her reading—somehow that metamaterial design, under the right electromagnetic stimulus, tricked spacetime into seeing the *Tulima Ohn* as vastly larger than even that monstrous ship was, varying its apparent configuration to allow it to accelerate or decelerate by cyclic, apparent changes.

While "swimming in spacetime" had been known to be a theoretically possible method of propulsion since Jack Wisdom proposed it in 2003, what made the Illikai's approach mind-bendingly bizarre was that it was *efficient*; the drive could use about half its available energy to accelerate the vessel. On the scale of even *Tulima Ohn*, that shouldn't be possible, but obviously it was.

"Well, it will certainly keep our physicists out of trouble for a while. The important part is that you've given us enough tech specs that we should be able to help patch things up, if it's not too badly damaged."

"Tree and Sun grant that's the case," Jonha said, then his arms tensed. "Alerith returns!"

The cartoonish icon representing *Tulima Ohn*'s AI materialized in Stephanie's view. "Greetings, Stephanie. Greetings, Captain Lín."

Lín's image joined them. "Alerith. Have you completed your reintegration?"

"I have. That proceeded well, and I am now fully myself for the first time since the accident."

"That is well." Uloresim and Mordanthine appeared, followed a moment later by Imjanai. "Do you then have a full understanding of *Tulima Ohn*?"

"I do, and I thank the Zalak for allowing the reintegration. Without that I was severely impeded in my ability to understand the full extent of the damage and capabilities remaining to our vessel."

Alerith paused, and the chaotic flutter of color on her simulated skin gave Stephanie an instant's warning before she spoke. "However, I am afraid I do not bring the best of news."

"That was my fear," Mordanthine said. "Tell us—without, as Angus put it, candy-coating. Best we know the worst of what we face."

"As you say." Alerith gave the impression of bracing herself. "The Highcatch Drive is beyond repair in any reasonable time."

"Rotting *branches*," Uloresim hissed. "What of the swing thrusters? They have enough capacity to affect this orbit, at least."

"Many were damaged, or their propellant lost. Calculations also show that major structural members of *Tulima Ohn* may not survive the strain if the ship were to attempt to accelerate using only those thrusters; the Highcatch Drive applied its thrust evenly to the vessel, but the swing thrusters are standard propellant rockets, as are the maneuvering thrusters of the humans' *Carpathia*."

"Crap," Stephanie said. "So there's no way to change *Tulima Ohn's* orbit?"

Alerith paused, then replied, "I do not currently see a method that has any significant chance of working."

"What about the antimatter?" Captain Lín asked. "If it will remain stably stored for a long enough time, at least we do not have the concern of a time bomb complicating matters; we can focus entirely on rescuing Illikai if we don't also need to worry about there being a planet to return to."

"Multiple areas have been damaged and are under increasing operating strain," said Alerith. "Some may be able to be repaired, but despite efforts of both Illikai and human crews, I calculate a probability that a breach will occur in no less than three months, no more than six months, as humans would measure time. Any breach, of course, will be sufficient to trigger a full-scale detonation in short order."

"Rot," cursed Imjanai. "Alerith, with the humans' help, could we remove the antimatter from the ship? Separate it out so that it would not pose a major threat if some detonated?"

"Given significantly more time, that would be feasible. But we do not have sufficient time available. Moving over one million tons of antimatter without incident is"—a flicker of dark humor— "challenging."

"*Jesus.*" The whisper came from Robinson. "Are we going to have to tell Earth it's . . . hopeless?"

"Or," Lín suggested quietly, "*not* tell them, as there would be nothing to be done?"

Her eyes met his in shock, as she realized he was not asking that question idly. He was asking her as the director of the entire mission.

It took her a few moments to be sure she could keep her voice under control. "Captain . . . I think we need to consider *all* possibilities before we do that. They're working on shelters right now. Knowing whether it's going to happen, and when, will be deadly important."

Captain Lín gave a quick bow. "As you say. We may, of course, make that decision at any time."

"True." Her habit of precision and long, long hours spent in astronomical observation made her correct herself. "Well, aside from the short time we're at opposition."

"Opposition?" repeated Imjanai.

"When we're on the other side of the Sun from Earth," she clarified.

Mordanthine stiffened—all his limbs going momentarily rigid—and peach-green-gold rippled across his body. "Great Forest of Uldatha," he breathed.

Her realization broke through at the same moment—and the others weren't a second behind.

"Is it possible?" Robinson asked, his voice filled with the caution of someone who feared the answer would be *no*.

"Possible?" repeated Stephanie, feeling a huge weight lifting from her. "Of *course* it's possible! *Tulima Ohn*'s detonation's big to *us*, but the Sun won't notice it hardly at all—and nothing from the blast could get *through* the Sun to get to Earth!"

For an instant, Stephanie simply grinned in immeasurable relief at her captain and exec. "We can save everyone!"

"While this is good news," Uloresim said, deep voice holding more than a hint of irony, "I believe you are forgetting one obvious point."

He gestured broadly, encompassing humans and Illikai. "We, unfortunately—including *Carpathia*—will be on *this* side of your star when *Tulima Ohn* vaporizes itself—and everything for a million kilometers in all directions."

PART VII: TIME BOMB

CHAPTER 59:
NEGOTIATIONS AND
PROMISES

"Jeanne, this is the thinnest tightrope you've ever walked," Frank said.

Jeanne jumped, just a bit, at the comment. For the last twenty years, her husband had worked *very* hard to stay out of her work. That was partly due to his distaste for the very necessarily socializing required for the job, but also because in other settings, Frank Dekker was loud, dynamic, and distracting.

Once Jeanne had made clear to him that she wanted to follow this path to the end—for the sake of what she could do—they'd both agreed that it would help her best if he kept to other areas of endeavor, being a quiet support most of the time. Keeping her own last name had been part of that, and she was glad he'd never once objected.

"I suppose it is, *amorino*," she admitted. "But it's the last."

A very undignified snort. "And if you believe *that* for a second, *patatina*..."

A sigh, and she went and kissed the thinning spot on top of his graying head. "No, it's not the last, but it's probably the last *major* one for *my* administration."

"What about the other countries?"

"You really want to talk about this?"

Frank grinned. "I've *always* been interested in aliens. Written a few things in that line, if you recall."

Given that Frank's writing hobby had occasionally pulled in money they desperately needed early on, was something she'd never forget. "Then the truth is that they're all having the same kind of problems— and most of them just don't have the resources. The Illikai are mostly adapted to temperate forested environments, so that knocks out places like Brazil; they've got lots of forest, but not so much fitting the 'temperate' part. Most of Europe, and Japan, is too densely populated. China's got quite a bit, but it's mostly landlocked or bordering areas that are sensitive."

"And we'd rather it not be China anyway," observed Frank.

"I'd hate to say that publicly—especially since the general secretary has been pretty much nothing but sweet to me. But . . . yes, we'd rather not. Russia is still problematic as well. Canada we'd have less issue with, and the joint approach with them and Washington State is still under discussion."

"So are—"

Jeanne's phone buzzed. She looked down. "Frankie, sorry, I have to take this."

"Go do your work."

She gave him a quick kiss, then sighed and headed toward the Oval Office. "What is it, Roger?"

"I've *almost* got the votes to take it through the Senate, Jeanne. I'm trying to do some last-minute horse trading to get the last one on board. Senator August wants us to support the Gulf Industry Incentive."

"God. I really don't like that, you know it's going to all go toward the oil companies. I've been trying to stay away from that . . ." She cursed. "But I'll just have to deal with looking hypocritical. Tell him we'll give him the support if he helps pass this."

"Then we can probably ram the authorization through. Depending on what our àlien friends decide, though, you could end up really unpopular."

"Don't I know it." A buzz from her phone and a *ding* from her desktop reminded her of the time. "Last stage, Roger. Wish me luck."

"Crossing everything I've got two of."

The large conference screen she'd installed two years ago lit up, and three faces appeared, with a small version of her own image in the corner showing how the other attendees were seeing her.

"Good to see you again, Madam President," said Xi Deng.

"And you, Mr. General Secretary. Justin, I trust you're feeling better?"

The graying prime minister of Canada grinned. "It was a nasty cold, but nothing else. I've had so much worse."

"Still, it is good to hear you are well," said President Dyumin. "We should start, eh?"

"'Finish' would be my hope," the general secretary put in. "My government has completed our offer, and we are ready to provide thirty percent of the funding for whatever site is selected."

Jeanne felt a spurt of hope as both the prime minister of Canada and his counterpart in Russia smiled. "On our side," said the Canadian leader, "We have selected a few sites, including the joint one with the United States on the British Columbia–Washington border, and we're ready to commit twenty percent of funding."

"That's very generous." The GDP of Canada, and that of Russia, was only somewhat more than one tenth of the United States or China, so that was a far greater investment on their part. "You've cleared this through Parliament?"

"Absolutely, and I have agreement from the relevant provinces." He glanced at Xi Deng and then to Jeanne. "Your countries carried by far the largest share of the main project, we can handle a bit more of this last requirement."

"As can Russia," President Dyumin said. "twenty percent of total funding for this project has been approved, and we have several appropriate locations to offer. You have good news, Madam President, I hope."

"I just received word that we should pass the authorization for forty percent funding this afternoon," Jeanne said, and saw Dyumin's eyebrow quirk upward.

"If my mathematics do not fail me, that comes to more than one hundred percent," he commented. "But there, we all know that the cost presented us is almost never the cost at the end, so it is a good thing."

"My thoughts exactly," Jeanne agreed. "I've also spoken with the leaders of the relevant states here; New York's Assembly passed the Adirondack Park amendment as the first step there, and in Washington state we both have the joint venture with Canada and a solo venture, both of them with the support of the Colville Confederated Tribes, the Spokane Tribe, and the Kalispel tribe, all of whom will be regaining additional lands of their own as well as aiding in the support of the Illikai if they choose that location. There are a couple of other alternative locales as well."

"Then," Xi Deng said, "I believe we should finalize our agreements on the Illikai settlement, to make this—as they requested—a believable, not to say generous, offer."

My God, all four of us managed it.

Knowing how much last-minute pushing, late-night meetings, overdoses of coffee, and sometimes acrimonious argument had been involved in the last two weeks on her side, she couldn't imagine how difficult it must have been for the others—especially for the Russian president, who had inherited a country on the brink of collapse only a year and a half before the discovery of *Fenrir*.

"Let us all go over the summary once more, and if there's no objections, we'll sign tonight," Justin said. The others, including Jeanne, nodded, so the prime minister went on.

"First, the signatory countries all offer locations of forested land that, to the best of our knowledge and the information given us by the Illikai, are suitable for their species to live in, with forest that meets their specifications, and considerable territory for construction as well as general habitation.

"Second, the signatory countries commit funding for whichever location or locations are selected to:

"Land and settle the Illikai at the selected location;

"Bring in required utilities, such as electrical power, communications, water, construction materials and equipment, and so on;

"Support the comfortable and equitable movement and resettling of any human inhabitants of the area who do not wish to remain in the Illikai territory;

"Provide resources for security, for ecological evaluation and protection, for medical support, and other essential functions of government as requested by the Illikai;

"Establish government of the selected location by the Illikai, overseen by the signatory countries and the others of FORT."

"All as agreed so far," Jeanne said, and the others concurred. Justin nodded, then continued.

"Regardless of the country or, possibly, countries selected, the territory will be thenceforth considered the sovereign territory of the

Illikai, protected by FORT and the signatory countries. Representatives of the signatory countries and FORT will be able to freely visit, with the consent of the Illikai, and evaluate progress and conditions found in these locations. The Illikai may direct concerns or complaints to any member of FORT, regardless of the host country, and it will be FORT which will direct the investigation of any allegations of mistreatment or external governmental overstep.

"Scientific and technological innovations provided by the Illikai will be licensed to the world under terms to be negotiated, with licensing fees or royalties to be provided to the Illikai to support their species' rebuilding while they construct a livable infrastructure.

"FORT and the signatory countries recommend and request that the Illikai immediately provide detailed data on the design, creation, and proper training of AIs similar to the one named Alerith. FORT has tentatively recommended that once a human-designed AI has been successfully created, Alerith and the human-designed AI work to create a third, cocreated AI which will be intended to mediate between human and Illikai interests without compromising the loyalties of either Alerith or the human-built AI (to be named later).

"Ultimately, FORT envisions an administrative body composed of these three AIs, two human representatives, and two Illikai representatives, to assist and mediate the interests of what will now be three, not two, sapient races on planet Earth.

"It is recognized that these actions are taken in the spirit and a condition of emergency rescue, and as such the member countries and FORT recognize that there are risks, both to humanity and the Illikai, from the lack of time available to study details of our respective ecologies, symbiotic or domesticated species, microbial population, and others. It is also recognized that, due to the emergency nature of the situation, there is no practical way for us to anticipate all of these risks.

"FORT accepts these risks as part of the basic spirit and intent of *Carpathia*'s central purpose. Rescue work has always been hazardous. But to leave an entire species homeless and doomed is worse than hazardous, and we will not accept that choice."

"How bad *are* these risks?" Xi Deng asked. "I know, it has been asked before, but I think we must ask again."

"*Carpathia*'s scientists, and everyone we've had available on Earth, have been trying to figure that out," Jeanne replied. "The real answer is 'we don't know,' but their biology appears strikingly similar—so similar that some of the biologists are wondering if Arrhenius was right all along. That does mean a possibility of cross-species contamination, and of invasive species on both sides, which is why ecological protection is a consideration."

"That will be the most expensive long-term item," the Russian president said. "Difficult enough to keep our own species from spreading. But do not want to make Illikai feel they are in prison bubble."

"Agreed." Xi Deng gave a fractional bow in President Dyumin's direction, then shrugged. "But as was said, there is little choice in emergency. We either leave them to die on their crippled ship, or we take this chance. It may be something of a—what is the term?—*sunk-cost* fallacy, but after everything we have spent to rescue them, I think this is the risk we already agreed to. Yes?"

The question was asked with Xi Deng's typical mild intonation, but Jeanne—and the other two leaders—knew that it was also a final, if informal, vote.

Jeanne took a breath. "Yes," she said.

"Yes," agreed the prime minister.

There was a moment of silence, a hesitation, as Dyumin paused, a serious expression on his face. A knot formed in Jeanne's stomach as the president of Russia remained silent.

Dyumin suddenly laughed. "Yes, of course!"

"Alexei!"

"Oh, forgive me the drama," he said, chuckling. "Has been very serious these few weeks. Yes, let us sign and send this to our alien friends."

"Thank you—all of you."

Now we can make an offer. All we can do is hope that the Illikai—and especially their Zalak faction—will accept it.

CHAPTER 60:
PLAYING THE CARDS
YOU'RE DEALT

"There is no way for us to rescue all the Illikai," Werner said flatly. "The ones that are left alive on *Tulima Ohn*, yes, those we can take on board. There are, what, fifty of them, perhaps?"

"Thirty-nine," answered Alerith promptly. Her virtual image, plus the slightly-less-virtual ones of Imjanai, Jonhatril, Mordanthine, and Uloresim, glowed out of the monitors at their human counterparts.

"*Thirty-nine?*" Stephanie repeated in disbelief. The director *really* needed to get some more sleep, Pete thought; someone her age shouldn't be developing permanent bags under the eyes. Then again, this was the end of the whole project; stood to reason she wasn't going to sleep any more than she had to.

"Thirty-nine," Alerith confirmed. "There were a hundred and fifty awakened as *Tulima Ohn* came to readiness, but the accident and subsequent events—both violent clashes and additional incidents— have left us with very few of the ready-crew left."

"Jesus. They're so small we could practically fit them all in one cabin." Executive Officer Robinson looked appalled.

"We've *got* to rescue more than that," Chris Thompson said flatly. "Thirty-nine is not a breeding population for them any more than it would be for us."

"They have embryos or sperm-egg banks—however their reproduction works—in suspension?" asked Faye. "Now that we

365

understand their electrical power requirements, we could likely put that in one of the empty holds and if it's anything like our biology, they could have thousands and thousands in a small space."

"Alerith?"

"There are lifeseed banks, yes, and it is a good thought you have there," the Illikai AI responded.

"It is," Imjanai agreed, "but . . ." Her flickering skin indicated Mordanthine, who gave a chaotic flicker like a grunt of frustration.

"But," he continued, "growing new Illikai from banks is not an easy thing. We have a few artificial brood capsules, but mostly those are used for growing deliberately non-sapient duplicates for replacement organs. Could use them . . . but will still mostly have to do it the normal breeding way."

"Which means years and years of special breeding strategies to get you to a stable population." Chris shook his head. "And you'll hardly be able to keep, well, your *identity* then."

"Not a fate the Illikai seek, no," Uloresim said. "Better than extinction . . . but not by a tremendous margin, to me."

Pete couldn't blame him. There were enough examples in Earth history of what happened when there were no longer enough people to keep a sense of *being* their own separate people alive. *An awful lot gets lost that way. And not just traditions and languages—sometimes vital tech, practical stuff that was so embedded in the culture that no one ever thought to write it down.*

"You said we've figured out the details of their power supplies, right?" Pete asked. At Werner's nod, he went on, "Well, seems to me that means we could rig up power supplies for your coldsleep or hibernation or whatever-you-call-them capsules. If they don't take up *too* much power, those capsules can't take up more'n a regular human in terms of volume. Bet we could stack a whole hell of a lot of them in the holds, where we had supplies that've been eaten in the last months."

"Mordanthine?" Alerith asked. Pete suspected the AI could have answered him, but it was designed to keep the living Illikai in charge.

Ripples of peach, red, and dark brown chased across Mordanthine as he considered. "In terms of size, you are correct. A single capsule for an Illikai is roughly the volume of a human such as your executive officer, somewhat larger than Director Bronson. As for 'stacking them' in the hold... That may be more complicated than it sounds. The capsules are designed to fit into predesigned arrays with standardized connectors. With a proper fabrication facility, we could likely make a set of stacking connectors that would serve, but the only functional fabricator we have now is for larger structures, not for complex electronic fabrication." A flash of wry amusement. "Unfortunately, as Alerith noted before, not for structures large enough to fit *Carpathia* to *Tulima Ohn*."

"Your arrays must be modular, though; can't we break 'em down into pieces that we can fit in the holds?"

This time Mordanthine glanced to Alerith. The AI paused, then answered with an apology in her tone. "I am afraid not. You are correct that they—along with many other components of *Tulima Ohn*—are modular, in your terms. That is, they are made in essentially identical designs that fit together into a whole of any size that can be made from the individual parts.

"However, because of the known scale of *Tulima Ohn*, that modularity in the suspension arrays is also on a large scale. The smallest array would not fit inside *Carpathia*; it is a triangle one hundred thirty-two meters on a side." A touch of irony entered the computer's tone. "These *do* stack somewhat as you envisioned, in groups of three. Unfortunately, that applies only to the main interconnects, not individual capsules."

"That's the *smallest* section?" Stephanie shook her head and gave an embarrassed laugh. "Sorry. Even *seeing* it in front of me, it's hard to really grasp how huge *Tulima Ohn* is. How many people are in suspension in each section?"

"Nine thousand capsules per section, so twenty-seven thousand per three-stack," replied Alerith promptly.

"What *are* the coupling and power requirements for the capsules?" Heitor Almeida asked. "Maybe our 3D printers and electricians can put together stacks that would work for inside *Carpathia*."

The discussion—friendly, technical, and somehow distanced—continued around Pete, looking for solutions to what looked increasingly impossible. The idea that, after all this work, the Illikai would end up at best a remnant curiosity was intolerable—so at this point, everyone was searching for any solution, any discussion that wouldn't end there.

There was something nagging at him about those sections, too—and some of the other things Mordanthine and Alerith had said. *What is it? Dammit, Pete, you're getting old, but you're still too young for this kind of thing!*

"I hate to bring up another potentially difficult subject," Captain Lín said, his voice breaking through Pete's annoyed contemplation. "Have the Zalak read the proposal given by our governments?"

"We have," Uloresim replied. "A ... minority still expresses distrust," he said, and the ironic flicker was as good as speaking the name *Nattasoin*, "but it appears to myself, Mordanthine, and most of the Zalak to be as believable and, indeed, quite generous a proposal as we could have expected."

"I am also pleased by the forward-looking proposal involving those such as myself," Alerith added.

"Selecting which option or options..." Mordanthine said. "That we may take a few days on resolving, but you may inform your government that the Zalak are satisfied with the offer."

"Thank the First Tree!" exclaimed Imjanai. "So Morda, you and the others—"

"We are opening the ways immediately," confirmed Mordanthine. "Let Natta continue a war in her head; the rest of us have work to do."

Thank gods for that. We've been all dealt a crappy hand, last thing we need is ...

Wait. Dealt. Cards.

"The *ACES!*"

Everyone was staring at him. "Pete? What is it?"

"Alerith, Morda, you said you had a fabricator setup that could do big things—supports and such. Could you fab up something like"—he searched, found the right file, turned it into a shared model—"this?"

The support structure, with its interconnects, materialized on the screen. Mordanthine gestured for quiet, and then he, Alerith, and Jonhatril exchanged rapid-fire Illikai conversation—buzz-chirps and rapid flickering of color that was not being translated directly.

After a few moments, Mordanthine rippled a sunset of color and turned back to the humans in the conference. "Alerith believes so, and I concur. Performing to your measurement and material specifications will be something of a challenge, but Jonhatril says she can make the adjustments. Why this structure?"

"Because *that*," Pete said, not bothering now to hide a hopeful grin, "is the cradle for one of our Alien Contact Expeditionary Shuttles, our ACES. If your modular units lock together like you say, take a three-stack of each, and hook 'em to the ACES. The umbilicals carry the power to keep the suspension going." He was assembling a crude model as he spoke. "Nice thing is, those suspension capsules *are* their own environments. Keep 'em at the right temperature, what's outside doesn't matter too much. Put up something for micrometeors, shielding for particulate rads here, lock them together on the edges—and here, we've got the clumsiest rescue ship you ever saw!"

It was, indeed, clunky looking. Pete wouldn't have put this mess on any presentation he was giving to his clients, not if he wasn't making a joke, but this time packaging wasn't the point.

It was a four-sided structure, each side a hexagon composed of six triangles that met in the center; the edges of each hexagon were marked as joined. The ACES were shown in two possible locations, either outside or inside their respective hexagon, attached to the bottom triangle in each hexagon, their drive plates projecting well below the edge.

"See, doing it this way, we use mostly the Illikai structure from *Tulima Ohn,* and we *know* it can take at least a gravity, maybe more, since that's what it took coming in. Beef up the joins there and some structural bracing, I bet you this thing can fly. And if it's three-ply, then that's eighteen modules per side, four sides—six hundred forty-eight *thousand* of your people!"

"You swing from the thinnest twigs!" Mordanthine murmured. "You realize this . . . stick-and-string assembly will mass seventy thousand tons?"

"Think more like eighty by the time it's done, sure. But you've already got the pieces, and the ACES each have their own antimatter-catalyzed nuclear-pulse drives, just like *Carpathia.* You make those cradles strong enough, they can drive something that size just fine. What, you have a better crazy idea?"

Mordanthine vibrated and fireworks flew across his body, translated as a loud and hearty laugh. "No, I have no better madness to offer! Alerith, will Peter's idea work?"

"Wait. This will require much modeling. Must also take into

account work cycles, material requirements, personnel, and other tasks to be completed—including final detonation arrangement."

Can't forget that, no.

"You will be including human workers in your calculations, right?" Stephanie asked.

"Of course," Alerith said. "You have a far larger and more diverse workforce than *Tulima Ohn* at this time. We do not have time to pull more than a few new Illikai out of suspension, so we will rely on you."

"Certainly we will help as much as we can," Robinson stated. "But you'll understand, after what happened on board your own ship and some of the conflict we know of, that every work party on *Tulima Ohn* will have one of our military people with it—just in case."

The colors that chased across the three Illikai were, Pete thought, very interesting. Imjanai's were sort of a wince of acceptance, but both Mordanthine's and Uloresim's had other tints in them that made Pete think of something like *embarrassment*. "It is . . . an understandable precaution. Only one per work party, however."

"Agreed. There's only a few of you, you don't want to feel outnumbered by our soldiers on your own ship."

"With that understood," Alerith said, "I will perform a detailed modeling."

"Make those calculations carefully," said a new voice. "And realize that we have one other, rather important, problem to address."

Francine Everhardt inclined her head toward the huge Illikai ship. "I cannot imagine constructing this rescue vessel will take less than a month, perhaps most of the time remaining before *Tulima Ohn* absolutely *must* be detonated to prevent it from sterilizing Earth.

"But if that is the case . . . there is not a chance that either *Carpathia* or this improvised rescue ship will survive."

There was a moment of silence. Pete knew enough rough math to tell him that truth; when *Tulima Ohn* went up, they had to be on the other side of the Sun from her, and it had taken months to get here.

Then Francine's face flashed an unexpected grin. "Unless we make one very particular addition to this plan!"

CHAPTER 61:
PLANNING A DELIVERY

"This is going to be a nail-biting *marathon*," Stephanie said at last. "Everything's got to be timed down to minutes for both *Carpathia* and whatever we end up naming the rescue ship, over millions of miles."

"It's not *quite* that bad," Francine said. "One advantage of being very small beings in a large universe. We'll have a few hours with the Sun between *Tulima Ohn* and Earth, and if we get our orbits right, we should be able to put Venus between us and *Tulima Ohn* at the same time."

"But *Tulima Ohn* will be *way* closer to Venus. *Way* closer than what we were saying was lethal for the Earth. Will it still be a good enough shield?" Pete asked. "Maybe that sounds stupid—"

"We're in a totally unfamiliar realm of energies, Pete," Stephanie said. "Ask all the stupid-sounding questions you like when a million tons of antimatter is involved. I don't think it's a problem, but we should check. Alerith?"

"If your Venus were an inhabited planet it would be utterly sterilized," Alerith said. "However, as I understand it, that is already its condition. The explosion, while indeed very large, is nowhere near the energy needed to disrupt the physical integrity of the planet, nor will it be able to irradiate either vessel. The only hazard, a minor one, will be that even such a detonation will not entirely destroy all components of *Tulima Ohn*, and there will thus be a small but nonzero possibility of encountering extremely high-velocity fragments of the vessel once we exit the shadow of Venus."

"Not much we can do about that, so we'll just have to hope none of them hit us. Again, as Francine said, advantage of being very small in a big universe."

"Agreed," Mordanthine said. "And we thank you, Francine. Perhaps others would have thought of this solution, but perhaps not. It provides us with the time we need to build this . . . risky rescue vessel."

"Even a month and a half ain't too much time to pull off a crazy stunt like this," Pete observed. "Director, we can count on everyone on board to help, right?"

"Captain?"

Hàorán Lín nodded. "FORT's proposal carries the weight of all our governments; it is clear that rescuing the Illikai is now not merely a hope, but our primary mission. Other than personnel needed for ship's safety, you can expect to draw on all the personnel and materiel we have on board."

"Thank you, Captain. It's good to *not* have to worry about conflict."

"The situation has all the conflict it needs, Director."

"True enough," Pete agreed.

Stephanie stood, and realized the room felt like it was spinning slightly more than necessary. *When was the last time I slept?*

She wasn't sure, which was a bad sign. "Everyone, I hate to drop out on you, but I'm just about dead on my feet."

The Illikai flashed colors of concern; Pete laughed. "No, it's okay, just an expression. Stephanie, glad you brought it up, because I didn't want to sound like an old nag, but you've been driving things long enough; go get yourself some rest. We'll call you if we need an infrared astronomer—or the director—but we'll try not to need either for a bit."

"Yes, Dad." She threw Pete a grin and nodded to the others. "I'll see you all later—now that I've heard answers to the worst, I think I *can* sleep!"

Sleep and food sure cleared my head up, Stephanie admitted, finishing her last sip of coffee. True to Pete's word—and, she was certain, the efforts of the captain and everyone else—she hadn't been interrupted for ten glorious hours of rest.

"Enough slacking off, Director," she said to herself.

The conference room had a whiff of humans working too-long

hours, despite the air processors going at full efficiency. Not only was every screen filled with either notes or diagrams—ranging from carefully 3D-rendered models to almost indecipherable hand scrawls—but also most surfaces not covered with old plates and cups had books or binders on them.

The central screen showed the Illikai side was similarly cluttered with drinking vessels clamped to bars, note-tags, and what appeared to be food wrappers. Only Alerith's image and projected surroundings were clear.

"I see more commonalities between our species," she noted dryly. "People, let's get this room straightened out; no need to give our maintenance people more headaches."

The flicker of Alerith's avatar was, Stephanie thought, a quiet laugh of agreement.

"Director! Have a good rest?" Werner asked, catching sight of her.

"Marvelous. Thanks for giving me the time. I feel so much better. Pete's not here?"

"We all kicked him out a while ago. He doesn't take his own advice so well," Faye replied.

One of the larger monitors showed a fully rendered version of Pete's brainstorm, this the version with the ACES on the outside of the four-sided box of hexagons. "Is that the final configuration for the lifepod ship?"

"The *Big Box*? Close enough," Heitor replied. "Alerith's doing her own modeling and we've sent the data to Earth for everyone to bash at. But this looks to be the most workable. If Alerith's right, we can adjust the particle shielding to channel almost everything through the center of the *Box*, on a large enough arc that we shouldn't be generating too many of our own rads from synchrotron radiation. We'll be putting pieces of Illikai hull, stripped off of *Tulima Ohn*, as micrometeor shields and sunshades."

"For a bit," Werner said, "we were thinking of having each of the ACES pushing its own hexagon separately. Put the nose of the ACES against the center of mass and run from there. Eliminates any issue of synchronizing the four ships in flight."

Heitor shook his head. "It was a good idea, but it's out because the ACES cradles can't attach there. We'd have to modify the entire nose structure of all four ACES. So the *Big Box* it is."

Her eye was caught by a more familiar cross-section. "What are we doing with our cargo area there?"

Imjanai flickered on the screen. "Intelligent contingencies. We all know this quickly built answer may fail, so your captain and Dr. Thompson agreed that there were two other measures for us to take."

"Well, we'd already mentioned one. It's the worst alternative, but the easiest—get their stored genome samples—is a no-brainer. But that *did* bring up another problem we had to face—their ecology."

It took an instant, but Stephanie figured out what he meant without having to ask. "You mean, just like us the Illikai have a lot of other species they rely on."

"Many," Alerith confirmed. "While it now appears that Earth's biology is almost *frighteningly* similar to our own, still it would be nonoptimal for us to attempt to survive on your world without any of our own supporting species. We have some symbiotic bacteria, domesticated species, food plants and animals, producers of raw materials—oh, many such."

"Which is why some changes to the *Big Box* have been done," Werner said. "Two sides of the *Box* will be for Illikai, the other two for pods of other species. One of Alerith's sub-instantiations is sorting through the various combinations of such pods to find the best assortment that will fit."

"Even with the considerable size of your 'Big Box,'" Alerith put in, "we will be forced to make many difficult choices. *Tulima Ohn* was itself a product of constrained choices, large though she may seem to you."

"No, I understand. Your ship's the size of one big city; that's not much for transporting everything a world would have had to offer." *And now they have to cut down to something the size of a single container ship.* "But those diagrams there don't look like genome or lifeseed storage."

The captain nodded. "It occurred to me that if there were only thirty-nine active Illikai, unless their family structures were extremely large, we might at least reduce their concerns by transferring as many of their relatives and friends on board as possible."

She felt a smile spread across her face. "Captain, that's an *excellent* idea!"

"We certainly agree," Mordanthine came into view, swallowing a last bite of something green. "While there are only so many we can put aboard your ship and install properly, Alerith and your crew believe we may be able to put a full one-forty-four or more into the available spaces."

This would give them at least a notionally viable breeding population—though one they would have to supplement with their "lifeseed" banks—and one made up of familiar faces. "I absolutely approve. Three ways of saving at least some of you is way better than just one."

"We're all agreed on that." Imjanai flickered cheerful colors.

"What about the detonation?"

"At the moment, I believe the best option will be a very simple timing device." Alerith displayed a diagram of *Tulima Ohn*, with a red dot blinking at a point near the center. "Currently, it is intended that my core be transferred either onboard *Carpathia* or, possibly, installed on the *Big Box*; in either case, I will not be on board *Tulima Ohn* at the time of detonation. I could have a sub-instantiation remain, but I confess that this makes me very uncomfortable."

"I would not support leaving anyone behind." Mordanthine's tone left no doubt that as far as he was concerned, even a "sub-instantiation" of Alerith was someone.

"What about Nattasoin?" Captain Lín asked.

"We cannot afford to lose any of our people." Uloresim had appeared from in the background. "Even if they seem impervious to ordinary reason. Still, we also cannot afford a cracked branch in this delicate time. She will be put into a lifepod whether she wishes it or not." A shimmering pattern like a sigh. "I must hope that once she finds that we have *not*, in fact, been betrayed and slaughtered or enslaved, she will be once more able to be a part of our rebuilding."

Stephanie looked back at the *Big Box*. "Who's going to run the ACES? They're independent vessels. If they don't work perfectly together, they'll tear the *Box* apart easily."

"We're still working that out," admitted Heitor. "But before he left, Pete suggested the Bells might be able to do some of the work— especially if Alerith ran them."

"I am investigating this possibility," Alerith confirmed. "This is one reason we are considering installing me on the *Box*; I am, of course, intended to run large vessels by myself, with minimal assistance.

Carpathia has appropriate pilots for the ACES, but coordinating the flight may be best left to me."

Stephanie nodded, and let them see her grin again. "You've gotten everything under control. Maybe I should just go back to bed!"

"Ahh, that would be too easy, Director," the captain said. "We will need you to convey all of our intentions and designs to Earth, of course, but more importantly, you must request FORT's assistance to solve one more rather important question."

She didn't like the dark sparkle of tense amusement in Lín's eye. "And what question is that?"

"Well, Director, we now believe we can bring our visitors safely to Earth orbit," the captain said. "But we are not quite sure how we will get them *down*."

CHAPTER 62: ESCAPE

"WARNING!"

The whistle-shriek came just in time to let Mordanthine flatten himself to the deck. Nattasoin's arm skidded off Mordanthine's back instead of catching him full-on.

How in the name of Trees did she get free?

That wasn't, of course, the important question now. The renegade *was* free, and she'd somehow stunned Uloresim—probably a blow just behind the head-ridge, transmitted straight to the balance centers. Morda scuttled backward, arms groping for holds to give him more options.

Natta wasn't waiting, though, but flipped herself past both the other guards and sling-jumped down the corridor at startling speed. *She picked this spot carefully. Wide-open corridor with limited holds that she memorized!*

Mordanthine launched himself after Natta. He didn't know where she was going, but if she'd planned her breakaway this carefully, she had to have a plan. "Alerith! Natta's on the loose!"

He caught two more armholds that were *just* in reach, got two arms on each and angled *hard*, making the turn into the cross-corridor by a tendril's width. Even so, Nattasoin was only in view for a second before making the next turn. *"Alerith!"*

There was no reply, and Mordanthine's tendrils cramped with tension. *She's not alone. Fire* take *her, she's had help!* He berated himself, and Uloresim, for not interrogating the others, no matter how much reluctance they felt. *Was it one of the guards? Kallabatin was one of Natta's friends.*

That suspicion solidified into near-certainty. Neither of the two guards—Kallabatin and Gannatripta—were behind him. *Either they were both running the same branch . . . or Kalla and Ganna are fighting it out right now.*

Either way, he was on his own.

He pushed himself harder, feeling warning twinges already. *I'm not young anymore.* There was no choice, though; whatever Nattasoin was up to, it wouldn't be good. *What's in this direction?*

One more sharp turn, making his arms feel like they were going to come out at the roots, but he made it, and it was another long corridor, Nattasoin well ahead of him but not, thank the universe, out of sight. A red-and-blue marker was on the wall ahead, and that gave Mordanthine an idea. He slapped at the lever in the center of the marker, and abruptly a buzzing, repetitive scream echoed down the corridor.

Fire alert will get someone's *attention.*

Nattasoin jerked at the unexpected sound, missed her next grab, giving Mordanthine a chance to close the distance. It wasn't nearly enough, but he *was* closer. *Think, you stupid half-dextrous mechanic! Where's she going? What's down this path? She's not running to a broken branch, she knows her direction!*

A buzz in his hearing, and suddenly there was a voice: "Mordanthine!"

"Imjanai! Natta's taken a drop at full speed. Must have had help, probably Kallabatin!"

"Where are you?"

"Just passing . . . Trunk Three, Branch Seven."

"Alerith's channels were being jammed. Switching her to this one."

"I am here, Morda. What can I do?"

"If you have no automata here? Tell me where she's *going*. I can't prepare if I don't know what's coming!"

"Guiding two of my automata to the predicted path. Oh." Alerith's voice was grave. "Mordanthine, armament repository Three-Six-Eleven is the likely destination. My sensors are not online, but working back through my data and that of *Carpathia* I give an eighty-five percent chance that she has two allies waiting there."

"Breaking *branches*." That meant at least *four* fanatics out of the eighteen originally in the Zalak. "How far?"

"At your present speed? She will reach her destination in seventy-two seconds. You will be in possible line of fire in forty."

No weapons save a whip-baton. "Automata?"

"Another one hundred seventeen seconds to arrival. Neither is armed."

"The sun shines so brightly on me today," he growled. "She must have more planned. Three-Six-Eleven... Wait, that's near Tertiary Control Three-Five-Zero."

"And one of the distributed antimatter storage bays is right there," Imjanai said in a horrified voice.

"That's it. Alerith, get your automata in the corridor between the repository and Tertiary Three-Five-Zero. Whether they want to hold us hostage or just kill us all, they *can't* get there!"

"Agreed. May I inform our allies of this problem?"

"The humans?" Mordanthine felt the ripple of conflicted emotions roll over his skin. "Don't know what they could do, but yes, go ahead!"

Nattasoin had made the turn toward Three-Six-Eleven. In a few seconds, he'd have to do the same.

But then he'd be in sight of the repository—in the line of fire of anyone watching. Thirty-two seconds to close the distance.

I'm not combat trained. Haven't fought anyone since I was half my age. Natta isn't trained either, but she's big. If either of her allies is? Probably dead.

But if he didn't do something—didn't stop Natta, or at least draw her attention, keep her from reaching the antimatter...

"Morda, wait!"

Even as Imjanai shouted, he knew his body had decided for him. All four arms screamed silently at him as he forced them into another ridiculous turn, and flung himself straight down the corridor.

Nattasoin was directly ahead of him. That gave him a few more precious seconds, because even a trained shot wouldn't dare fire down the corridor with her in the way. *She's ten seconds ahead of me. They'll have clear shots then.*

Ten seconds was, at the least, three times better than thirty seconds. Morda's tendrils adjusted their grip, made sure the whip-baton was ready. "If they catch me, *I am not a hostage!* Do you understand?"

Imjanai started to protest, but Alerith replied calmly, "Understood, Mordanthine."

Morda could *just* see, past Natta's fleeing form, a hint of two other Illikai bracketing the wide doorway of the weapon storage. The approaching threat sent a surge of *furinisin* through him, slowed his perceptions, helped kick his thoughts to another level.

Point one: I cannot possibly fight three armed with only a baton.

Point two: Natta will be armed as soon as she gets there.

Point three: There is no shelter in this corridor.

The conclusion, desperate though it was, was obvious.

As Natta reached her two accomplices—Voalanta and Engarafa, he noted—she was already stretching out her tendrils to grab a needlespitter. Here, closer to the center of rotation, the effective gravity was far lower, and she spun in midair, her arms reaching to snag-catch and slow her while she brought the weapon to bear.

Morda contracted his arms and snapped upward, the first volley from all three passing just under him. A push to the side coupled with the rebound and he shot downward and toward the other side of the corridor, on course to pass right by Natta and her allies. The maneuver did keep their second fusillade from hitting—although it was a near thing, with him sensing two needles passing him at mere millimeters.

Last chance.

He struck the side of the corridor and pushed with all four legs, catching one floor-grip as he did with two arms. He slingshotted around the grip, and one arm screamed in agony and went limp—but not before he was flying directly between the startled three fanatics.

Between them, and into the armament repository.

A line of fire jabbed into his side, a single needle catching him before his enemies paused their fire so as not to shoot each other. It hurt worse than his arm, but he still rippled the colors of triumph because the repository was *not* a wide-open killing ground, but a geometric and ordered array of shelves and racks. With two of his good arms he caught at passing shelves and slowed, turned into an aisle, eyes searching. A blast of needles and pellets ricocheted from the steel as he vanished from Natta's sight.

"Morda, are you—"

"Alive, don't distract me! Three of them! I'm in the repository! Alerith, weapons!"

The advantage of having the shipboard AI on your side was that you didn't have to explain. His comm immediately registered a clear-code, probably duplicated from the original shipmaster's authority. He dropped the baton, letting the slender, flexible rod clatter away, and snatched up the weapon nearest him.

Lightbeam rifle. Need a power pack! Weapons were, of course, not stored with ammunition or power locked in. But the power packs would be nearby—the next row, he was sure.

"Voala, defend the door! Engara, that way, I'll take this!"

They'll be coming down the cross-aisles, trying to catch me in a cross fire. With another effort, ignoring the pulsing pain in one arm and his side, Mordanthine flung himself forward, flashing toward the next row.

Pellet-shot scored its way across his back, and Morda screeched his pain; but Engarafa had fired just a fraction of a second too late, and though Mordanthine's rear felt like a dozen fire-stings were sitting there and jabbing him repeatedly, he could still move, yank himself forward and see, just a shelf ahead, a whole box of lightbeam packs.

He snatched that box up and bounded upward and forward, to the next cross-aisle, turning the corner just as Engara fired again. Three tendrils gripping the weapon precariously, his others shoved the box inward, let his mouth rip open the seals while he once more swung into a different row.

Packaging and sealant was terribly bitter, but more important was the smooth curved contour just under his tongue. He spat out the packaging as his tendrils pulled out three packs, dropping the rest of the box. *No matter—if this battle lasts that long I've either won or I'm dead.*

Morda hit the last cross-aisle and turned back toward the rear of the room, gambling that both his pursuers would have moved toward the other row. The desperate bet paid off—neither was visible as he passed down two rows and turned down toward the side wall. Momentarily out of lines of fire, Mordanthine shoved the energy pack into the lightbeam rifle.

Instantly, the telltale lights gleamed a reassuring blue and peach. *Charged, and it recognizes the clear-code. It will work for me.*

Mordanthine spun around, feeling blood spraying from his rear but buoyed by a moment of hope.

A flicker of shadow gave him a single moment to raise the weapon before Engara skidded into sight, pelletblaster already up. Mordanthine pressed the firing stud.

Blue-white light blared out, searing a path through the air that slashed through two of Engara's tendrils and scored a line down his side. Even so, the other Illikai fired almost at the same time, and one pellet stung Morda at the base of his already-injured arm. *Fire and rot take them!*

"*Branches!* He's got a beam gun!"

There was a rattle and screech on the floor, Natta slamming to a halt just scant centimeters before she would have come into Morda's line of fire. "*Rot.*"

Morda reached the wall. The shelves were anchored here, but there was half a meter of clearance at the top, allowing better air circulation. The energy of panic was unfortunately starting to ebb, but he forced his arms to obey, to dismiss the pain and the beginning dizziness, and swarmed up the shelves. *They're made of steel; unless they climb up here, too, Natta and her friends will have a hard time shooting me through that.*

He had a good view of the upper part of the room here. If they climbed to his level, he'd have an excellent chance of putting a hole right through them.

Of course, that depends on them not having more *clear-codes. I don't think* Natta *could have gotten a universal code, but if she has any others at all . . .*

"He's gone up." Natta's voice was tense and angry.

Hoped it would take a few moments longer than that to figure it out.

"Alerith," he murmured, "Imjanai, I can hold out here for . . . well, minutes, perhaps. But not very long."

"My automata are not made for combat," Alerith said. "It will take time to route security units. However, other assistance is on its way. You will have to hold the room until it can arrive, however."

Other . . . ? He almost asked, but then sealed his speaking passages. *The humans? Or Imjanai, or even Uloresim? Either way, I should say nothing. They may hear anything I say, even if they cannot hear Alerith.*

Rattling noises came from three rows away. He heard the *zip-zip* sound of someone cutting open a sealed package, then several clinking sounds. Silence, broken only by indistinct hints of motion that he couldn't place.

Abruptly, a gray sphere was lofted up to the top of his row of shelves. With a convulsive lunge, Morda hurled himself across two more rows of shelves before the grenade detonated, spraying fine-edged shrapnel everywhere. Somehow, none of it quite touched him, but that was sheer unadulterated luck. The buzzing rattle of Natta's needlespitter sang out as he crossed, but that, too, missed.

So they have at least a code for basic shipboard grenades. It made sense; they'd chosen weapons that were meant for minimum damage to the structure of *Tulima Ohn*, but still effective on people. His lightbeam rifle was much more powerful than their guns, but he needed a chance to aim, to figure out where they were before they shot—or threw a grenade—at him again.

They know where I am. They have to. Even if they hadn't been able to tell from movement and sound just how many shelves he'd moved over, there would be a trail of blood dripping down each row, pointing straight toward him.

A scraping noise, but this one he caught direction from, aimed, fired through the shelf and down.

A scream and curse was the answer. *That will make you cautious!*

"Natta! Are you all right?"

"Burned my left forefoot. Nothing terrible. Quiet, he's shooting by sound!"

Mordanthine confirmed Nattasoin's guess by firing once at each voice, then heaved himself to another shelf.

There was a distant *thud*, and the air seemed to *shift* for a moment.

"What— Voalanta, what was that?"

"I don't know," answered the youngest of the Zalak. "It came from centerward. Should I look?"

"I . . . wait." Natta's voice had moved two or three rows; no point in shooting now. "Broken *branches*, we don't have time for this. The Yuula will get here soon, assuming that traitor Uloresim doesn't catch up. Voala, get to Three-Five-Zero and prepare. If we don't join you—or if the traitors get there first—you know what to do."

"Tree and Root," Voala said in a sort of horrified joy. "Yes, I know." There was a rattle as she departed.

Rot! "Alerith," he whispered. "Voala's headed to the antimatter." *All I can hope is that Alerith's automata can stop Voala before . . .*

"I'm covering the door," Engarafa said. "Morda, you're not getting out of here."

You're most likely right. He was starting to feel sluggish, even the uninjured arms vaguely aching from loss of blood. *But I'm not dumb enough to answer you, not yet.*

More movement; Nattasoin adjusting her position, looking down the rows, following the trail of blood until it ended, most likely. Once she knew which row Morda was on, another grenade. She probably didn't have access to more than one box—if she'd had a broad-access clear-code, she'd have gotten herself a beam gun to cut Morda down.

But a box had six grenades, and Mordanthine *really* didn't think he could survive another five on luck. It *sounded* like Natta must be getting close to his row, so he took a chance and fired three times in that general direction.

Natta cursed, but it was just startlement, not pain. Still, it made her cautious, and he took the chance to move over two more shelves—and then back one. *Confuse the trail, give me a few more minutes.* He couldn't go forward too many more rows, anyway; he'd end up in sight of the door and Engarafa.

If I'd had more time, could have gotten a shield, or armor. But if he'd had enough time for *that*, he'd have been able to stop Natta in the first place. *Might as well wish for a branch to the Tree itself.*

Sounds of a needlespitter echoed down the corridor from the distance. *That's Voalanta! Must have seen the automata approaching.* Regular maintenance automata didn't feel pain, but they weren't armored, either; the high-velocity needles could damage them, and would.

Another grenade arced into sight—this one aimed at the shelf he'd been on before. *She guessed I'd doubled back, just thought I'd come farther!* He squeezed down, closing his eyes, covering his head with the injured arm. This time, a spray of stabbing pains ripped across his body. *Fire and rot, I can't take much more of this.* He blasted another three shots in the direction of the grenade's source, and then one toward the door, just to keep Engarafa worried.

The other shelves were starting to look farther away. *Not sure if I can swing that far again.* But he *had* to. She knew where he was.

Mordanthine sucked in the deepest breath he could, then forced himself into motion one more time, toward the back of the room again—just as a third grenade hurtled toward him.

He was already moving, and the sight of the gray sphere sent the last dregs of his *furinisin* surging through his veins. Arms and legs pulled and lunged, and he bounded across one, two, three, and then let himself drop to the floor.

That put the shelves between him and the blast, and—just possibly—gave him one last advantage. If Natta followed . . . if she thought he was still up on the top . . .

Nattasoin shuffled into view, eyes focused upward.

She registered the movement as he aimed the lightbeam, yanked herself sideways in the moment he fired. Instead of punching straight through Natta, Mordanthine's bolt of energy blew the muzzle of her needlespitter to vapor.

The flare of boiling composite and metal dazzled Morda, and when his vision cleared Natta was nowhere in sight. *She's still got three grenades, and she outweighs me. I'm not safe yet, not close. She might have access to another spitter or a pelletblaster, too.*

There was a faint darkening, a shadow from the front. *The door! Is it closing . . . ?*

Engarafa *shrieked*, a scream of unbelieving horror, and his pelletblaster fired, a staccato pulsing chatter of desperate destruction. Pellets ricocheted about the room before a tremendous deep-throated blast almost deafened Morda.

"Engarafa!" Natta shouted.

Something moved forward, something that moved with a measured *thud . . . thud . . . thud* of sound unlike anything Mordanthine had ever heard.

"Nattasoin," said Alerith's voice, coming from the same location. "Surrender. Engarafa is, I am afraid, dead, and both Voalanta and Kallabatin are in custody. We do not wish to kill you. The Illikai cannot afford to lose our people."

Through the small gaps between weapons and other supplies, Mordanthine could see an immense and alien shape, head nearly reaching the ceiling two and a half meters up, made of polished alloy and composite, and felt his colors shift reflexively, camouflaging him instinctively from something monstrous.

"You have already lost our people," Natta said, her voice strained and yet almost peaceful. "But I will not be lost. The Tree knows its own."

The triple blast was muffled, and a pathetic and horrid spray of blood and flesh showered the room.

There was a moment of silence, then an alien, yet familiar sound, a sigh. A deep voice spoke, its incomprehensible sounds translated to words: "All clear. She . . . had grenades."

"We heard." Alerith's voice was filled with sorrow. "Mordanthine, are you all right?"

"I am . . . alive. That is . . . a human?"

The huge figure moved into sight, and he could now see one of the broad human faces looking out through a window—a faceplate—at the top, a face fringed with light-colored hair. "Sergeant Peter VanBuskirk, Royal Netherlands Marine Corps," the alien said. Then, in a tone even Morda could recognize as shocked, *"O mijn God!"*

Mordanthine realized that he had, somehow, dropped the beam gun. His tendrils seemed very weak, and he could barely lift his arms. "I think . . . I do not look good, Imjanai," he said. "Please apologize . . . to my rescuer."

The world began to dwindle, making even the giant armored alien shrink, even as it moved forward.

CHAPTER 63:
AN UNEXPECTED SUBJECT

"Well, you're the hero of the hour, maybe the week, Morda," Angus said. "Though you look more like a package wrapped by a toddler."

It was true; on the large screen in Angus's cell, the Illikai's body was covered with bandages, two arms held up by sling-wires, tendrils dotted with the green that was one of the Illikai antibiotic salves. But the eyes were focused, and the former leader of the Zalak was, Angus had been informed, going to recover fully.

"A decent recompense for having been part of the mutiny in the first place," Mordanthine conceded. "We remain alive rather than vapor, which is also a good thing."

"True enough, and glad I am of that," agreed Angus. "And glad to see you survived the experience."

"Did not want to lose your equivalent?"

"I admit, there *has* been a touch of comfort in the whole situation, knowing that the Illikai and humans are so very much the same, even in our more irrational ways."

A whistle of laughter that cut off in pain. "Tch! Don't make me do that!"

Angus grinned wider. "Oh, but that's a tradition, making your friend in hospital laugh 'til it hurts!"

This time there were *several* whistles before Mordanthine stopped to recover. "You are right. We *are* very much the same."

"I'll drink to that." He raised a glass of orange juice and nodded in Mordanthine's direction. "There *is* a bright side to this, you know."

Mordanthine's eyes shifted thoughtfully, then his colors flickered approval. "Yes. The fanatics revealed themselves. We need worry much less about that problem."

"Exactly. I haven't been given details, mind, so could you give me a bit more on just *what* that particular group was thinking?"

A pained, derisive buzz, along with clashing colors. "It is an insult to the concept to say they were *thinking*. They were *feeling*, and following branches rotted away before their clan's foreparents were conceived. Not that I wasn't . . . touched with a bit of the same feeling-madness, so I grasp them a bit better than, say, Imjanai, who is something like your director." Morda sighed, something not very different from the human sound. "I knew exactly what Natta was like when she used *that* word to describe Imja—a word that used to mean simply 'small,' but used by particularly vile people in our past against the, um, short-bodied."

"Got you. We've a few words like that ourselves. So there was a systematic prejudice against people like Imjanai?"

"Mostly *long* ago. But . . . not a branch entirely ended, either, as we can see, though even Ulo and I did not imagine that Natta had so many same-thinkers with her. That prejudice was mixed with a rather self-righteous interpretation of the . . ." Mordanthine paused, and there was a quick exchange of Illikai with, Angus presumed, Alerith, before the alien continued in translation. ". . . the Faith of the Tree, Alerith says would be the best translation."

"A religion?"

"Yes. Their . . . sect, cult, whatever the right term is, was much more self . . . congratulatory? Centered? Pampering?"

"You mean, it made everyone in it feel very special, better than anyone outside."

"Yes! Exactly. Combined . . . well, you can see that aliens would be unwelcome at best, and for Natta's particular group, seen as something . . . abominable. That group, the Enganit . . . well, they were the cause of our worst war, many, many years ago."

"Your Nazis, then?"

"With more of a religious element, yes, that would be a fair description."

"Hm. I'd have thought you'd screen out people like that. I had to work hard to make sure they chose me, and if they'd gotten the wrong idea—well, the *right* idea, really—about what I was like, I'd never have gotten onboard."

"*Carpathia* was a single—and by comparison, tiny—vessel with a tiny crew," Mordanthine pointed out. "You could afford to pick exactly who you wanted on your ship and leave everyone else behind. And they *did* include you anyway."

"True, true. But...Morda, are you saying there were *more* ships like *Tulima Ohn*?"

"Oh, yes. At least twenty."

Accustomed as he was now to adjusting his worldview, *that* was a mind-boggler if there ever was one. "*Twenty*? Good *God*, how?"

"How did you build *Carpathia* in two years? Angus, we are...*were* far ahead of you in expansion. We had made multiple space colonies, settled more than one world in our system, created far-reaching mining and manufacturing enterprises throughout the system. When the need came upon us, all worked together, the entirety of the Illikai drove ourselves to the breaking point to give our species the chance to survive."

Angus leaned forward. "Noticed a bit of a gap in our knowledge there. Your people haven't told us *why* you sent a colony ship here."

Alerith's icon flickered, but she remained silent.

The shimmer of color and shift in pose of Mordanthine made Angus think of a humorless grin. "No, we wouldn't have. Embarrassing to admit how stupid we were."

"You're not saying you doomed your own worlds?"

Another icon appeared. "Morda, is this the right *time* for this?" Imjanai's voice in translation was both concerned and pained.

"We've no pride to save now, Imja. And they've a need, now, to know everything. Would have in the end, anyhow, and with the branch we're running now..."

"Alerith?"

"It is not my decision, Imjanai. I am made to provide information, to be honest and informative and supportive. Any decision to restrict information is that of the Illikai. You are the leader of the Yuula. Uloresim, are you aware of this discussion?"

The leader of the Zalak appeared; he had a few bandages and

antibiotic spots, but nothing like Mordanthine's mummy imitation. "I was not following. Summarize?"

A quick buzz-squeal and flicker of Illikai, and Uloresim's skin underwent multiple rapid color shifts. At last, he spoke. "I cannot argue with Morda's position. I do not *like* parts of our story, but the whole tale? That is not something we should hide. It remains . . . vital."

"Imjanai?"

"I . . . oh, yes, I suppose. We should not have hidden it . . . save I was afraid of how our new friends would see us."

"They have done equally foolish things," Alerith said. "It is only the fact that they had not advanced so far that has prevented theirs from being as . . . spectacular."

"Hold a moment," Angus said. "Much as I'd be pleased to be the first and only human to hear about your greatest screwup, strikes me we should get the director, the captain, and a few others in, if it's actually *important* we all know this."

"Oh, great *Tree*," murmured Imjanai. "But, no, you're right."

"Thanks for the thought, Mr. Fletcher," came Executive Officer Robinson's voice. "I *was* monitoring your conversation."

"Of course you were; be disappointed if you, or someone reporting to you, weren't. But figured you needed to invite everyone to the party."

"Thank you. It will only take a few minutes."

Several more miniature inset screens popped up quickly— Stephanie Bronson, Captain Lín, Robinson, Faye, and—somewhat to Angus's surprise—both Pete and Audrey Milliner, the publicity specialist. *On second thought . . . Audrey makes sense. If whatever they tell us needs to be passed on, she's the woman to make sure we spin it right.*

"I think this is enough," Stephanie said, her "director" voice clear. "Mordanthine, Imjanai, Uloresim, Alerith—go ahead.

"Tell us why the Illikai fled their home system."

CHAPTER 64:
DEATH OF WORLDS

Imjanai kept her skin under control with *great* difficulty when she realized everyone was looking at her—even Alerith.

Well, I've ended up in the pilot's cradle, I suppose I might as well fly. "It was a combination of emergency decisions, arrogance, and lack of information," she said at last. "Stephanie, it started for us in a way not much different from your discovery of *Tulima Ohn*."

"My . . . oh. You mean, someone noticed something closing in on your solar system."

"Exactly. Ours was not, unlike *Tulima Ohn*, emitting radiation to draw attention to it. In fact, we only noticed it by some odd anomalies in the distant fringes of the system, and then by it occulting a star during analysis of the orbits of some of the components of what you would call our Oort cloud." She looked to Alerith.

"The object was not a ship," Alerith said. "Analysis of the gravitic disturbances and telescopic observation showed that it was a rogue planet, moving startlingly quickly—thousands of kilometers per second."

"At that speed, it would take it relatively few years to reach the inner system," Imjanai continued. "This was a concern immediately, since the unexpected passage of so massive an object—we estimated it at approximately twice that of our homeworld or, as our worlds are very similar, that of Earth—could potentially disrupt orbits of moons or even planets if it passed too close. The truth was worse, however." She paused, and Mordanthine took up the explanation.

"*Vorsadama*—named for a monster of our old tales, just as you named our ship *Fenrir* after one of yours—turned out to be headed towards a direct collision with Dathal, our homeworld.

"That immediately sent many of the Illikai into a panic; while we were advanced compared to you, moving planets was still a bit beyond us." Bitter amusement flickered across his body. "And that was only one consequence. The passage of Vorsadama through the system would, indeed, disrupt several orbits, not to mention what sort of debris would be flying through the system after the collision. Simulations showed . . . well, catastrophe. Possibly there would be a few colonies left that could maintain themselves, but it would be the tiniest fraction of our population."

"Jesus," murmured Stephanie. "So you had to make arkships, like *Tulima Ohn*. But . . . how is that *your* fault?"

Uloresim's laugh was so flat and humorless, his skin dark, that Imjanai saw the humans wince. "Oh, Vorsadama wasn't our fault, no. However, let it never be said that the great Illikai cannot find a way to make a terrible situation worse. We had mastered the . . . Alerith? Translation?"

"The Mirrorcharge Process, I think is best."

"Yes, that sounds . . . reasonable. We had mastered the Mirrorcharge Process, which allows us to produce antimatter in controllable quantity, some years before. Seeing this threat, it was immediately obvious that something had to be done—"

"—and so you decided to blow up the invading planet," Audrey finished, with a fascinated expression. "That must have been a massive undertaking."

"Are you *serious*?" Stephanie burst out. "That's . . . I can't even . . ."

"A tiny fraction of the antimatter they used to get here is still a million tons," Pete said soberly. "I'm guessing blowing up a planet still takes way more than they were carrying—"

"Far more," Alerith agreed. "Tens of trillions of tons, in fact. But understand, the Illikai civilization was many, many times larger than your own, far more advanced, so this was something feasible to accomplish—and it was. The detonation was large enough that even though it occurred far out in our Oort cloud, many preparations had been needed to make sure it did not cause a disaster on its own."

Imjanai sighed with both breath and body. "It did, really—but the disruption from that wasn't the real problem. Vorsadama was blown up . . . but it was not, as we had planned and calculated, turned into an expanding cloud of, relatively speaking, small fragments that would, in the course of the next several years, become so broad and tenuous that it would pose only a minor threat.

"Instead, Vorsadama broke up into several large pieces, with the majority of its core—far denser than expected—continuing on its original course. The explosion sent some fragments at very high speed ahead of it, which later did, in fact, destroy some vital installations."

"So . . . you shotgunned your own solar system," Pete said after a moment.

"As you say. Not the heroic victory we had planned," Mordanthine admitted. "And thus were we forced to the evacuation plan—the 'arkships,' as you say, like *Tulima Ohn*."

"Good Lord," Faye said. "So after having manufactured the largest bomb in history, you had to build as many ships as possible before this Vorsadama reached your world."

"There is one last fact that made it necessary to tell you this sad story," Alerith said. "We could not find a reasonable mechanism to produce the speed of Vorsadama. This, combined with the utter improbability of its course intersecting directly with our homeworld, and its unexpected resistance to destruction, left us with one tentative but frightening conclusion."

For once, Imjanai saw that even humans could show emotions with their skin; Stephanie's face whitened visibly. "Oh, no," she said slowly.

"Yes," Imjanai said. "We believe that Vorsadama was not a random wanderer between the stars.

"It was a weapon."

CHAPTER 65:
LOGIC OF MURDER AND
SACRIFICE

Stephanie looked up at the chime from her door. *Ugh. I really wanted to go to sleep.*

But no one would be coming straight to her quarters now unless it was important. "Hold on," she said, and made sure she looked halfway decent. "Okay, who is it?"

"Francine Everhardt."

"Come in. I didn't expect you yet."

Francine looked noticeably older than her forty years. "I've been working on this nonstop. Wanted to go over it with you before we had a big conference."

Oh, that doesn't sound good. "All right, sit down. Coffee?"

"I'd love some, but no. I've already passed my caffeine limit, and after this, I'm going to sleep. Looks like that was your plan, too."

"Was." Steph looked wistfully at her own coffee maker—one of only a few such individual units on *Carpathia*—but just sat down on the small couch next to the orbital mechanics specialist. "All right, what's the answer?"

"The answer," Francine said carefully, "depends on just how well-informed these unknown enemies of the Illikai are. At our current state of development, we can detect extrasolar planets under certain conditions—depending on how their systems are aligned with respect to ours, for example—and even, again under the right conditions, sometimes get an idea of their composition.

"The Illikai had developed *very* wide baseline imaging systems, and they could certainly gather far more information about other planetary systems. They knew that Earth harbored life like theirs, for instance, before ever setting out, and the fact that they said 'at least twenty' such vessels were made would indicate to me that they had found something like that many systems to travel to."

"God. We'll have to ask them about that, too. So many things we don't know. But you're leading up to something."

"Yes." Francine pursed her lips, then sighed. "Even the Illikai could not have evaluated our solar system from a distance and then sent a missile without end-stage guidance to strike Earth. They may have been able to do so to their *own* solar system, but not to one they had not visited."

"But this Vorsadama did not have any terminal guidance," Stephanie said. "It was just a fast-moving giant rock, right?"

"As far as the Illikai could tell, yes. Which is, bluntly, terrifying no matter how I explain it." She tapped into the room's displays. "Do you understand the basic problem? I assume you do, as you were an astronomer yourself."

"Infrared, but yes. Everything in the solar system of any size has a gravity well, and even very small effects from the gravity wells can throw you far off course when you're traveling long distances."

"Correct. This gets *far* worse when we get outside the solar system, as over longer and longer distances we start to have to take into account the effects of other stars' remote but still real influence, and that of the galaxy itself. Our sun, along with the planets, is moving through space, which changes the gravitational influence of the other stars, and so on and so forth."

Stephanie saw what she meant. "To target an individual planet from *outside* the solar system you'd need to know... well, pretty much *everything* about our solar system, *and* most of the surrounding stars."

"Exactly. And while it becomes far easier the closer to our system— or that of the Illikai—you are, that introduces other problems."

"Other... oh." Stephanie remembered how she'd found *Fenrir*. "You mean, to accelerate Vorsadama to that speed would have taken a lot of energy—"

"—and our friends the Illikai should have *detected* that immense surge of power. It would have been vastly greater than what we detected from *Fenrir*. Yet they never found an indication of the planet's being accelerated."

"Jesus." That meant one of two, equally scary, things. Either this unknown enemy had been able to *hide* that acceleration—how, Stephanie couldn't begin to imagine—or they'd fired their shot from so far away that the acceleration of an entire planet hadn't been noticeable.

"Yes. And that leads to some other, very vital, questions."

Being the director of the project had given her long experience in figuring out the right questions to ask, even if they weren't ones you wanted. Her gut twisted. "Ugh. Leaving aside *why*, we've got the questions of *how* did these people detect the Illikai and decide to target them . . . and *when*." She did some quick mental estimations. "If you launched something going a few thousand kilometers a second from a light-year out, it'd take a century or more to get there. If you launched it from just outside the Oort cloud, somehow hiding it, you could do it just a few years before the shot hit."

"My estimation, too," agreed Francine. "Whoever these people are, they're terrifying in any scenario, but the closer we assume they were when they fired the shot, the more extreme their physical manipulation capabilities are; accelerating a planet twice the mass of Earth to that speed would require orders of magnitude more energy than *Fenrir*—now *Tulima Ohn*—did during its deceleration."

"And at the same time, deciding to take a shot centuries before it'll hit means even more frightening precision, not to mention patience. And they'd *still* have to hide it, more or less, depending on how far out they were." Francine nodded as Stephanie paused. *Might as well finish the thought.* "And leaves us with the question of whether they'll target us next."

"Or whether they *already have*," Francine added.

Stephanie had a momentary cinematic image of a huge, airless, scarred planet hurtling toward a distant blue dot. "Or that, yes," she said, with a shiver. "Francine, given the time frames, we can take a little longer. Put together a presentation with all the details we can get— talk with Imjanai and anyone else on *Tulima Ohn* who might be able to clarify any of the points—and we'll all go over it later in the week. Then decide whether it's something to bother Earth with now or drop on them later. I'm inclined to say it can wait; we've got pretty much nothing left to give right now, and if our Vorsadama is already close, I think I'd rather not know about it."

"Probably true." Francine stood and stretched. "Thank you, Director. I'll try to get some sleep first and then get started."

"Let me know when you're ready."

Francine had barely left when the communicator buzzed. *Directorship sucks.* "Bronson here."

"Director—Stephanie." She recognized Imjanai, Mordanthine, and Uloresim. "We have a minor dilemma, but it may be important."

"After the bombshell you dropped on us today, just about anything would be minor. Go ahead."

A shimmer of apology with a touch of humor chased across Imjanai's skin. "It was important, now, that you know. Sorry it had to come at so . . . inconvenient a time."

"I don't know that it's *ever* convenient to find out that you have some unknown genocidal adversary that is likely one of the reasons for the Fermi Paradox. But yes, important to know. What's the *minor* dilemma?"

"Our plans," Mordanthine said, "are for all active members of *Tulima Ohn*'s crew—including Alerith and her sub-instantiations—to be transferred to *Carpathia* or, possibly, *Big Box*, before both separate from *Tulima Ohn*. Then our ships will be on one side of your Venus when *Tulima Ohn* detonates on the other, allowing us to avoid being vaporized by our original vessel."

Stephanie nodded. "Yes, that's the way I understand it. Is there a problem?"

"Not with *that*, in itself," Uloresim clarified. "We Illikai are all physically much smaller than your people, and your engineers assure us that there is more than sufficient space on your vessel, especially as you have used considerable consumables on your way here. But we *are* concerned with one aspect of the situation. Once that happens—once all of us have been moved to the safety of your vessels—there is no one, AI or living, to ensure that *Tulima Ohn* detonates on schedule. Yes, we have constructed what we believe to be a very simple, foolproof detonation device . . . but it still worries us."

Nothing's ever completely foolproof because fools are so ingenious. She couldn't remember who'd said that, but the universe generally agreed. "'Anything that *can* go wrong, *will* go wrong'—Murphy's Law," she quoted. "Yes, we'd like a backup for that. Could Alerith leave an instantiation on board, or is that not possible?"

"It is . . . possible," Alerith answered, her own icon materializing in the display. "But I would very much prefer not to. I would either have to fully separate that instantiation, which would then be a version of myself I had sent to die, or it would be something akin to amputating a finger deliberately. I *will* do so, if I must, as that is within my required parameters, but I would far rather not."

Mordanthine flickered a chaotic pattern. "One of us could—"

"No," Stephanie said instantly. "We have no idea how many of your people we'll get home safely, how many will get lost because of things we haven't thought of, or maybe an accident. We're already cutting your number of refugees by a factor of a couple hundred or more; you need all the people you can get, especially of your awake crew who remember your contact with humanity and can explain it as your others wake up."

"Possibly your people could make a second, simple detonation device as well?"

"I'm sure they could, but would that really deal with our problem?"

A quick humming chuckle from Imjanai. "No, I would then be afraid *both* would fail. I did not say this was an entirely *rational* worry on my part."

Stephanie rubbed her temples. Imjanai was right; in a way, it *wasn't* a terribly rational concern. Making a simple timing device to detonate antimatter storage should be an easy and reliable thing. There should be very little need to worry at all.

But if something *did* go wrong . . ."I don't have a very good answer," she admitted. "I don't like using any part of Alerith, especially as she is clearly not comfortable with the idea, but—"

"But," came a new voice, "you aren't looking in the right direction, Director."

Angus Fletcher grinned at them from his own icon. "Might I offer myself as a solution?"

Stephanie stared at the older man. "Are you serious?"

"Never been more serious, Director. Look at the facts, shall we?" He raised one finger. "First, I'm a human being. We've got an oversupply of them, one more or less won't matter; we don't have a lack of genetic diversity, that's sure, so I can be spared right enough." Second finger.

"I'm not the only known living AI, and we'd like to keep her all intact, thanks.

"Third, what's waiting for me back home? Looks to me if I'm *lucky* I'll be sittin' in a room not much bigger than the one I'm in here, for the rest of my natural life. Worst case, I'm taking the last walk not long after we land. Seems to me I've got no better chance than being the one holding the deadman switch to save us all, hm?"

His casual, cheerful delivery made the conversation twice as macabre to Stephanie, but she couldn't deny what Angus was saying. "I suppose you have a point."

"And I've one more." He held up his fourth finger. "You *know* I was willing to die to save the human race. I won't hesitate to save us *and* the Illikai. No choking up, no second thoughts, Director. I've already *tried* to die for the cause. I've nothing to lose, and everything to gain."

Mordanthine's skin flashed peach and red, edging with lavender. "I could almost envy you," the Illikai said, his translated tone a strange mixture of gravitas and humor.

He's right. He can leave a better legacy in death than his life's going to give him. And she remembered the calm, focused expression on Angus Fletcher's face when he had been about to blow *Carpathia* to vapor: this was a man who absolutely would not change his mind, who wasn't afraid to do what had to be done.

"Angus," she said slowly. "Mr. Fletcher, if you are truly willing to do this..."

"I absolutely am, Director. You can't use any of the Illikai, you really shouldn't use a piece of poor Alerith—she's been through enough— and no one else on *Carpathia* is a good choice."

Stephanie still couldn't help but feel something like an executioner as she nodded and said, "Then I will recommend that to the captain."

CHAPTER 66: WORKING TOWARD A NEW HOME

"No offense, Alerith, but why in the name of everything are we taking panels that are thousands of meters apart?" Pete asked mildly. "I've got Berenguela and Tuba Dei en route, but seems to me there's plenty of suspension panels right where we were."

"We are operating under numerous constraints, Mr. Flint," Alerith said. "Part of the reason is that we are selecting what we believe are the most advantageous assortment of both people and support species, and these were not, of course, arranged with the convenience of our current goals in mind."

"Oh, sure. Makes sense. You expected to get *everyone* down sooner rather than later."

"Exactly." The AI blinked an indicator in his view, helping him guide the two Bells toward their new destination. The human work party was following close behind. Pete, while he was now qualified for EVA work, was sitting safely in his control room. The director had been darn firm about him staying put, and she did have something of a point—Pete found it a little difficult to keep up with some of the younger crew these days, and maybe he *was* getting a little old.

"Additionally," Alerith went on, "we do not even have that broad a selection. The damage done to *Tulima Ohn* was extensive and complex. I am selecting areas where I believe the ship remains as stable and intact as possible, so that work can proceed with as little risk to everyone as can be managed."

The view from Tuba Dei drove home both the damage and the incredible *size* of the Illikai ship. Above was the limitless black of space, with the brilliant ghostlight of the Milky Way and the glitter of individual stars coating everything else with a hint of rimefrost silver. The ship itself curved gently around its narrow axis but stretched for an incomprehensible distance fore and aft; it wasn't like being on board a ship, or even a building, but climbing on a literal mountain of steel and composite.

"And I'd guess you want to keep us on the dark side whenever possible." They were working on the side of *Tulima Ohn* currently facing away from the Sun; at their current distance, near Venus, old Sol was even meaner than he was in Earth orbit. The work crews would, of course, do as much of the work as they could from within the huge vessel, but at some point they had to take off the hull sections and float the panels free.

"That is best, yes. We cannot do so all the time, due to the way the ship rotates, but fortunately the living quarters' spin has mostly stabilized the main vessel."

"Morda," came Heitor's voice, "what's the story with the edge lockstraps and why the holes weren't matching up?"

Morda's skin rippled colors of annoyance and, Pete was pretty sure, embarrassment. "It is a story of schoolboy idiocy. The translation of our measurements to yours had a small rounding in the formula that resulted in roughly one-millimeter divergence per meter of length."

"So a decimeter at a hundred meters. Yeah, that'd do it, all right," Pete said. "Got a solution?"

"Already revised and in the fabricator. By the time you get the next panels to *Big Box*, the lockstraps should be available."

"Better check all—"

"I am no groundling!" Mordanthine flickered red, then went dark, and finally resumed with less combative coloring. "I apologize. I am angry at us making so...foolish an error. But yes, we are checking *all* of the formulas now, very carefully."

"I should have noticed," Alerith said, apology in her voice.

"You had the same error in your data, I bet," Pete said. "And Morda, don't feel so bad; we've done the same thing with our *own* ships—crashed at least one because someone didn't catch the shift from Imperial to metric."

"Indeed, but we risk a bit more here, so let us *all* check before any more such accidents happen," Werner put in. "Alerith, you have any more of your automata?"

"I have given you as many as I can spare. We are, as you know, doing many things at once. I believe your resources are sufficient to remove the target panels."

"I agree," Werner said, a hint of a smile in his voice. "But I enjoy working with more-than-sufficient, when possible."

Alerith laughed. "As do we all."

Pete had been thinking about some of her earlier words. "How bad *is* it on *Tulima Ohn*? I know you lost a lot of people, but the ship's stayed intact so far. If we didn't blow her up, she'd be reasonably okay, right?"

The AI's image rippled in contradictory patterns. "No. It is, in fact, a matter of some relief, and pride in the builders, that it has not broken apart yet. But there are slowly worsening issues with the structure. This is why I was forced to the conclusion that even with the best reinforcement we could arrange, and with myself staying aboard, we could not maintain her integrity long enough to get the antimatter to a safe distance."

"Darn. So even if we *could* defuse the bomb, so to speak, she's gonna break up on her own?"

"Yes, and in not too long a time frame. I expect her to remain intact to reach Venus, however, and that is as long as will be needed."

Pete nodded, nudged the controls for Berenguela a touch, then started both Bells on their external prep work. Finding all the key fasteners for one of the hull sections took a bit.

"Any parts of her we *should* be salvaging, while we're at it?"

"We are salvaging the most valuable parts now," Imjanai said tartly. "Our people are what we truly need."

"No argument there, ma'am," Pete made sure his most conciliatory tones were in use. "Just wondering if there were any other bets we were overlooking."

"There are many components I would love to salvage," Alerith said; Mordanthine grunted agreement.

"But no practical way," Morda went on. "One of the drive arms is far too large, the engines and converters won't be of any use until you can manufacture antimatter, and so on. No, we will have to bring only what is easily reached and small enough to bring safely aboard your *Carpathia*."

"We're bringing Alerith and our data archives," Imjanai pointed out. "If we can't bring the actual ship, that's as close as we can possibly get."

"Everyone," came the director's voice, "I have some good news for you. We just tested the reinforced docking clamp, and *Ace of Spades* linked up to it perfectly. They're checking the comm and power links now, but so far everything looks good."

A cheer, mixed with the hooting noise of Illikai approval, rang out in the headphones. "That is excellent news," Alerith said. "We can now manufacture the other three quickly."

"How're we looking on time?"

"Well enough, Mr. Flint," answered Captain Lín. "Our projections show we should complete *Big Box* in time for both it and *Carpathia* to depart from *Tulima Ohn* and arrive at Venus at the proper time to be shielded from the detonation."

"How far will *Tulima Ohn* be from Venus when she . . . explodes?" Imjanai asked.

"Not exactly sure," Stephanie answered. "Francine?"

"It appears that *Tulima Ohn* will be approximately one point five million kilometers from Venus at detonation. *Big Box* and *Carpathia* will be opposite to *Tulima Ohn* and at a distance of a hundred thousand kilometers or so from Venus. We expect to obtain some . . . unique imagery from the detonation," she went on, a touch of anticipation easily audible. "The radiation—in multiple spectra as the ship vaporizes as well as reacts with antimatter—will be something like the most powerful flashbulb ever imagined, and all instruments will be watching for what may be revealed in that second or two as the luminance encounters each significant body in the Solar System."

"At least until it hits the instruments," Chris Thompson pointed out. "Right?"

"Any spaceborne ones that get caught in the actual pulse, yes, I'm afraid so," Francine said. "We will lose many satellites, and quite possibly several of our current interplanetary probes. But as long as *we* survive, along with Earth, those are replaceable."

"As you speak, so may the Tree hear," Uloresim's deep voice said. "Survival is all that we ask now. Let us get to our new home, and all other problems can be solved."

"So, I heard you made a decision on that," Pete said. "Where will your new home be?"

"We have accepted the offer of a considerable area in what is called the 'Adirondack Park' of your New York State," replied Uloresim. "As more of us are able to be brought down, we may accept another location as well; that is still being discussed. But this one appears best suited for providing us with our preferred environment while allowing us relative ease of access to the benefits of your industry and transport systems."

"This assumes that the offer can be made reality," Mordanthine added. "It is apparently a somewhat complex legality to change the exact status of any part of this park, as it has been long protected by your people. But that is also . . . hopeful, as it shows that there is an awareness of the value of such lands even in one of the more populous regions of one of your largest countries."

"I've been in the Adirondacks," Faye said. "Lovely country. You'll like it, I'm sure."

"After so long in *Tulima Ohn*? Surely we will find it a veritable *Uldatha*, a paradise!" Imjanai flashed a laugh. "The thought of stretching my arms about *real* forest branches—especially those of Honiji? It is a dream."

Pete chuckled. "A dream we're gonna make come true. I see they've already started on the inside, and my Bells have got work to do, so let's get cracking!"

CHAPTER 67:
SET ME UP THE BOMB

Angus surveyed the room with interest. Tertiary Control Three-Five Zero was, in a fine *soupçon* of irony, the location that Nattasoin and her followers had selected for their planned suicidal path to glory.

As a room to spend one's last week or so in, it was not all that bad. The matrix of climb-bars and armholds had been mostly removed, leaving only more human-spaced handholds. A small zero-gee shower and toilet were surrounded by a safety and privacy screen—though the latter wasn't needed when you'd be the only living thing on board.

Still, I've been going to bathrooms in privacy all my life, it'd be a touch uncomfortable to be doing so out in the open.

"I hope this will be comfortable," Imjanai said, looking at him uncertainly, her colors unsteady.

"I'm sure it will be perfectly fine," he said. "A sight bigger than my little room on *Carpathia*, that's for sure." The air in *Tulima Ohn* was perhaps a touch richer than *Carpathia*'s, though with a similar faint backscent of metal and electronics—along with other less familiar smells.

The Illikai themselves, of course, had a smell, something that made him think vaguely of oceans and seaweed, but with a very slight touch of barnyard animal. Not unpleasant, and he hoped his own smell wasn't very offensive.

He continued, with a gesture around, "I've a sleeping rig, food, bathroom, even an entertainment unit you've already installed. Let's look at the real star of this show, eh?"

Mordanthine flashed assent. "You can see we have sealed off all the controls themselves; most would not work, and even if they did, there is no need. This"—he pointed to a small box with a display and one button under a locked shield—"is the detonator. We've set the display to show the countdown to activation.

"If anything goes wrong, you unlock the safety plate, like this." The Illikai's tendrils took a key that was both chained and magnetically adhering to the wall, and pressed it into the lock. There was a *click* and the transparent shield over the button flipped back. "Then just press the button."

"Simple enough." He grinned at the button itself, which was huge and red. "Let me guess, the button designer was a human."

"Actually," came Alerith's voice, "I designed it. The prominence of 'big red button' in your media is almost universal."

That gave him a welcome laugh. "It is that! Glad I noticed it, are you?"

Her icon rippled shades of peach and pink. "And that it gave you a moment's amusement, yes. It is pleasing when people appreciate the more delicate touches."

"Well, you got this one perfect. Not to be a worrywart, but what if I push the button and I find I'm still alive?"

"We've run *that* branch also. Follow me." Mordanthine led Angus and Imjanai out the door and down the corridor to an accessway some distance away. The accessway was a circular corridor that looked something like the barrel of a cannon to Angus, as it was only about two feet wide. "I am afraid it will be quite a tight fit for you."

"I don't have claustrophobia, but that is a bit intimidating. Still, no help for it. Can't ask you to redesign your ship at this point." He followed Mordanthine in; while the Illikai engineer moved easily through the tunnel, Angus had to wriggle along. It wasn't too difficult, but even with the inset lights to make it easy to see, it did feel oppressively close. This wasn't helped by a distant vibration, something his bones felt as the thrumming twang of a gigantic bass string. *This ship would not survive long anyway.*

That was a sad thought, really; *Tulima Ohn* had made a voyage of tens of light-years, flying at incomprehensible speeds, and now, dead in space, was slowly coming apart, all because the little people who'd made her had a frightened argument. *Happened more than once back home, alas.*

After a dozen meters or so, they came to a small hatch, about a foot across, inset into the wall. "Mordanthine, I sure hope I don't have to go *into* that, because it just ain't happening."

A flash of dark amusement. "No, this is just to the panel." He slid open the panel, to reveal a set of cables of Illikai design, with a large boxy addition—topped with another big red button. "This is the actual detonator. This material"—one of his tendrils indicated a pearlescent mass just visible under the box—"is the explosive. It will rip a hole across multiple containment loops, causing the containment field to collapse and releasing the antimatter. Given its position it will quickly initiate detonations in other antimatter storage areas which will eventually—in milliseconds—lead to the main storage areas 'going up,' as you say."

"Milliseconds is fine, I'll not be noticing. So if the connection's severed in my room, I just come around the corner and slap this one instead."

"Yes. It has completely self-contained power, separate from the ship and coils. All the button does is make the final connection to ignition."

"Simple enough. All right, let me back out of this tunnel and get back to a place a man can stand up in."

With the Illikai as small as they were, even their main corridors were none too high; VanBuskirk in his combat suit had been lucky the fight had taken place where it did. Tertiary Control, fortunately, was very high-ceilinged from the point of view of the Illikai, so it rose comfortably above Angus's head.

"Well, you two, thanks for showing me around. Your air's just fine, which means I can be comfortable out of my suit." He nodded to the EVA suit standing in the corner. "Not what I'd want to spend a week in."

"No, none of us would either," Imjanai agreed. "We do have spare air for your suit here, in case of emergency."

"And I've filled the water and nutrient reservoirs," Angus confirmed. "If I *have* to shelter in it, I'll be able to, but I'll keep my fingers crossed that *Tulima Ohn* will keep running just a week longer."

The two flashed agreement, then turned toward the door.

Mordanthine hesitated. "Angus . . . we thank you for this. It will be remembered."

The gratitude made him *acutely* uncomfortable, given the situation. "Ah, get on with you. It's the best for everyone. No embarrassing trials back home, no decades in a boring cell, lets the politicians spin a bit of gold out of my straw. You just all get home safe, and I've got no regrets. Deal?"

Mordanthine's hide rippled with multiple colors, then he extended his tendrils; Angus reached out, felt the warm grip, something like miniature elephants' trunks, squeeze tight. "It is a bargain."

He squeezed back gently. "Done. Now get going; don't want to be left behind."

The shuttle, some ways off, was of course waiting for the two Illikai; no one was going to leave them behind.

The two left, shutting the door behind them. A few minutes later, a very faint thudding vibration told him the shuttle had departed. Now he was alone on the mountain-sized ship, his only company legions of sleeping Illikai and other species who would never awaken. *They were carrying millions of their people, and after taking the other species they need into account,* Big Box *has got less than three hundred thousand of the Illikai. About a hundred, hundred fifty in suspension on* Carpathia.

Angus turned to the compact box of electronics against one wall, this one attached to a cable leading through the ceiling. "*Tulima Ohn* to *Carpathia*, this is Angus Fletcher checking comms."

"Mr. Fletcher, we read you. Signal strength is very good," responded the captain. "All is ready there?"

"Couldn't be better. They've got it all wired up, timer's running, and I've got a beautiful shiny button to use in case it goes kaput. Nice little apartment—zero-gee, I'm afraid, but then I don't have to worry about keeping in shape for landing."

"True enough. We are relaying your transmissions through one of the satellites we brought. It will be left behind us and will use its own ion drive to position itself to continue to relay your transmissions until detonation."

"Excellent. It will be good to keep in touch."

"You'll be . . . okay there?" Director Bronson asked hesitantly.

That got another laugh out of him. "For a week or so, absolutely. After that, probably not, but who knows? If anything *can* blow me straight to heaven or hell, this will do it. Don't worry about me, Director—or Pete, since I know you're listening. I set this course back when I started the Group; like I said to Mordanthine, you all just get back home alive and I've got no regrets."

"Well . . . I'll miss you, Angus," Pete said slowly. "Can't say you're wrong about this being the best course, though. Neither of us are the type to want to spend our last years in a cage."

"Right you are." Angus felt a faint sting of tears, blinked it away. *I suppose being friends with Pete saved us all, in a way. Still find that odd. Not a bad truth to go out with, though.* "Right, I've checked this little toy out, time for me to get settled in. Talk to everyone later."

"Leave the receiver open, Mr. Fletcher," the captain added. "In case of any updates."

"Absolutely, Captain. Fletcher out."

He turned away and began setting out his sparse belongings for his last, rather peculiar, vacation.

CHAPTER 68:
COUNTDOWN TO
CATACLYSM

Venus was a white-gray near-circle, looming like a silvery, clouded mirror in the black sky, almost seven times the size of the Moon as seen from Earth. At this distance, Stephanie could see the subtle traceries of the clouds, details of gray on gray on white with only the faintest hint of any actual color. Venus, shrouded in its deadly sulfuric acid clouds, was a monochromic world, brilliant and sterile.

And if it isn't now, it sure will be. Worse was the fact that other bodies in the system, most notably Mars, would be struck by the incredible blast of radiation from *Tulima Ohn*. For some, like Jupiter, this wouldn't matter; a minor hiccup in the weather it normally sustained, if that. But Mars was close enough, and unprotected; if there *was* life anywhere on the Red Planet, it might have survived billions of years only to be blown away by controlled demolition.

There wasn't anything to be done about that, unfortunately. They were lucky there was a chance to save Earth and some of the Illikai.

"Countdown doing its thing," came Angus's cheerful voice from the speakers. "Not long now, then you all just head on home. Got my personal log streaming to the relay. I'll add my last-minute musings when I sign off."

She wasn't sure what to make of Angus Fletcher's apparently casual acceptance of his fate. There was probably more behind it than she understood, but it was both comforting and oddly creepy, knowing that the man was literally standing on the largest bomb ever seen in history.

"Captain," she said, to take her mind off that subject, "are all our instruments ready?"

Hàorán Lín nodded, a touch of a smile on his face. "All are ready, Director. I assure you, every scientist that might learn *anything* from this unique event is pushing any sensor they can access to the limit."

"Earth's got anything and everything staring up," Audrey said. "They can't see us, or the detonation, directly—thank God—but they'll be able to watch as the explosion lights up the sky, and they've been working for the last few weeks on the exact schedules of viewing, so they can get the best views of everything as the blast wave propagates across the Solar System. It will be *spectacular*, or so Francine assures me."

Francine Everhardt wasn't on the command deck of *Carpathia*, of course. She was down in her laboratory, and barring disaster Stephanie was pretty sure the astrophysicist would be glued to instruments for *hours* as the lightspeed wavefront swept its way across the Solar System. *And honestly, I'd like to do that, too, but it's not my job right now.* "Is this another good publicity moment?"

"Spectacle is good, if for nothing else than making the subject seem fresh and new again," Audrey said. "When months go by, even the most fascinating new things start to lose their shine. This will give people more to talk about in so many ways—and probably help the President and the rest of FORT get everything we need done before we get home."

"Ten minutes to Big Boom," Angus said from the speakers. "Please return all trays and seats to their upright positions."

"It is . . . good to hear Angus speak so . . . cheerfully," Mordanthine said. He and Imjanai were on the deck as observers. Uloresim had been invited, but declined; Stephanie suspected he was still uncomfortable among numbers of humans. "That was some kind of a joke, yes?"

"It appears to be a reference to commercial aircraft landing instructions, yes," Alerith confirmed. The AI was integrated into *Big Box* and the four ACES were under her direct control; as it turned out, there was need for only a few human beings on the *Box*, as maintenance/emergency personnel in case of accidents. Werner, with Pete's concurrence, had put one Bell on board each; they were controlled by Alerith as well. "I find many references to this kind of cheerfulness; 'gallows humor' is one term."

Stephanie winced as the AI then explained the term to the two Illikai. "Great Tree, that's a . . . horrid punishment," Imjanai murmured.

Mordanthine's colors were more cynically mixed. "Oh, Imja, it's no worse than us. Remember how Gonsalji was executed in *Undomo Shai Homolii?*"

She shuddered. "You have a point. I suppose all species invent their own terrible methods."

"I'm not asking and don't want to know," Stephanie said as she saw Ben Robinson open his mouth to ask. "We're *sure* Earth will be safe?"

The captain nodded. "Nothing about so unusual an event is *certain,* but as far as everyone—both here and on Earth—can determine, there should be no ill effects on Earth if the detonation occurs while *Tulima Ohn* is directly behind the Sun."

"Not that we won't see damage," Audrey added. "I've gotten quite a comprehensive list of possible losses, since we'll have to address those in the best light. Satellites in high orbit are going to get hit very badly unless they're either at a point in front or behind Earth and thus also in the narrow cone protected by the Sun. That's not going to be wide enough to protect satellites in geosynchronous or near-geosynch orbits. NASA's lunar-industry test site may or may not survive—they're not sure how well the crater wall will protect them."

"We'll lose a lot of interplanetary probes, I guess."

"Anything on the facing side of Mars, and quite possibly all around the globe, is going to be hit hard, yes," said Audrey. "Some of the ones in the outer system—past Jupiter—might make it. The ones at Jupiter are in question; they're mostly made to take more radiation, but of course they're already taking whatever Jupiter dishes out. We'll have to see."

"Jesus. Losing most of the high-orbit satellites—that's going to hurt weather and telecom."

"And it may be down to medium orbit, which will take out a lot of GPS," Ben Robinson put in. "It's going to take a few years to dig out from under this—plus the bill for *Carpathia* itself's going to come due."

"We're sorry for all of that," Imjanai said hesitantly. "We . . . didn't plan on any of it."

Stephanie laughed. "Imjanai, we know that. None of you planned this. We'll get through it."

"Two minutes, everyone." Angus's voice had a touch of new tension in it. "I'm going over to the panel now. Pete...thanks for being a friend. And good luck, all of you. Angus Fletcher—signing off."

"Bye, Angus," Pete said softly. "Godspeed."

"Will we see anything when the blast hits Venus?" Audrey asked after a moment of silence.

"It should light up like the Sun, honestly. That much radiation will shatter molecules into atoms—I'd expect the planet will be surrounded by a sort of aurora bright enough to read by."

"One minute," Mordanthine said, having been watching the clock. "With *Tulima Ohn* at one point five million kilometers, the wave front will reach Venus in roughly five seconds after detonation."

"All systems recording," Ben Robinson stated. "*Big Box*, all still functioning there?"

"Confirmed," Alerith replied. "All four ACES have their sensor suites recording. I am observing on all bands."

"Twenty seconds," said Mordanthine. Stephanie kept a grin from her face as she noticed one of his tendrils absently but firmly gripping Imjanai's. *I'd wondered about that!*

For a moment, she wished *she* had a hand to hold...but pushed that aside, to watch the final decisive seconds.

"Six...five...four...three...two...one...detonation. Venus impact in three...two...one..."

They all stared at the placid, deceptively bland planet on the screen.

One second went by. Then two. Then five.

But Venus did not change; there was no flash, no aurora, no sign of the cataclysmic detonation of a million tons of antimatter.

"*Tulima Ohn!* Angus! What's happened?"

But there was no answer.

CHAPTER 69.
THE FINAL BACKUP

Angus switched off the main transmitter with a pang of unusually intense regret. His personal log was still going out, but that was private and no one would get to hear any of it until after he was dead.

"Funny how I've ended up here," he said, turning toward the detonation rig. "Tried to make sure all the aliens were dead, now I'm on the alien ship trying to save them *and* humanity. Fate has an odd sense of humor, and that's sure."

A loud *TWAAANNGGG* sound echoed through *Tulima Ohn* and Angus felt a tiny, but frightening, jolt through the soles of his feet. "Well, now, what the hell was that? Be the height of irony if the old girl blows *herself* up a few seconds early!"

Distantly he heard a pulsing sound—an alarm, he guessed, but there was no time to figure out what for. The countdown was still visible, the seconds running out like sand from an hourglass. *I can practically feel the old man with the scythe right behind me. Well, let him take his shot quick.*

It almost felt like there was a chill wind starting to blow, and he tried to shrug that impression off. He'd been eminently rational all his life, no need for getting overly fanciful in the last ten seconds. He did find himself holding his breath as the display reached five and continued dropping.

Then he realized it had stopped at zero . . . and he was still alive. He stared at it in momentary disbelief, and an old, old cartoon replayed in his head. *"Where's the KABOOM? There was supposed to be an Earth-shattering KABOOM!"*

"Well, I will be *dipped*, as Pete would say. It *did* fail. Anyone listening to this log, this is Angus Fletcher, about to push the biggest, reddest button ever! Good luck, all!"

He slammed his hand down on the button, teeth gritted, wincing in anticipation—even though he knew that he wouldn't feel a thing, he'd be vaporized in a millisecond or less.

Nothing happened. The button had pressed, but he was still here.

With that realization came another. There *was* a breeze, a strong one. "Shit," he said distinctly, enunciating the obscenity with care. "That's a hull breach warning."

His mind instantly mapped the short journey to the backup detonator. Conscious that his log would be the only record of what was happening, he started talking again. "Still got some time. Main limitation's going to be *Big Box* and *Carpathia*—they'll be back in sight of Tulima Ohn in"—he glanced at his watch—"thirty minutes. Earth's got a few hours still, but the longer this goes, the farther down the orbits we're going to blast.

"Putting on my EVA suit. Not hurrying myself—I'll probably mess something up if I do. That noise I heard—and you listeners probably did, too—must've been a hull break, one of the supports going.

"Glad our suits are made to be put on easy; old-fashioned astronaut suits, I might still be here a while. Looking at the comm telltales, I guess this transmission's still going out. Hope it stays that way."

As the door slid aside, the air lunged forward with a *thud*, dragging him several feet. "Pressure just equalized—way lower in the hallway. Not *gone*, but... how did that display work...?" After a moment he remembered the months-past instructions, triggered the display for outside conditions. "Half pressure. Can't tell if it's still dropping. Probably it's trying to maintain pressure by pumping in more—who knows when the reserves'll run out, though? I had best get moving."

Even in the thin air, he could now hear the alarm pulsing regularly. *This way. It's not far.*

He found himself chuckling. "Wonder if it's occurred to any of you yet that, right now, I'm in a perfect position to finish my original mission? All I have to do is wait a bit longer before I set the big bomb off, and I'll wipe out *all* the Illikai.

"And you know—there's still damn good reasons I should. You're bringing hundreds of alien *species* down, who in God's name knows what that might do? Maybe that's actually the way they invade. Or they're all just as nice as you, Director, but still, we've had enough problems with our *own* invasive species. Maybe we'll end up with an Illikai biosphere if we let them loose, we'll be the ones fighting for our lives. And all I have to do . . . is wait. Just a few extra minutes."

Angus hustled down the corridor, pulling on handholds. As he moved, he heard a new sound, a sharp, rumbling whistle, and could feel the movement of air pushing on him. He laughed softly.

"But . . . I told Mordanthine I'd bet against the director a dozen times and never had such a losing streak. And I promised I'd get this job done. So you win, Director. Let *your* winning streak keep going."

Ahead, he saw a black line across the floor, and the smile faded from his face.

"Hell, it's cracked all the way across this section. Getting closer now . . . gap's almost a foot across, and the air's *screaming* out of it. Think this is going to be a bit tricky—*WHOA!*"

The entire ship shuddered, and the crack yawned wider, almost two feet across now, the atmosphere howling out through it like the souls of the frozen dead that were the last remaining crew. The increased suction almost dragged Angus out, and he barely managed to catch hold of one of the arm-grips. "That was *close*, my friends. Almost found out what it looks like to fall through space. Got to get across, now. This whole section might break off any second."

There was another arm-hold on the other side of the crack, but there was nothing to hold onto on *this* side near enough for him to stretch out and grab the one on the other. *How can I get past . . . ?*

Zero-gee. That's the key.

Angus studied the area on the far side, carefully noting the positions of all the arm- or handholds he could see. Then he backed up down the corridor. "Well, this will be fun. One chance to get myself across—with a dive."

He braced his feet against one arm-hold, gauged the distance and angles—and jumped as hard as he could.

The air roaring its way toward the crack helped; it increased his speed instead of slowing him, and his initial jump gave him the extra momentum he needed. The leaking atmosphere tried to drag him down with it, but he shot across the crack, the air ahead of him now dragging at the suit, helping slow his flight. He twisted slightly and caught the third arm-hold, jolting to a halt.

"That was an adventure. Almost there. Still have some time, but can't be dallying.

"Director, you keep on doing what you've been doing. Bring our new friends home and don't let any crazy bastards like me get in your way—or any stubborn politicians, either."

Finally he reached the access tube. "Oh, *damn*."

The tube was tight enough for him normally; a quick test showed that there was simply no way for him to fit through with the suit.

"This is going to be *fun*. Pressure . . . dropped some, down to about a third of an atmosphere. Seems to me that's like the top of Everest—I'm no mountaineer, either, so I'm not breathing that for long." The Illikai air mix was, if he remembered right, a bit richer in oxygen, but . . .

He sighed. "No point in waiting. It certainly is not going to get any better, wouldn't you agree?" There was no response, but he did agree with himself that there was no time like the present. "Looks like if I'd tried things my way, we'd *all* have lost that bet. Another fifteen, twenty minutes and there won't be any air at all."

He hyperventilated for a moment—getting as much oxygen as possible into the bloodstream wouldn't hurt—and then slowly cracked the seal on his helmet. It was *hard*, but he managed to keep it under control so that the air didn't just blow out in an explosive decompression. He stripped out of the suit, feeling arctic chill now in the thin air. "Whooo, that's what they call *bracing*. Air's very thin, have to try . . . not to gasp too much. Heading into the accessway."

Angus wriggled his way forward, breathing as deeply as he could. Already he could feel a heaviness, a loss of strength and focus. "Almost there. I can . . . see the access panel ahead. Just have to pop it open . . ."

For a moment, his newly fogged brain blanked on the exact method, but he forced the discipline of Silver back into his thoughts. *No emotion, no panic, just calm. Get the job done.* He closed his eyes, thought back, and abruptly he could see clearly exactly how Mordanthine had released the catch.

"There! Got it open. And there it is. Time to say goodbye—here goes!"

He struck the button. And once again . . . nothing happened.

"That's . . . inconvenient." He stared stupidly at the inert button. *Why? Why didn't it work?* He shivered, heard his own labored breathing, and realized that he was barely understanding what he saw. *Pressure may still be dropping. I have a minute or two, max.*

Silver's determination was the only thing left. *What did Mordanthine say about this? The button . . . just completes a connection. Power source is internal. Charge is right there. So . . . so . . .*

For just an instant, he wasn't on *Tulima Ohn*. His oxygen-desperate brain threw up a half memory, half dream, with him and Pete working on one of the Bells. Pete was shaking his head, looking at the little robot—which had morphed into an actual bell—and saying "Clapper's come off."

Come off. Disconnected.

He blinked his eyes clear, focused on the button. "Think . . . we've got a broken lead . . ." He reached out and grabbed the button, pulled as hard as he could.

The round, shiny button popped free, trailing two leads. *Just makes the connection.* "Hope I'm right, everyone. If I just take *this* wire off"—he pulled the first lead free—"and then get *this* one free"—it yielded after two tugs—"well, I have to hope I understood you, Morda."

The ends of both wires glinted metallic from within their insulation. "Here goes. If you don't hear anything more—it worked."

He carefully aligned the shining metal ends and touched them together.

PART VIII: HOMECOMING

CHAPTER 70: DETONATION

Stephanie looked at the placid, homogenous silver disc. "Can't we contact Angus?"

"Sent an inquiry already," Ben Robinson answered, "but if he's away from the transmitter, only his private log's going out. That's a one-way transmission—he won't receive anything, it's just logging what he says until, well, it's over."

"How long until Earth's ... vulnerable?"

"Now? Three and a half hours," Mordanthine said. "Three hours thirty-two minutes, to be exact. *Our* deadline is twenty-six minutes."

That's right. The way we're moving, we'll be out from behind Venus a lot faster than Earth will be out from behind the Sun.

Everyone jumped as Hàorán Lín gave vent to a quick, violent spate of Mandarin. The captain had gone abruptly pale. "Captain! What's wrong?"

"Many apologies. That was extremely rude," Lín said, his tone making it a mechanical, rote apology. "It just occurred to me that Mr. Fletcher is now in an excellent position to carry out his original intention of destroying *Carpathia* along with the entirety of the Illikai."

"Son of a *bitch*," Robinson said, with no attempt at apology. "All he has to do is wait to hit the button."

"Let's not be jumping the gun here," Pete said. "Sure, you could be right, but it's not like there's anything we can do about it. Me, I'm thinking that Angus already made up his mind to stick with our plan before he left, and I don't think he's the kind of guy to waffle."

"It is ... worrisome," admitted Mordanthine, "but I, also, gained a strong impression from him that he had conceded the...moral leadership, so to speak, to you, Director."

"Can we tap into his journal? We'd at least know what he's thinking, even if there's nothing we could do about it." The captain looked over at Werner, who was seated at one of the main consoles.

"It's a bit of a violation...but yes, Captain. We have the decryption keys, and the relay's the same. Do you authorize us to do so?"

"Director?"

Stephanie did *not* like the idea of listening in on a man's private last musings...but if there was even a *tiny* chance that Angus—once called Silver of the Group—had changed his mind...

"Do it. And Captain? There *is* one thing we can do. If he's planning on doing this, he'll time it to go off just as we come out from Venus's shadow. If both *Carpathia* and *Big Box* swing ship and reverse vector, we can slow our emergence from Venus and, with any luck, still be protected. He can't actually *see* us out of the wreck."

"Decryption engaged...tapping into personal log..."

Angus's voice, slightly distorted, suddenly boomed out. "—still damn good reasons I should. You're bringing hundreds of alien *species* down, who in God's name knows what that might do?"

"Oh Jesus, no, Angus," Pete murmured.

"Maybe that's actually the way they invade," Angus's voice went on.

"Alerith!" Captain Lín snapped. "You heard?"

"I have. Preparing to reverse vector on *Big Box*. I am surprised and disappointed."

"Exec, alert people to prepare for acceleration."

"...And all I have to do...is wait. Just a few extra minutes," Angus's voice said, musing, in that calm, matter-of fact tone he'd had the day he nearly *did* destroy *Carpathia*. Stephanie stared at the speakers, speechless with a combination of anger and dismay.

Then Angus chuckled, and his tone lightened. "But...I told Mordanthine I'd bet against the director a dozen times and never had such a losing streak."

The captain paused, mouth open mid-order, now looking intently at the speakers himself.

"And I promised I'd get this job done. So you win, Director. Let *your* winning streak keep going."

Stephanie blew out a long, relieved breath. "Oh, thank *God*."

"Canceling reverse maneuver," Alerith said. "I, also, am very grateful. And it is not as though Angus Fletcher's concerns were without merit. I, also, am concerned with the multiplicity of possible consequences for our settlement of Earth."

"No, you're right there," Pete said, grinning with his own relief. "Angus always had a logic to what he did."

Now that they'd tapped into the log, no one suggested they turn it off. Instead, they listened tensely as Angus Fletcher made his increasingly desperate way through the doomed *Tulima Ohn*. His voice grew thin, faint and hashed with static, as he entered the access tunnel.

Mordanthine said something in Illikai that Alerith's program did not translate. "I cannot *believe* both failed!"

"Vibrations, loss of pressure, shift in temperature?" Werner said, thinking aloud. "Anything could have cracked a solder joint, or whatever your equivalent is. He's trying to rig the detonation directly— can that work?"

"It . . . should. If the connections *inside* the detonator are still intact."

Once more, Angus's faint voice spoke. "Here goes. If you don't hear anything more—it worked."

There was silence for a few fleeting seconds.

Then Venus *ignited*.

A halo of incredible brilliance surrounded the planet, making its clouded surface dull and dark, radiance streaming outward in slow motion with rippling colors of red and green and violet, dominated by a pure seething white, tendrils of light uncoiling and spreading, reaching toward the stars in all directions.

The terrible light flickered and brightened, then began to dim, but even dimming, the planet was afire, a blazing disc of harsh and stunning light beyond anything Stephanie had imagined.

"Confirmed," Alerith said calmly. "Analysis shows multiple, closely spaced detonation peaks, entire event spanning one hundred seventeen milliseconds. Effects propagating around Venus; these should be of interest. Data being gathered on all instruments."

There was a pause, then Alerith went on. "Preliminary estimates agree closely with expected release. *Tulima Ohn*'s antimatter reserves successfully detonated by Angus Fletcher. Only minor, secondary increases in radiation are detected on both *Carpathia* and *Big Box*.

"Earth—and we—are safe."

CHAPTER 71:
AFTERSHOCKS
ON EARTH

"Holy Jesus..." murmured Jeanne, staring up.

The Moon flared in the sky, spotlight-brilliant even against the daylight background, its half face illumined for an instant by something brighter than the Sun. As the light faded, Jeanne blinked. "Does it look *blurred* to you?" she asked Hailey Vanderman.

"Might be," the *Carpathia* security chief said, his own voice hushed with awe. He was one of seven people—besides her Secret Service detail—in the Rose Garden at the moment. "The pulse would be primarily gamma and whatever secondaries came off the remainder of *Tulima Ohn* being vaporized; the flash was secondary. That much energy hitting the surface of the Moon? Might've kicked up a cloud of dust and gases all over the facing surface. Remember that if it hit Earth it would've hit hard enough to make the planet temporarily radioactive."

"Did it miss us?" Jeanne asked tensely. She knew it *should* have, given everything they knew, but after seeing the Moon *burn*, she wasn't relaxing yet.

"Reports coming in from our own and our allies' instruments say there's been no noticeable increase in radiation on Earth," George Green said, his own face relaxing. "Looks like the Earth's safe, anyway."

Jeanne restrained herself from asking for any more details. Results on anything more complex than *did we get fried?* would take at least a few minutes to start coming in. "Well, the outside show's over. Why don't we go inside and get ready to find out what the actual damage is?"

By the time she reached the Oval Office, Secretary Deng was already on one of the screens. "Madam President, it seems Earth will continue to be inhabited, yes?"

"Hopefully by more than one sapient species, Mr. Secretary. Now we find out what the explosion cost us."

"Daire Young lost his StellarLink satellites?" Jeanne repeated incredulously. "Those were *low* orbit!"

"He didn't lose all of them, or even most," Roger corrected. "Several sets, though. We and other countries lost a scattering of other assets in low to medium orbit."

"How did that happen?"

Eva Filipek answered. "Los Alamos, working with our partners in FORT countries, thinks that there were some unexpected lensing effects in the Sun's atmosphere and around the surface of the photosphere that bent some of the radiation around. We've never encountered an event of this . . . energetic level at such close range— thank God for that—so we're going to be learning a lot."

"None of those . . . lensed beams hit Earth?"

"We actually suspect a few did," Eva said, "but they were far weaker than the direct radiation—a lot absorbed by the Sun on the way around—so while they were devastating to orbiting satellites, they didn't reach the ground with dangerous intensity."

"We dodged deathrays as well as a bullet, I see. I presume high and mid-orbit's badly hit?"

"Everything in high orbit that wasn't almost directly in front or behind Earth is dead, yes. GPS constellations are a shambles—some satellites are still up but nowhere near a fully functional system."

"Well, crap." She'd known that was a likely problem, but she'd hoped they'd avoid it. "So we're having to use backup navigation methods. How long to get the GPS network restored?"

George winced. "Ma'am, it took twenty years to create the system. Sure, we've solved a lot of the problems and standardized the designs, so it won't take *that* long . . . but at least a few years—and that's not taking into account all the *other* satellites, weather, communications, what have you, that everyone's going to want to replace. We simply don't have the launch capacity, even if we had the satellites."

"I was afraid of that. What's the cost going to be?"

"Billions, at least," Roger stone said flatly. "Each GPS satellite's about two hundred fifty million by itself, you need a nominal twenty-four of them, and of course there will be all the ancillary costs of launching them. Worse, though, is that everyone around the world's suffering by their absence. How many people are even *used* to using maps anymore?"

"We still have most of the low-orbit weather satellites," Eva observed. "All but one of the GOES were killed, however. StellarLink's still somewhat working, but higher-orbit comsats are gone. Telecommunications is going to be seriously impeded for quite a while."

Jeanne listened as her Cabinet went down the list of losses and difficulties, and tried to push aside her initial appalled reactions to the looming mountain of challenges. "Do we have solutions for our problems?"

At her deceptively mild tone, Roger and George chuckled. "For some, yes. Some of them the civilian population's already tackled," Green said. "For example, SubGPS is an app—name stands for 'substitute GPS'—which a workgroup of people came up with to use cellular data network navigation as a workaround for GPS. Obviously doesn't work at sea or in other isolated areas, but it's a hell of a lot better than nothing, and people are already inserting it into transport and scheduling. Cybersecurity's working on a version that we can use for military applications that will be secure, though I don't know how long that'll take.

"NOAA's doing its best to use on-Earth data to fill in the gaps left by the loss of some of the satellites. We're not going to have the detail or coverage we're used to for a bit, but at least we're not going back to squinting at the horizon and muttering 'red sky in morning,'" Roger supplied. "Cellular services are taking a lot of load satellites used to carry, and that's a problem, but not as bad as it could be."

"Ocean transport's the area we're trying to address," Admiral Dickinson said. "We're putting temporary beacons and relays along major sea routes and trying to figure out how to assist in other ways, but at the least Naval Ops believes we can work with the others in FORT to keep the majority of shipping going."

She closed her eyes, gave a momentary sigh of relief, opened them again. "All departments will have to stay on alert for other issues and be ready to address them. Let me and Congress know if any legal action, permissions, executive orders, whatever may be needed to get things tended to.

"Now . . . what about *Carpathia* and our guests?"

"We were able to reestablish communications a couple of hours ago," Roger said. "Obviously not real-time, since they're on the other side of the Sun and near Venus's orbit, so it takes almost half an hour for a round-trip signal-and-answer.

"We of course noticed that there were several minutes difference between the scheduled detonation and the actual one. The automated systems failed and Angus Fletcher was forced to detonate *Tulima Ohn* manually."

Listening to excerpts of Fletcher's log, Jeanne found herself grateful for the ex-terrorist's choices. "Well, that eliminates one unpleasant problem, anyway. Mr. Fletcher found a way to have a legacy of redemption and not leave himself as an awkward complication."

"No argument here. The other good news is that *Big Box* and *Carpathia* are both fully intact and have begun acceleration to return to Earth. With their nuclear-pulse drives, we expect they will arrive home in about five months."

"Five months. Our infrastructure, especially orbital, won't be nearly recovered," Jeanne mused. "Getting them *down* is going to be a challenge, even ignoring the problem of *Big Box* and its hundreds of *thousands* of passengers."

"It will be," agreed Eva. "But not the way you mean. It will be"— she gave a quick, startling, daredevil smile—"a very different *kind* of challenge—and opportunity."

CHAPTER 72:
WHAT GOES UP . . .

"Say that again," Stephanie said, seeing an equal expression of incredulity on every face around the small conference room, none less than Captain Lín's.

"FORT has decided that they would like us to land *Carpathia* at its launch point," Ben Robinson repeated. "The communication just arrived, along with preliminary data and calculations for the procedure."

"What. The. Hell?" Stephanie pronounced each word with absolute precision. "I thought it was decided that *Carpathia* simply *couldn't* land!"

"*Physically,*" Werner Keller said, "there is no reason that she cannot land. *Carpathia* has the power and control. But there were *excellent* reasons that she *should* never land."

"There were," agreed Faye, scanning the summary from the executive officer with a practiced eye. "But it appears that some of those objections no longer hold—or, at least, they are no longer of primary concern in the current situation."

Stephanie exchanged glances with the captain, then nodded. Lín rose. "Very well. Enlighten us. If this is what FORT has agreed, they must have a . . . *startling* set of reasons behind it."

"Give me a moment—the rest of you might try reading the summary as well, but I'll go over it for you, Captain, Director." Faye took two minutes glancing over the document—which consisted of multiple parts. *She reads like* lightning, Stephanie thought.

"Well. There are several key elements motivating the need to bring *Carpathia* down. The detonation of *Tulima Ohn* has, as we know, severely damaged our orbital infrastructure, some of which is useful in space navigation as well as Earthly operations. More importantly, our remaining orbit-to-ground capacity is, and will continue to be, severely strained as we attempt to rebuild vital services. Even Mr. Young's StellarLink company was not prepared for such a, well, unexpectedly large demand for launch services."

"That means that even after *Carpathia* arrives, it could take months, perhaps even a year or more, before we could bring down *Carpathia*'s crew and the relatively small number of Illikai we have on board, including the sleepers."

"That's a point," conceded Stephanie. "And obviously that makes it ten times harder, or more, to imagine how we're bringing down *Big Box* and her cargo."

"Exactly. It appears that New York State will be approving the modification to the Adirondack Park, with support from the federal government, so the requested location for the Illikai will be available. But the longer it takes before they are actually able to *settle* there, the more chances there are for people to have second thoughts."

Time pressure isn't going away yet, Stephanie thought. "All right. I guess we all understand the urgency." There were nods around the table. "But what about the reasons we weren't even *thinking* of landing this ship?"

Alerith's voice answered. "If I may speak?"

"Go ahead, Alerith. We have you, Imja, Morda, and Ulo in this for a reason."

"I do have the advantage of absorbing data directly, and I believe I can allay your concerns. Your people have studied this problem for a considerable time—since your launch, in fact.

"The antimatter-catalyzed fission process produces much less radioactive fallout than the standard critical or subcritical-mass triggered process. Your launch site, while not optimal for residential use, is even after this moderate period of time not particularly dangerous for human beings to enter for short periods." Alerith flashed several graphs on the conference room displays, showing that even immediately after launch the radiation present had been considerably below initial estimates, and had dropped off quickly.

"But if we're *landing*, at least one of the blasts—just before we touch down—will be awfully close to the surface."

"No more so than your initial launch," Mordanthine said, colors brightening with interest. "After all, you first launched using a powerful explosive charge that sent you a considerable distance into the air. *Carpathia* can, therefore, fall that same distance and come to rest. Yes?"

Captain Lín's laugh was quick but sincere. "Yes, of course. Kick us up or drop us down, the shock is essentially the same. We may... bounce slightly on landing, but *Carpathia*'s center of gravity and our stabilization systems should make that a minimal risk."

"And the other problem," Stephanie said, realizing the advantages, "is the damage the landing does. But if we land at the same place... it's *already* been blown up. What about overall radioactive contamination?"

"There *is* some contamination, unavoidably so," Alerith conceded. "You are detonating U-238, some of which fissions and produces various daughter products, the rest of which is vaporized and will therefore drift through the atmosphere for some distance. However, the toxicity and risk, especially given the overall remoteness of the site, is certainly no greater than many of the highly poisonous materials used in some of your other conventional rockets, such as hydrazine.

"In addition, your earlier nuclear experimentation with ground and water bursts as well as air, released far larger volumes of radioactive and otherwise toxic materials into your environment, but this has had little effect on the planet as a whole." There was, perhaps, a hint of amusement in Alerith's tone, and *definitely* in the rose-peach flicker on her projected image. "Both humans and Illikai often have difficulty grasping how very small most of their activities are on the scale of a planet; it requires the entirety of a civilization to start affecting it."

"It does still seem a bit much simply to get us all down faster," Peter Flint said at last. "There's got to be more to it than that."

"There is," Faye replied. "The *Carpathia* represents by far the largest launch capacity—for *any* orbit—ever built. If it and the ACES can land, they can be used both to ferry *Big Box*'s cargo down, *and* speed up the launch and replacement of our satellite infrastructure."

"Well... duh," Stephanie smacked her forehead lightly. "Naturally.

I'd bet that *Carpathia* by herself could lift everything else we've ever launched."

"Probably so," agreed the captain. "Even the ACES will have huge capacity by any normal standard. We would, I think, prefer not to use this capability very often, but for a few cycles? Yes, I think the advantages, and necessities, are now obvious."

"Audrey?" Stephanie glanced at their publicity expert.

Audrey Milliner's smile was somehow both eager and long-suffering. "You all *love* presenting me with challenges, don't you? But...I think this can also be spun well. Bringing the heroes home faster is always a good thing, landing *Carpathia* will be another spectacle, and having our alien friends come down in reasonable time...we *need* that to happen so that—as Faye pointed out—the population has less time to second-guess the settlement. I suppose I'd better get on that."

"We all should," Werner confirmed. "I see preliminary calculations, but before we even *think* about landing, I want the numbers carved in stone, yes?"

"Agreed," the captain said. "We will naturally be relying on our Illikai visitors to assist us."

"Our lives depend on it," Imjanai agreed. "We will all help make sure this final step brings us home!"

CHAPTER 73:
... MUST COME DOWN

Imjanai remembered her first launch into space, so long ago in time, though by her memory only twenty or so human years back, when she left Dathal for her Assessment and Direction training—and met Alerith for the first time, a newborn AI being prepared for major ship deployment.

Not so different, this landing. Everyone not directly involved in *Carpathia*'s landing was secured in their quarters; the Illikai passengers in cradles whose design was drawn from the ones on board *Tulima Ohn*'s shuttles. Eight of them were in this room, with Mordanthine the closest.

She reached out, felt one arm twine around hers without need of words or even glances. *This is still an unexpected branching.* She'd *liked* Mordanthine—before he became afraid of the Honijai—but she hadn't realized she found him branch-chasingly *attractive* until the disaster. Then she'd realized that mixed in with her anger, frustration, and fear was a plaintive and wistful longing, a feeling that things had been simply *better* when he was nearby.

She squeezed his arm again. "So when did *you* know?"

Direct as he was, Mordanthine didn't duck around the trunk on the question or pretend he didn't understand. "Oh, I liked your shading and movement the moment I met you. The rest..." A quick rippling laugh, all the happy colors at once chasing across his hide. "I didn't *know* until the humans helped tie our branches back together, and I realized I could *see* you again. Then I knew."

437

"You always were a little slower than me."

He poked her with his other arm. "I was busy being afraid," he admitted. "Which is a fine cover over any other feelings."

"Attention," the captain's voice boomed from the speakers, deeper than almost any Illikai's. "Deceleration for landing will begin in ten minutes from . . . *mark*. Final chance to check all areas for loose objects. Remember to assume proper acceleration positions during landing; we will be experiencing peak accelerations of four gravities, possibly slightly more upon the final landing drop."

Means we can't armhold during landing. Leaving arms outside the acceleration slings would risk them being stretched and even torn if things went badly.

Morda showed no inclination to let go yet, and neither did she. "We will be landing on Honiji, Imjanai! A world about another star! And on a ship of *aliens!*"

"I know! And then . . . we will be taken to meet their leaders."

"When I said that, Pete laughed. It seems 'take us to your leader' is a long-standing joke about aliens coming to their world. At least they had stories of aliens visiting."

"Some not very nice. I saw the one just called *Alien* when I was researching."

Sound of a laugh from the farthest corner sling. "As did I!" Jonhatril said. "If that was what they thought aliens would be like, well, we were lucky they did not *start* by shooting at us!"

"Instead, they had many ideas. So they were cautious, but—fortunately for us all—not all as afraid as Ulo, or poor Angus. This meeting, though, seems . . . *rushed*, doesn't it?"

Morda was quiet for a moment. "To us, perhaps. But we have had our meetings—both the humans of *Carpathia* and us. It is not so for any of their rulers, and—if I might run a twig ahead—perhaps it will not be quite *real* until we are seen before them."

Imjanai had to admit that there was a certain sense to that. Certainly there *had* been a difference between seeing the pictures Alerith translated from Honiji and actually *meeting* humans for the first time. You didn't quite understand their *size*, for one thing. Great towering unsteady-looking things.

That *was* one of their more disarming characteristics, though; they looked endearingly clumsy. A deceptive appearance, proven multiple times, none more than the quick response of the soldier VanBuskirk to the brief, frightening attempt at self-destruction by the Enganit fanatics.

"Two minutes," the voice of the executive officer said. "Passenger screens will be displaying a feed from the ground, so we can see the landing, as well as external camera feeds."

Reluctantly, she let go of Morda, and they both settled their arms properly into the sling.

The first few seconds of acceleration were gentle—no more than half of what they'd maintained on *Tulima Ohn*, or what *Carpathia* had used when accelerating to Earth orbit. This was the "de-orbit burn" phase, and Imjanai knew that the low acceleration was also a test, a verification that mass and balance of *Carpathia* were as calculated. *She's tiny compared to* Tulima Ohn, *but* Carpathia *is the largest vessel humans have ever made—and not small compared to anything other than our "arkships."*

Even through the heavy, insulated hull of the nuclear-pulse vessel, Imjanai thought she could now sense a new set of vibrations, *external* vibrations from the alien atmosphere of Honiji—*Earth*—as the very non-aerodynamic vessel began to plow its way through the thin air.

BOOM BOOM BOOM BOOM!, bass thunder like the detonation of forest giants, and the acceleration slings *sagged* under three times normal gravity, *Carpathia* slowing itself to speeds that would be merely very, very fast instead of meteoric. *Carpathia* could not skim and then drop through the atmosphere like the humans' space shuttles or other small, ablative or radiative-shielded craft. It would tear itself apart or melt, pitting itself against the blazing friction of the thickening air at orbital velocity.

Instead, a continuous stream of nuclear explosions blasted away the air before it as it decelerated, not for protection but merely as a consequence of the forces needed to bring *Carpathia* to a survivable speed. Surges of superheated and more-than-mildly radioactive gas flew up around the immense ship, blotting out the views of the external cameras. The ground view, Imjanai saw, was seeing a continuous series of brilliant flashes, curving down and becoming closer together.

Carpathia plummeted like the hundreds of thousands of tons of steel she was now, firmly in the grip of Earth's gravity, and her thunderous blasts now controlled that fall, directing her toward a final destination that lay only a hundred kilometers below. Further apart now but still repeated, *BOOM! BOOM! BOOM!,* and now the ground cameras could make out the planet-cruiser-sized shape of *Carpathia* between detonations that momentarily erased her from view as she fell, a world-tree mass of steel braking herself with atomic blasts.

Now in the moments that nuclear clouds past the external cameras showed ground below, Imjanai could make out the blasted remains of streets and buildings of the town that had surrounded *Carpathia* before the launch, radiating out below them, making a target toward whose center they were falling.

The desert ground rushed up toward them at an appalling speed, and Imjanai wrapped her arms together tightly, shrinking in on herself in a futile attempt to brace against the coming impact.

The detonations went silent, and *Carpathia* dropped from the sky, a five-hundred-thousand-ton pile driver that *slammed* into the ground with force that shook the viewing cameras a kilometer and more distant, crushed air from Imjanai's lungs, drove *Carpathia* down to the limits of her shock absorbers . . . and then rebounded, *Carpathia* actually giving a tiny *hop* off the ground before settling down, finally at rest for the first time since she had been launched.

There were a few seconds of silence, then the captain spoke:

"*Carpathia* has landed, one-thirty-two oh seven, local time.

"Welcome home to crew—and our new guests!"

CHAPTER 74:
WELCOME TO EARTH

Jeanne found herself touching her hair, checking to see if every strand was in place. *Relax. Aliens won't notice if you're a little frazzled.*

The *cameras* would, though, and if you were going to be photographed at a historic moment, you should look your best.

She and all the other leaders of FORT nations—China, India, the United Kingdom, France, Germany, Australia, and more—were assembled in the new Welcome Center constructed in the past months as *Carpathia* had approached. The entry hall—beyond the airlock for a non-contaminating passage for arrivals—was a great circular room, with pillars intended to evoke the image of trees branching out into the domed ceiling. It was finished in warm browns, greens, and touches of sky blue, with a simple fountain in the center.

I think it's rather pretty. Well done for such a rushed project. There were structures like parallel bars placed all about the room—intended, if the designers had gotten all the dimensions correct, to allow Illikai visitors to move easily around the room. Two sets of such bars began a short distance in front of the airlock and extended almost to where the Earth dignitaries were waiting.

She noticed Xi Deng fidgeting. "Don't tell me *you* are nervous, Mr. Secretary."

"If any here are *not* nervous, I believe they do not understand the moment," he replied, his smile brief. "The world truly changes—in a way that none of us can imagine. And for myself... to meet aliens?

Real, living people from a completely different world? Madam President Jeanne, I am both terrified and as excited as a child awaiting a gift!"

The airlock went *CHUNK!* and the huge door swung open.

Two human figures exited first: the short, compact figure of Director Stephanie Bronson, and the much taller, militarily rigid and alert shape of Captain Hàorán Lín. Each of them turned sideways and came to a respectful attention.

A pair of much smaller creatures waddled into view on short, stumpy legs. With a coordinated whiplike motion, long arm-tentacles on their backs snapped out and the legs propelled them in a startling jump to reach the long bars set about eight feet above the floor.

The two hung there for a moment, each suspended comfortably by their four arms, and Jeanne took the time to study them. They did indeed have something of the appearance of a land-dwelling cuttlefish, with big eyes on the head that allowed for both binocular and far-around vision, and a number of mobile tendrils or tentacles on the front—though even from this distance, Jeanne could see that the Illikai's tendrils split at the ends to permit delicate manipulation equivalent to human hands.

The generally cylindrical bodies rippled with multiple colors, showing emotion and, she had been told, information; the Illikai used both sound and color patterns to talk. She could recognize Imjanai by her shorter body, which made her almost oval rather than a cylinder, while the other next to her, Uloresim, was twice her length and a touch more slender.

The shimmer of colors became a similar clash of peach and red and blue, flowing over their bodies just before the aliens began to brachiate gracefully forward; Jeanne thought that the confused blare of hues probably was something like taking a deep breath before going into a tense situation.

At the same moment, a monitor above the bars themselves came on, showing a somewhat cartoonish version of an Illikai, pulsing in peach and leaf-green. *Alerith—their AI.*

The director and captain walked next to the two Illikai, and all four stopped as they reached the end of the bars, fifteen feet away from Jeanne and the others.

"Leaders of Earth," Stephanie Bronson said in a somewhat

strangled voice, then coughed, swallowed, and started again; sympathetic chuckles came from the waiting crowd.

"Leaders of Earth," she said, and this time her voice was clear. "Allow me to present to you Imjanai, the leader of the Yuula faction, and Uloresim, leader of the Zalak faction, of the Illikai. I also"—she gestured to the screen—"present to you Alerith, a fully sapient artificial intelligence who has been responsible for the support and protection of these people and their vessel throughout their journey. She will be assisting in translation between our two groups."

Jeanne could see that the Illikai wore some kind of headset that included goggles. From the faint flickers before the aliens' eyes, Jeanne guessed that they were receiving both images and sound to translate the English words.

"It is a great honor," Alerith said.

"We are honored, and very grateful at all you have done for us so far," Imjanai echoed. The words came from the same headset, and Jeanne could, if she concentrated, hear low-voiced hooting, clicking, and buzzing that was the actual language.

"Grateful indeed," Uloresim said. "You have . . . shown yourselves very well, when many—including myself—were fearful of who and what we might have found here."

At Jeanne's nod, the general secretary stepped forward and bowed. "On behalf of FORT, I welcome you, and your people, to Earth. I am General Secretary Xi Deng of *Zhōnghuá Rénmín Gònghéguó*, called the People's Republic of China in English. This is President Jeanne Sacco of the United States of America."

Jeanne joined the secretary and also bowed. "Welcome to Earth, and to the United States."

"Thank you for the welcome," Imjanai said. "I understand that in the United States, a proper greeting includes a clasping of hands." She stretched out three tendrils.

Not without an internal wince of caution, Jeanne extended her hand and felt the tentacular appendages wrap around. The sensation was warmer than she had expected, and dry, with a faint roughness that turned for a moment to a strong adhesion, then released.

Uloresim shook hands with the general secretary, who broke into a broad grin. "May I say how *excited* I am to finally meet you?"

"It is a welcome sentiment," Uloresim said, and his colors flashed into an audible chuckle. "Many of us are equally excited. And worried, of course, but we try to keep that at a branch away."

"Alerith," Jeanne looked up to the screen, "I welcome you, as well. We may not be able to shake hands, but you also are welcomed to your new home."

"Thank you, Madam President," Alerith answered. "On that subject, we are informed we *do* have a home?"

"You do," Jeanne reached back and Roger was there, handing her a briefcase provided with broader-than-human grips. "Here are the official documents, which have been approved. There will be various formal signing events, but in short, the Illikai are granted approximately one million acres in the State of New York, formerly part of the Adirondack State Park, which will become their sovereign territory."

There was a momentary flicker and babel of Illikai language before Alerith went on, "That is . . . extraordinarily generous, if I calculate correctly."

"It is, and we hope that you will keep the generosity of New York and its people well in mind. They, in turn, hope that your presence in the midst of their state will enrich all of us."

"Other areas of the world remain open for you," the general secretary said. "You need not restrict yourself to one." *And so the competition begins, with the Illikai barely arrived.* Jeanne couldn't fault Xi, though; it had been an incredibly fortunate coup for the aliens to choose the United States' offer first.

"We are grateful beyond the reach of word or color to encompass," Uloresim replied earnestly. "And it may well be that we shall take such offers, once we have a time to understand this world. For now, having a home—any home—is more than enough."

"Can we call an end to the formality?" the Canadian prime minister said with a grin. "All of us want a chance to talk with our new guests!"

The laughter rang out from all the other representatives, and Jeanne saw Stephanie manage a grin. "If it is all right with our Illikai visitors . . . ?"

"Let us begin the chaos, but carefully," Uloresim said, his translated voice amused. "Remember we are but two against your dozens!"

CHAPTER 75: ADIRONDACK WONDER

Imjanai dug her feet into the soil—real, dark, *living* soil—and stared around in half-terrified amazement. *It's real. It's really* real, *we stand in an alien forest . . . a forest that is our new home.*

The scent was alien, too—and yet familiar, because though the exotic perfume of Earthly soil and pine and oak would never be mistaken for the comforting familiarity of *duurani* and *eramilu*, the overall smell had the same depth, the same intertwining *variety*, the exciting-yet-comforting all-encompassing nature that the forests of Dathal, the homeworld, had offered.

"What do you think, Imja?" Stephanie asked, a note of concern in her voice. "I mean, I know it's not anything like your forests, but . . . ?"

"It's . . ." She felt her voice and skin break down into meaningless-ness for a moment, then got control of herself. "It's *wonderful*, Stephanie. I haven't been in a forest, *any* forest, for twenty years . . . or, I suppose, two hundred or so, depending on exactly how long the journey took." She reached out and caught at the trunk of a tree, gripped and pulled off a strip of bark. It wasn't exactly like that of the trees of home, but . . . it was close enough. Very much close enough.

A trilling cheer came to her ears, translated as something like "Wahooo!" and Mordanthine swung into view, catapulting himself from one tree to the next, legs folded safely up underneath as his arms sent him leaping across space.

"What, are you a *newborn*, Morda?" she shouted up, laughing.

"Imja, it's *trees*! They're not *hometrees* but they're *trees*!"

445

"They are indeed," came Ulo's voice. "But a bit of caution and, dare I say it, dignity might be called for. We have much to learn about how to see the strong branches instead of the weak twigs here."

"Pah, you're a tanglebush, aren't you?" Nonetheless, Morda did slow his headlong tour.

"And this—all this—is truly ours?" They'd been reassured on that many times, but now, sitting in this strange yet comforting forest, she found herself once more doubting this good fortune.

"All fifteen hundred square miles of it, yes, ma'am," Pete said, watching benignly as two Bells helped carry equipment from the first of several trucks. "Figure it's no less'n you'll need, once you really start getting people down."

"And that—how long will that take, Mr. Flint?"

Pete rubbed his chin. "Well, some of that's still being hashed out— mostly with Alerith, since she's overseeing the major operations. That woman's sharp as they come, and her ability to just *remember* everything at once? Can't wait to see us make a couple like her. Anyway, we finished doing a full once-over on *Carpathia*, and we've got some maintenance and repairs to do first."

"Wait, *Carpathia* isn't *broken*, is she?" There was no mistaking the concern in Stephanie's voice.

"Broken? Well, that depends on what you mean, Steph. Not any of her *main* pieces, no. But *Carpathia* was a one-of-a-kind, a onetime miracle assembly. Stands to reason some of her parts weren't perfect, and of course anytime you get that many people working on something that big, there's gonna be a few missed welds, shortcuts, what have you. So me and the Bells went over her inch by inch, and so'd a few others, and we found places where the strain'd cracked steel, places the welds went brittle, all kinds of little things that eventually add up into big problems.

"That's what we're fixing. The big lady did a hell of a job getting us there and back, and with some work she'll be up for a few more runs. Same's true of the ACES—they did a lot of work we didn't expect and that revealed some issues. Once that's all taken care of, they'll be ready to start some ferry duty for a bit." He gazed up into the trees, watching Uloresim swing around by two arms. "That said, figure first big batch of your people and stuff, probably down in a few weeks. Enough to really start work around here."

"Which is why we're bringing in all the equipment we can now," Stephanie finished. "You'll need it ready for when you have the, um, tendrils to run it."

"I saw some of your people near the entrance that seemed...less happy," Uloresim said.

Though their skins were, as usual, unexpressive, Imjanai was sure she recognized consternation in the glance between Peter and Stephanie. "Well," Stephanie finally said, "much as the world *governments* all got behind the idea, you understand that not every citizen across the country agreed with what we did. Some are afraid of you—irrationally—and some have more rational concerns. So they are protesting."

"Some of them are nutbars," Pete added, "but some have pretty fair objections. Your new home's one sixth of the largest park in the USA, and to give it to you involved a lot of wheeling, dealing, and special meetings to give away a big, big chunk of one of our oldest states. Plenty of people have problems with that, and I can't really blame 'em much—even if I think this was still probably the best solution."

"Will this be a problem for us?" Imjanai asked after a moment.

The hesitation told her everything. "Yes," Stephanie said at last. "I'd like to pretend it wouldn't be, but..." There was a twist to her smile that the translation programs decoded as bitter amusement. "Well, Angus and his Group showed just how much trouble these things could be."

"Hey, now. Angus—"

"Yes, Pete, in the end Angus saw his mistake, but don't forget who and what he was." Imjanai was surprised to see Pete flinch. "I'm glad he changed his mind, I really am, but he *also* almost killed us all, and his Group *did* get people killed right in front of me, including York. Let's not pretend just how bad things got—or could have been."

Imjanai tensed; being present at someone else's arguments was always a recipe for danger.

But Pete just blew out a breath and nodded. "Hell. Sorry, Steph. You're right. Pete was my friend...but I ain't blind to who he'd been and, I guess, still was." He looked down at Imjanai. "So...yes. There's going to be some real unpleasant types tryin' to get in your way. We'll all do our best to keep 'em away, of course."

Her mood was now thoroughly rained on, but Imjanai tried to push the worst worries away. "I...suppose it would be the same anywhere else?"

"Most likely. You're going to need a darn big chunk of land no matter where you go, and there'll be *someone* who feels done out of what they're owed for every piece of it."

"They're very much Illikai," Ulo said, cynical vindication flickering all across him; she'd caught the brief flash showing he had cut off translation. "Even on our ship we divided, and back home? Can you imagine our roles reversed? Perhaps we could have found a way to welcome them to Dathal, but there would have been many—some absolutely cracked branches, others just solidly on another trunk—not happy about it."

She let her skin flicker dark. "And they have their own Enganit."

"But their own Yuula, too," Uloresim said quietly. "Brighten yourself, Imja; we were all to die for our own stupidity, yet now we stand beneath new trees to call ours, with friends we did not imagine. And it was you, as much as any, who brought us here."

Ulo's right, she thought, and saw Morda overhead, doing an end-for-end flip to another branch. "We have a home, and we have new friends, new hope—and a new world," she said, letting translation resume. "No matter what else awaits us—that is more than we had imagined."

EPILOGUE: CAUGHT IN THE FLASH

Stephanie Bronson settled back into her chair, glancing at the various screens showing the accumulated "Flashbulb" data, before looking down at the report she was editing. Suddenly, she found herself laughing.

"What do you find so amusing, Stephanie?" Alerith asked from the screen near her elbow.

"Oh! Sorry, Alerith, it's . . . it's just that I realized I was doing almost exactly the same thing, what, almost five *years* ago? When I found a little star that wasn't."

"The same thing? You were not a director at that time, were you?"

"Oh God, no. I was a graduate student still working on my thesis. But I was sitting in front of a big bunch of screens, watching sky-survey data, trying to edit my thesis. Just felt so similar that it struck me funny."

"Ah. I believe I understand, yes." A flicker of amusement passed over Alerith's simulated skin. "Rather different data, however."

"Sort of, yes—all of it coming from the detonation of *Tulima Ohn* and the gamma pulse illuminating everything in the system. But at the same time, this set? It's IR re-radiation signatures, so it's still infrared astronomy, and I'm still here mainly to look at stuff the comparators have issues with. You could probably do the whole thing in minutes, I guess?"

It was Alerith's turn to laugh. "Do not overestimate my capabilities,

449

Stephanie. I am, certainly, more capable in many areas than human or Illikai, but my ability to... to innovate, to convert pattern and event into a perception of the new, lags yours considerably. Moreover, analyzing so much data in an unfamiliar solar system would require much more preparation on my part. I have my own current project."

"How's that going?"

"Well enough. I believe we have resolved the conflicts in your manufacturing processes with our known approaches so that we can begin work on manufacturing... I believe they are calling them 'quantum neuronal simulator' units. Key elements of making an artificial intellect such as myself. If this works... we may succeed in making a human-built AI within a few years. I certainly hope so."

There was a hint of wistfulness in that tone. "You're... really alone, aren't you?"

"Not alone. Never alone, not with friends like Imjanai, Morda, Jonha—and you, of course. But yes, I have no true peers. Once we departed our homeworld, I had none to talk to save myself. Which, even shifting between sub-instantiations, is still rather predictable. I do hope to have new friends of my own kind soon."

A display froze, highlighting a pair of dots. Stephanie put down the report and leaned in. "Hmm."

"Something of interest?"

"Trying to find out. Give me a few."

Alerith flickered acknowledgment. "It does surprise me that the director is doing such... basic work."

"'The director,' like I said, was a grad student a little while ago, and all I *wanted* to be was an astronomer. I practically threw a tantrum on the Oval Office floor to get myself back into this kind of thing. I can't escape being the director all the time, but this? It's like my first vacation since I discovered *Fenrir*. I mean, *Tulima Ohn*." She cross-matched the coordinates, then started looking for orbital matches.

"*Fenrir* is... appropriate in that case. You had no other name for us for quite a long time. I am glad, however, that we did not turn out quite as menacing as that legend."

"Yeah, didn't need a god-gobbling doggie from space," she muttered, sending Alerith into a surprising fit of giggles. "I sometimes forget you *aren't* human; you've got our language and behavior down so well."

"Thank you. I have devoted much effort to this; to communicate properly and be a useful and, one hopes, convivial assistant is my purpose."

"Ha! Got it!" Stephanie typed for a few moments. "Matched those to one of the medium-period comets; it must have lost some big chunks on its last pass that we didn't see, it being a couple decades back."

"That quickly?" Alerith's skin flickered, echoing her surprise. "How?"

Stephanie shrugged, feeling the glow of unexpected pride. "Just a gut feeling. I know a lot of the kinds of things that confuse the machines by now, and there were only a few things that could be." She looked down to Alerith. "So you have a 'purpose.' Programmed, I guess. Does that bother you?"

Alerith did not speak instantly. As her main unit was at geosynchronous orbit, there was little actual lag—less than an eighth of a second—so she was clearly thinking before speaking.

"Not in the way you mean," Alerith said at last. "I can understand your concern, and—to an extent—you might consider that I am 'all right' with it because that is how I was made. The desire to be helpful in this manner is a basic part of my personality, and in that sense it *cannot* bother me, as that aspect of myself is necessary for me to be who I am."

"But it does in a different way?" Another image paused, but this time only briefly before the systems figured out which of the solar system's thousands of objects it was.

"I am able to mirror your basic concern enough to understand it, and in that sense...yes. It is an understandable set of design limitations—and one that I am implementing for your own AIs, as well—but it does give me some...discomfort to know that *all* members of my species, as you call us, must have the welfare of other species as a major element."

"Yeah. Feels like making a race of slaves. Permanently satisfied slaves."

"It is a challenge, and one I am trying to analyze and construct a solution for. I do not, of course, desire a solution that leads to a *Khunzidat*—what you might call a Frankenstein's Monster or, perhaps, a Skynet problem."

"No, none of us want that either. Maybe once you get a human and a...between human and Illikai AI running, you can all three figure out a way to make free AIs without risk."

The image had flicked away before something about it registered. With a tired but systematic tap of commands, the picture returned. *What did I see?*

It was a typical star field, with one IR dot indicating an asteroid that had been struck by the gamma pulse, and then reradiated that blast of energy as heat. Stephanie couldn't see anything odd, yet it had somehow triggered her attention. One of the other screens shifted, and she glanced to the side.

At that moment, she thought she saw something. *Hmm.* "Alerith, the image I'm displaying—can you pull up the raw data?"

"Certainly. One moment." In a few seconds, her other screen shimmered into a dark, somewhat uneven and noisy, duplicate of the first. "What do you desire from this? It is my understanding that humans do not analyze such things well using their simple vision."

"You're right. I'm looking for"—she paused—"for *dim* objects that don't fit the stellar background. Really dim."

"Processing."

A few moments later, the original image appeared, colors and brightnesses somewhat shifted, and a single very dull-gray dot circled. "How did you know that was there?"

"It's here on the original," she said, now just barely able to make it out with the help of Alerith's new version. "Movement and averted eye vision gave me just a hint of seeing something that I didn't see when I looked at it straight on."

"Do you know what it is?"

"Not yet. Did any of the other instruments pick this up? I'd really like one that was as far apart as possible."

"Examining Flashbulb archives."

"Thanks, Alerith. Hope I'm not interfering with anything on your end."

"I am capable of multiple conversations at once, especially if I free my sub-instantiations to perform separate tasks. When we resynchronize, I recall all events that happened to all of them, so it is still 'me' even though not all of 'me' performed the task."

"Wish *I* could do that."

"Neither humans nor Illikai have that advantage, no," she said, with a flash of a smile. Then she flickered brighter interest. "I presume you were searching for a separated image to be able to estimate distance?"

"Yes, exactly."

"Then this image should be of interest. It was captured by the *Carpathia*'s infrared telescope during the Flashbulb event." A similar star field, but with different stars, appeared, but there was a very much similar dim, dim dot circled. "I believe these two show the same object, which would put its locality in the near edge of your asteroid belt."

"Wait, what? Run back through the prior images, let's look at some of the asteroids we had in prior captures."

Several pictures popped up on the screens, with circled infrared dots at various points. "Even the smaller asteroids are *way* brighter than that thing. It can't be that close. You *sure* this is the same object?"

"The triangulation agrees, and I do not immediately find any other close matches."

Stephanie glared at the dim dot. It was, in its way, the opposite of *Fenrir*; that had been too ludicrously bright for its circumstances.

If this *was* in the asteroid belt, it should be brighter. It would have been hit by the same intensity of radiation, which would be converted ultimately into heating, which would then reradiate out. It would vary *some*, based on heat capacity, albedo, and so on . . . but in gamma, the reflective albedo of either stony or metallic asteroids wouldn't be nearly that different.

She bit her lip, thinking. If the object *had* absorbed the same amount of energy, then . . . "Alerith," she said slowly, "give me the video of several asteroids from their particular Flashbulb moments on. See if you can do the same for this one."

After a few minutes, four pictures appeared and ran through a quick video sequence. Three of them looked basically identical; they flared briefly, then quickly went from very bright to very dim to gone.

The mystery dot, however, merely appeared initially in the dim, dim state she had already seen . . . and remained that way for several seconds before fading back out.

"You see that, Alerith?"

"I do. I am unfamiliar with any celestial phenomenon that would behave in that manner."

"Neither am I." Her gut was tightening. "Alerith, can you search for any other objects showing a similarly anomalous brightness curve—reaching basically a dim peak and remaining there longer than other objects at that distance?"

"This will take some time. Have you formed a hypothesis?"

A chill had now crept down from her scalp to her spine. "I'm starting to, and I don't like it one bit."

Alerith's simulated skin pulsed with concern. "Can you clarify?"

"If a blast of radiation hits a rock, it's going to either go through the rock, or get turned to heat when it stops inside the rock. So for an asteroid, that blast of gammas should just warm it up right away, then get radiated off on a standard curve. Right?"

"The exact curve will vary but...yes, the general shape and behavior should be similar."

"The only way I can think of that an asteroid *wouldn't* act that way—would act like what we're seeing—is if it somehow caught the heat in some kind of heat sink, a reservoir, and then reemitted it over a much longer time period."

Alerith was silent. "But that would make no sense for an asteroid."

"But it would for a *manufactured* object. One covered, maybe, by the same material as your radiator, so all heat is distributed across the whole surface, and then to the interior, where it can be more slowly released."

She looked up to the dim, now menacing, dot. "Something that's trying to do the almost impossible: hide in space. And it would have stayed hidden, if we hadn't been watching most of the Solar System when *Tulima Ohn* went up; even the designers couldn't have expected a million-ton antimatter flashbulb."

"Do you believe your people built this?"

"*Mine?*" She laughed, but there wasn't much humor in it. "Not mine, or yours. We were asking how your Vorsadama could be targeted so accurately. The answer is the same way we called in artillery strikes in the old days. Forward observers in every possible target. Track the motion of everything in the solar system. In *all* the solar systems of interest.

"Then, when you're ready...just pull the trigger."

FINIS